THE PRINCESS POSE

The Modern Royals Series

AVEN ELLIS

The Princess Pose

Copyright © 2019 Aven Ellis

Cover Design by Becky Monson

Formatting by AB Formatting

For Amy Barnes
Thank you for being my cheerleader, making me laugh, and being
my royal expert in crime.

ACKNOWLEDGMENTS

Thank you to my copy editor CeCe Carroll, for cleaning up my words, for my content editor, Joanne Lui, for loving my characters and story and making sure they are the best they can be, and for my British proofreader, Alexandra Morris, for your eagle eye and thorough red pen in making ALL THE BRITISH things British.

A special thank you to Stephanie Kay and Samantha Wayland for pushing me through this book and getting me to this finish line, which seemed so far away at some points. I love you girls and our daily chats.

Finally, thank you to my readers. You embraced this adventure into royals with gusto and I love you so much for reading my words.

A NOTE FROM THE AUTHOR

Because this story is told from the point of view of a British heroine, I decided it would be true to the character to write her speech and thoughts in UK English. So some of the terms are different (like a jumper for a sweater) or spelled in the UK way (realise instead of realize.) I hope you enjoy this authentic take on Elizabeth of York.

CHAPTER 1

THE WARRIOR POSE

I pull my long, blonde hair up into a ponytail. Then I pick up my pink baseball cap, threading my hair through the back opening and working it into a messy knot on the back of my head. I check my appearance in the mirror. I'm wearing a striped, black-and-white T-shirt, black yoga leggings, my Puma shoes, and warmup jacket. I retrieve my sunglasses off the dresser—even though it's a dreary, drizzling grey day in London—and put them on.

I'm a total idiot if I think I'm incognito.

I sigh. I might as well head out the front gates of Kensington Palace wearing a "YES, I'M PRINCESS ELIZABETH OF YORK" T-shirt and pause for selfies with people. Despite my predicament, I smile.

Wouldn't my dear aunt, Queen Antonia, love that?

I stifle a laugh, because I know my current outfit will turn my narrow-minded aunt upside down and result in lectures from her press secretary, but in order to move forward, the House of Chadwick can no longer remain locked in an ivory tower and appear pristine every day of the year. People relate to us as modern people. My cousin

Christian and his fiancée, Clementine, have started to turn things in this direction by being true to themselves and bucking some of the expected behaviours and traditions. Clementine, an American with no noble lineage, has soared near the top of the popularity charts for royals, and she's not even an official one yet.

Because they blend that mystique of being royal with being *real people.*

And I don't care what Antonia says, I'm going to follow in their footsteps.

I turn around and review everything I have gathered for my outing this Saturday morning. I have my mat, water, towel, and a yoga bag. I'm ready for class.

Then my stomach turns upside down, and I rethink the whole thing.

It's not just a yoga class.

It's a yoga class in a greenhouse.

At Cheltham House.

Where Roman Lawler is.

Oh, what am I doing?

This is a terrible idea.

Roman might not even be there; it's a Saturday, after all.

I should be going because I want to learn yoga in a beautiful greenhouse setting.

Not for the one-hundredth of a chance he *might* be there.

I haven't seen Roman since this summer, when Clementine introduced us whilst they both worked at Cheltham House. He drove up on a motorcycle to Kensington Palace and revealed himself to me when he took off his helmet. I was stunned by how handsome he was, rugged with stubble shading his strong jaw. He had thick, luxurious, dark brown hair and intense hazel eyes. I was furious at the press that day, and his intense eyes observed me, never wavering, until I stopped speaking.

I remember hearing his deep voice for the first time when he said, quietly, that he liked when I was angry Liz, the one who wanted to change the world with my platform as a working royal. Shock waves reverberated through me, knowing a stranger liked that side of me, the side I never dared show on the public stage. When Clementine made the introduction, he extended his hand. When I close my eyes, I can still feel it touching mine, the callousness and roughness of it. I had never before touched such a deliciously masculine hand as his, one worn from working the earth as a gardener.

I didn't want to let it go.

Then he rode out of the gates of Kensington Palace, and I haven't seen him since.

But I haven't forgotten.

Which causes two simultaneous—albeit conflicting— emotions in me.

The first one is worry. Am I going mad? I never give men a second thought, ever. There are multiple layers to unpack on this particular issue, starting with the fact that I'm easily disappointed in the ones I've met. Guys like the idea of access to *Her Royal Highness Princess Elizabeth* more than Liz. It became so apparent in men I talked to that I could identify them within minutes and make a polite exit, ending any hope they had of making an entrance into the mysterious world of the monarchy.

I take that one out of the mental suitcase and lay it on the bed. Next up is the fact that there is so much sameness to the men I have been exposed to. I've mostly met earls and viscounts. Even my friends at Oxford, which I graduated from this past year, all seem the same. Heat colours my face as I think of how limited my world has been. I was always disappointed in the monotony that made up my world, when I longed for something *different*. I couldn't identify what exactly that meant, but I always told myself I'd know what it was when it came upon me.

Little did I know it would come to me in the form of a gardener on a motorcycle.

This is why I should worry. Roman shook my hand, told me he liked my fire, and left. There was *nothing* to this interaction on his part. Yet here I am, revisiting it often, like those screaming girls who go mad for Xander whenever he's out in his army uniform, waving to crowds at one of our royal family events, and go online to add pins of him to their Pinterest boards at night.

I always snickered at that and teased Xander about how all those girls had visions of being the future queen consort to his future king, without even knowing a single thing about him.

Oh, irony, how delicious you are, I think, grabbing my keys and phone and heading out of my room. Because I can't forget a man I spent mere minutes with, and now I'm going to a yoga class with the single hope that I *might* see him.

I put my hand on the doorknob, about to exit my cottage at Kensington Palace, and freeze.

What do I expect to happen if I do, on the tiniest remote chance, see Roman? Will he remember our introduction? The conversation we shared?

My God, I am mad.

Roman, of course, will remember me not because I was Liz, but you know, because meeting a ranting princess at Kensington Palace is not an everyday occurrence.

The *Liz* version of me doesn't matter.

I turn around, putting an end to this hare-brained idea. If I go, I will be disappointed. I'll feel like a fool.

I'm used to being disappointed. But I can't stand being a fool.

Before I can take a step away from the door, the determined side of my brain takes charge.

You've never met a man like Roman. How do you know if he will disappoint you?

Hmm. Valid point, determined side.

Then a different voice speaks up, one that rose within me the second I met Roman.

The romantic side of my brain, which I thought I was born without.

What if it's fate that you have this opportunity to see him again? What if this is your moment, and you don't take it?

I have a flashback to the old Gwyneth Paltrow movie *Sliding Doors*, which shows the path her life takes if she catches a different train. I stumbled on it one weekend years ago when I was sick and flipping channels, and I got sucked in by the parallel universe plot.

I wrinkle my nose.

What if the greenhouse is my train? What if I don't go, and it alters the course of my life?

I exhale. This conversation with all my multiple selves is not only making me think I'm crazy, but it's becoming tiresome. I throw everything back into the mental suitcase —my disappointment and the advice from all the corners of my brain, except for one—and put it away.

I allow my decisive voice to take charge.

Which means I have a greenhouse yoga class to attend.

Warrior pose, here I come.

And amongst the hanging plants and potted poinsettias, I hope to find one special gardener.

Who might change everything.

⚜

The drizzle stops by the time I pull my Range Rover into the car park at the Cheltham House estate. The wind gusts, blowing golden leaves from the trees in the park across the street, sending them up and down in dips and swirls as they are taken on a new journey. I exhale as I turn off the engine. I watch a solitary leaf dance in the wind, passing my windshield and, as if drawn to it with a magnet, heading in the direction of Cheltham House.

Hmm. Symbolism.

I feel like that leaf, being drawn and pulled in a direction of somewhere new. The wind represents fate, pushing me where I need to be in this moment.

I laugh out loud at my deep, philosophical thoughts. All without my usual cuppa, Twinings Earl Grey tea with a splash of milk, which is how I always start my day. I'm ritualistic that way. Cup of tea, always in a fun mug, sitting at my table and reviewing my notes for my appointments for the day.

Except for today.

I was too nervous for tea this morning.

I see a woman in yoga pants and a hoodie, with a yoga bag slung over her shoulder, headed up the path in the direction of the estate.

I tighten my grip on the steering wheel. It's time to go. If I come across Roman, I'll take it as a sign that I was meant to see him today, to have the chance to talk to him and discover whether there is more to him like I suspect. Or I might discover that it was a great moment, but that is all it was ever meant to be between us.

A moment.

At least I'll know I didn't leave anything on the table. I don't want to have any regrets like "I wish I would have gone to find him" or "What if we would have met a second time? What if we would have talked?"

No. I don't do regrets.

I glance in my rear-view mirror, then turn over my shoulder and look backwards. I check each side of me and to the front before I slip out of the car, as I always do, to become oriented with my surroundings and familiarise myself with the cars and people in my vicinity. This is part of the self-defence training I have had because, unlike Xander, Christian, and James, who are direct heirs to the throne, I do not have a personal protection officer.

Which I'm glad about.

I don't know how they handle always having someone around. You'd never have complete privacy, and I'd hate that. I give up enough of that as it is; I feel the girl with the yoga mat eyeing me as I slam my car door shut.

This is where I'm so different from my sisters. Bella is insecure and hates the attention that comes with being a princess. She tends to keep her chin tucked down and eyes glued to the pavement, trying to be inconspicuous. Victoria, my youngest sister, is always in pose mode, walking straight, as if cameras are on her—acting as if they are completely invisible, while well aware she is on display.

Neither response to attention would be mine.

I flash the woman a smile and greet her with a cheerful "hello." I've been accused of exhibiting a fake persona—of a sweet princess who is trying to stay in the good graces of King Arthur and Queen Antonia—so I can remain a working royal when they are trying to cut the costs of the monarchy for the British people.

But that isn't true.

I like people. I enjoy being friendly. One of the best parts of having this platform is the opportunity to meet so many people from all walks of life. While Arthur is supportive of me being a working royal, my aunt is not and thinks this work should only be reserved for her children, Xander, Christian, and James. She thinks I'm "freeloading" off the royal payroll and taxing the public.

I set my jaw as I walk, my heart going as cold as the crisp autumn wind around me. Arthur stood up to her for me. I will never forget his kindness or belief that I can use my role as a working royal to do good things for children, my most passionate cause. Antonia, on the other hand, suggested I save the monarchy the bad publicity and get a "real job."

I cringe as I have a flashback to the family dinner where that exploded. My father, the Duke of York, was enraged at the accusation. My mother, the Duchess of York, was tearful, while I was left angry and humiliated.

But it was my cousins Xander and Christian who backed up their father and insisted I would be nothing but an asset to building the young, modern monarchy of the future. Xander went a step further and implied it would be a pity if a story was leaked to the press about the queen being so secretly jealous of Princess Elizabeth that it pushed her to the point where she threw a fit to keep her out of public service.

I smile. I thought only the carpets of Buckingham Palace were red, but the shade Antonia turned was on a whole new level after that comment.

Xander won. Arthur said there would be no more discussion on it, and I was going to be paid to work as a royal. Now it's up to me to prove that their unwavering faith in me is right. I must go above and beyond what is called for. Pack my diary with engagements, perform them well, and raise money for charities and bring awareness to their needs. Be the face of the monarchy and show that the next generation is hard-working, and eager to do well and embrace the life we have been most fortunate to be born into.

I will be the best advocate for the monarchy. I will be the face of the future, along with my cousins and my sisters, if they choose to follow the path I'm determined to make available to them. I will be kind and compassionate and thoughtful in all my endeavours on behalf of the family business, as Christian calls it.

I set my jaw.

I won't fail them.

I can't.

As I close in on the beautiful estate, where people are headed in for tours of the home or to take a stroll through the gardens designed for winter viewing, I shift my thoughts to one thing.

The opportunity to reconnect with Roman.

I go to the front of the estate, where a few other people in athletic wear are waiting in the queue. I've already purchased my admission for the small group yoga class, but we must check in for admission to the gardens where the greenhouses are.

I wait in the queue, and this time, I don't feel eyes on me. I might slip by relatively unnoticed today after all. When it's my turn, I approach the admissions lady and smile at her.

"I'm taking the yoga class at ten," I say, retrieving my phone and bringing up my proof of paid admission.

"Ah, lovely, yes," she says, peering down at my receipt.

"You'll need to wear this band." She slips a green wristband across the counter to me. "If you'll wait with this group down at the end of the steps, a staff member will lead you to the gardens through the side entrance."

"Are the gardening staff working today?" I ask, hoping against hope that she says yes.

"Oh, no, you'll be let in by the yoga instructor, dearie," the older woman says sweetly. "Our gardeners don't work weekends. Well earned, I say, as they are here working before I even get my morning coffee brewing."

I'm taken aback by how disappointed I feel at this news. *Roman Lawler isn't here today.*

"That's all you need; have a lovely time," she says, urging me to move forward in her own way so she can take care of the rest of the customers in the queue.

"Right," I reply, nodding.

So, this is where my no-regrets journey ends. Not the romantic movie version I scripted in my head, where I saw him, he saw me, and something magical happened, proving the moment we exchanged months ago was meant to be something more. I resolve to bury the letdown feeling. I took the opportunity presented to me, and it wasn't meant to be.

Yoga in a greenhouse, however, is.

I gather with the small group of people set to take the yoga class. It was limited to ten, and while Roman was my motivating factor, I am lucky to have received a spot before it sold out.

A woman on my left accidentally bumps into me. "Oh, I'm so sorry," she says quickly as the strap to my yoga bag slides off my shoulder, dangling oh-so-ungracefully off my arm.

"It's quite all right," I assure her, adjusting the strap. I meet the deep brown eyes of a woman my age. Her brow wrinkles as her eyes meet mine.

She's in recognition-mode. Either I seem familiar, but she doesn't know from where, or she's about to ask if anyone has ever told me I look *just like* Princess Elizabeth.

"I'm Jessica Lui," she says, smiling at me. "Greenhouse yoga virgin."

I chuckle. "Liz, also a greenhouse yoga virgin."

Her eyes widen. I'm guessing her suspicion has been confirmed by my name.

"You are her," she says, dropping her voice as to not draw attention to me.

"I am," I confirm.

This is always the point where things get interesting. I have had people freak out, act shocked that I'm real, or stare at me in disdain as a worthless waste of taxpayer money. What will it be today?

"Well, it's a pleasure to meet you," Jessica says. "I hope they let us in soon; it's so cold out here. I can't *believe* how cold it is. Ha, isn't this stereotypical British conversation? Remarking on the temperature."

I smile. She is treating me like anyone else she might have bumped into.

"Or how damp," I joke back, following British conversational norms. "Since it's morning, and I can't say the typical 'I can't believe how dark it is' comment, I'll go with, 'I can't believe how *damp* it is.'"

Jessica flashes me a wicked grin. "Or you could ask how much a Freddo is," she says, referring to the Cadbury chocolate bar shaped like a frog.

"You must have seen the same 'Things British People Say' post on Instagram that I did," I reply, giggling.

Jessica cocks an eyebrow. "You have an Insta?"

Crap. Nobody knows I have a secret Instagram except the squad: my sisters, my royal cousins, and Clementine.

"I had a friend show me," I lie.

Then I think how stupid it is that I have to lie about having an Instagram account. Millions of people around the world have them. Doesn't it make me human to have one and allow the world to see it?

Determination sets in. I think I'm going to approach Arthur about being the first working royal with a public Instagram account—not the one run by the palace, but my own. A personal account of my life as Elizabeth of York.

It's time.

More than time.

"We haven't ticked off everything on the list," Jessica says, moving ahead with the conversation. "We need to comment on how fast the year has gone and that Christmas will be here soon."

I'm about to reply when a tall, willowy woman approaches the garden gate from the estate side. "Hello, is everyone here for greenhouse yoga?" she asks. "I'm Lydia, and I'll be your teacher."

The first thing I notice is that her voice is incredibly mellow and soothing. Hmm. Combine her voice with the warmth of the greenhouse, and not only will I be incredibly relaxed by the end of class, but I'll also, quite possibly, be asleep on my yoga mat during the final relaxation exercise.

She leads us through the private gate and down a path. My stomach tightens as I peer out over the carefully manicured estate, wondering what part Roman played in this. I see evergreens and carefully sculpted topiaries. There are hedges with not a single leaf or branch unclipped, every row kept in perfect, uniform shape.

A flash of his hand touching mine fills my head again. Did those hands create this living art I'm looking at?

My cheeks grow hot as I remember how large and strong his hand was, and how warm it was when it grasped mine. I really had never in my life felt a hand like Roman's.

Perhaps that's why it's so hard to let the memory go.

I shift my thoughts back to the class as I walk behind Jessica. We stroll down the narrow path, and as the drizzle begins again, I shiver inside my light warmup jacket. Lydia is talking about embracing the beauty around us, the blessings of nature, as she leads us down a private section of the estate, marked off for employees only. We step through the area, and I spot the greenhouses. There are three in total, and Lydia explains that one has been reserved for us this morning.

I am grateful as we enter the greenhouse to be warmed by the rush of tropical heat. The centre of the greenhouse is cleared for us, but potting benches are filled with bulbs being forced in pots, no doubt to decorate the inside of Cheltham House for Christmas. Poinsettias in hanging baskets are overhead, and assorted large palms and house plants surround us. My mood instantly brightens from the surroundings.

"I ask that you disconnect from the outside world now," Lydia says. "Please turn off your phones and leave all your personal possessions at the back of the room. This is an hour not for your outside life, but for you to connect with your body and mind."

My bright mood becomes as strong as the sun in the Outback. I don't have to worry about anyone trying to sneak a picture of me during class now.

Complete freedom.

I unzip my jacket and peel off my T-shirt, revealing a

black-and-white, piped, cropped yoga top that matches my athletic leggings. I carefully remove my baseball cap, pulling my hair back into a top knot after I do. A few more eyes widen in recognition, followed by whispers. I continue to smile as I place my mat next to Jessica's at the back of the class.

"In case I think of more completely British things to say," I explain, sitting down next to her, "it will be easier to share them with you."

Jessica returns the smile, and we chit-chat as everyone gets situated for class. I find that I enjoy talking to Jess, as she has asked me to call her. She is from London and teaches at a nursery school, so we have a love of children in common. She's funny and down to earth, and she reminds me of Clementine, who has become one of my best friends since she came into Christian's life.

Clementine. Guilt twinges through me. She has no idea I'm here at her former place of employment. She used to be a tour guide and antiques specialist here but renounced her position after her engagement to Christian was announced.

She offered multiple times to reintroduce me to Roman, but each time I declined. I didn't want Roman to do it as a favour to Clem; I wanted to meet him again on my own, to gauge his actual interest in me.

I repress a small smile. Clementine was incredibly frustrated by me and my total stubbornness on the issue. My stubbornness, one of my greatest attributes, is also one of my biggest weaknesses, according to her. But I didn't want Roman to feel like he had to meet me. I wanted it to be natural.

Apparently, natural means not meant to be.

"Let's start," Lydia says, instructing us to stand up on

our mats, and we all comply, following her melodic instructions.

As I go through the movements to get into chair pose, I hear shouting outside the greenhouse. "Tune out the outside world," Lydia says without missing a beat, but I can't help but look, along with a few of my other classmates.

My stomach drops as I see a photographer with a huge lens on his camera. I know he's here to photograph me. A picture of the princess in workout clothing would be a huge score for a tabloid.

Anger surges through me. If that's what he wants, I'll give it to him. I'm a woman taking a yoga class, and if the world is going to go mental over it, so be it. He can have his picture, but it will be outside the greenhouse. I'll leave the class if I must. The one thing I won't do is let him ruin this yoga class for everyone else.

Fired up, I rush outside, ready to confront him, but I stop dead in my tracks.

"You're invading their privacy," a baritone voice says in a low, warning tone. "You will leave. *Now*. I will escort you out. You will not take those pictures without consent. This is a *private* class. You are violating that with your camera. It's disgusting, and I won't permit it."

I stare at the back of the man in front of me. He's dressed in jeans, a work jacket, and Wellingtons.

The man with the voice I can't forget.

My heart thunders against my ribs. I don't care about the soft rain falling on my skin, how cold I am dressed in only my yoga outfit, or that I'm standing barefoot on the icy, wet path. I'm only aware of one thing.

The man standing in front of me, the man furious at this paparazzo, is one I know.

It's Roman Lawler.

CHAPTER 2
HER ROYAL HIGHNESS

"I don't care about the class; *Her Royal Highness* is the prize I'm after," the photographer sneers. I don't recognise him from the usual pack of paparazzi. "And there she is. Liz, how about a smile so you'll look pretty online later?" He's trying to get a rise out of me as he raises his camera to his eye.

Roman turns around. The second he sees me, his eyes widen in complete surprise.

"*Liz?*" he asks, his voice resonating with shock.

I shift my attention to the photographer, who is moving to get Roman out of his frame. Roman follows my gaze, and as I'm about to tell the photographer he can take a picture if he promises to leave, Roman whirls back around, quickly grabbing my hand and using his huge frame to shield me from the lens of the camera.

I gasp as Roman, in a flash, has me behind him. One hand is spread out to hold the photographer at bay while the other has a grasp on my wrist, drawing me close to his back.

"No. You're not taking a picture of her," he says, his deep voice defiant.

I'm so stunned by Roman protecting me that I can't even formulate anything to say.

"Aren't you a ballsy one, grabbing a hold of royalty?" the photographer says.

Roman's fingertips flinch against my wrist, as if he's suddenly aware of what he has done. I hold my breath, wondering if he will release his hold on me.

But he doesn't.

"Get out," he orders the man. "Now."

"I'm not leaving unless you throw me out," the photographer tosses back.

"You do not," Roman warns, his voice rumbling, "want me to do that."

"It's not necessary," I say, not wanting Roman to get into an escalation on my behalf.

Roman shifts and, still shielding me, moves me back towards the second greenhouse, making it impossible for the photographer to get a shot of me that isn't completely obscured.

"Your Royal Highness, please go into the greenhouse," Roman commands, glancing over his shoulder at me.

In shock, I open the door and slip inside, once again wrapped in the scent of flowers and heated by warm, tropical air. Roman shuts the door, and I watch as he strides back to the photographer, towering over him. I hear Roman's voice again, and there is no mistaking his patience has run out. The photographer steps back from him, and as Roman looms over him, I see the photographer is nervous. The photographer suddenly leaves, but Roman tails him, probably to ensure he is kicked off the grounds and not allowed back in.

I whirl around, pressing my back against the door, my heart thundering against my ribs, my brain whirling.

Roman is here.

I begin to pace across the floor, moving around the bags of potting soil and organic fertilisers, eager for him to return. Scared for him to return. I grabbed this moment and took this chance, but I have no idea what will happen next. Do we have anything in common? Will he want to talk to me, other than brief chat about the paparazzi and our initial meeting because of them following Clementine?

I stop walking and touch my wrist, where his fingertips were a few moments ago. He didn't hesitate to protect me. My pulse is still galloping at the spot where he held me. I draw an anxious breath as I realise Roman is the only man who has ever elicited this kind of response from me.

Merely from the touch of his hand.

The doorknob rattles, and I lift my head in the direction of the sound.

It's Roman.

If I thought my heart was wild before, it has gone crazy now. It's pounding so loudly, and I can feel it against my ribs. The blood rushes to my head, and my throat goes dry as he steps inside and closes the door gently behind him.

I drink him in with all the thirst of someone who hasn't had water in days. My memory of him didn't fail me. The tall frame, the thick, espresso-brown hair, the olive skin with the shading of thick, dark stubble on his face.

Roman approaches me. My nerves accelerate with each step he takes. Finally, he's before me, gazing down into my eyes. I notice how his eyes are more brown than green, but now that I'm close, I can see flecks of a golden honey colour in them.

"Are you all right?" he asks, his voice gentle as those unique eyes lock on mine.

"Yes. I'm so sorry you were put in that awkward position because of me."

"What? No," Roman says, shaking his head. "You were the one who had your privacy violated."

"Well, I ended up having it protected, thanks to you," I say, smiling softly at him.

"Where was your protection officer?" he asks.

I laugh, and Roman appears confused.

"What's so funny?"

"I don't have protection."

Roman's eyes widen. "What?"

I shake my head. "I'm not that important in the royal line of succession. There is pretty much zero chance of me ever being Queen Elizabeth, so I don't have them. No need to spend money to protect Princess Elizabeth of York."

"That's not right," Roman says firmly. "You're important to the monarchy. Look at all the work you do for children. You are a famous figure. You bloody well should have a protection officer. What if that photographer had been a stalker? You shouldn't be put in that kind of vulnerable position."

"I've had self-defence training," I say.

"Liz. That's not acceptable."

"I promise you, I prefer it. I couldn't bear to have someone follow me around at all times, or live in my house. No. I'm too independent for that. I'd rather learn how to throat punch someone and gouge eyes out with my fingernails than have a protection officer with me twenty-four hours a day for the rest of my life."

The corners of Roman's mouth twitch, as if he's repressing a smile.

"What are you about to smile at?"

"How do you know I'm about to smile?" he challenges, those hazel eyes shining teasingly at me.

"The corners of your mouth are curving up. Do you not believe I can throat punch? Because I can."

"No, because you are the same as when I met you the first time. You are quite the firecracker off the public stage, aren't you?"

My breath catches. He does remember me, and for more than being Her Royal Highness.

"There are certain ways I'm expected to be when I'm in the public eye," I say. "But that's only one part of who I am. It's hard, though, for people who only see me in that forum to believe I'm otherwise human. Like how I am now, standing before you barefoot and in yoga clothing."

Then I remember that I am in form-fitting yoga clothing, with a cropped workout top showing off my midriff. Something that I was willing to pose in for that idiot photographer now leaves me feeling almost vulnerable in front of Roman.

As I say the words, his eyes flicker over me, moving over my body and causing me to grow hot as a result. His gaze is intense and lingering, but abruptly, as if the move was instinctual, he quickly brings his gaze back to meet mine.

"My jacket is in the other greenhouse," I explain. Then I wince. "Along with my bag and my mat."

"Would you like me to retrieve them for you?" Roman asks, as if knowing I don't want to interrupt the class any more than I have.

"Thank you," I say. "My mat is at the back of the room, next to a girl with long, jet-black hair in a yellow-and-black outfit. My bag has my royal coat of arms on it."

Roman nods. He's so earnest, I burst out laughing.

"I do not have a yoga bag with my coat of arms; I'm teasing."

He rubs his hand across his jaw. My pulse leaps when I see once more how large and masculine his hand is. What I wouldn't give to feel that protective hand on my skin again.

"But it is a Sweaty Betty bag," I offer.

Roman stops rubbing his jaw and furrows his brow.

"The royal coat of arms would be infinitely more helpful." Then his mouth twitches again, toying with me, as if maybe, just maybe, I might be rewarded with a full smile at some point.

"It's a black quilted bag, with a zipped compartment on the bottom. That should help."

"Right," Roman deadpans. "Easy."

"I have infinite faith you will find the right bag," I tease.

Roman's brow furrows again.

"What?" I ask, curious as to what is causing that expression.

"You're surprising."

My heart flutters. "How so?"

"You just are," he says, his deep voice quiet.

I hold my breath. Roman stands still. Our eyes remain locked on each other.

"I'll be back," he finally says, turning and heading out the door.

As I watch him leave, I know I'm not crazy.

There *is* something crackling between us.

I draw an excited breath as I pace the greenhouse floor again, eager for him to return. Within minutes, my wish is granted, and Roman, who has my bag slung over his shoulder and a yoga mat tucked under his arm, opens the door.

"The woman on the mat next to yours assured me I was correct," he says, stepping inside the greenhouse. "She also asked if you were okay."

"Thank you," I say. Then I make a note to contact the instructor and see if she will forward a note to Jess on my behalf. I like Jess, but I don't know her. I must be careful with any private information, like email addresses or phone numbers, until I'm sure of the person I'm talking to.

I should say the same about Roman, but my instincts tell me, beyond a shadow of a doubt, that I can trust him already.

He gently places my bag on a clean area of the workbench, and I reach inside for my T-shirt and tug it on, feeling it's more appropriate for the situation. Then I almost laugh. Modern Liz, who I'm trying to be, has suddenly gotten all shy and prim in the presence of one Roman Lawler.

After I get the shirt on, I find him watching me.

"I'm sorry your class was ruined," he says.

I blink. He has no idea that I've never been happier to have my life disturbed by the press. "It's okay. The class wasn't meant to be," I say, staring into those gorgeous eyes with the flecks of honey.

But this moment is.

"I'm sorry I interrupted you when you were working," I continue.

Roman begins to take off his coat. As I watch him shrug out of it, butterflies spring out of nowhere, attacking my stomach as a feeling of eagerness, of pure excitement, surges through me—a sensation I have never felt before.

He's getting comfortable because the room is warm.

Because he's going to stay.

"I'm not working in the true sense of the word today,"

Roman explains, placing his coat next to my bag on the bench. "I came in because I got bored. I'd rather be outside. There's a lot to do at this time of year, contrary to what people think about gardening when the weather turns cold."

He is standing before me now in a dark green tartan shirt. His eyes take on more of that greenish hue because of it, but much to my delight, the golden flecks remain.

"I would think summer is your busy season," I say, curious.

"No, it's not. But I'm sure you don't want to hear the intricacies of cutting back trees and planning for the winter kitchen garden," Roman says.

"That's a bit presumptuous."

Roman's brows knit together. "I'm sorry?"

"You presume I asked you a question that I didn't want to know the answer to. In fact, if I had my normal cup of Earl Grey, I would ask you that question, and many more."

His lips part in surprise.

My heart is roaring in my ears again. What is it about Roman that makes me want this so badly? Makes me so bold? I've never yearned for conversation like this with a man in all my life.

He falls silent. I still hear the blood pounding in my veins. To my shock, he picks up his jacket and walks towards the door. I'm so stunned I can't speak. Was I too much? Too forward? While I might not think I'm crazy, maybe Roman does. As he walks away, my stomach drops out.

The moment is over.

As he reaches the door, he turns to face me. "Milk or sugar?" he asks.

I gasp. "W-What?"

His mouth curves up again, but this time, he rewards me with a smile. It is genuine and real and lights up his face.

"How do you take your Earl Grey? If I'm going to bore you with details of bulbs, the least I can do is bring you a cup of tea."

CHAPTER 3
DARJEELING WITH A DROP OF LIME

I watch as Roman strolls across the garden grounds, up towards the main house.

He wants to have a cup of tea with me.

The excitement that races through me is beyond compare. My pulse is still rapid, and if Roman's fingertips were to graze across my wrist now, he'd know the response he elicits within me.

Joy is equal to my eagerness. I can't stop the smile that is spreading across my face, because for the first time in my life, I have zero fears of being disappointed. In fact, I'm eager to sit down and learn all about him.

I gaze up at the poinsettias hanging overhead, filling the greenhouse with vibrant shades of deep crimson and rich cream. I feel like I'm dreaming. Is this real? I'm truly going to have tea with an intriguing man in a greenhouse filled with vibrant Christmas blooms? I trace my finger around the edges of a full-grown amaryllis plant, with velvety red petals with white stripes down the centre of each. This is no dream. I'm here. In this cosy, warm greenhouse.

Waiting for Roman.

I let my gaze wander, taking in this foreign environment. I've been blessed enough to grow up in palaces with breathtaking gardens—like the lush grounds of Buckingham Palace and my own home, Kensington Palace—but I've never thought much of the labour that goes into maintaining their beauty and keeping them pristine and healthy for the public to enjoy.

So many questions fill my head. When did Roman know he wanted to work in landscaping? Has he always loved the outdoors? Is he living his dream, like I am mine?

I trace my hand over the old bench, thinking of how, when I speak of my dream, I'm not thinking of the ballgowns and diamonds and palaces but the fact that, every day, I get to wake up and help children. For example, on Monday, I'm attending an event for Scout 4 Girls, a group promoting confidence and self-esteem in girls. The girls are going to show me their projects in robotics, graphic design, and financial independence, which I'm most keen to see. I can't wait to ask them about what they are creating and learning. With the press following me, I'll be able to give this non-profit organisation a spotlight to increase awareness of what they do and bring attention to their needs.

I stare down at the grooves on the wood, ones well-worn over time, feeling blessed that the monarchy has immense power to help these wonderful organisations and charities. There have been snarky articles in the press about how my father demanded this position for me so I didn't have to get a "real job" upon graduating from university. They don't understand how real this job is.

I stand straighter as I think of the criticism that has been laid at my feet all summer. I have never worked harder than I have these past few months. This is not me working through my diary and going through the motions with a fake smile on my face to justify my princess title. I'm not doing this work to keep myself in a palace. I'm not doing this work to be famous.

I believe in the work I'm undertaking. I believe it's important, that I can make change in the world, and that the things I do will somehow, in some small way, make this world a better place for someone.

I'm called to do this.

I'm doing this work because it's in my heart.

The doorknob rattles, and my nerves jump as I turn around. Roman is back, balancing two cups in his hands as he pops open the door. My breath catches in my throat again the second I see him, this gorgeous gardener who wants to share a cup of tea with me.

"I'll close the door," I say, moving towards him.

"Thank you," Roman says.

I head over and slip behind him, pulling the door shut. He turns to face me, and I have to gaze up at him. He is tall, easily six foot four, and towers over my five-foot-four-inch frame.

"One Earl Grey tea with a splash of milk for Elizabeth of York," Roman says, handing me a paper cup with a cardboard holder around it. His fingertips briefly graze against mine as I take the cup from him, sending a delicious shiver down my spine.

"Thank you."

"And one Darjeeling tea with a drop of lime for me," he says. He sets his tea down on the work bench and takes a moment to remove his jacket again.

"A drop of lime?" I ask.

"All it needs is a drop," Roman explains.

"But lime, not lemon?"

"Has to be lime. I hate lemon."

I'm about to ask him how on earth he can live without the joy of eating lemon curd out of a jar with a spoon, like I'm fond of doing, but I'm distracted by the fact that he's now taking off his shirt.

Oh. My. God.

I hold my breath for fear of gasping out loud. Roman is standing before me in jeans and a simple white T-shirt. The shirt fits him snug across his massive chest and reveals beautiful arms, ones that have been tanned by time spent in the garden and are muscular from all the manual labour he does. My eyes start at his wrists and move up along his powerful forearms to biceps that are straining against the sleeves of his cotton shirt.

"I don't know where we can sit except for the floor," he says, rubbing his hand against his cheek. "I'm so sorry. I can't believe I'm telling you to sit on the floor of a dirty greenhouse."

"It doesn't bother me to sit on the floor," I say, lowering myself to the spot where I was standing.

Roman winces as he peers down at me. "Liz, no. Please stand up. I can go find something for us to sit on."

"If I wanted to sit on something, I have a yoga mat. I don't care."

Roman's hand stills on his face as his eyes meet mine.

"You honestly don't care, do you?" he asks softly.

I can't breathe. This is already becoming the most real conversation I've ever had with a man. I don't want Roman to see me as Her Royal Highness Princess Elizabeth of York.

I want him to see me as *Liz*.

"I'm more bothered by your use of the word 'hate' to describe your feelings on lemons. I'm troubled by this, as lemon is one of the most delightful things in the world. It's vibrant and tart, yet it can be wonderfully sweet, like a delicious lemon curd, or lemon bars dusted with icing sugar. It's a bite of sunshine. I'm disturbed that you are missing out on such a luscious experience."

Roman's hand slowly moves down his jaw to his mouth, and his index finger draws back and forth over his full lower lip. He appears to be thinking.

This greenhouse is going from warm to stifling hot as I watch him touch his mouth. I stare at that full lower lip being brushed by that oh-so-wonderful rough and masculine hand, and now I'm about to break out in a sweat.

"Hmm," Roman says, picking up his cup of tea and sitting down across from me on the floor. "Interesting."

He pauses to take a sip of his tea, and I do the same, needing to forget the image of him touching that lip and stop wishing I was the one touching his hand.

Or his mouth.

I blink. I take a sip of my tea, although my hand is jittery as I put the cup to my lips. "What's interesting?" I ask after I've taken a moment to recover.

Roman sets his cup beside him and stares at me. "You aren't what I'd thought you'd be."

I furrow my brow. "What did you think I'd be?"

He clears his throat. "This is embarrassing to admit. Please keep in mind I'm not exactly a royal family watcher, so I'm basing this only on media that happened to land in front of my face."

I take another sip of tea. "I see. So, I take it you haven't told Google you are interested in stories about Princess Elizabeth?" I tease.

I see the start of a small smile on his face. I realise Roman doesn't give them easily.

"Um, no. I hope you aren't offended, Your Royal Highness," he counters, sexily lifting an eyebrow at me.

My heart does a zigzag.

"No, I'm not."

"Good."

"Please, don't keep me in suspense," I implore. "Tell me what you thought I'd be."

"In the snippets of you I've seen on TV, you had a… a…" Roman stops.

I will him to go on with my gaze.

"Damn it," he blurts out, shifting from a sexy, flirting man to one who is developing a flush up the sides of his neck and appearing incredibly uncertain. "What am I doing? I can't tell you this. Geez, Darcy is right. I'm awful with women. It's been too long. This is why I belong in a garden, where I spend all day amongst the plants and trees who don't care what comes out of my mouth."

Now I'm the one surprised. Roman, who says what he thinks and rides a motorcycle, who protected me from the paparazzi, who has been flirty and charming in our brief exchanges so far, is now showing me a vulnerable side. As I watch him, a new feeling comes to the surface, one I've never experienced before.

I like the fact that he's showing me all of him, including his insecurities.

"I promise I won't be offended," I reassure him.

Roman sighs heavily. "I thought you had a 'sameness' about you. Your expression was always the same in pictures. You were always shown doing the same things: meeting people, taking flowers, posing. You always wear white. I assumed—wrongly—you were one-dimensional."

I blink. While I was running from the sameness of the

men in my social circle, Roman was perceiving the same thing about me.

Yet, I understand his assumption.

"That is my work," I explain. "People expect me to show up dressed as Princess Elizabeth, in the image I started to curate last year for myself. Do you know why I wear white? Because when I see white, it feels optimistic. I read about colour, and when a person wears white, along with innocence, the colour projects optimism. That is how I want people to see me: as an optimistic woman championing for change."

"I think you can be optimistic and let people see some more of you," Roman says slowly. "I know I liked what I saw this summer. That unexpected passion from you to protect Clementine from press attacks stayed with me. You stayed with me, Liz."

"You stayed with me, too," I admit, barely hearing my own words over the sound of my heart racing in my ears. "You told me, upon meeting me, you liked the side of me I don't allow people to see. I was angry and unwound, and you didn't flinch. Instead, you encouraged me to live as I feel, something nobody in my entire life has ever encouraged me to do."

Roman's eyes grow more intense. I feel nothing but chemistry filling the space between us. This feeling makes me brave, so I go on.

"Roman," I say—oh, how I love hearing his name fall from my lips— "did you ever think about asking Clementine about me?"

His mouth parts in shock.

"No, no, of course not. You're a princess. I'm a gardener. Even taking that out of the equation, it felt impossible."

"How does it feel now?" I ask.

"Surreal," Roman whispers. "Crazy. I can't believe you thought of me at all, let alone for months. But you don't know me, Liz. Compared to everyone in your world, I'm different."

"Exactly," I say.

Roman's mouth turns down in doubt. I know I'm going to have to convince him to take a chance.

On me.

"I want you to put aside Princess Elizabeth," I ask. "See me as I am. Sitting on the dirty floor of a greenhouse, in yoga gear, wearing my hair in a knot and drinking a cup of tea, only wanting to know the man sitting across from me. Not the man known as a gardener, but the man known as Roman."

He doesn't say anything.

"All I need to know is that you want to do that," I continue. "That you want to know me, as Liz, and all the things that make me more than the title I was born with. Just as I want to know you, as Roman Lawler. All you have to say is yes, Roman, if you want to get to know me."

My heart stops as I wait for his response.

As the seconds go by, I realise the answer, after the reality of a princess sitting in front of him hits him, might be no.

Roman exhales loudly. My heart sinks.

With a sickening sensation gripping me, I know his answer.

He's changed his mind.

"Liz," he says, his voice grave, "we're so different. I don't want to make a mistake. What's the point of this? You like *lemon*. What will I find out next? That you have a black thumb?"

Oh so slowly, the corners of his mouth turn up. My heart roars back to life.

Roman flashes me a big smile, one so rare and radiant that I feel my soul light up the second I see it.

That smile tells me everything.

Roman is willing to take a chance on getting to know me.

And our time starts now.

CHAPTER 4
LIMES OR LEMONS

I smile back at him. I'm elated that he wants to spend time getting to know me.

Not as Princess Elizabeth of York.

But as Liz.

"This could be dangerous, Roman," I say, dropping my voice. "It's going to take a lot for me to comprehend selecting lime when you can have the seductive tartness of a lemon instead."

His eyes lower to my mouth for a moment. I grow hot from the intensity of his stare.

"Has to be lime. It has more zing, in my opinion," he says, shifting his attention to my eyes.

"So, zing is important?"

The curved smile appears. "Yes."

Zing, indeed.

"I think you are entirely dismissive of the lemon."

"It should be dismissed," Roman asserts, his smile broadening. "Key lime pie proves it. I love Key lime pie."

"Oh, no, a classic lemon tart is by far superior to Key lime pie," I insist. I pause and take another sip of my tea. "I have another question. Who is Darcy, and why does this person think you are rubbish with women?"

The flush creeps up Roman's neck again. My heart *zings* upon seeing it.

"Darcy," he says slowly, his deliciously low voice rolling in the air between us, "is my cousin. We were born in the same year, grew up together, and he's like an annoying older brother. We share a flat in Shepherd's Bush."

I nod. That is a neighbourhood in West London, known for being multicultural, near the massive Westfield London shopping centre.

Roman rakes his fingers through his hair, which causes it to stick up messily on his head. I find myself wondering if that is how he looks when he wakes up in the morning.

"But I'm not telling you why Darcy thinks I'm crap with girls," he says.

"Oh, intrigue. Now you have to tell me."

He chuckles. "No, I don't."

"Do you want me to guess?"

"Oh, God, no," Roman grimaces, but I see a playfulness in his eyes.

"I'll make a deal with you: I cannot ask why this infamous Darcy thinks you are rubbish with women, and you can't ask me any questions about being a princess today."

Inwardly, I wince as the word princess escapes my lips. I glance down, staring at the lid on my cup. It sounds *ridiculous* that, in this day and age, I exist. I am a modern-day, real-life princess, something that seems like it should only exist in fictional Disney fairy tales, or in those TV movies that Clementine introduced me to this summer. But as I think about it, they never have princesses anyway. The heroine is, ninety-nine percent of the time, some plucky

American who lands the heart of some prince who is from a fictional foreign country but speaks with a perfect British accent.

I feel heat radiating across my cheeks now, which I'm sure matches the flush on Roman's neck.

"Damn, I've boxed myself into a corner. I was so hoping to hear about your tiara collection," he says, interrupting my thoughts. "But in order to avoid talking about my rubbish skills with women, I'll forgo hearing about your royal jewellery vault."

I shift my attention back to him and find his eyes are shining brightly at me. Then he smiles, that brilliant, gorgeous smile that he is starting to bestow upon me more liberally now.

My heart does that now-familiar *zing* once again.

I laugh. "Ha! I don't have a single tiara in my collection. I do, however, have a collection of adult colouring books I can tell you about, but somehow, I don't think you care to hear about the specific brand of colouring pencils I'm obsessed with."

Roman's eyes widen in surprise. "You colour?"

I nod. "I love it. It's one of my favourite things to do."

"What do you like about it?" he asks.

"It makes me feel grounded," I explain. "It requires focus. I lose myself in the colours and patterns. I love the sound of the pencil strokes. I usually do it at the end of the day as a form of meditation."

Roman nods. "I feel that way about planting. It's just me and the dirt. I lay out the garden the way I designed, and I go to work, digging up the earth and watching things come to life. It's peaceful. Quiet. I like that. I'm not always good with people. Plants are much more forgiving of my flaws."

My ears perk up. I wonder if that comment is connected

to whatever his cousin Darcy told him about his skills with women, but my instinct tells me not to ask about that.

"How did you get into gardening?" I ask instead.

Now I see something new filter across his handsome face. His eyes are lit up, he's smiling, and there's joy expressed in his features.

"When I was little, I spent a lot of time with my grandfather, Clive. He's the head gardener here. My grandparents have lived here, at Cheltham House, as long as I've been alive. My parents aren't into gardening at all, so when I'd come visit here on weekends, Grandfather would take me out and teach me things. He let me get my hands dirty. I could dig up stuff, pick up worms, all the things that little boys love. Grandfather has infinite patience, and he loves explaining things. He talked to me about respecting the land. He said, if we nurture it, we can be blessed by what grows from our efforts. I still remember the first garden I planted with him. It was the kitchen garden here. I was so excited to come each week and see if anything was growing. I was the proudest boy in the world to be able to pick tomatoes I grew."

My heart flutters as I see the little boy who knew his destiny early on.

"I never outgrew that interest," Roman continues, pausing to take a sip of his tea. "I found solace in the earth. I wanted to do everything Grandfather did, and I began working at Cheltham House as a teen. I would have been happy to go straight into work after completing my A levels, but Grandfather had none of it. He said I needed to go to university and study horticulture. He said he wanted me to take over for him when he retired, and he would only recommend me if I had a degree."

I smile. "Blackmail."

Roman laughs. "It was."

"Where did you study?"

"I have a bachelor's degree from the University of Glasgow. I did course work at the Royal Botanical Garden of Edinburgh, which was a fantastic experience. Now, I'm gradually taking over work for my grandfather. I think he should retire, but after losing my grandmother a few years ago, he needs the work to keep his mind busy. They were married forty years. She had Alzheimer's and spent the last few years in a memory care home. Grandfather went every day, without fail, even when she didn't know who he was."

"I know someone who lost her husband to the same disease," I say, as the image of Jillian, the older woman Clementine used to live with, pops into my head. "It was incredibly hard on her."

"Grandfather tried to take care of her, but as the disease progressed, he couldn't give her the care she needed. It gutted him to have to put her in a home. I think he's only starting to come back to life now, and it's been seven years."

"A broken heart can take time to heal," I say.

Roman studies me. "Have you had your heart broken?"

"By a man? No. By my family? Yes."

The words come out so easily that I'm shocked to hear them escape my lips. Nobody—not even Clem or Lady Amelia Westbrook, my best friends—know that truth. It's such a secret, such a hurt on my heart, that I haven't shared the story with anyone. My sisters, Bella and Victoria, don't even know what is going on behind the closed doors of St. James's Palace, where my parents live.

I feel Roman's gaze on me. Once again, a deep blush colours my ivory skin. I know because my cheeks are burning.

"You know, we've gotten way too serious here," he says,

as if knowing I cannot speak of what I alluded to. "I need to ask the important questions now, excluding any princess-type inquiries."

How did he know I couldn't tell him my truth? I stare at him in a mixture of amazement and pure gratitude.

"I'm ready."

"Green thumb or black thumb?" he asks.

"Black of blackest death," I say.

"What is black of blackest death?"

"Well, I moved into my cottage over the summer," I explain. "I love fresh cut flowers, so I always make a point to get those when I do my shopping—"

"You do your own food shopping?" Roman interrupts, obviously surprised.

I can't help but grin. "I even push my own trolley."

"You don't have people for that?"

I burst out laughing. "No, I don't have those kinds of people. I do have a secretary, Cecelia Green, who is based at Kensington Palace. She handles my engagements and accompanies me if I need her to. She's incredible. I'm always well prepared for my engagements with detailed notes and counsel from her. She has truly guided me into my role. Sameness and all," I tease.

Roman's hand flies to his hair, and he quickly begins raking it again. "I'm such an arse."

"No, you're not. You're being real. I appreciate that. More than you could ever understand. People are incredibly keen, at least to my face, to tell me what they think I want to hear. They are also equally keen to say terrible things about me on social media."

"This is why I like poinsettias," Roman says, glancing at the baskets that hang overhead. "They don't judge. But let's come back round to the black of blackest death."

I groan. "I buy fresh flowers because I can replace them weekly. Unlike plants. I had houseplants. I say had because I forgot to water them. Then I watered them extra to make up for not watering them. And then—and this was a tragic day indeed—they all died."

Roman is grimacing.

"You've put a stake in my gardening heart," he declares, putting his huge hand over his chest.

I study that hand, the large, strong hand that touched mine earlier, and with a ping in my chest, I realise I want it back over mine again.

But I stay in the conversation instead.

"Shall I gather my things?" I tease.

Roman smiles. "No. My guess is you've had no gardening education, so you were destined to kill plants with precision."

"You make me sound like a murderer," I giggle.

"Aren't you?" he teases.

"I'll have you know that I will not have a single poinsettia plant in my cottage for fear of killing it within days upon arrival. And I love them. They are my *favourite* Christmas flower. I love the red petals."

Roman smiles at me. "I think," he says slowly, "it's time for Poinsettia 101."

I watch as he stands. He moves around the greenhouse until he finds a hook, and then he removes one of the plants that is hanging overhead. He grabs the plant and places it on a work bench.

"Come here, Liz," he says.

My heart does a *zing* the second my name escapes his lips. I unfold myself off the floor and move next to him at the bench.

"What you think are petals," Roman says, "are actually called bracts."

"Bracts?" I repeat.

"These," he says, putting his fingertips on one of the red bracts, "are not petals, but leaves."

His bare arm brushes against mine. A frisson of excitement shoots through me, causing goosebumps to sweep over my skin. As Roman leans in, I don't smell any kind of posh cologne, or any cologne for that matter, but what I do detect is the lingering scent of sandalwood soap, combined with an outdoorsy smell. He smells like grass and dirt and sandalwood, and the scent of him — rugged and all masculine — is uniquely him.

And all I want to do is drink it in, absorb it, and get drunk off it.

"These are the actual petals of the flower," Roman says, snapping me from my thoughts. "Right here."

His enormous hands delicately lift the centre of the bracts to reveal little yellow flowers. At the same time, I move my fingers to touch the flowers, and our fingertips collide.

I suck in my breath as a jolt rips through me. Roman doesn't flinch, nor does he remove his hand, but instead, he hooks his index finger over mine. I stare up at him. He's already gazing down at me, the golden flecks in his eyes dominate now in his soft expression.

"Liz," he says, his deep voice sending an electric feeling through me, "is it wrong that it already feels right to touch your hand?"

He begins rubbing his index finger lightly up and down mine. Heat spirals through me. The move is gentle and soft, and I feel like he's taking care of me, like I'm something special that he's discovering.

"No," I whisper in the close space between us.

We remain silent for a moment, connected by the barest of touches but not willing to give it up.

"You're dangerous," Roman says quietly. "You make me want to know you. I haven't felt this way in a long, long time." His eyes never leave mine as he speaks, and I know my gaze is as intent as his.

"I haven't either," I murmur.

The truth is, I've *never* felt this way. Only Roman has elicited this excitement in me. This desire to get to know him is unique to him, and him alone.

"Is this crazy?" he wonders out loud. "You. Me. We've only talked about plants and lemons, yet I feel... I can't describe it."

My heart bangs loudly against my ribs. Roman is feeling it, too. He doesn't have to say it, but he's known since that day at Kensington Palace. There's something magnetic between us. We don't know each other. I'm a modern-day princess. He's a gardener. We grew up in completely different worlds. No matchmaker would ever put us together.

"I don't want what has been in my limited world," I say, continuing my thoughts out loud. "I want something different. I think you do, too."

Roman's finger travels down to my wrist, trailing across my pulse point. "Your pulse is fast," he whispers. "It matches mine."

I suck in my breath. This is the most intimate moment I've ever had with a man, and we haven't even kissed.

"I need more time with you," I say without thinking. "But nowhere public."

"No. You... you wouldn't... um, want to come over for dinner, would you?" The flush sweeps up his neck again.

"Mind you, my flat is probably the size of your wardrobe, and my cutlery doesn't match, among many other things that could disappoint you."

I read between the lines. Roman is worried what Princess Elizabeth of York will think of his life outside of this greenhouse moment. As if I, Liz, will disappear.

"There's only one thing that could disappoint me about this invitation. Can you cook? Or do you at least have a good takeaway place nearby? Because food is *all the things* to me."

The flush fades from his neck. Roman's other fingers encircle my wrist, grasping it gently and sending my heart fluttering. "Can I cook?" he asks. "Of course I can. Farm-to-table is my specialty. Lady Cheltham gives me full range of the kitchen garden, so I make use of what is in season."

Roman just became the sexiest man alive.

Oh, who am I kidding? He's been the sexiest man alive since the moment he removed his motorcycle helmet in front of me.

"Shall I pick you up around six?" he asks.

It takes all my learned princess restraint not to burst out in joy.

"Yes," I say. "Will you bring your motorbike?"

"No," Roman says, his voice firm. "It will be cold, and night riding is more dangerous. I won't put you in that position. I'll drive my car."

He's protective. My heart flutters, seeing this trait in action for me.

"All right. I assume casual dress?"

A smile twitches at his lips. "What is casual in your world?"

I allow my own lips to twitch back in the same flirtatious smile. "Jeans. How about in your world?"

"Joggers. But I won't wear joggers if you are my guest."

Roman could wear joggers and a T-shirt and be barefoot, and I'd be happy, but I keep this thought to myself.

"So, jeans it is," I say.

"Will you wear a tiara?" he teases.

"You insult me. I'm still Liz," I chide.

"I stand corrected. Liz wouldn't own a tiara. I apologise."

I grin. Roman must think I have a collection of them back at the cottage, but the truth is, I don't own a single one. Though I'll save that jaw-dropping fact for later.

"I'll have you put your number into my phone," he says, still holding my wrist and tracing circles along the inside with his thumb. "I'll walk you out to your car in case that sleazy photographer is milling about."

Warmth fills me, the effect of his calloused thumb circling my skin and the fact that he's so protective of me. When he releases his grip to retrieve his phone, regret surges through me.

What are you doing to me, Roman? I think as I watch him move over to his jacket, withdrawing his phone out of his pocket. *You are making me feel things I didn't think any man could stir in me.*

He stands before me, typing on his screen. "Here. I've set you up. Enter your number, please."

I nod and take the phone from his hand. I glance down at the screen, and my heart stills as I see how he's entered my contact information:

Liz

To my surprise, tears of happiness prick my eyes. Many

people *call* me Liz, but they don't *see* me as Liz. There's always that title, my blessing and my curse, hanging over their impression of who I am, or why they want to get to know me.

I glance up at Roman, who is watching me with a gentle smile on his lips.

He is different.

He wants to know me. Not the woman attached to the British monarchy, but me, as the real person I am underneath the title.

And that is exactly who he will get tonight.

CHAPTER 5
FLAT NUMBER FIVE

I'm a jumble of feelings as I let myself into Wren House, the two-story cottage that I call home at Kensington Palace. I drop my yoga bag on the floor and kick off my shoes the lazy way, by stepping on the back of the heel to pull them off so I don't have to untie them. I stroll over to my oversized cream sofa and flop down backwards, sinking deep into it. I pick up one of the many cushions and cradle it over my heart, closing my eyes so I can visualise Roman like a favourite dream I want to revisit. I feel his fingertips against my skin. Smell the scent of soap and the outdoors on him. See the golden flecks in his hazel eyes.

I have a date with Roman tonight.

A squeal of joy bubbles up my throat, and my cheeks flush with excitement. I'm excited and nervous and eager. I've never, ever felt like this. Not because I didn't allow myself to, but because no one ever elicited these feelings in me. I feel like a new princess now, just like Sleeping Beauty, who has been arisen by her prince from a deep sleep.

Before Roman, I was sure all men would somehow disappoint me. I shut myself off from any who showed interest. Or at least that is what I thought. But maybe my head knew the right man hadn't come along.

Until I met him.

He is the dangerous one, I think as I run my fingers over the fine-piped edge of the cushion. Roman is the man who made the impression my head couldn't let go of. He is the one I want to take a chance on.

I bolt upright. I have a million things I need to do. I need to pick out my outfit, soak in a long, hot bath with rose oil, and take care to apply my makeup. I want to turn up some music and dance around my bathroom and embrace every wonderful, exhilarating feeling that is sweeping through me because of Roman.

But first, I want to tell a few people, ones in the circle of trust. Normally, this would include my cousins Christian and Xander, who are like brothers to me, but this is going to be strictly girl business right now.

I pop up and move back across the oriental carpet to the hallway where I dropped my yoga bag. I tug on the zip, remove my phone, and before I can even send a single message, I see I have a slew of texts to read.

I head back into the living room and sink down on the sofa again, grabbing the thick, soft throw across the back and tucking it over my lap. I review the texts I need to answer:

Amelia

Clementine

Mum

Bella

I wrinkle my nose. Mum's texts are never good. Usually, she texts me when she needs to vent about my father, the Duke of York. I hate that I am in the middle of their marital drama. The drama that I have been dragged into by accident and now has each of them trying to play me against the other.

What truly hurts is that they don't care that they are hurting me. They don't care that I've been sick to my stomach worrying about this secret, shedding tears over them for fear of what would happen if anyone were to know.

I frown. I wish I didn't know anything. I'm envious of my sisters, Isabella and Victoria, who are off at university and unaware of what I stumbled upon this summer at St. James's Palace.

In a moment of self-care—another cause I would like to encourage in my position—I put a stop to all the bad feelings. Today is my day to be excited and happy. Mum and Dad are not going to ruin this for me. I won't let them.

Instead, I read the text from Amelia:

OMG OMG. There is a picture of Xander holding hands with a girl in Windsor on the Dishing Weekly website. And it's INDIA ROTHSCHILD. Her Majesty must be OVERJOYED.

What? *India?*

I quickly go to the website of that heinous rag—the worst for gossiping and spreading horrible, nasty, mean-spirited stories about my family. This time, I assume, they must have reached a new low with some made-up story, including split side-by-side photos of Xander and India to make it look real, because there is no way he'd be with her.

Xander is in the army, serving in the Household Calvary at Windsor, and will be retiring in January to focus on his royal duties. The media will start applying pressure, along with Antonia, that it's time for the clubbing to end and the search for a wife to ensue. I roll my eyes at that perfectly archaic way of thinking.

But Xander with India? I nearly snort-laugh at the thought.

Actually, it's hard to picture Xander with *anyone*. He loves the ladies, but he's like me for a different reason. He keeps his space to keep his freedom, I keep mine because I don't want to be disappointed, but we both throw up bars around ourselves for —

My brain comes to a screeching halt as soon as *Dishing Weekly* finishes loading on my phone. Sure enough, there is a picture of Xander walking in Windsor this morning and holding hands with Lady India Rothschild.

I gasp. India is gazing up at him with starry eyes, while Xander is smiling and staring straight ahead.

What fresh hell is this?

I zero in on India, who is the daughter of a duke and duchess and *the* socialite on the London scene. She does absolutely nothing but shop and attend specific charity events that she deems worthy. She is a fixture in the chicest clubs in Mayfair and always places herself in Xander's sight if he happens to show up. She's beautiful, of course, with silky blonde hair and a body built by Pilates and a militant diet she makes known to anyone who eats in front of her, but her personality is horrid. She's stuck up, elitist, and has no ambition in life other than to spend her inheritance.

And be the Queen Consort when Xander becomes king in the future.

I immediately call Amelia. She is also a lady — as her

father is the tenth earl of Westbrook—and my kindred spirit. She is down to earth, loves to give back to her causes —one of her big ones is supporting aspiring youth in fashion design in the United Kingdom—and, like me, prefers to keep her socialising out of the trendy nightclubs, opting instead to hang out with groups of friends and have dinner parties at home.

She answers as I head up the stairs to my room. "Hello?" she asks.

"Amelia! What is Xander doing? Has he lost his *mind?* When did this come out?" I say rapidly, needing more facts, and not the ones provided by the idiot crack journalists at *Dishing Weekly.*

"I nearly spat out my coffee when I saw it," Amelia exclaims. "Apparently, they went out for a coffee and a stroll around Windsor."

"I don't get this," I say, reaching the top of the stairs and move across the landing, passing by the portraits Arthur was nice enough to loan me from his personal art collection.

I pause at my favourite one: my role model, a young Princess Helene, my great aunt. She has given her entire life to promoting the monarchy and used her position to do as much as she could, but she is one of the few who realise the monarchy is getting stagnant. She is strongly against the elitist, archaic ideas my grandmother, the dowager queen, as well as Antonia want to hold on to. Over cups of tea, which I take weekly in Apartment 1A here at the palace, she has said the future lies with me, my sisters, and my cousins. She has encouraged us to find new paths to serve.

I study her younger face. She will not be pleased about this India development, as Helene has called her a wannabe queen, as real as cling film. Helene took back the comment, citing it as an insult to cling film.

"I don't understand it either," Amelia says, interrupting my thoughts. "Xander has never shown any interest in her at the functions or parties I've seen them at."

"No, and he's never talked about her. Ever. Nor has she been on the list of girls that he's flirted with or gone out with," I add.

"You don't think he's going to do the old idea of 'get on with marriage' now that he's going to retire from the army, do you?" Amelia asks.

I blink. I never thought of that. But God only knows how much pressure he will get from not only the media, but also from Antonia, to find a suitable wife.

Then it hits me. I wonder if she is pushing this on Xander because Clementine, an American with no wealthy background or aristocratic lineage, is her worst nightmare as a future member of the family.

I gasp. "She thinks India is the antidote to the popularity of Clem!"

"Liz, what are you talking about?" Amelia asks.

"But why would Xander do this? He's always stood up to Antonia," I say, continuing my thought process out loud.

My phone beeps. I see it's Clementine. Maybe she knows the real scoop.

"Amelia, it's Clem. Let me see if she knows what is going on, and I'll call you back."

"Believe me, if you don't, I shall ring you incessantly until you pick up," she declares.

I hang up with her and take Clem's phone call.

"Clementine! What the hell is going on with Xander?" I blurt out, continuing to my room and pacing across the shining hardwood floor.

"I know, Liz. It's crazy. Christian is freaked out. He called Xander as soon as the picture went viral across social media. He asked Xander if he pulled this stunt to deflect from my first walkabout on Tuesday. Which I still want to puke about, by the way."

Oh, I hadn't thought about that. Maybe this wasn't an Antonia stunt but a clever one by Xander to take some publicity pressure off Clementine and Christian. Relief fills me, and I sink down onto the edge of my duvet. "So that's why he did it," I say, nodding.

"No!" Clementine says sharply. "He told Christian it's time to grow up and get serious with someone."

I bolt right back up to standing. "What is he doing? He picked India because she fit the role? He's never found her interesting!"

"Christian is as baffled as you are. If anything, he thought he'd pick someone the opposite of India because his mom adores her."

We both fall silent for a moment, as Xander being with anyone—and now choosing boring, stuffy, snotty India—is truly baffling. I need to get out my colouring book while I work this out in my head.

"I'll talk to him later," I say. "There has to be more to this."

"I don't know. Xander was clear to Christian that this was something he wanted to do."

"Ew, but India? Does he not see that she is Antonia two point oh?"

"She is," Clementine agrees. "But for reasons we don't know, right now, she's his choice for romance."

I resist the urge to throw up at that visual.

"Well, tea with Helene will be even more lively than usual next week," I say.

"Forget that. We need Jillian to come over and mix up gin and tonics to sort this one out."

I smile. That would be fun. Maybe I'll suggest that to Helene.

"Now we," I say, shifting away from Xander drama for a moment, "are going to go over everything you need for your public appearance this week. I'm sharing all my secrets, including how you must exit the car on the photographer side so they can get good pictures of you. You need to pose for a few seconds so they can do their job. They will love you if you do that."

"I'll make sure to turn the droopy side of my face towards the *Dishing Weekly* guys," Clementine quips.

I grin. She has handled being thrust into our world amazingly well, and when *Dishing Weekly* exposed her facial paralysis from her brain tumour surgery, she ended up finding one of her new causes—helping people with permanent illnesses—and sharing her own journey with the world.

"You will be amazing, and people will love you. For this week, at least," I half-tease.

One thing I will do is always be honest with Clementine. Right now they all love her for being a breath of fresh air in the monarchy, but I've also prepared her for when they will come after her with pitchforks for wearing the wrong shoes, or not curtsying deep enough to Arthur.

"You are so right about that," Clementine laughs. "I can't wait for them to start watching my stomach for a baby. It wouldn't be proper protocol to yell out, 'It's a sandwich!', right?"

I giggle. "A sandwich can't give you a baby belly."

"Speak for yourself. I bloat with grain."

I clear my throat. "So, Clem, I have something to tell you. I don't want you to get all excited or anything, but I have a date tonight."

Clem is silent.

Hmm. Maybe, on the heels of Xander dating, this is too much. If I hear a thud, I'll know that she has passed out and hit the floor, as both developments are equally shocking.

"What?" she finally asks. "A date? Are you joking?"

I smile as Roman comes to the forefront of my mind instead of Xander and Ms. Cling Film.

"I'm serious. I'm having dinner with a gorgeous, sweet man. And his name is Roman Lawler."

Dead silence.

"Clementine?"

"No," she gasps. "No way! Roman? My friend Roman from Cheltham House?"

I grin. "That is indeed the same Roman Lawler."

I hear a happy shriek on the phone, then her dogs, Bear and Lucy, barking, and then Christian's voice in the background.

"Christian! Liz has a date with Roman!" she yells out gleefully.

I blush as I hear the excitement in her voice. So much for keeping this in the girl circle of trust.

"Liz, how? How did you connect? How did this happen? I have so many questions, but they don't matter because he is wonderful. I'm so happy! Wait, I'll come over. You can tell me in person because, unlike Ms. Cling Film, this is news to be celebrated, and I need all the glorious details."

※

I put the last pin in my messy bun, which is loose at the nape of my neck, and study my reflection in the full-length mirror in my dressing room. The chandelier light flickers softly overhead, and I'm surrounded in the large walk-in space by my clothing, shoes, hats, and bags, all organised by colour and style. Each handbag has a place, as well as each pair of shoes and every hat box. In the centre of my room, there is a long glass cabinet that holds my jewellery, gloves, and other accessories. My clothing diary is kept on a tablet in the top drawer so I know what I've worn to events and appearances and when.

But I don't need a designer gown tonight, or a smart clutch.

I'm dressed for a casual night in.

A first date.

With one Roman Lawler.

I study my reflection in amazement because I've never seen this glow on my skin before. I'm excited and nervous and filled with joy about tonight.

After Clementine came over and we reverted to sixteen-year-old school girls talking, as Clem said, about *"all the Roman things,"* we came upstairs to my dressing room. We spent another hour sorting through my wardrobe to find the perfect casual outfit for tonight, and I ended up selecting a pair of Rag & Bone jeans and a cream V-neck cashmere jumper. But then, to surprise Roman, I picked a Burberry wool check scarf in rose, which adds a pop of colour next to my ivory skin. A simple pair of antique pearl studs, given to me by Helene from her private collection, complete my outfit.

I study myself again. I spent the rest of the afternoon getting ready and thinking about how I was more excited to dress for this date than I have been for any formal party I've attended at Buckingham Palace. I pick up my black leather motorcycle jacket, slip into it, and then move over to my vanity. I reach for my signature scent, Shay & Blue

Black Tulip, and spray the beautiful floral perfume on my wrists and the base of my neck. I close my eyes, remembering Roman's fingertips over my wrist and how he felt my pulse.

Will he feel my pulse racing for him this evening, too?

My heart does that zigzag inside my chest as I head down the stairs to wait for him. I alerted security that he would be here to see me this evening and to allow him in at the gate.

I draw a nervous breath as I try to anticipate opening the door to him, seeing his handsome face, and sitting next to him in the car. I wonder if his hand will reach for mine.

I tug on my tall, black boots and try to tamp down the butterflies fluttering within me. My mind skips ahead. What will our dinner be like? What's his flat like? Will our conversation be as natural as it was this morning?

I wrap my arms around myself, willing him to get here as soon as possible. I want to know what it's like to see him working in his kitchen. I want to sit across the table and see him reward me with that beautiful smile for something I've said.

The sound of a car cuts through my thoughts. Roman. I know it is.

I allow myself to pause at the window as the sound comes closer. A small Land Rover slows in front of Wren House and pulls up to the curb. I watch as he steps out of the car, and my heart comes alive when I see him rake his fingertips through his hair, smoothing it so it looks good for me.

I hurry away from the window and wait for him to ring the doorbell. I can't believe this is happening. After months of thinking about him, I got my chance. I can't believe the chemistry and connection I felt sitting in the greenhouse with him. Now we'll see what the evening brings us.

The doorbell rings.

My heart beats rapidly against my chest. I breathe in deeply. I don't even think colouring could calm the emotions I'm feeling right now. Nor do I want them to, because they are all magnificent. Wonderful. Real.

I open the door and stifle a gasp as Roman stands before me. He's ruggedly handsome in a black leather jacket, jeans, and brown boots. I shiver, not from the cold December wind that whips across us but from the way his eyes are lingering over my face. He hasn't even glanced at my outfit. Roman's hazel eyes are simply staring into mine, almost disbelieving that he's gazing at me.

"You're actually standing in front of me," he says, his deep voice low. "This is going to happen, isn't it?"

The chemistry from his words is palpable. I can feel it between us without even touching him.

"I'm here, hardly believing I'm looking at you. I wondered for months if I was crazy to keep thinking of you after that brief moment right over there," I say, gesturing towards Christian and Clementine's cottage. "Did I make it more than it was? Di—"

"No," Roman interrupts, "you did not."

My heart is pounding in my ears.

He turns and takes in his surroundings. Then he faces me again, a mystified expression on his handsome face. "I'm at *Kensington Palace*. With you. How am I not dreaming? How does this make sense? How am I here, in my beat-up car, to take you to my small flat? It can't be real."

"Because this is my home," I remind him, not wanting Roman to be skittish because of my situation. "You're picking me up here, like you'd pick me up if I lived in a flat in any other neighbourhood. You're taking me in the car you own to the place you live to make me dinner. My situation is unique, with my family and what I do and where I live. I know that. But I'm still the same girl as the one in the greenhouse, Roman."

He remains silent as he stares down at me. "Which I'm glad about."

Ooh!

His mouth curves up into a gentle smile. "Are you ready?"

I nod, thinking he'd never ask. I take a moment to lock the door and drop the key into my Anna Walker cross-body bag.

Roman smiles down at me, and it illuminates my heart.

"Shall I take you to flat number five, Liz?"

Then he offers me his arm.

I'm shaking as I wrap my hand over it. I glance up at him, wanting to remember this moment and the way the moonlight is dancing across his face, the way I smell the leather from his jacket, and the way he's smiling down at me, only seeing me as Liz.

"Yes," I say eagerly. "Take me to flat number five."

CHAPTER 6

CHRISTMAS CAKE AND A GLASS OF PORT

Roman escorts me to the passenger door. Like a true gentleman, he opens it for me, and I reluctantly release my grip on his arm so I can slip inside. While he is walking around to the driver's side, I take a deep breath and try to calm myself.

Oh, screw it, I think as he opens his door. *I've never been so excited to be on a date in my life, and I want the nerves and butterflies.*

The second Roman is in the car with me, I drink in the scent on his skin again, the familiar smell of sandalwood soap. Oh, that's sexy. I study his profile as he starts the car, and I notice he's shaved. I fold my hands in my lap to resist the urge to lay my hand against his cheek to feel his smooth skin.

"You look lovely, Liz," he says, interrupting my thoughts. He shifts his attention to me as the car idles. "This is surreal. I can't stop staring at you for fear that you'll dissolve the second I touch you. Not because of your last name or because I'm in Kensington Palace, but because you're the girl from the greenhouse today. You're *Liz*, the girl I thought of for so long but never dreamt could be anything more."

Emotions swell within me. Roman has connected with me in the way I hoped.

With the real me.

"I promise I won't disappear if you touch me again," I say softly.

Roman's eyes spark. Even in the darkness, I know the golden flecks have grown brighter with my words. I hold my breath as he slowly lifts his hand and hovers it over mine, which is still folded in my lap. He picks up my right hand, and I stifle a gasp as he slowly, deliberately, pushes the edge of my jacket sleeve up so his fingertips can slide to my wrist. He begins stroking my skin, carefully, as if his fingers are imprinting the feel of it to memory.

Heat ignites inside me as he draws his fingertips oh-so-slowly from my wrist to my hand, continuing to rub his calloused fingertips back and forth across my skin. They travel with a slow, tortured speed towards my knuckles, where he slowly skims each one as he stares deeply into my eyes.

Roman's fingertips travel up to my fingers now, moving over them and making me go mad with desire as he caresses each one up to the fingertip, gazing into my eyes as he touches each one. I have never had a man touch me like this, with such sensual deliberation. It makes me wonder how he kisses.

I shiver as he draws my hand to his mouth. I suck in a breath of anticipation, desperate to feel those warm lips against my flesh. My pulse·ignites the second I feel his breath hit my skin. Roman turns my hand over and slowly, reverently, places his warm, soft lips against my knuckles.

It's the sexiest, most romantic kiss I've ever had.

I'm trembling all over as he turns my hand over again and rubs his thumb along the inside of my wrist, down to where my pulse is beating furiously. He draws my wrist closer to him, and I yearn for the next kiss. Roman replaces his thumb with his lips, pressing another gentle kiss onto my skin.

The desire to kiss him becomes more acute.

It's now a need.

"I'm real," I whisper to him.

"I know," Roman says, his deep voice low. "Believe me, I know."

He lowers my hand and places it back on my lap, and I feel a pang in my heart when he releases his hand from mine.

He clears his throat. "I hope you're hungry," he says as he shifts the car into first gear.

"I hope you're cooking a lot, because I'm famished," I tease.

We talk as we head out of the protected gates of Kensington Palace and into the city. The conversation between us is as easy as it was in the greenhouse, which makes me happy.

"Do you like living in London?" I ask as Roman drives in the direction of the neighbourhood where he lives. "With your love of gardening, it almost seems like you'd be happier out in the country."

"Oh, no, not so," he insists. "Don't get me wrong, I love the country for the beauty of it, but I actually find a lot of visual inspiration in the city for what I do in the garden. Like I'll see a sign with interesting colours put together, and I'll get an idea of how to replicate that with flowers. Painting with nature, so to speak."

"But do you enjoy city life?" I ask.

Roman grins, and my heart flutters at the full smile. "It doesn't matter where I live because, most of the time, I'm in the garden or at my flat. With the outside possibility of going to a Spurs game with Darcy or maybe to the pub for a pint."

I smile, now knowing Roman's favourite football team is Tottenham Hotspur.

"That sounds like the confession of a hermit who is lured out if there are tickets on match day."

"Not true. If you offered me Man United tickets, I'd say no, unless they were playing the Spurs."

"What about pub quiz nights?"

Roman groans. "Oh, God, no. Darcy loves them, but I hate pub quiz nights. I find trivia games boring."

"You must be bad at trivia then," I tease.

His smile broadens. "No, I'm not, but sitting still and answering questions for hours is not my idea of fun."

I feel like I'm colouring now, starting to add contrast and shading to fill in the blank spaces. I see Roman as someone who gets antsy sitting still for long periods. He needs to be active, outdoors, and doing something with his hands.

I get a flash of his fingertips exploring my hand in that sensual way. Yes, Roman is exceptionally gifted with his hands.

"How do you spend your nights in London? You aren't a regular on the Mayfair scene," he says, interrupting my thoughts.

"How would you know?"

"Google."

"And when did you Google me?" I ask, laughing so he knows I'm not mad but intrigued by this development.

"After I rode away from you this summer."

Zing, zing, zing!

My heart dances from this revelation.

"What did you discover?" I ask.

"That you work incredibly hard. All the time. You aren't snapped at the clubs. Most of the pictures, outside of work ones, were of you getting a coffee or shopping on Oxford Street," he says.

I grimace. The press loves to go after me when I buy clothing or things for my home. "But none of me pushing a trolley while doing the shopping?" I ask. "Those exist. Try 'Princess Liz plus trolley' for your search."

Roman chuckles, and God, his deep voice makes that an intoxicating sound to my ears. "I will, but you are evading the question. What do you do for fun? Besides colouring."

"I love decorating my home. That's why I'm out shopping quite a bit. I'm always searching for things that will make my house a home. It's not like I have a list, per se, but when I see something, I know if it belongs in Wren House. I can spend hours even on the little things, right down to the tea towels that hang in my kitchen."

"That's how I am about gardening tools and seeds," Roman says. "I can spend hours studying seed catalogues. I love finding heirloom seeds and incorporating them into the garden." He groans. "I'm talking about seeds. What is wrong with me? I sound like all I do is live in a garden."

"Well, don't you?" I tease.

"No," he insists. "I cook. And I like woodworking. I'm working on some bookshelves now."

Again, always busy with his hands.

"You don't like idle hands, do you?" I ask.

Roman chuckles again. "No, I don't. I've never been good at it."

"My brain is always operating like that. It won't stop.

I'm learning things to calm my mind, which is usually operating five steps ahead. I think it stems from my work. I have to prepare the day before. I study all the people I'm going to meet, learn who they are and what they do. I study current news articles about the charity or organisation. I get an agenda from my assistant that breaks down how everything will be timed. If I have to speak, I practice my speech several times. My outfit is selected and catalogued. If I have multiple events that day, I refresh in the car between them, studying my notes. Then if I have an appearance at night, I go through the same preparation and do an outfit change."

I take a breath. I never realised how much I go and go and go until I said all of this out loud to Roman.

"You have a hard time shutting work off, don't you?" he asks as we enter Shepherd's Bush.

"I do. I'm trying to be better, though. I made myself sick in the beginning because I couldn't sleep at night. My brain wouldn't shut off. So, I began searching for solutions. I picked up an interesting book on self-care, and that is something that I'm working on. I mindfully try to do things that ease my stress. Colouring is one. Yoga is another. I try to eat better, but that one is harder for me because I crave pastries when I'm tired or stressed."

"Lemon curd tarts?" Roman says, a slow smile spreading across his face as he turns down a residential road.

"No, sir, you are incorrect," I say emphatically. "Lemon bars. A cup of tea and a stack of lemon bars. With extra icing sugar."

He laughs. My heart flutters.

"The Christmas season is upon us now. Do you ditch the lemon bars for this occasion?"

"What madness do you speak of? 'Ditch the lemon bars?' No! I always have lemon bars. Though I do love a good slice of Christmas cake."

As I talk about the cake, I suddenly get an urge for it, all studded with fruit and topped with marzipan and royal icing. So. Good.

"My Grandmother used to make Christmas cake," Roman says, turning down another road. "We haven't had one since she became ill. I think it used to make everyone sad, you know, as a reminder of her, but I miss them. I think it would be a lovely tribute to her to have a slice in her honour every year."

Sentimental, I think, my pulse skipping a beat. *Roman is sentimental when it comes to his family.*

"I think that's a lovely idea," I say softly.

"We changed to brandy butter on Christmas pudding," Roman says. "But I do miss Grandmother's cake. She always had it with a glass of port. I can still see her in the kitchen, making her cake and drinking port at the same time. Sometimes, that resulted in some... interesting décor on the cake, like lopsided Christmas trees. One famous year, we celebrated a 'Hapyp Chrismas.'"

I laugh. "No!"

"Yes. That was classic. Grandmother was so embarrassed. Obviously, she hit the port harder that year."

I smile, my heart warmed by the fact that Roman treasures these little memories of his past.

"Do you know what I've never done?" I say as he draws to a stop near a vacant parking spot on the street.

"Misspelled 'Happy Christmas' on a cake because you were too deep into the port glass?"

I laugh. "No. I've never decorated a Christmas tree."

Roman's brows knit together as he manoeuvres the car into the spot. "What? Never? Not even as a little girl?"

My cheeks pool with heat. "No. My parents always let the staff at St. James's Palace do that. Wait. I'm lying. The staff would leave out a small box of decorations, and Bella, Victoria, and I would each take one and put it on one of the trees. That was our version of decorating."

Roman frowns. "I'm sure the trees at St. James's Palace are incredible, but that seems wrong. Your parents didn't even have a family tree?"

"No," I admit. "It's funny. As a kid, you see things as ordinary because you don't know any better. But as an adult, you look back and think, 'that would have been a nice thing for them to do for us as children.' It would have made our Christmases more... normal."

Roman finally has the car in the spot and turns off the engine. He faces me, his hazel eyes shining in earnest.

"But it's something you can change for yourself. You can have that tree, Liz."

"Like you can have Christmas cake and port."

He stares at me. "Yeah, like that."

Our eyes remain locked, and suddenly, I have a vision of decorating my first tree with this man. I imagine us also attempting to decorate our own cake and drinking port and toasting his Grandmother as we each have a slice.

Crazy, right? The fact that that thought slid so easily into my head?

Roman clears his throat, and I'm grateful he can't see the picture of Christmas bliss I had coloured of us. Otherwise, he'd be turning the engine right back on and speeding back to my place so he could throw me out in front of the gates of Kensington Palace.

"Well, this is it," he says, inclining his head towards my

window. "We're on the ground floor. It's not much, but it's where I live."

I study the Edwardian-style building, one of many identical ones up and down the street he lives on. I'm about to say something about it, but Roman has already opened his car door and is dashing around to my side to open mine for me.

Once again, his thoughtful side shines through.

"You don't have to always open my door, Roman," I say, smiling at him as I exit the car. "While I appreciate it, and I do thank you, I can get it myself."

"I know you can," he says as he offers me his arm again.

Gentleman. Gallant. Thoughtful. Sentimental.

I am the luckiest woman in all of England, and it has nothing to do with palaces or titles or spending Christmas at Sandringham.

But I hesitate to take his arm in public.

"Liz?" he asks, his brow knitting together.

"I shouldn't take your arm in public, even though I want to," I say gently. "If someone takes a picture, we'll have no privacy to get to know each other."

Recognition dawns in his eyes. "You're right," he says. "I'm sorry."

"Don't be. And I'll gladly take your arm the second we are inside."

We stroll up the path to the front door.

"You caused quite a stir in the media this summer when you shut your own door going to an event," Roman says.

I laugh as we walk. "I had no idea closing my own door was such a big deal."

"I didn't even have to Google that one," he says.

"No?" I ask. Then I grin. "Did Google alert you to

Princess Liz breaking news? That she—gasp!—opens her own doors?"

"No," he says slowly, stopping as we reach the door. "That was on the telly during breakfast. I couldn't avoid you, even when my brain told me I should."

Bam! My heart slams against my ribs with force.

"Why did your head want to avoid me?" I ask, staring up at him.

Roman swallows before answering. "Because this was *a fantasy.* You're Princess Liz. I saw you once; I knew I'd never see you again. There was no way a woman like you would have thought for a second about a man like me."

Roman unlocks the door and we step inside the small hallway. As soon as the door is shut behind us, he reaches for my hand again, this time turning it over in his as if it's a newly treasured object he can't believe is his but has had the good fortune to have found. His thumb caresses the top of my hand, and I break out into goosebumps.

"I thought about you for many seconds, feeling like you were just as elusive to me," I admit.

He draws my hand to his lips again, and tingles run through every inch of me as his warm lips graze my knuckles.

"This is crazy, me inviting you here. Crazy to cook for you, to think I can impress you in some way when your life is so—"

I take my fingertips and press them against his lips, causing his eyes to flip wide open in surprise.

"I'm here because I want to be. There's nowhere else I want to be right now than in your flat, getting to know you."

Roman takes my hand again. "I have a feeling it's going to be hard to say no to anything you ever ask me to do."

"Good. Now let's go inside."

He grins and opens the door for me, and as I enter his world, I know I will never be the same as I was before this moment.

And I have a good feeling about what this evening will bring.

CHAPTER 7

A COSY DINNER FOR TWO

"You don't have to stand in the corner," Roman teases as he chops up some veg. "Although standing in the corner in this flat means you are only three steps away."

I take a sip of my chardonnay and smile. His kitchen, while fully refurbished with white cupboards and marble worktops, is impossibly tiny. I feel as though Roman's massive frame needs all the room he can get as he works at the short worktop crammed with ingredients. When I was next to him, he kept bumping into me as he tried to prepare everything in the small space, so I decided to give him some room by backing up a few spaces and parking myself against the door that leads to the garden.

"I don't want to be in the way of you creating a culinary masterpiece," I say.

Roman smiles as he dumps parsnips in a bowl. "I'm just hoping it won't be burnt. I'm not used to being distracted when I cook."

"By talking?" I ask. Because from the second we entered his flat, that's all we've done as he has prepared dinner for us.

Roman turns his head to face me. "No. By the beautiful woman who has agreed to dine with me this evening. It's distracting knowing you are a few feet away from me."

My heart does another zigzag from his compliment, and my stomach does a summersault from the way he's gazing at me.

He shifts his attention back to the chopping board, and I notice the flush has returned to his neck. Swoon. If this were my great-great-great-so-many-greats Grandmother Victoria's time, I'd be on the verge of needing smelling salts.

"I assume parsnips and kale are in season right now?" I ask.

Roman nods. "Yes. I grew all the produce we're having tonight. All in season for December."

"I love that you are so passionate about eating food in season," I say.

"Food tastes so much better when it's fresh from the garden," Roman says, discarding a kale stem. "I'm picky about that."

"What else are you picky about?"

His mouth turns up in that teasing, "I'm not going to give in to that smile yet" way.

"Do you honestly want to know?"

"I do."

Roman pauses for a moment. "I'm picky about clothing. I feel out of sorts in a suit and tie. Restricted. I'm much happier in jeans and a T-shirt."

Restricted, I muse, absorbing his words. I imagine he would be restricted in an office job, wearing a suit and a tie and being in a building all day.

With a sharp pang, a doubt comes to life in my heart. My life is incredibly restrictive. In what I can wear. How I can act. What I can say. Even how to stand on a balcony at Buckingham Palace is organised.

Is it fair to flirt with the idea of something with Roman, knowing how much he would hate my life if we started to see each other? How on earth could he be happy in my world? Would it make him miserable? I couldn't bear it if it di—

"Your turn." Roman's deep voice interrupts my thoughts.

I blink. I'm having dinner with him. That's it. I need to, no matter how impossible it seems, not think five steps ahead and enjoy this evening for what it is meant to be.

Which is sharing a cosy meal for two with this man.

I steel my resolve to focus on the now and smile at him. "I'm picky about pens and pencils."

Now I get an amused smile from him, which sets my heart back to happy. "Pens?"

"I don't like light pens. I like a good, solid fountain pen. With a nib, you can write so elegantly. I sometimes will use multiple pens a day because I want different nibs. I have one I like for everyday writing, like in my diary, but if I'm writing a thank you note, I have a different preference."

Roman stops what he is doing and turns around to face me completely. "So, a fine evening for you might be studying nibs on a website?"

I smile coyly and take a sip of my wine. "Perhaps."

"Perhaps?"

"Only if I'm not on a pen forum talking about pens and answering questions for people new to fountain pens."

His beautiful eyes widen in surprise and amusement.

"Pen forums?"

"Oh, yes, they exist. There are pen meetups, too."

Roman tries to repress his smile, but he can't.

"You hang out with pen people?"

"I do. I talk about pens, nibs, even coloured ink. It's awfully exciting."

His smile reaches up to his eyes. "It sounds like it."

I can't help but laugh. "Do you think people have any idea that we like to spend our free evenings studying pens and heirloom seeds?"

"No, but why make them feel inadequate for being out at a nightclub having cocktails? Only bitter jealousy would ensue."

I can't stop smiling. "Did you think we'd be the same? Preferring to stay in and pursue our own interests?"

"No," Roman says, shaking his head. "I didn't."

Our eyes lock again, and my breath catches as I see how he's gazing at me. His eyes are full of surprise, happiness, interest, and attraction, and I know, without a doubt, they mirror the expression in my own.

"Can I please help you?" I ask. "I feel wrong standing over here drinking while you work."

"No," Roman says, shifting back to the task at hand. He picks up the parsnips and moves over to the oven. "I'm going to pop these in to roast. Then I'll sauté the guinea hen and kale. Then we can sit down to eat."

He reaches inside the fridge and juggles a few things in his arms. I see one package is about to slip, so I rush forward to catch it. I forget about the wine in my hand, so as I do, I catch the butter but spill my chardonnay all over his chest.

I watch in horror as the wine sloshes across his jumper and all over the food he has gathered in his arms. His hand instinctively takes a hold of my elbow, holding me close to him, with butter, mushrooms, cream, and parsley squished between us.

For a moment, I don't move. It's bliss to be this close to him, to feel his touch, breathe in his scent, and gaze upon his beautiful face, which is now inches from mine.

Bliss indeed.

I'm snapped back to reality when I feel wine dribble down my jumper sleeve.

"Oh!" I gasp, "I'm so sorry, Roman! I reacted without thinking."

His fingertips don't move from my elbow. "Do I seem upset?" he asks.

I blush. Furiously.

"I appreciate your eagerness to help," he says, letting my arm go. "Or your excuse to be near me." His eyes are dancing. His mouth is curved up.

The game is on.

"You're right. I was looking for any excuse to crash into your massive chest, and butter in a perilous state was just the invitation I needed."

"You've noticed the size of my chest?" Roman asks, twitching his full lips in amusement.

I want to kiss that twitch right off his sexy face.

"What if I have?"

"You see me as a sex object then," he declares, moving back to the worktop and shoving things around to make room for the new items.

I furrow my brow. I wish Roman had more space to cook. It has to be hard to have to utilise this small space every night.

"You know I'm teasing, right, Liz?"

I lift my eyes from the worktop to his face, which is etched in concern that perhaps I took him seriously when, in fact, I was thinking about his kitchen. I'm about to answer when the sound of the front door opening catches both our attention.

"Darcy," Roman says, nodding. "Don't worry, he knows to make himself scarce this evening."

Because you can see everything in this tiny flat, I keep my attention fixed on the door. It swings open, and in walks Darcy. I see so much of Roman in him. He's tall, dark, and handsome, though not quite as tall as Roman, and his hair is longish and wavy. As soon as he sees me, he stops dead in his tracks.

"My God, you *are* Princess Elizabeth," he declares, his voice echoing with amazement. "I thought Roman was *joking*."

I feel Roman's eyes land on my profile while Darcy remains frozen in the doorway. Nervousness seeps through my happy feelings. I've always been strong in my identity. I know what I was born into. I accept my position with great pride, responsibility, and patriotism. Unlike my cousin Christian, who wrestled with his position in life until he met Clementine and discovered his true self, I've been happy with my station.

But now, at least for tonight, I don't want to be Princess Elizabeth of York. I don't want to be seen as a member of the monarchy. I don't want to scare Roman off with my reality. Not tonight.

Tonight, I just want to be Liz, a woman on a date with Roman.

I decide to take action. I smile brightly, move across the living room, and extend my hand to a shocked Darcy. "Liz," I say simply. "I've heard a lot about you, Darcy."

He stares at my hand as if it's not real. He lifts his brown eyes—ah, another difference: they aren't beautiful and unique like Roman's, with all the flecks of brown, green, and gold—and he gawks at me, his mouth slightly open.

"Please shut the door and shake her hand, *Mr. Darcy*," Roman says.

I repress a smile. I know from his tone that Mr. Darcy must be a name his cousin doesn't like.

"Shut up," Darcy says, yanking the door shut behind him. He quickly extends his hand towards me. "It's a pleasure to meet you, um, Your Royal Highness."

"Liz," I repeat again, shaking his hand firmly in mine.

"Er, Liz," Darcy says. He drops his rucksack on the floor and rakes a hand through his hair, which makes the waves appear higher on his head.

"My aunt Lisa named him after Mr. Darcy; I assume you know what I'm talking about," Roman says.

"All women know what you're talking about," Darcy says, slipping out of his coat and dumping it on top of his rucksack.

I remember how Roman helped me out of my coat, then took off his, and neatly hung them on a coatrack next to the door when we entered the flat, as opposed to Darcy dumping everything on the floor. He reminds me of Victoria, who was a nightmare for the housekeeping staff at St. James's Palace growing up.

"Mum was a huge *Pride and Prejudice* fan, I take it?" I ask.

Darcy flashes me a cheeky grin. A sense of relief sweeps over me. Conversation is reminding him I'm a normal human being.

"God, yes," he says, heading into the kitchen. He moves to the fridge and pokes around for a minute before pulling out a takeaway foil tray and standing back up. "Growing up, I hated it because everyone thought I was a girl with the name Darcy. Then it became Mr. Darcy. Now it's to my advantage. Girls obsessed with Jane Austen love it." He grins broadly at me. "Hmm, and you're Liz. Short for Elizabeth. Are you the Lizzie to my Mr. Darcy?" he jokes, his deep brown eyes sparkling at me.

"No," Roman says, picking up the guinea fowl and giving it a hard whack with a meat cleaver, "she is *not* your Lizzie."

"Oh, he must like you. One, because you're here—that's a first—and two, he doesn't like me joking about you being my Lizzie. I'm kidding, Roman. He," Darcy says, leaning closer to me, "is a serious one. Loosen him up, would you?"

I'm about to reply, but Roman beats me to it.

"Don't you have more books to read?" he says pointedly.

"Yes, yes, I'm taking my cold sweet and sour pork and conveniently hiding in my room for the rest of the night to study," Darcy promises. He smiles at me. "It's a pleasure to meet you, Liz. Surreal, but a pleasure."

I smile. "Nice to meet you, too, Darcy."

He takes a few steps towards his room but pauses and glances back at Roman, who is breaking down the bird with his knife.

"Roman?" he says, and I see mischief in his eyes.

Roman glances up.

"Use the words 'most ardently,'" Darcy says, referring to a phrase used in *Pride and Prejudice*. "Women love that."

"Shut up," Roman says, his neck growing redder by the second.

Darcy laughs, and Roman appears to be mortified by his suggestion. I have a feeling if his hands weren't engaged in a bird, he'd be ruffling his hair right now in embarrassment.

Or personally shoving Darcy down the hall to his room, I think with a smile.

I move back into the kitchen, closer to Roman this time. "You're flushed."

"He's annoying," Roman says, quickly cutting apart the bird.

I take a moment to watch him work. Wow, he's like a professional butcher. I can't even get the leg separated from the thigh when I attempt to cook at home.

He places all the parts on a new chopping board and moves to wash his hands.

"I think you're cute when you get flustered," I bravely admit.

Roman turns on the tap with the back of his hand and uses his wrist to pump soap into his open palm. "You must think I'm cute a lot when I'm around you."

Ooh!

He scrubs his hands and dries them on a tea towel.

"You say what you think," I tell him. "I like that about you."

His honesty and openness with his thoughts is downright intriguing. I've never had a man be this honest with me. But I've also never cared until now whether they were or not.

"Shall we reset now that Mr. Darcy is out of our hair?" Roman asks.

I giggle at his annoyance with his cousin. They truly are like brothers. "Yes, and I believe you were about to tell me all about your ex-girlfriends when Darcy interrupted us," I say, curious with how Darcy brought that up, as if it's a novelty that Roman invited me home.

And not because I'm a princess.

Roman laughs deeply. "Oh, you lie. That's a conversation for another night."

"Is it?" I ask, now extremely curious about the women in his past.

"I'll share that when you share your royal history. We'll share our history another time. Tonight, I don't want the serious past. Only the now. If you agree, that is."

Once again, his honesty touches my heart.

"Agreed," I say, nodding.

Roman smiles. "Good. Now let me get this bird in the pan so we can eat."

I can't believe the evening has come to an end.

I stare at Roman as we drive through the gates of Kensington Palace. It's well after one in the morning, and I would have happily stayed in his flat until the sun comes up if it wouldn't have been too imposing on him.

I think of all the dinners I've had in my life, from Christmas Eve at Sandringham to elaborate state dinners at Buckingham Palace and feasts at the top restaurants in the world to meals prepared by private chefs, made to my exact specifications.

But nothing, and I mean nothing, compared to having a meal with Roman.

He prepared it for me as a sign of affection. I would have loved it if it would have been a simple toastie, but he is a chef. The guinea fowl was pan seared with truffle butter and was absolutely decadent. I had pureed parsnips with freshly grated parmesan cheese and kale with white wine. I savoured every moment of the meal, talking with Roman at the intimate table for two that he built himself.

Once again, I found myself drawn to his hands. Ones of great talent. Ones he uses for things he cares about, like gardening. Cooking.

And me, I think as my heart beats faster.

We stayed at that table for *hours*, talking about our likes and dislikes and discovering more about each other. We're both morning people. We get up early, have quiet time, and prepare for the day ahead. We both run. We're both news junkies, but while I read everything on my laptop, Roman prefers to have a physical newspaper in his hands, which made me smile. We talked of our families, with me discussing my sisters and my parents and cousins, and Roman doing the same. His parents also live in Shepherd's Bush, and he usually goes round with Darcy for Sunday lunch, while I normally have that at St. James's Palace with my parents. I confessed to not having much of an affection for chocolate and having a mortal fear of spiders. Roman forgave me for not liking chocolate and told me spiders are important to the eco system and I should embrace them.

We talked about world issues and politics. It was a luxury to have an opinion on the topic with another person, as I'm not allowed to give any hint of my personal feelings in public or in interviews. But as I spoke, I discovered our thoughts aligned. I shared my thoughts of the world we live in and how I wish things could change for the future. He did the same. I talked about my work and my causes for children, and Roman talked about his longing to protect the environment and raise awareness about sustainable farming.

Our conversation confirmed what my heart hoped it would find this evening.

Roman is a man who lives his beliefs, as I do. He's true to who he is. He is passionate about things he loves, and he's determined to know what goes on in the world around him. He's a knowledge seeker, and his seed-loving soul seems matched to my fountain pen-loving heart.

When we are parked outside my cottage, he asks in a low voice, "May I walk you up to your door?"

Zing! "Yes."

The air is sharp and cold. Normally, I'd race down the path to my door to get away from it, but not tonight.

Roman opens my car door, and once again, I feel that swoon from his manners.

You are such a gentleman, I think as I tuck my arm around his and we walk, safe from wayward cameras now that we are inside the palace walls. I'm a bundle of nerves. Will he kiss me goodnight?

Oh, how I want him to kiss me.

Nothing is said as we reach the door. Roman unhooks his arm from mine, and I lick my lips as I gaze up at him. I lose my breath. He is so beautiful, from his chiseled features to his full lips, but his eyes are my undoing. They are unique and changing, and I don't think I'll ever grow tired of looking into them.

"Liz," Roman says slowly, "thank you for coming to dinner this evening. It was an honour getting to know you."

My stomach flips in excitement. My heart is fluttering.

"I enjoyed it so much," I say, nodding. "Everything about tonight was wonderful."

Because it was spent with you.

His eyes lock with mine. I wait for him to lower his head, to put his hand on my waist or against my cheek. My pulse grows rapid in anticipation of this moment.

Roman doesn't move. Instead, he gently takes my hand. "I owe you nothing but honesty about what I'm thinking," he says softly.

My heart stops. My stomach drops with a huge thud.

No, I think, my mind reeling. *Is this where Roman, in all his honesty, tells me dinner is it? That can't be.*

"I could tell you I'm going to text you later, but that would be a lie," he continues, his voice low. "I would prefer to call you, so I can hear your voice."

My heart roars back to life, and I find myself grinning at him. "I'd prefer that, too," I say.

Roman lifts my hand to his lips again and turns it over so my palm is facing him. He gently presses a warm kiss against it, and heat shoots through me from the sensation. He turns it over again and presses another kiss against my knuckles, and the warmth of his lips, the softness of his mouth, and the thought of those lips against mine someday unravels me.

"One more thing," he says, lowering my hand but still holding it in his.

"Yes?"

"May I call you Lizzie?"

While I detest it when the press does it, Roman would bring a thrilling new association to the name.

The name that will be his and his alone to call me. "Yes, you may," I say, my heart pounding in wild excitement.

Roman releases my hand. "I'll call you when I get home."

"Fifteen minutes," I say.

"Fifteen minutes," he confirms. "I'll say goodnight then."

"Okay." I watch him as he walks up the path.

Roman slips into his car and turns the engine on, and I realise he won't leave until I'm safely inside my house. I take out my key and unlock the door, waving as I step inside.

As soon as the door is shut and locked behind me, I lean

against it for support. I'm trembling with pure electricity. My heart is beating like mad. My pulse is racing, and oh, these butterflies are making up for years of never needing to take flight.

That moment, while no first kiss was involved, was magically, wonderfully, romantically, *most ardently* perfect.

With a huge grin, I dash up the stairs, practically counting the minutes until he's home.

And calling me Lizzie.

I don't even have to ring the bell at Christian's cottage on Sunday morning. It's nine o'clock, and since we all moved into Kensington Palace this summer, Clementine and Christian always have their door open for Sunday breakfast for members of the squad.

I open the door, step inside, and call out, "I'm here."

Which is a miracle considering I talked to Roman until three in the morning, and then spent another two hours lying in bed thinking about him. I have no doubt I appear haggard and tired, but I have never felt such exhilaration and so much anticipation to see what happens next.

Luckily, I won't have to wait long. Roman is coming to my place tomorrow night, and it's my turn to entertain him for dinner.

I hang up my coat and walk towards the back of their house, to the kitchen. Clementine is poring over her diary, scribbling notes and sipping a hot chocolate in a Princess Fiona mug from the movie *Shrek*. She's wearing a Cambridge sweatshirt and is fresh-faced, with her hair hanging loose around her shoulders. Christian, on the other hand, is standing at the hob, flipping pancakes. There is no chef employed in their household, although few would believe it. This is part of doing things their way. Both of them like the routine of cooking together and decided to continue it. Apparently, according to Xander, it caused a row between Antonia and Christian, as she called them undignified and the beginning of the unravelling of the monarchy.

Dear old Antonia. Such a proper ray of sunshine and modernity.

"Good morning," Christian calls out cheerfully. I notice he has a bag of mini M&Ms out and is sprinkling them over the tops of the pancakes on the griddle pan. "Do you still want eggs and avocado toast? Or pancakes? I got these mini M&Ms from America, and they are perfect for pancakes."

"Oh, did any fun flavours come in your shipment? Did Bryn find those hot cocoa-flavoured M&Ms?" I ask, sitting across from Clementine. Bryn is one of Clementine's old roommates from Stanford, and she's Christian's source for all the fun flavours available in America.

"Who cares about M&Ms?" Clementine cries impatiently. "How is Roman? How did it go last night? I'm dying. Dying!"

"Please tell her," Christian says, expertly flipping his pancakes. "I'd hate to have her die before our first walkabout and public engagement on Tuesday. I'd rather not be stuck with Xander and Cling Film for future appearances as a substitute for my Fiona."

I burst out laughing at his dry humour. "I want to talk about Xander and India. What is he doing? Outside of being stupid at nightclubs on a few occasions, he's never done anything so… so…" I stop, as the behaviour is so un-Xander that I'm at a loss for words.

"So smacking of Xander having a quarter-life crisis?" Christian supplies as he stacks pancakes on a plate.

Ooh. Christian might be right. Xander is leaving the military at the start of the year to take on more royal duties. With Christian getting married in the spring, he will face even more media pressure than before to find a wife before he turns thirty. Personally, I think Xander should marry if and when he wants. He always does what he wants normally, so this sudden dive into a relationship with India surprises me.

There has to be more to it than a quarter-life crisis, I think.

"No, no, I want to hear about Roman first," Clementine says firmly, interrupting my thoughts of Xander. "I want good news first. Not news of my beloved future brother-in-law making a huge mistake with his first dive into romance. So, tell me about your date last night while I get water for your tea."

Warmth spreads across my cheeks as I remember Roman pressing a kiss upon my palm. Making me dinner. Telling me about his childhood in Shepherd's Bush and the Christmas cake his grandmother loved to make half-sloshed.

"He's *real*," I say without thinking. "Kind. Genuine. Down to earth. We talked for hours, and then for hours more on the phone after I got home. I've never wanted to spend this kind of time with any man."

Clementine brings me a mug and the box of Twinings Earl Grey teabags she keeps for my visits. I put my tea bag in, and she pours water over the top of it. Christian comes over to the table and places a stack of pancakes at Clementine's place.

"There you go, Ace," he says.

I see the look of love they exchange over simple gestures like these. Christian makes her breakfast and calls her Ace, while Clementine has her friend in America buy special treats because she knows Christian loves them.

"Thank you, love," she says, smiling at him.

He sinks down in the chair next to me. "That's how I felt about Clementine," he says, dousing his pancakes in syrup. "When we started talking, I knew she was different."

"I'll start your toast," Clementine says.

"Please sit down and eat your pancakes," I insist, rising from my seat. "I can get my own eggs and toast."

"Fine, this one time, I'll let you," she replies, smiling and taking a seat as I pop some bread into the toaster. "But back to Roman. I'm telling you, he is a good guy. There's no pretence with him. Everything you described about him is the man I know."

"He's so grounded," I say. I pluck an avocado and a lemon from the basket on the worktop. "Roman is honest about what he likes and what he wants. He's sentimental when it comes to his family. He's passionate about horticulture, and he even wanted to hear about my fountain pens. Can you believe it?"

I abruptly stop. I'm babbling like a girl with her first crush. I feel giddy as the things I discovered about him yesterday replay in my mind.

"You told him about the *pens?*" Christian teases, spearing some of his pancakes and popping them into his mouth.

"Yes," I say as I open the avocado and put it into a bowl so I can mash it. "Roman found my interest in pens intriguing."

"Oh, he must have it bad if he can indulge your pen talk," Christian says.

"You shut up," I reply, trying not to laugh.

I feel Clementine's gaze on me and turn my attention to her. She's smiling happily, and I know she's excited for the possibility of me and Roman dating.

My toast pops up, and I put the avocado on it, followed by a drizzle of olive oil and a squeeze of lemon. I decide to pass on the eggs for now, as I'm eager to sit down and talk more about Roman.

"He's a tremendous cook," I say, gushing as I take my place at the table. "He grew all the vegetables he served at dinner."

"A shocking twist, with him being a gardener," Christian says dryly.

"Stop it," Clementine chastises, giving him a look.

"All right, I know that look. Go on, Liz," he says.

"We talked all night, long after dinner was finished and we had cleaned up. I stayed there for *hours*, and it felt like mere minutes. We're so different in so many ways. We grew up differently, in different worlds, but so much of him resonates with me. His work ethic is like mine. We both want to inspire and create change in the world as part of our work. We both love our own time, alone or with our circles of friends."

"The differences can be strengths," Clementine says, gazing lovingly at Christian.

"I want what you two have," I admit, pausing to take a bite of my toast. "The only fear I have is, if Roman truly sees my world, will it scare him off? Will it be too much for a man like him, who loves the solitude of the garden?"

I can't believe I admitted that to them. We've only had one dinner and not even one real kiss on the lips, yet I'm trying to plan for future problems, much like I do when I prepare for an event. I'm always looking for potential problems and planning for them.

Because I know those things could happen.

Just like my royal life becoming something that turns Roman away from me.

"I think I can speak to this better than anyone," Clementine says. "I knew I loved Christian. Just Christian. I understood his world was going to be hard on me. Sometimes, it's harder than I thought it would be, and I know six months from now, when the press gets bored of being nice to me, they will try to turn my world upside down with horrible stories.

"But the love I have for this man sitting across the table from me," she continues, beaming at Christian, "is what matters at the end of the day. I will get through whatever happens in this gilded world because I love him. I'll have my hard day, and I'll text you to come watch movies with me or grab Jillian for some gin and tonics. But I'll always go straight to Christian the second I see him and wrap my arms around him and know all of this is worth it because I love him. Whoever loves you for you will feel the same way."

I glance at Christian, whose eyes have nothing but love and admiration for Clementine in them.

"You can find someone who doesn't care about the monarchy, Liz." he says. "Who isn't trying to use you, who is willing to come into this world and live in this goldfish bowl. Is it harder bringing people like Clem and Roman into this life? Of course. But is it worth it? Yes. If you fall in love with him, and he with you, and you both want to be together, that is all that matters."

I study my cousin and his fiancée, and I can only hope that I can find what they found: a love that is strong and a true partnership. They are two people who celebrate their individuality but love what they share together equally as much.

"And if you dare go out and find someone who is supposedly easy and knows the family business," Christian continues, "and pursue a relationship for that reason like my brother Xander the former Philanderer, I shall never speak to you again. If Roman is the man for you, and you're willing to guide him into this world and protect him as much as you can, you do that. Because I don't believe for one second Xander will be happy with India."

"Is that why he's testing the waters with her?" I ask.

"I talked to James this morning," Christian says, referring to his younger brother, who is away at university. "Xander told him he knows it's time to start being serious. Even in this day and age, he knows his role is to secure the future of the monarchy, and he has to think about getting married at some point. Which means no more club philandering. India, as he told James, understands this world. She knows the part to play, and he feels it will be easier to find a woman from his own social circle as opposed to going outside it, like we are."

Oh, no. The idea of Xander settling and spending the rest of his life with someone he doesn't love passionately because he thinks it will be easier breaks my heart.

"I'll talk to him," I say, nodding. "I think a quarter-life crisis—combined with the reality of how hard it is to bring someone into his life is as the future king—is driving these decisions. As hard as it will be for Clementine, and let's, for sake of conversation, say Roman, it will be so much worse for someone who will be the future queen."

"He's going to end up like our Father," Christian says, sighing heavily. "He'll pick the *right woman* and screw himself. Xander will be stuck in a marriage with a woman he doesn't love."

I swallow hard. If Christian only knew he could be talking about my father with those same words, too. Except my father didn't take the road Arthur did. My fa—

"All right, enough of this," Clementine says quickly, interrupting my thoughts. "Maybe India will bore him to tears, and he'll move on."

The conversation shifts to the big week ahead, with Clementine and Christian doing their first public appearance since their engagement photocall. Clementine has had Buckingham Palace staff working with her on what to expect, like how to exit a car and not to pose for selfies or sign autographs. She's received her first stack of notes on who she will be talking to, with their histories, and has been counselled on what to wear.

"You are going to be overwhelmed with how excited people are to see you and Christian," I say. "But you are going to be utterly fantastic as the duchess you soon will be."

Clementine exhales loudly. "Next spring, I'll be a duchess. Of something," she says, shaking her head. "This is insane."

I smile. Arthur will give them an official title that will be released after they are married.

"Yes, you are marrying me to be the *Duchess of Something*," Christian teases.

We sit around after we've finished eating, lingering over our hot drinks, the conversation rolling from how the members of the squad are doing to what is going on in the news and how soon Christmas is coming.

Clementine snickers after I say that.

"What?" I ask.

"That is such a British thing to say. I hear that several times a day. You all are obsessed with how soon it's coming, and it's only the first week of December."

"Well, it is *soon*," I say, grinning at her.

"Christmas isn't soon," Clementine counters, "but your second date with Roman is."

I blush at the reminder, as if I needed one.

My second date with Roman is tomorrow night. While I'm looking forward to my adventure with SCOUTS 4 GIRLS on Monday, I'm eagerly anticipating the moment when Roman shows up at my door at Wren House.

And even more eager to see if we will share our first kiss.

CHAPTER 9

PRETTY IN PINK

I review the notes in my diary as Cecelia, the personal secretary assigned to me from my father's staff at St. James's Palace, drives us to the school that has the chapter of the SCOUT 4 GIRLS group that I'm visiting today.

"May I tell you something?" she asks as she stops in London traffic.

I glance up at her profile. "You may tell me anything. You know I value your honesty and guidance." And I do. Cecelia is a veteran of the Royal Household and knows how to navigate the press better than almost anyone.

Her lips tip upwards in a small, approving smile. I almost laugh. She tries so hard to be business all the time, but in our months together, we've grown close. I can tell she views me as more than an assignment now, which makes me happy.

"You are beautiful in colour," Cecelia says softly, referring to the bright pink cashmere jumper and wool overcoat I selected for my visit today. "I always thought you would be, but I knew your theory on wearing white. I thought you used white to protect yourself, as your armour."

"Armour?" I ask, confused.

"White is safe. Expected. You are so careful of making a misstep, either with the press or with Arthur. But it's good to take chances, Liz. They don't always work out, but you are a vibrant young woman, and the future of this monarchy. It's good to see you show more of your true self with your clothing."

I know she's right. I carefully thought out my strategy with white and the image it projected, and I wanted to be safe. I didn't want to fail. But since taking a chance to try and find Roman, I've seen the wonderful things that can happen when I do take a risk, even a small one.

"So why pink today?" Cecelia asks as the light turns green.

I blush. I turn my head and stare out the window of the Range Rover so she can't see my expression of happiness. I can't tell her the truth, that when Roman and I talked on the phone last night, he mentioned how beautiful I was with my pink scarf on the other night, how it lit up my face. I'm wearing this as a secret hello for him, before our date this evening.

I paired my colourful jumper and coat with winter white trousers and black high heeled boots, but pink is the dominant colour today. I told him this morning to pay attention to my appearance and look for a hidden message for him. After hearing Cecelia's words, I think I'll start to incorporate more colour into my appearances.

"It was just time to try something new," I tell her.

I pick up my phone and go to the Twitter list I've created for the royal reporters I follow. A stream of coverage for Antonia's event pops up. She is visiting a neurology wing at a London hospital as part of her new cause in honour of her most beloved future daughter-in-law, Clementine, who had her own battle with a brain tumour.

My stomach recoils with nausea. Antonia hates Clementine, but since the public adores her, she has shifted her strategy to ride that wave of popularity and be the doting future mother-in-law.

For a moment, I wonder if Xander is right. If he did marry a girl like India, his life would be much easier. India would be entering a world she knows, one she is at ease with, and she would do it with the full support of the queen and her staff, unlike Clementine.

I swallow. Antonia would view Roman the same as Clementine, as an intruder unworthy of the monarchy.

She would never support Roman in this world.

I shake the thought from my head and scold myself for planning ahead again with him. I come back to today and focus on the load of press Antonia is receiving, which is good. I know not to upstage her, so I made sure to schedule my appearance after hers. I am hosting a reception at Buckingham Palace tomorrow night, but I made sure she wasn't appearing *anywhere* that night before I put the event in my diary.

I exhale. It's such a balancing act, more than I ever dreamt it would be. But it's crucial to never upstage *Her Majesty.*

Cecelia draws near the school in Islington. I see crowds have gathered outside the barriers, and of course, the press and paparazzi are waiting for me, too. I close my diary and put away my fountain pen. I already have planned who I will meet upon entering the school, who will show me around, etc., but I always go off-script a bit, too. People know I will pose for pictures before going in, to make the press's job a bit easier. I always stop and talk to some of the people kind enough to wait outside, in the cold, to greet me, and I do the same on the way out, too.

Cecelia drives into the car park, and the crowd cheers when they see me. I wave and smile, and for me, it's genuine. I still can't believe these people are here to see me. This is where clothing and appearance are important. They have an image of the monarchy in their head, and I want to live up to the mystique. Even if I feel bad, I have to give them what they want to see. For all the good I can do, and how wonderful my life has been, I'm more than happy to square my shoulders and give it to them, even if I feel sick or sad inside.

Today, however, I'm happy and excited to see what these girls are doing with robotics. I can't wait to see what they have come up with.

A man from the school moves forward and opens my car door. As soon as I step outside, the crowd gasps and phones go up in the air. The comments are carried towards me with the crisp December wind.

"Oh my god, do you see that? She's in pink!"

"Pink? Have you ever seen her in pink?"

"LIZ! LIZ!"

"We love you, Liz!"

"She is a princess. She's so beautiful!"

"She's wearing pink; I can't believe it!"

I hear more comments about pink than anything else. I turn and face the cameras, smiling brightly as the photographers call to me, too.

"LIZZIE! Why the pink?"

"Pretty in pink, are you?"

"Finally, a colour!"

I stand still for a few seconds, giving them their shot,

and then head towards the members of the school and organisation who are waiting for me.

"Welcome to Greenwood Primary School, Your Royal Highness. I'm the headmaster, John Giles."

"Liz," I say, extending my hand. "It's a pleasure to meet you, Mr. Giles. I can't wait to see what the girls are doing inside."

I'm introduced to the scout leader and other school officials, but before we head inside, my eyes scan the crowd, where I find an elderly woman in a wheelchair, bundled up against the cold.

"If you will allow me a moment, I'd love to meet some of the people out here," I say, knowing full well Cecelia built time into my schedule for this. It's brief, five minutes, but at least it's something.

"Of course, Liz," Mr. Giles says.

I walk across the street, and the crowd cheers. While there is a police presence, I'm aware there are no protection officers surrounding me like Christian and Clementine have, so once again, I do an assessment with my own eyes for anything suspicious, smiling the entire time as I do. Nothing catches my eye, so I proceed straight to the white-haired woman in the wheelchair.

"Hello," I say, kneeling down so I'm eye-level with her. "I'm Liz."

"Oh, heavens, I know who you are," she says, laughing. "I haven't missed a chance to see you since your mother stood outside the Lindo Wing with you in her arms."

My heart is touched. The Lindo Wing at St. Mary's Hospital is where I was born, and where all royal babies have been born since Antonia had Xander there. "That is so kind of you," I say, placing my hand gently over hers. It's cold and paper thin, and I suddenly feel the years of living in that hand that has now turned delicate from time. "I truly appreciate that."

"I knew you were destined to do great things," she says sagely as people snap pictures of us. "I've always been a royalist, you know, and I had a feeling you would be a special one. You have proven me right, Your Royal Highness."

I swallow hard. I don't know what I've done to deserve such confidence. She thought I would be special, and I'm grateful to have people like this woman on my side.

"What is your name?" I ask.

"Margaret Snyder."

"Well, Ms. Margaret Snyder, it's a pleasure to meet you. Thank you for your kind words; they mean everything to me."

"Thank you for carrying on the name in such a good way," she says. "You are extremely pretty in pink. I was quite shocked to see colour on you, I must admit."

"I was inspired to try pink today," I say, thinking of Roman.

"Keep trying it," Margaret advises. "One never moves forward repeating the same steps."

I let go of her hand and wish her well. I make a few other stops in the crowd, shaking hands and taking a bouquet of flowers and a teddy bear from a little girl, but I'm urged away to keep things on schedule.

As I hand the gifts to Cecelia, I turn and take one last look at Margaret, who is waving at me.

One never moves forward repeating the same steps, I hear her say in my head again.

I smile at her. Margaret is right.

Pink is a new step forward for me.

As is my date tonight with Roman.

"That was incredible," I say as soon as Cecelia and I are back in the car. "Did you see how excited the girls were to talk about their robotic projects? The energy in that room was brilliant, absolutely brilliant to behold. Those young women will shape our future, from medical advances to technological changes. I can't wait to do that fundraiser luncheon for them next month!"

Cecelia nods. "They were so excited to see you, Liz. All the questions you asked, all the encouragement you gave them — not to mention the publicity for their organisation — you are the difference in them bringing the programme to more schools, to more girls."

I retrieve my phone and swipe it open. "I truly hope I can be a part of giving them the donations and visibility they need to expand. I want those girls to believe they can do anything in this world and to encourage them to seek opportunities in science and engineering."

"I think you are a good role model for that. You are creating your own opportunities in the monarchy, so you live what you encourage. Being genuine is important, and you recognise that."

I shake my head. "I've been blessed to be in this position due to birth, not because of anything I've done."

"Liz. A lot of royals can appear at an event and shake hands. You make connections with your audience, and with the press. Your energy lights up a room. Not everyone has that genuine interest."

I know she is referencing Antonia.

"But with you, Christian, and Clementine, I see such a vibrant future ahead for not only the monarchy but the organisations you wish to support."

I hope Cecelia is right. I want to follow in the footsteps of my father and uncle, but I feel as if they still have that reserve left from the last generation. The modern royals, as my sisters and cousins and I say, need to bridge this gap.

I go to Twitter and open my media list, eager to see the publicity that my visit has generated today. But the first thing I see makes me gasp. "Oh, no," I whisper. "No, no."

"Liz?" Cecelia asks as we head out of the car park.

I cringe as I see the *Dishing Weekly* article pop up on Twitter:

LIZZIE IS PRETTY IN PINK! HER MAJESTY BORES IN BEIGE

My stomach rolls over as I see side-by-side photos of our appearances today. One shows Antonia with an unflattering, serious expression on her face posing with doctors in the hospital, wearing a beige dress, beige wool coat, tights and nude pumps. Her brow is furrowed, her hair back in her signature chignon.

In my picture, however, I'm shown smiling and talking with girls about their mobile phone-controlled robot, my rose lipstick and pink jumper and coat lighting up my face as I give the robot a try with their help.

I can't bear to read the article. I don't want to see the ugliness that is going to be laid out, comparing me to Antonia, but knowledge is power, so I force myself to read it. My stomach sinks even further.

The author points out my joy and uniqueness, while mocking Antonia's expression and saying she's tired and boring and appeared as if she'd rather be anywhere else. Then I read a sentence that makes me gasp out loud:

The queen could take a lesson from her son, future daughter-in-law, and niece. The times are changing in the House of Chadwick. Perhaps it's time for Her Majesty to inject some life into not only her wardrobe but her personality, too.

"Crap," I murmur, shoving my phone into my cross-body bag. "This is the worst thing that could have happened. That magazine has no idea of the bomb they've thrown in my lap, none!"

"What? What are you talking about, Liz?" Cecelia asks as she drives us back towards Kensington Palace.

"*Dishing Weekly* has done a side-by-side comparison of royal appearances this afternoon," I say.

"That is not even a magazine; it's a piece of rubbish," Cecelia huffs.

I relay the headline to her. I watch as she winces in response.

"Antonia is going to be furious with me for upstaging her."

Cecelia remains silent. She has never involved herself in the family drama, and I'm about to apologise for bringing it up when she speaks.

"We need to have a meeting with Sydney tomorrow," she says. "She can help us come up with a strategy to deal with the fallout that is going to happen."

"No," I say sharply.

There is no way I can sit across a table from Sydney Cross-Jones and put my future in her hands. Sydney is part of my father's staff. She was hired a year ago to be my father's top advisor and prepares him for all of his appearances and meetings with heads of state. She has corporate experience that has taken her around the world, and she's intelligent. Quick. Savvy.

She is also the woman who made my dad realise he no longer loved my mother.

"But she's sharp, Liz. She will know how to work through this and keep your confidence from Antonia's camp," Cecelia protests.

Yes, Sydney is good at keeping secrets, as she has been sleeping with my father for a year now and nobody knows. I only know because I accidentally walked in on them kissing in my father's library the weekend I moved home after graduating from university. Dad saw me, and all hell broke loose. He explained that he fell out of love with Mum many years ago. It took meeting Sydney to bring his heart back to life. I went through all the emotions—disgust, rage, disappointment, heartbreak. I asked him why he didn't divorce Mum, which is what rational people do, but he said no one in the monarchy would divorce.

Ever.

He was going to live with love and told Mum to do the same, to discreetly find someone that made her happy. Mum didn't accept their marriage falling apart, and the affair turned her toxic against Dad in private. She knows that I know, so she uses me as a sounding board on schemes to try and win him back and to get Sydney out.

I press my head against the car window. God, how messed up is this? These are my *parents*, living in a pretend marriage because the monarchy can't bear to admit a marriage failed, and I'm trapped in their lie. I haven't whispered a word of it to anyone. I'm too ashamed. I don't want to burden Bella and Victoria whilst they are at university. I also feel it's not my story to tell them. So, at family dinners, I'm part of the lie, sitting there and acting like nothing is wrong. My sisters think they live in a happy family, when in reality, that is an illusion.

To my surprise, my throat swells. I've pushed this so far down that I can't believe these feelings are rising to the surface. The questions I had in the beginning roll up on the shore for me to think about again.

Is this the normal thing for people to do? My aunt and uncle don't love each other. My father stopped loving my mother. Amelia's parents are divorced. They all loved each other at one point. How does an emotion so deep that it leads you to marry someone stop?

I think of Roman. For a moment, I have an urge to head right back into my protected walls. What is the point of this? Even if he can adapt to the confines of the world that I live in, would he stay in love with me? Or would he fall out of love, like my dad did with my mum?

Another thought hits me.

Even if Roman did fall in love with me, and got past the monarchy, what would he think of my family if I were to confide in him what I know? He has two normal, loving parents. Good god, what would he think of this mess of a family I have?

I wince. Why didn't I think of any of this when I decided to see if I could find him? How could I have buried this so far down that it interfered with my logical, planning self? If I would have thought this through, beyond my attraction to him, I would have stopped myself. No normal man would want any of this for the long term.

As Roman's hazel eyes fill my mind, I know exactly why I ignored the obvious.

All the thoughts of my family slip away, and I replace them with Roman having tea with me in the greenhouse. Of him showing me a poinsettia. How he made me dinner and pressed his lips against the palm of my hand. How his eyes, with their flecks of gold, seemed to intensify when he gazed at me.

I knew from the moment I met him—from how he protected Clementine and told me the world should see angry Liz—that he was different.

Tonight, I promised him I'd tell him about this side of my life, the one I lead as Elizabeth of York.

Which will include the truth about the Duke and Duchess of York.

Should I trust a man I barely know with such explosive information?

Despite the logical answer of "no," my head and heart say "yes."

For the first time in my life, I have met a man I trust implicitly with my truth.

I only hope Roman still wants to take a chance on me after he learns it.

CHAPTER 10

THAT'S WHAT TAKEAWAY IS FOR, RIGHT?

I scurry around my living room. Roman will be here in about ten minutes, and I want to make sure everything is perfect for our date tonight. I have a wonderful meal planned. Rather, I have a meal that the chef at my favourite Italian restaurant in Chelsea prepared for me to reheat once Roman is here. Wine glasses are out, and I have the pinot noir ready to be uncorked.

Now, the living room. I anxiously fluff the cushions I already fluffed a few minutes earlier. I glance around. I have lit candles that smell like oranges, cloves, and woodsmoke, creating a cosy glow in the room.

I take a step back. I have a fire roaring in the fireplace, candles, and cushions. If I only had a Christmas tree, it would be perfect. But for a December date tonight? It's incredibly romantic.

Wait. Am I trying too hard? Do women actually do these things for a man coming over on a date? Or am I relying on unrealistic scenes from movies I watched with Clem over the summer?

I'll skip music, I decide, nodding to myself. *If I put on music, that will scream over the top.*

Or would it be okay if I played Christmas music? I picture "Santa Baby" or "All I Want for Christmas is You" being played. I'd probably blush a thousand shades of red.

No. No music.

But what if Roman heard one of those songs and asked me to be his Christmas present? That is the cheesiest thing I've ever had come into my brain.

But I like it.

Roman is igniting all these new thoughts and feelings in me, and I want to embrace them all.

Music, it is.

I turn on the TV and find a channel that plays popish-sounding Christmas songs. Music fills the air, and happiness fills my heart.

Roman will be here any minute now, if his punctuality holds true for our second date. I move restlessly around the room, studying the oil paintings of flowers on the walls and absent-mindedly moving my colouring books on the side table a millimetre. While I'm excited and eager for tonight, I can't help but allow the thoughts from earlier today to creep into my brain.

I'm going to tell him the truth, over dinner, and hope that the tabloid life that is my world doesn't scare him away.

The sound of a motorcycle pierces my thoughts. My heart jumps. I part the curtain to peek outside, and sure enough, Roman has driven his bike over, despite the dangers of driving at night that he warned me about. I watch as he removes his helmet and rakes his fingers through his dark brown hair.

My breath grows rapid as I watch him get off the bike. He moves around to the back and unlatches a case. He lifts something out, and I see he's holding a small box. Oh! Anticipation rushes through me, wondering what it could be.

He glances up and catches me staring at him. Roman flashes me a huge smile that lights up his face, and my knees nearly buckle in response. I smile back before heading to the door to greet him.

He's coming up the path as I open the door. He looks dead sexy in a black leather jacket with a silver helmet tucked under his arm.

"Are you that eager to see me?" he says, raising an eyebrow.

"Most ardently," I say saucily, quoting Jane Austen.

Roman reaches my doorstep. "I hope I'm the only man you are saying most ardently to, Lizzie."

Oh!

Electricity surges through every inch of me from his words. Roman's mouth is now set to serious, as are his eyes —with the flecks of gold growing even more dominant as he gazes down at me—intensely searching mine.

"Indeed."

I see his lips twitch upwards again, sending my heart racing. "Good."

Oh, so incredibly good.

"You're stunning in red," he says, his eyes moving over my outfit. "You're incredibly beautiful tonight."

"Thank you," I say, ushering him inside. I'm over the moon that he noticed my red cashmere V-neck jumper. From the way his eyes drank in my jeans down to my tall, black suede boots, I knew he liked my outfit before he even spoke.

As Roman steps through the door, my excitement intensifies. He's the only man I've ever invited past the palace gates, either here or at St. James's Palace. Yet he has no idea of the significance of this moment.

"Where should I put this?" he asks, lifting his helmet. He looks around at the Chippendale tables and cream furniture. "I don't want to get anything dirty."

"You won't, and this console table is fine," I say.

Roman sets his helmet down, as well as the white box, tied with a beautiful red ribbon. He slips out of his leather jacket, and I greedily drink in his massive chest, which looks brilliant in a fitted black jumper. I've never seen a chest this broad. My instincts tell me it would be solid and sculpted if I were to slide my hand up underneath his jumper and T-shirt to explore it.

Heat spreads through my body from the mere thought of intimately touching him. I shake the thought from my head before I do something stupid.

Like grab him by the jumper and draw his mouth towards mine.

"I'll take that," I say, grateful for the momentary distraction of hanging up his coat.

I feel Roman's eyes on me as I put his coat in the cupboard. I shut the door and turn around, and his eyes haven't left me.

"I can't believe I'm with you again," he says, his eyes searching mine. "If it hadn't already happened at my place, I wouldn't dare believe it."

He reaches for my hand and links it with his, drawing it to his chest in an intimate manner. The second I feel the warmth of his wool jumper, the caress of his huge hand over mine, all I want is to be in his arms.

And discover what his kiss is like.

"Believe it," I say softly. "I'm so happy you're here."

The gold flecks in his eyes shine brightly. "Me, too."

"Would you like a glass of wine? I have canapés, too, in the kitchen."

"That sounds good. As I'm drinking, I'll call Darcy to come get me. I can get my bike tomorrow, if that's all right with you."

I love how responsible Roman is. He has no idea that this is a huge turn-on for me, a man who takes care of himself. "It would be a reason to see you tomorrow for breakfast, wouldn't it?" I ask.

His lips turn upwards. My heart flutters.

"You'd have to get up early. I need to be at work by seven," he says.

"I'm always up early. You know I'm a morning person. I'll have already gone for a run through the garden by that point."

A crease of concern forms in Roman's brow. "With no protection officer?"

"None, and I'm fine. See? I'm right here, holding your hand."

His chest rises and falls against my hand. How is it I feel so connected to him at this point? Without even kissing him?

Because he's exceptional, that's why.

"Roman. Remember I can throat punch. And scratch eyes out."

"Lizzie. Remind me not to cross you," he teases.

I grin wickedly. "You're the one who wanted to see Angry Liz, remember?"

"If that's how you are feeling, then yes, I do."

I stare up at him, grateful once again that he wants to see me as I truly am. "I like that you want to see all sides of me and don't expect me to be perfect."

"I wouldn't want you to be any other way. Especially for me."

A silence falls between us. I'm falling for this man. I have no doubt that is what all these new feelings inside of me are.

I only hope he can handle my story once he hears it.

"It feels festive in here," Roman says, shifting his focus to the living room. "Candles. Fireplace. Music." He turns his attention back towards me. "Down to the red lipstick on your lips."

His eyes land on my mouth. My throat goes dry.

Never have I wanted someone to kiss me like I do Roman.

"I think it's as Christmassy as I can get without a tree," I manage to say.

"That is something you need," he concedes. "And a poinsettia. Luckily, I know the person to help you with that."

"Hmm, but can this person help me keep it alive?"

Roman squeezes my hand affectionately. "I believe so."

I clear my throat. "Good, because you know I have the blackest thumb of death."

He smiles, and so do I.

"All right. Since Darcy is your Uber tonight, let me pour you a glass of wine and get dinner started."

I take his hand and lead him towards the kitchen, but he stops walking after a few steps. "Wow," he says.

I turn around to find him staring at the picture above my fireplace, his eyes large in wonder. He leads me over to the large oil painting of an arrangement of flowers. "This is stunning," Roman says. He glances down at me. "Is this from the royal vault?"

An uncomfortable, anxious feeling rises within my

chest. I wanted to be Liz for a little longer before I started blurring the lines with Elizabeth of York.

"Yes. My uncle is awfully generous in allowing me to borrow some furniture and art from the family collection."

Roman's eyes hold steady on me. I swear I feel a flashing neon sign over my head that is blinking *royal* at him. "Uncle," he repeats, and I can see the image of King Arthur in his head.

Silence follows that comment, and dread nearly swallows me whole. Roman is seeing my reality. It's hitting him what my last name means, and my heart hurts, thinking this could snuff out what we are exploring tonight.

"This uncle must have some good connections," he says. Then he gives me his beautiful grin.

My anxiety fades away, as if Roman flipped a switch with his smile to turn it off.

"He might know a person or two," I say, leading him back towards the kitchen again.

He follows me inside the space, which I made improvements to over the summer. I had the cupboards re-done and new appliances put in, and now it's fresh and white, with some personal touches, like my mug tree, full of mugs with funny sayings, and festive tea towels, edged in a red-and-green tartan fabric.

"So, this is what a good worktop is like," Roman teases.

I laugh. "Yes," I say, moving over to the wine bottle on the worktop and picking up the corkscrew. "I'm not exactly the world's greatest cook, so I don't use most of it."

He takes a place next to the oven, leaning casually against the worktop. "Should I be afraid that you are cooking for me?"

I hand him a glass of wine. "Who says I'm cooking for you? That's what takeaway is for."

Roman chuckles, and goosebumps prickle my skin from that low, throaty sound. I pour a glass for myself and move closer to him. He lifts his glass.

"To getting to know each other better," he says, clinking his glass against mine.

I tap my glass against his. "Cheers to that."

We each take a sip.

"That's nice," Roman says. "Although, I can't tell you why. I merely go by whether I like the taste or not."

"Me, too," I reply. "Although, we should be tasting black cherry and vanilla. According to the label, that is."

He takes another sip, and I wonder if I'll be tasting the wine on his lips later tonight.

"Hmm," he says slowly. Then he glances at me. "Still tastes like good wine."

"I agree."

Roman moves towards the kitchen table, where I have set up a cheeseboard of cheeses, figs, grapes, prosciutto, and some baguette slices. "This looks fantastic. Do you mind if I tuck in?" he asks.

"Please. Perhaps while you dive into that, you won't notice I'm putting takeaway food into the oven," I say.

I'm rewarded with a full smile. Electricity sweeps through me as a natural response to it.

"No need to pretend. You don't cook. I should know this about you."

I open the fridge and remove the tin with the food. I lift off the lid that has the directions on top and find the steaks on one side, the risotto on the other.

"Whilst I can't cook, I'm superb at following reheating directions," I declare as I read. "For dinner tonight, I'm warming the steak in the oven and bringing the risotto back to life with stock in a pan on the hob."

"Then I'm in good hands," Roman says gamely. He moves back towards me and leans against the worktop again, watching me work. "May I help?"

"No, you may not," I say. "This is my turn to treat you to dinner."

He studies me as I slide the steak into the oven. "I don't consider it a burden to stir risotto."

"This is my burden to bear, and mine alone," I say dramatically.

Roman chuckles. The sound wraps around me and warms every inch of my soul.

As I heat the stock in a small saucepan on the hob, he studies me. "How was your event today?" he asks.

"Oh, Roman, it was incredible. These girls are so bright, so full of passion for what they do. I love how the programme encourages them to expand their minds and gives them the confidence to go for anything. I'm so glad to be involved. My goal is to help them expand across the UK and bring this programme to any girl who wants to be a part of it."

"Those girls sound like you," he says. "I knew from the first day I met you that you had that kind of passion inside of you."

I frown as I turn the heat up on the saucepan. "The press infuriated me that day. They went below the belt with what they did to Clementine. That's why I had to write that letter from the palace, to express my disappointment with it."

An image of that tabloid headline flashes through my head, the one dragging up her medical history for everyone to see and pointing out the paralysis on her face as a result of her brain tumour surgery.

Roman is quiet as I add the risotto to another pan. Then

he asks, "How do you handle that? The press recording everything you do?"

My mood shifts. We've come to the moment faster than I wanted to this evening.

"Lizzie. You can tell me the truth," he says gently. "I want you to know that."

I feel exposed now, vulnerable to the reality that Roman is a good man, who might not want the crap that would come into his life if we were to start dating.

I slowly lift my gaze to meet his. "I'm going to be painfully honest with you, Roman. If you change your mind about seeing me after you hear everything, I will understand."

I reach for my wine and take a sip, to delay the inevitable, even if for a second.

"I am Liz. But I'm also Princess Elizabeth of York," I say. "I'm proud of who I am, and of the family I've come from. I have expectations to bear, but I not only understand that challenge, I embrace it."

To my surprise, Roman moves closer to me. We're inches apart. He reaches up and brushes his fingers against the side of my face, gliding his calloused fingertips across the top of my cheekbones. Heat flares within me from his masculine skin making contact with mine. My heart beats faster as I try to find the courage to say more.

"I know Christian struggled to accept his role in the monarchy, a fate he was born into and has no choice about, being a prince. However, I relish mine. I always knew I could make a difference. I can represent my father and uncle in a positive way. I was—and am—honoured to have that opportunity.

"I know the world is changing and the monarchy has to embrace that," I continue. "I believe in that, too, and I want to do everything I can to make our role an important one in the modern world. I know there is a part of society that thinks we are irrelevant and outdated, but I want to prove them wrong. We have a purpose. The monarchy performed two thousand engagements last year. We support more than three thousand charities. We entertained more than seventy thousand guests. We travelled the globe to promote relationships with the United Kingdom. We brought tourism to the UK. Did you know that Clementine and Christian's wedding is expected to generate three hundred million pounds for the British economy?"

I pause for a moment. Roman's fingertips are still gliding across my cheekbone in a comforting manner.

"I admit," he says, a flush climbing up his neck, "that I didn't understand all that you did. I saw it as an outdated part of history that should be that—history. But that's changed. Because of you."

I hold my breath as I wait for him to go on.

"After I met you, I went online and read about you. I went to the monarchy website and saw how you are one of the hardest working royals, with a diary that is always full. You've travelled abroad, no doubt to do things that don't interest you, but you did it with enthusiasm and a smile on your face to represent the United Kingdom. You throw your passion into your causes, and I saw that at the conference you had with Christian, Clementine, and Xander, where you announced the launch of your foundation. All of this makes us a better country. I'm sorry I never saw it before. I once saw the monarchy as a financial drain and woefully outdated. But now I see the truth," Roman says, reaching up and trailing his fingers along my hairline. "I was wrong. I owe you an apology."

"No, you don't," I say.

"I do. Because I learnt not only what you do but that there is a deep personal price you pay to do it. Yes, you have castles and luxury, but you have your privacy taken away and horrible things written about you. You're judged, every day, yet you are more than willing to pay this price."

My heart throbs in pain. I have to lay everything out for him. Now.

This moment may be the last I have with him after I speak.

"Roman, you know the price Clementine has paid for being involved with Christian. I'm not an easy person to date. Your life—your wonderful, quiet life with the land—will be exploited and turned upside down. The world will know you. And they will never know *enough* about you. Ever since Christian proposed to Clem, the world is hungrier than ever for our stories, of the young royals. You won't be able to avoid this."

Roman doesn't say anything. His eyes grow darker, and I know I've lost him.

"I understand if you can't do this. It's too much to ask anyone," I say, desperately trying to keep the shake out of my voice. "You don't even know about my family and the skeletons that are buried over in St. James's Palace, Roman. It's messy and complicated, and I'm afraid t—"

Suddenly, Roman's massive hands are framing my face.

"I'm not afraid of any of that," he says, his voice commanding.

"But you don't *know*," I implore.

"I don't need to," he says, his eyes bearing down into mine. "I only have one fear. One."

"What is that?" I whisper over my pounding heart.

"I'm afraid that if I kiss you, I'll never want to kiss anyone else."

I part my lips in a gasp, floored by this confession. A kiss, to Roman, means no turning back. He would be risking his heart and opening himself up to be vulnerable if our lips meet.

And now I'm *desperate* for him to kiss me.

He begins caressing my face. My hair. Roman lowers his forehead to mine. I close my eyes and breathe him in, the scent of sandalwood soap on his skin, trembling from his touch the entire time.

"I have my own skeletons. I'm terrified I'll disappoint you," he whispers, his breath warm against my mouth.

His mouth hovers near mine, and my body screams inside for his kiss.

"I'm not afraid of that," I whisper back.

His fingers trail down to the nape of my neck, stroking it and sending desire through me. Then his hand finds its way to the side of my face.

"You're a fear I'm determined to face, Lizzie," he murmurs. "I have to. I'll die if I don't."

And then his mouth touches mine.

CHAPTER 11

A KISS IS BUT A KISS...

Roman's lips are like velvet against mine, delivering the softest, sweetest kisses over and over as his calloused fingertips stroke my face in a reverent manner. My emotions swirl in growing intensity. I'm shocked that he kissed me. Ecstatic from his lips on mine. Eager for him to part the seam of my lips with his tongue and taste me.

His slowness now, however, makes me feel cherished by this man. This first kiss is more than a kiss—it's a connection between us that will change everything.

I instinctively move my hands to his chest and find his heart is beating furiously under his jumper. Roman slips his hands underneath my hair while sliding his tongue between my lips. Heat erupts in me as he demands more. I've never had desire ignite in me from a first kiss, but now it has. My tongue eagerly explores his mouth, wanting to take everything I can from him, to feel all the currents running through my body from this shared intimacy.

His tongue is lush, and I curl mine with his, eliciting a low groan from his throat, which heightens my excitement.

His mouth is warm and inviting, and he tastes of the wine we drank.

All I want to do is get drunk on him.

Roman moves one hand down my back, drawing me closer to him as the other hand caresses the hair at the back of my head. His lips grow more demanding with each kiss. My heart pounds fiercely, in the same rhythm as his. I move one hand against the side of his face, sending a shudder through me as his freshly-shaven skin glides under my fingertips, and I make my own assault on his mouth, feeling my lips grow more swollen with each needy kiss.

"Lizzie," Roman whispers between kisses. "I can't... stop... kissing... you."

"Then don't," I murmur against his lips. "Kiss me. Again."

He kisses me harder. I'm on fire. Every single inch of me is responding to this man like I've never responded to any other man in my life.

They say a kiss is but a kiss.

But not this time. Not with this man.

And definitely not this kiss.

Roman finally breaks the kiss, and I allow myself to come up for air. He is breathing hard as he slides his hands up underneath my hair again, caressing it gently and sending shivers down my spine.

"The butterflies are going like mad," he murmurs, brushing his lips against my forehead.

Zing! He has butterflies for me?

A loud hiss from the hob gets both our attention.

A light bulb goes off in my head.

"Oh, no, the stock!" I say, untangling myself from his arms and hurrying over to the saucepan.

The stock has boiled away, leaving a brown burnt crust

in the bottom of the pan. I quickly take it off the flame and dash to the sink, turning on the water. The pan hisses in response, and I know it's going to have to soak before I can scrub it out. I squeeze in a bit of washing up liquid and let it sit.

Roman chuckles as I run around.

"I told you I can't cook," I say, reaching for a tea towel and drying my hands.

"No, I'd say you were otherwise engaged," he replies, the gold flecks in his eyes growing more intense.

I put the towel down as Roman moves closer to me, and my breath hitches in my throat. His hands frame my face, and then he drops the gentlest of kisses on my already swollen lips. He lifts his head. His hands slide round to my waist, and they are so huge that they practically span my waistline.

"I was right to be afraid," he says, his voice low.

Elation fills me as a gentle smile lights up his face.

Roman doesn't want to kiss anyone other than me.

"I have the same thought," I say, moving my hands up to his neck. "I like the way you kiss me, Roman."

He bends over so he can press his forehead to mine. "If you didn't have dinner in the oven, I'd be content to forgo food and kiss you for the rest of the night."

I close my eyes and breathe in the scent of him. "You'll be hungry."

"I don't think so."

I laugh and put my hands on his, and he laces his fingers through mine.

"Come on. Let me try this stock one more time and get the risotto back to life. By then, the steaks should be ready."

I retrieve the ready-made stock from the fridge and a clean saucepan, vowing that no matter what Roman does,

I'm going to pay attention this time. He makes it a bit easier for me by picking up his wine glass and taking a sip a few feet away from me.

In other words, out of kissing range.

Which is good.

No. That is bad.

"Lizzie?"

I turn towards him. A serious expression is etched across his gorgeous face.

"Please don't be afraid of anything in your family changing how I feel."

My heart stops. I don't know what to say, but Roman continues.

"We all have crazy families and exes, and yes, you have this whole princess thing, which is a bit of an unusual layer," he says, running his hand through his hair and messing it up. "But I don't care. I promise you, there's nothing you can tell me that will make me change my mind about what I want."

I think he might be able to hear my heart beating now.

"So, what do you want?" I ask, my voice quiet with hope.

"I want a chance to see what we can be," Roman says simply. "That's all that matters to me."

"That's all I want, too."

"I don't date," he continues, putting his wine glass aside. He moves behind me and slides his arms around my waist, nuzzling my neck as he does.

"Good, neither do I."

"So, we'll not date. Except to date each other."

I laugh, and Roman chuckles into my skin, his warm breath a delicious sensation against my neck.

"Perfect plan," he says, standing upright and dropping a kiss on the top of my head.

I somehow manage to successfully heat the stock, which I add to the pan of risotto. Before long, dinner is ready. We move to the dining room and sit at one end of the table.

"Tell me more about Elizabeth of York," Roman asks quietly.

This time, I feel more secure in the truths I'm about to tell him. Because the man who has held my hands so lovingly, who kissed my palm, who protected me from the press, and who risked his heart by kissing me so passionately this evening isn't going to be scared off by the reality of my life.

I trust him.

Over dinner, I tell him what it was like to grow up inside palace walls. I explain how I knew early on I was different, and I share the rich experiences this life has afforded me, like being able to travel the globe, live in palaces, and enjoy holidays in places like Africa, Biarritz, and Monaco. I've eaten dinner with heads of state in elaborate, beyond reality-type dinners, steeped in that royal magic and protocol.

"I saw a picture of you at a state dinner last summer," Roman says, gazing at me. "You were in a white evening gown and gloves, and you were breathtaking.'

I blush from his compliment. "Thank you. That was the dinner for the king and queen of Spain."

"You had some bling that night," he teases.

I laugh. "Yes. I had a pair of diamond and aquamarine earrings that were a gift from my grandmother."

"I bet they matched your eyes," Roman says, gazing at me affectionately. "Your eyes are aquamarine."

"They did," I say.

"How come you weren't wearing a sash like Antonia?" he asks before taking another bite of his risotto.

"Those are royal orders, given as a reward for service," I explain, taking a sip of wine before continuing. "I have not been awarded one."

"And no tiara?"

"You are obsessed with the tiara, aren't you?"

Roman chuckles. "I've never had a date with a woman who owns a tiara."

"You still haven't," I say, arching an eyebrow. "I do not have a tiara. In our family, you don't wear one until you are married. Clementine will get the next tiara to wear in the spring when she marries Christian."

Roman furrows his brow. "That sounds so archaic."

"It is. A lot of things about the rules in my life are, from who you talk to at a state dinner and in what order you turn to talk to the next person to the clothing we are expected to wear at traditional events, like Trooping the Colour, down to the necklines and hemlines. Victoria, my youngest sister, loathes it. She once picked out an off-the-shoulder suit, and my parents forbade it, saying she would catch so much hate in the press for being that far off from what we are expected to wear," I stop for a moment and give Roman a small smile. "She wore it anyway. My parents were upset, Antonia was furious, and the press had a field day, calling her a disrespectful royal, a rebel in clothing, while simultaneously giving her credit for moving the fashion forward a notch."

I reflect on the memory. Victoria is on Antonia's bad list after that episode. She barely acknowledges her now, which makes Victoria gleeful. But Victoria doesn't want to undertake a working role like I do. I'm reminded of my pink outfit today, the awful headline, and how I've become a threat Antonia will seek to eliminate.

"Where did you go?"

I blink. Roman is studying me with concern in his eyes.

"I might have gone too far by wearing pink today."

"What? That's crazy. It's a colour."

"No, I upstaged Antonia's press today," I say, treading into the area of family secrets that only Clementine knows.

Now Roman will, too.

"Roman, my family is full of craziness and ugliness," I say, my face growing warm. I avert my eyes from his and stare down into the deep red wine in my glass instead. "We are worse than any reality TV show you can think of. The public has no idea, none. Palace employees sign confidentiality agreements to keep our secrets. People have been paid off to eliminate things from being revealed. And it's all so stupid and ridiculous, and I can't believe the things I'm going to tell you."

I glance up. Roman reaches over and places his hand over mine in a gesture of comfort.

"The king and queen despise each other," I admit. "If it weren't against what was expected, Arthur would have divorced her decades ago."

Roman's eyes grow wide. "You're kidding."

I shake my head. "I adore Arthur. He is everything you see on TV: strong, quiet, solid. He's a good man who wants nothing more than to help the people of the United Kingdom flourish."

"And the queen?"

"She's an awful person. I know people shouldn't be black and white, Roman. Nobody should be that one-dimensional. But she is. Antonia cares about her position and hanging on to her youth. She was horrible to Clementine, as she saw her as unworthy of being in this ridiculous family, when she's been one of the best things to ever happen to it."

Roman stares at me, stunned. "She is an evil queen? This sounds like a book, Lizzie."

I can feel my blush extend to the roots on my head, and I know I'm bright red in shame. "Antonia likes being Her Majesty. She fell in love with the spotlight, and she can only find value and happiness in adoration from others. Clementine is a threat to that."

Roman is silent for a moment. "And so are you."

"Yes," I say. "She will make my life difficult as long as I'm a working royal. She fought against me taking on this role and suggested I go find a real job. Arthur won that battle, but she isn't about to let me forget where she thinks I should be."

"You've been nothing but an asset and ambassador for them. People love you. You've touched them. If Antonia was truly about serving her kingdom, she'd be proud of you. Not jealous."

"Thank you for saying that."

"It's the truth. Those little girls today will never forget the encouragement you gave them. Your words were from your heart. Anyone who hears you speak knows that."

I'm nothing but grateful for his words. His understanding encourages me to continue to the most painful part of my story.

"My parents are miserable," I say, diving deeper into the cupboard of Chadwick secrets. "I... I found my father in a compromising position with his top advisor. He's having an affair."

Roman's mouth drops open.

"I have to keep that secret. My sisters don't know, and the guilt of keeping the secret eats me alive. But it's not my story to tell. Mum knows, of course. Dad simply said he fell out of love with my mum. But since divorce isn't an option within our gilded walls, he lives and works with his mistress under the same roof. Mum is a mixture of sadness and fury, one moment raging at him, the next wanting me to help her win him back."

My voice wobbles. Roman squeezes my hand.

"All of them would be better if they could divorce, but they're trapped. And while we all act happy and joyful and like the perfect family when outside the beautiful palaces, there is pure misery simmering beneath the surface. Now I'm put in the middle of Mum and Dad and terrified this story will somehow find its way out of St. James's Palace."

Roman moves his hand to my cheek. "You don't deserve this. Any of it. I'm so sorry you've had to bear all of this."

"See?" I say, forcing a smile. "We're regular, messed up people, too."

"You're messed up with better holidays, but yeah, I agree."

I laugh. He smiles in response.

"I bet you don't have this kind of crazy."

Roman shakes his head. "My family is pretty normal. Sure, we have our rows and stuff, and our hard times, like when my grandmother died, but nothing dramatic."

Once again, I think of how normal and quiet his life is. He has his family, who live in the same neighbourhood he does, and his garden. It's simple and straightforward, whereas mine is like a snow globe. It's a glass bowl that people stare at and like to shake up, to watch the glitter swirl and fall.

I'm worried that by bringing Roman into this world, I'm about to shake it up in a way he might hate.

Which will lead to him hating me.

Tears fill my eyes. "I like you. I like you more than I should," I say, forcing the words out of my thickened throat. "But Roman, I could upend your world. Do you see now what I mean? If you date me, you'll eventually have to face all of this, along with a media who will want to dig up everything about you."

To my surprise, he gets up, moves next to my chair, and drops down on one knee, taking my hands in his.

"Maybe I'm ready for an upending," Roman says, his voice commanding. "My life has been stuck, Lizzie. I've been in love only once in my life. Once. I fell in love with a girl called Felicity when we were sixteen. We were together all the way through until my last year of university. We commuted to see each other, texted, and spent hours on FaceTime, dying to see each other again as soon as we could. I thought that was it. Forever."

I search his eyes. I don't see sadness there, or lingering desire, but simply a man sharing his story.

"I thought I would marry her," Roman admits quietly. "Then she broke up with me, over the phone after she picked a row. She told me there was more out there in life, and I wasn't enough. Felicity said she had fallen out of love and had been faking it for a while, until she could find the nerve to break up with me. She said she needed to find someone who could add the excitement to her life that I couldn't."

I wince, as I can't imagine the kind of pain that must have inflicted on his heart. "I'm so sorry, Roman."

"I was gutted. I shut down. I buried myself in work; that's all I did. For *years*. I decided I'd rather be alone. I didn't need to open myself up to disappoint someone else. I didn't date. I didn't mess around. I chose to close myself off and remain alone."

He stops speaking for a moment. I remove one of my hands from his and caress his face.

"But one day I found myself inside the gates of Kensington Palace, and I was rescued by this princess with no tiara, but with aquamarine eyes and fire in her heart," Roman continues. "And I was *alive* again. Now that I've been given this chance, I want to take it. With you."

My heart is filled with relief. I exhale. Roman's mouth curves up in response.

"Were you worried I'd leave? I told you I wouldn't. If anything, you should leave after my confession of living as a hermit gardener."

I lean forward and press my lips against the bridge of his nose. "I happen to fancy hermit gardeners. And you've made me exceedingly happy tonight."

Roman backs up. "Wait. You have a reason to have a mad crush on me that you don't even know about. Hold on."

"Where are you going?" I ask as he walks out of the dining room.

"I'll be right back."

I smile. If he only knew I already have a mad crush on him. Because I do. An impossible, fully-fledged, I'm-tumbling-for-this-man kind of crush.

And it's only our second date.

Roman comes back carrying the white box he had left on the console. He places it in front of me and takes his seat at the table. "For you."

The box is adorned with a red ribbon, which I untie. "You didn't have to get me anything," I say.

"Oh, I know, but you'll be happy that I did."

Hmm. I get the ribbon off and lift the lid. As soon as I

do, the scent of butter and lemon waft towards me. "Roman!" I gasp.

Because underneath the waxed paper, I find two perfect lemon bars.

"I'm not a baker, but I found one who makes lemon bars."

"I haven't had one in so long. Thank you so much!" I cry in delight.

I lift my gaze back up to Roman, this man who wanted to surprise me with my favourite treat, and who decided to protect his heart from any chance of hurt until he met me. The fact that he wants to take this chance with me, with all the drama and baggage that is attached to my name, touches me more than he could ever know.

I'm about to tell him so when I hear my mobile ringing from the living room. I instantly sit straight up. "Oh no," I whisper as the ringtone I have set for Buckingham Palace fills the air.

"What? Liz? Who is that?"

I draw a deep breath and exhale.

"It's Antonia."

CHAPTER 12
TRUE COLOURS

"The queen is calling you? Don't you need to get that?" Roman asks, as I remain seated.

Do I need to get it? I ask myself as the mobile continues to ring. She is the queen—a powerful woman who is already jealous of the attention I've been receiving. And now she will be in full-on threat mode because of what the tabloids were saying about her today.

But she's not my boss. Arthur is. It's nearly eight o'clock, and I'm not working on behalf of the crown at this moment. "No," I say, standing up. "I'm going to get some plates for the lemon bars. Would you like a cuppa to go with it?"

Roman studies me carefully. "You are letting Antonia go to voicemail?"

"Yes. She's not calling to congratulate me on my engagement today. She's calling to invite me to tea, to mark her turf and send me scurrying away. That is not a phone call I care to take in my off hours, and best of all, I don't have to. Antonia doesn't own my time, and she won't get it until business hours tomorrow."

A slow smile begins to form on Roman's face, which blossoms into a beaming grin. "This is why I couldn't stop thinking about you," he says. "This fire. You're confident. Strong. You don't take rubbish from anyone, whether it's the press or the queen. Do you know how attractive it makes you?"

My heart swells. He's not turned off by the fact that I assert myself; in fact, in his eyes, it makes me sexier.

And the fact that he thinks so makes him hotter to me.

"I'm glad you like strong women," I say.

Roman rises from his seat and moves closer to me. "Not just any strong woman."

Ooh!

He reaches for my waist and draws me to him.

"What about the lemon bars?" I tease.

"We'll have them when I come back for breakfast tomorrow," he says, dropping his mouth on mine.

❦

"I think I could get used to this," I say, gazing at Roman across the table. "I have my Earl Grey. I'm indulging in this scrumptious lemon bar for breakfast."

"Scandalous," he says, cocking an eyebrow.

I smile and continue. "And I'm sharing this meal with a devilishly gorgeous man. That is the best bit."

Roman's neck begins to turn red. He ruffles his hair, which makes it stick up, and oh, I am deliciously smitten with this man.

We stayed up until midnight talking and sipping wine in front of the fireplace, cuddling and kissing. Lots and lots of kissing.

Wonderful, sexy, slow, sizzling wine kisses that are now seared in my memory.

And in my heart.

So much so that Antonia's voicemail—I've been summoned to tea on Wednesday to discuss "proper engagement etiquette"—didn't even make me mad. I was able to put it in perspective. Meaning, while this tea is code for "don't ever show me up again, you millennial twit," and she added a veiled warning that she hoped to see me in a more "appropriately-coloured" dress for my reception tonight, it wasn't the most important thing in my life. Even a summons from Her Majesty couldn't ruin my blissful state of mind.

Instead, I filed her away to be dealt with in a firm, yet respectable way over tea in china cups and watercress finger sandwiches. Rather than plot out what I will say, when I will say it, and what expression will be on my face, I went back to thinking about Roman. A first for me.

I come back to the present and drop my gaze to his mouth, and the soft lips that caressed mine until the moment Darcy picked him up. The second I think about kissing him, my pulse quickens.

True to his word, Roman returned this morning at six for breakfast. It was a night of little sleep, but I feel exuberant.

"The gardener and the princess," he says, shaking his head as he reaches for his mug of tea. "Sounds like you got the wrong end of the fairy tale."

I watch as his mouth curves up as he taps the top of his egg with a spoon. This is something else I've learnt about him. Roman takes his tea black and likes dippy eggs with toast. He eats one slice with butter—the dipping piece— and another with marmalade.

My gorgeous gardener has no idea that I have found the man I didn't think could exist until I met him. The truths I whispered to him last night were ones nobody else knows. I let him inside not only the walls of Kensington Palace but inside of my heart, too.

"How can you say this is a fairy tale? I didn't have Darjeeling tea or lime to give you at breakfast. This is a *nightmare*."

Roman chuckles, and my pulse quickens at the magical sound.

"So, you have an event this evening?" he asks.

I nod. "Yes, a formal reception at Buckingham Palace for a young entrepreneur group," I say. "I'm presenting the awards to the top five entrepreneurs."

Roman shakes his head. "I could never do what you do. Get up in front of people and speak like that? No. Nooooooooooooooo."

I laugh. "I actually like giving speeches."

Roman shoots me a repulsed look. I grin.

"Is that it?" I ask. "Will you delete my number from your mobile now?"

"No, you'd have to do something more offensive. Like kill a poinsettia."

I reach for his phone on the table. "Then I'll do you a favour and delete myself now."

Roman grins and snatches his phone back. "I won't let you kill a poinsettia. In fact, I believe in you so much, I might bring you one."

"I'm terrified. For the poinsettia."

"I have complete faith that after my lesson, you will not kill it."

"When can I expect this lesson?"

"When's the next open date in your diary?"

Zing!

"I'll be home tomorrow night."

"Who do I call at St. James's Palace to get an appointment with you in the evening?" Roman says.

I want to kiss those lips that tease me with a hint of the smile I know he's suppressing.

"Well, seeing as how I'm a modern royal, I'll handle that engagement request directly."

"I'd like to request seven o'clock."

"Confirmed," I say, taking another bite of my lemon bar.

Roman appears thoughtful. "Can we meet here?"

I nod. While we are getting to know each other, Kensington Palace is easier for privacy.

Where I can protect him, I think determinedly.

"Yes. What takeaway sounds good to you?" I ask.

Now I get the full smile.

"Let me handle dinner," Roman says. "Do you like seafood?"

"Now I get to let you in on more weird things about being a royal," I say. "Did you know I'm not supposed to eat shellfish while travelling or dining out because of the risk of food-related illness?"

Roman wrinkles his brow. "You aren't serious."

"Oh, I am."

"They tell you what to eat?" he asks, incredulous. "That is so… three centuries ago."

I laugh. "We can't afford to be sick in public or on tour. But I do love sushi, lobster, mussels, all the usual suspects."

Roman nods. "Well, maybe I'll make something with seafood."

"I'm already looking forward to it."

He smiles at me. "Me too."

Before I know it, Roman needs to head to work. I

picture how his day will be, all rugged, digging in the dirt, and how hot he must look doing it. He retrieves his helmet, which has remained on my console since he left it there last night, and I walk him out to his motorcycle.

"Have a good day at work," I say, putting my hands on the lapels of his leather riding jacket. I laugh. "Wow, I sound incredibly old and domesticated saying that."

"No," Roman disagrees. "It's hot when you say that."

I blush. He chuckles.

"Come on, Lizzie. We like seeds and pens. Conversation about having a good day at work is sexy."

I smile. "I agree."

Roman leans down and drops a kiss on my lips. "Call me after the reception is over?"

It is ridiculous how giddy I am at this moment.

"Yes."

He steps back from me and is about to put on his helmet when he stops. "Not that you would ever take my advice on anything related to receptions, but I don't think you should wear white tonight," Roman says, his hazel eyes growing darker with intensity. "Your aunt might be the queen, but you are *Liz*. I see all the colours in you, and so should the rest of the world. No matter what her majesty dictates."

Then he puts on his helmet, straddles his bike, and zips away.

I watch Roman until he's out of sight, my heart full of joy knowing he sees me as vibrant and passionate.

And ready to show the world my true colours.

I hurry back down the path and into my cottage. I return to the dining room table and retrieve my phone. I have a meeting with Cecelia at St. James's Palace this afternoon to go over all the details for this evening, but I managed to convince her we didn't need to meet with

Sydney about the headlines comparing me to Antonia. That leaves this morning free.

I pull up Amelia's contact info and tap on the message icon. I type:

> **Super short notice but are you free this morning to go shopping? I want to get a different dress for my reception appearance tonight, preferably by a British or commonwealth designer/design house. Would need alterations done on site. Am I crazy?**

I hit send as I pick up my mug and head back into the kitchen for a fresh tea bag to make another cup. Amelia loves formal wear and bridal gowns, and I've never seen anyone as obsessed with the show *Say Yes to the Dress* as she is.

While I wait for her to respond, I check my other messages. I smile when I see the ones Victoria sent yesterday, approving the fact that I wore pink and usurped Antonia. The jumper I chose is already sold out online. I wonder if my wearing colour will have an unexpected impact on designers and fashion houses, with consumers demanding any eye-catching pieces because I have worn them.

Next, Bella texted me with concern, saying I shouldn't cross Antonia in any way as my position is so new. She thinks I should take care of myself and not incite any kind of response from her.

I take a deep breath and exhale. Out of the three of us, she is the most vulnerable. Bella is a sensitive soul, and she reminds me of Christian. She's hiding away at university, where the press respects her privacy, and I think, deep down, she's terrified of what will happen when she graduates and becomes fair game for the media. Right now, she's happily cocooned in Scotland with her study of history, but I worry about what will happen when she leaves the protected walls of St. Andrews.

My phone vibrates, interrupting my thoughts. It's Amelia with a response:

YES YES YES, Liz! I know the place to go. It's in Teddington, and the stockist strictly carries UK designers. I'll get us squeezed in—obvs they'll make time for Her Royal Highness, ha ha! Shall I pick you up around 9ish?

I can practically hear Amelia squealing with joy from her flat in Chelsea at today's prospect of shopping for a formal dress. I confirm that is perfect and put my phone down to prepare my tea. I glance down at the time on the phone. It's quarter past seven.

I move back into the dining room, the warming cup of tea in my hand, and glance down at the name on the pastry box that held my lemon bars.

The Biscuit Cutter

The address and hours are printed underneath the logo. It's located in Belgravia and opens at eight. That's perfect. I take a seat and peruse the website on my phone, selecting an assortment of themed biscuits, and choose the option for delivery so I can surprise Clementine with a gift in honour of her first charity engagement and walkabout this afternoon. Then I read the morning news on my phone, as I always do, and yes, there is tons of press for SCOUT 4 GIRLS because of my decision to wear a pink jumper and coat. I'm amazed, but if I can further my message and help my patronages by wearing colours, I'll do it.

I take a sip of tea and consider Roman's words. I was so certain I had to be safe, to make optimistic white my colour. It was a way of building my presence, but by remaining colourless, I was hiding myself.

As I skim through the pictures from Antonia's appearance, I notice she is so carefully restrained that her choices are never wrong, but boringly safe. She's a stunning woman, and she would be beautiful in jewel tones, but that is not in her crafted image.

My eyes widen as I realise the truth.

By sticking with white, I was following in Antonia's image, although my brain refused to see it that way. There's no difference between her neutral sheaths and coats and my hues of white.

It's all manipulated.

I blush in shame. Then I sit up straight and square my shoulders. I'm changing this. I'm going to wear colours of my choice. I'm going to show more of myself to the world through my fashion choices. I know some will be criticised in the press and talked about by the public. I can't control that. But at least I'll know the woman outside of the palace walls is closer to the one who lives inside them.

Today is the start of something new for me. The idea of turning things on their head tonight with a shocking choice of evening gown is not terrifying to me. Thanks to Roman's words, it's exciting.

And I can't wait to get to it.

CHAPTER 13

FLOWERS AND BUTTERFLIES

Amelia is chatting away as she drives into Teddington. She has been talking non-stop since she picked me up this morning.

"They have the most exquisite wedding gowns at Beautiful Days," she says, referring to the by-appointment-only bridal and evening gown boutique that she is taking me to.

I listen as I scroll through my phone. When Amelia is excited about something, she talks a mile a minute, going into fantastic detail about the topic of interest. I glance at her. Her dark hair is pulled back into a messy bun, and her green eyes sparkle as she goes on about one of her favourite designers, who has amazing fabrics and techniques that make women look elegant.

"The bodices have such incredible attention to detail, and all of the work is done in London, down to the delicate hand-embroid—"

She abruptly stops speaking. "Liz! I'm so sorry, I've been rambling on forever about silks and bodices and all the designers this stockist has, and I know this isn't your thing."

She stops at a traffic light, chewing the inside of her lip anxiously. "I'm so sorry."

"A, would you stop?" I say, smiling at her as I use my favourite nickname for my dear friend. "I'm relieved you know fashion down to the last detail. I know if I'm going to change things up tonight, you will make sure everything is fitted appropriately and in fabrics that flatter my frame."

"Gowns make me happy," Amelia says simply. "The stories and memories that each one can create for a woman take my breath away. If I didn't have the title in front of my name, I would have studied something in fashion."

A long sigh escapes her lips. I frown. Amelia has been told since she was a little girl that Westbrook women have a great legacy of service to the world and must prepare accordingly. It's weird. In some ways, her family is more archaic than mine. She was given a list of "Westbrook-approved" studies for her university years, and fashion wasn't one of them. It's one of the things we bonded over: being born in to a world of amazing privilege, with such restrictive boundaries in return.

My phone vibrates in my hand. I'm overjoyed to see it's a text from Clem, and from the picture, I can tell my gift from The Biscuit Cutter has been delivered to Buckingham Palace, where she and Christian are preparing for their visit and walkabout this afternoon.

"Clem got the biscuits," I say happily, staring at a basket of the most elegant bespoke iced biscuits I have ever seen.

"What did she say?"

I laugh softly. "That as soon as the appearance is over, she will dive in and eat all of them to relieve her stress. And that the one of Buckingham Palace is her favourite."

"I need to go with you to this shop," Amelia says as the traffic light changes.

"I want to see it, too," I reply. "I picked out my items on the website, but I must visit in person soon."

"I have no talent for baking," she says. "We always get our Christmas cake from a bakery and decorate it ourselves."

An idea hits me as Amelia navigates towards the shop. I need to get a Christmas cake for Roman. I think of his grandmother, of how much he misses that tradition of port-induced decorating, and I want to give him that tradition back.

And make a new memory of doing it with me.

"Here we are," Amelia says, driving her Volvo down a tiny street. "Isn't it adorable?"

I stare at the shop, which is tucked into a quaint building, with a gorgeous bridal gown on display in the window. I groan. "If I'm snapped going into a bridal shop, the media will have a field day," I say, thinking of what stupid, far-fetched stories will soon pop up, with ridiculous headlines to match.

"No, they'll merely say you are getting another white gown," Amelia teases.

"That stops today," I say firmly. "I don't need white as my security blanket anymore."

Amelia keeps her eyes ahead as she searches for a parking spot. "Thanks to a gardener with an eye for colour. And you."

My face instantly burns as she teases me.

"Look at you, blushing over a man," she says, surprise in her voice. "I never thought I'd see it, Liz. Since I've known you, you've always pushed them away. Now you're blushing at the mere mention of one."

"You know what's weird? I knew he was different the

first moment I met him. I just knew it. Have you ever felt that way?"

Amelia appears thoughtful as she waits for a car to reverse out of its spot. "No. When I first met George," she says, referring to her last boyfriend, "we were friends first and kind of fell into dating. There was never this *knowing* moment. Obviously, or we wouldn't have broken up. I think we dated because it was easy… What is this woman doing? Knitting a jumper while she reverses? Come on!"

"Roman has stirred up feelings in me that I didn't believe could exist," I say as Amelia impatiently strums her fingers on the steering wheel. "When you meet someone like that, Amelia, it's not like what you had with George. Not that your relationship with him was wrong or bad, but the feelings are intensified. Your senses are alive. You can spend hours with him, and it's not enough. But I'm comfortable, too. We sat in front of the fireplace sipping wine and talking and holding hands, and it was magical."

As the car slowly begins to back out of the space, Amelia studies me. "You're going to fall in love, aren't you?" she asks, her voice incredulous.

If she had said that to me with any previous man who came near me, I would have snort-laughed, rolled my eyes, and hit her playfully on the arm.

"I hope I do," I say out loud.

Amelia's eyes widen at my confession. "You're serious," she says, parking her car.

"I am. I never wanted to date seriously. Nor did I want to fall in love and end up being disappointed by the experience. But now I do. And it's because of Roman. He has changed my mind on everything I thought I wanted."

"You know that after two dates?" she asks.

"I do. I've realised it's not that I didn't want to take a

chance on love before, like I thought. I just needed Roman to come into my life to wake me up to the beauty of it. He makes me want it, and he's worth risking disappointment. Roman," I say firmly, "is the only man worthy of this risk."

Amelia turns off the engine and shoots me a beaming smile.

"I feel two things right now."

"Oh, please, share," I say, dropping my phone into my bag.

"My heart is giddy to see you happy with a man who is worthy of you."

I take a moment to check my surroundings before exiting the car, grabbing my tote bag of shoes to try on with the different dresses. "And the second?"

We both exit the car, and Amelia comes round to join me on the path. "The other," she says, her eyes twinkling, "is that I want what you have. You are glowing."

"That's compliments of my face mask from last night," I tease as we begin to walk. I see people approach us on the street, but nobody recognises me. Yet.

Beautiful.

"It's not your face mask," Amelia declares as we walk in the direction of the shop.

I laugh. "No, it's not. And the way I feel, I might never need a mask again."

"I should hate you for all of this."

We reach the shop, and now I feel eyes on us from behind. I can always sense when I've been spotted, and I have since I was a little girl. I tuck my head down and quickly pop open the door, knowing there will be pictures of me going into a bridal boutique on social media before I get my first dress to try on in the changing room.

The boutique is small and full of gorgeous bridal gowns

made of the most exquisite fabrics, with intricate details. Elegant chandeliers hang from the ceiling, and the scent of freshly-cut roses fills the air.

"Oh!" Amelia gasps, moving towards the gown that is on display to my right. "Isn't this gorgeous? See the fullness of the skirt?"

I grin. The way I can go on about pens and Roman can talk about seeds is how Amelia can speak about wedding dresses.

"Your Royal Highness?"

I turn around and see a sales woman approaching me. She is elegantly dressed in a black wrap dress, her silver hair cut into a chic, pixie-like cut.

"I'm Pamela. I will be your fashion consultant today." She extends her hand, and I shake it.

"Please, call me Liz," I say, smiling.

"Amelia, welcome back," she says brightly.

I cock an eyebrow, and Amelia blushes.

"Cocktail gowns," she says firmly. "Family business, you know."

Yes. With a huge side of wedding gown daydreaming, I think.

"Amelia tells me you are looking for a reception dress for tonight," Pamela says, opening her leather journal.

"Yes, I have a formal reception at Buckingham Palace."

Pamela doesn't bat an eyelash.

"I have a seamstress on site ready to go, so we can accommodate you today," she says swiftly.

"Thank you," I reply, grateful that I am able to get such service.

"We have some lovely winter white gowns that would make stunning evening wear," she says, leading me towards a display of dresses.

"Oh, no. I want colour."

Pamela freezes as another sales woman walks by, her heels clicking against the floor and a garment bag rustling as she takes a discreet, one-second glance at me. "Colour?" Pamela repeats, as if she heard me incorrectly.

"Yes. I want colour."

A smile brightens her face. "Then let's get you into something fabulous and statement-making."

Statement-making, I think with excitement.

Yes. That's what this dress is: a statement that I'm no longer playing it safe. I'm ready to take chances. I want to be seen as a vibrant woman who is confident enough to let the world see my personality in my dress. I'm smart and worthy of the position I have, and no matter what I'm wearing, people can be confident I'm doing the UK proud.

We follow Pamela to the back of the boutique, where the formal dresses are. "A lot of our orders are custom, so we'll need to find something off the rack that we can alter immediately."

I glance at Amelia, who gives me a reassuring nod. They begin flicking through gorgeous gowns. I'm shown dresses in rich red, shimmery silver, and deep pink.

I begin to doubt my choice to not wear white. Ugh, I shouldn't have decided to do this for tonight. As with everything I do, this needed a plan, with examples of what I like, the colours I'd like to try, and plenty of time built in for alterations.

The fact that I'm here, thinking of going so far off my script, should terrify me.

But thanks to Roman, I'm inspired to leave the plan in my diary.

While Amelia and Pamela discuss the merits of a coral twist satin dress, I move down the row, to a rack filled with dark gowns.

Then I freeze.

I see my dress.

I move towards it, drawn to it, needing to touch it.

I pull the dress out, and a gasp escapes my lips.

The dress is a long evening gown in navy. It has a plunging V-neckline, but it's underneath a sheer navy top with long sleeves. The waist is fitted, and then the dress is straight until it flares a bit at the bottom.

But the best part of the dress is the embroidery. It's covered in exquisite vines, flowers in full bloom, and butterflies, in shades of rich violet, pink, and greens. I run my fingers over the sheer fabric covering the delicate work, and excitement surges through me.

I draw an anxious breath of air and dare to read the size on the tag. Please be a ten. Please be a ten...

I close my eyes for a brief moment, then make myself check the sizing.

10.

It's all I can do not to squeal in excitement.

If this dress fits like I think it should, at the most, I might need only minor alterations here and there to perfect the fit. I brought a couple of pairs of heels that would work with assorted colours, but my silver Jimmy Choo heels will be beautiful with this stunning dress.

This dress represents my growth and change in my role.

In myself.

And it's for the man who has his soul tied to the earth, and who nurtures the land and is passionate about the environment. The man who is bringing beauty in the world to life, and who is stirring this new view of myself.

This dress is not only for me tonight.

It's for Roman.

Cecelia escorts me as we walk towards the Picture Gallery at Buckingham Palace, the majestic room where the reception will begin this evening. I will meet and talk to guests over cups of tea and canapés before moving to the ballroom to give my brief remarks ahead of the presentation of the entrepreneur awards.

"I can't get over the change in you," Cecelia says as we move from one long corridor to another on the world-famous red carpeting covering the floors. "You're wearing colour. Actually, multiple colours, and a pattern!"

"I've come to the conclusion," I say slowly, "that I can prove my value and worth in colour as well as white."

"The press is going to eat this dress up, as much as they did the red draped coat Clementine wore this afternoon. That asymmetrical cut, with the tartan black-and-red wool sheath underneath, was lovely."

"She was radiant in all the pictures," I say, thinking of her and Christian smiling, shaking hands, and talking to the people at their walkabout. "People loved her. Did you see all those American flags woven in with the British ones?"

"I've never seen Christian appear more comfortable with the crowds than he was today," Cecelia adds. "He was smiling and engaging. The sad prince is gone."

"Did you see how he put his hand on her back protectively?" I ask, warmth filling my heart. "He loves her so much, Cecelia. Clementine is so bright and vivacious, and she brings out the best in him. You could see it today. And he does the same to her."

My mind shifts to Roman. He has already brought out a change in my clothing, and in my approach to my work.

"You could see how they connected with the people in the senior centre, too." Cecelia says, interrupting my thoughts. "You would never know it was Clementine's first event."

"Clementine is a natural at this. You could see in her reactions with the public that she was sincere."

"Sounds like someone else I know," Cecelia says.

I smile as we near the Picture Gallery. It's one of my favourite rooms in the palace. Its pink-flocked wallpaper is adorned with some of the best pieces of art in the world, including works by Rembrandt and Rubens. I first fell in love with it for a different reason, however. As a little girl, the pink wallpaper was magnificent, but it was also the place I used to chase Xander up and down when he was annoying me by snatching my doll and then throwing it to Christian as they engaged in a game of keep away, until one of our parents broke it up. Even then, Xander was mischievous.

I pause as I think of India, and how serious and rigid she is, and once again, my gut screams at me that this is not the girl for him. He needs someone to settle him down, yes, but he also needs someone who can push him, challenge him, and keep that spark in his eyes while doing it.

That reminds me: Xander hasn't returned my phone calls. But he should know he can't avoid me—or my questions—for long.

I stop as we approach the corridor that leads to the gallery.

"Liz?" Cecelia asks, coming to a stop beside me.

I realise what I'm about to do. While guests are enjoying their cups of tea in fine china and picking up canapés off silver platters, as soon as I enter, the talk will be of me. They will gossip about my dress and wonder why am I not wearing my signature white.

Like the old British saying, I'm about to put the cat among the pigeons. Antonia will be *furious* that I defied her tonight and didn't slip back into my non-threatening custom white.

I hold my head high. I'm proud of the decision I'm making. Yes, there will be consequences, but I've learnt that taking risks is important for evolving. It's how I found Roman. It's how I'm finding my true identity as a royal, one that is as unique and individual as I am.

As Liz.

And there is no better time to do it than now.

The evening was magnificent.

I feel radiant as I slip through the halls of Buckingham Palace. The reception has ended, and everyone left buzzing about the organisation's direction for the upcoming year: to help young people get their businesses off the ground. The energy in the room was full of excitement for the future and the young minds who will shape it.

I head back to my office at the palace, which Arthur

gave me upon graduation, and slip inside. Normally after an event, I like to sit down and write a report of it while it's still fresh in my mind, listing what went right, what went wrong, and what I could improve upon.

I sit at my desk, still dressed in the evening gown, and open a new word file on my laptop. As someone who plans everything, I love this part of my work. Dissecting the event to see how it worked and utilising that information for the future is a planner's dream.

But tonight, I'm distracted. My thoughts aren't locking into the event post-mortem like they normally do. I glance at my clutch. My mobile is safely tucked away in there, so I can focus on this task and then head home for the night. I don't need to read press reports or see the first pictures that have shown up on social media, but I'm desperate to know if Roman has texted me.

I want to rehash the night with him and find out if he has seen any pictures and figured out this dress was chosen to honour the way he's made me feel.

No, I scold myself. *You are working right now.*

I begin to type:

04 December

I lift my eyes from the screen to my clutch.

I wonder if Roman messaged me.

We exchanged a few texts as I was getting ready, and I told him to pay attention to my dress this evening. He guessed—incorrectly—that I would be wearing pink.

I tear my eyes away from my clutch and exhale loudly as I watch the blinking cursor on the screen.

Okay. I will write this report, and my reward will be

checking my phone for texts from Roman. As soon as I get this done, I will do that.

I dive into my work. Though not completely, as visions of Roman's smile dance in my head as I go through my usual list of questions and jot down notes on each one.

The second I hit "save," I reach for my clutch, eagerly retrieving my phone. I feel anxious and excited as I scroll through my messages: one from Amelia, one from Clementine, Victoria...

I stop.

There's one from Xander, which I am eager to read, but I scroll past that one for now.

Then I see the one I'm looking for:

You were breathtaking tonight in that dress, Lizzie. I can't imagine what you looked like in person. I'd have a hard time believing anything that beautiful could be real.

My heart is racing from his heartfelt words. I decide to be bold in my response:

I know we don't have an official engagement on the diary until tomorrow, but I am still in this dress if you would like to verify it is indeed beautiful in person.

I hit send and take a moment to retrieve my navy overcoat from the coat stand.

Ding!

I hurriedly tie the sash around my waist and retrieve my phone to read his reply:

**If this is an invitation to meet you at Kensington
Palace, it is accepted.**

Electricity fills me. I reply that I will meet him there and
that I'm leaving Buckingham Palace now.

I slip out of my office, practically floating down the
regal halls in exuberance. I can't wait for Roman to see me
in this dress.

And to see how he'll react when he finds out the
inspiration for it.

As I walk down the corridor, still thinking of Roman, I
pass a bust of a young Arthur along the wall, from when he
was the Prince of Wales.

Prince of Wales.

Xander.

I can't believe I forgot to read his message! I quickly
retrieve my mobile, amazed at how Roman can distract my
thoughts, though in the best of ways.

**Daring gown tonight, Your Royal Highness.
Besides the motivation of pissing off my mum,
which puts this in the win column, what is the
reason? Oh, and your texts about India? I'm
avoiding them. I'm no longer a philanderer, but
I'm still annoying.**

How does Xander have the amazing ability to be both
charming and exasperating within the few characters of a
text message? I reply as I continue my journey through BP,
as the family calls it, to the car park.

**I have been inspired by someone new in my life.
His name is Roman, and he's a gardener for the**

estate where Clementine used to work. I'm one hundred percent falling for him, Xander. He's smart. Sensitive. Kind. We're alike yet different. He challenges me in all the right ways. I know if we get serious, the road ahead will not be easy for him, but I don't want what is easy. I want what is right.

I hit send. Xander will know that last line is a reference to him choosing India.

By the time I have reached the car park, Xander has replied:

Liz. You can choose the harder path because you aren't going to be the king. I see what the press has done to Clem. I see how hard it was on Christian. I know she's being adored now, but we both know that will change. Now that I'm at the point where I need to think about a relationship, I'm not willing to do that. India is a safe choice. She knows this world. More to the point, she can handle it.

I freeze as I reach my car. I'm alarmed that he used the word safe. One thing that has never fit his personality is the word safe. Xander will regret the safe choice for the rest of his life; I know he will. But his words also send a reminder of reality to me, words that make my heart freeze over in fear.

Will Roman be able to handle my world once he is truly inside?

I turn over my shoulder and stare at Buckingham Palace, all lit up against the midnight-blue sky. This isn't

Roman's world. The man I'm falling for is happy in solitude, in his gardens and home in Shepherd's Bush, building tables and peering at seeds online.

I bite down hard on my lip. Will he hate this world, even if I'm in it? Will he be wounded by the intrusion and judgements that will enter his life? Is it fair to do this to him? To my surprise, tears fill my eyes, and the palace swims in front of me.

With a jolt, I understand that while I have lived my whole life afraid of men disappointing me, the shoe is now on the other foot. I don't want to disappoint him. I can't bring him into my world and have him hate me for it.

Or leave me because of it.

Ding!

I blink back the tears and glance down at my phone. It's a message in the squad's WhatsApp group chat. I click on it and see a picture of Clem and Christian, dressed in hoodies and joggers and all cosy on the sofa, their faces lit up in joy. The message underneath reads:

Successful day for the squad! Clementine nailed her first engagement, and Liz knocked that reception out of the park. Anyone up for late night pizza and beer? Let us know.

I re-read the message. Clementine and Christian are happy and in love. They are meant to face this life together. Christian had to take a risk to know that Clementine could be happy in his world, and despite the hardships, she chose this life because she chose him. I have to shove these fears down and allow Roman to make that same choice.

I open the door and slip inside my car. I draw a breath of air. I'm going to do this the right way. I'm going to keep this relationship a secret until I know Roman can handle what is to come, and he is sure he wants to try this world on for size.

I'm going to protect him with all that I have.

But tonight? I think it's time for Roman to spend some time with the people who know me the best, and who are closest to my heart.

I'm going to bring him into the squad.

CHAPTER 15
PARMA HAM AND ROCKET

As I finish touching up my makeup in the hall mirror, I hear the sound of a car travelling down the road. As it grows closer, my stomach tingles, wondering if it could be Roman.

I've already asked the squad if he can join us tonight, and the responses ranged from Christian's "Don't be daft, of course he can" to a "Squeee! YES!" from Clementine and a "Who is ROMAN?!? You're bringing a MAN? HOW DID I NOT KNOW ABOUT THIS, ELIZABETH?" from Victoria.

Ha! When my baby sister uses "Elizabeth," she's pissed.

But the second Victoria sees me with Roman, she will forget all about the fact that I hadn't been giving her all the details. All she has ever wanted was for me to stop shutting down around men, and now I can tell her she was right. I realise I do want a man in my life.

And that man is Roman.

I go to the window and part the curtains. I see his Land Rover pulling up to my cottage, and excitement surges through me. I force myself to step back so he won't find me with my face practically smashed up against the glass in eagerness to see him.

Within seconds, my doorbell rings. Feeling beautiful in my evening gown, I can't wait for him to see me in it, to see if the gold in his hazel eyes darkens in approval. I slowly open the door, but Roman gives me a surprise of his own. My mouth drops open as I take him in. I can't speak. My heart is pulsating at a rapid rate. I feel breathless staring at him.

He's wearing a dark navy suit, showing off his broad shoulders and trim waist. The pale blue dress shirt is beautiful against his olive skin, and he's even worn a navy and platinum dotted tie to bring the suit together. I'm about to speak, but when my gaze meets his, I'm rendered speechless by the adoration in his eyes.

"Lizzie," he says, his voice low, "my God, you are the most beautiful woman I have ever laid eyes upon. It's your eyes. The light in them, it's different."

He lifts his hands to my face, and I shiver the second his deliciously rough skin meets mine. "They are sparkling, like sunlight on the aquamarine sea," he whispers, staring deeply into my eyes. "I've never seen you more radiant." As Roman says the words, his gaze remains fixed on mine. Not on my dress. Not on my body.

He's telling me all the beauty he needs to see is reflected in my eyes.

I stare back at him, seeing the gold flecks growing more intense.

"Thank you," I murmur, still revelling in joy from his response.

Roman takes my hands in his and steps back, viewing my dress from head-to-toe.

"So beautiful. I lost my breath when the video came up

on my phone, but you are even more perfect in person. You chose colours for a high-profile event," he says, as if hardly believing I took his advice to heart.

"I chose a pattern," I say as Roman studies me, "of flowers and leaves and butterflies, like the place where your heart is the happiest."

His eyes widen as he takes in my words; then I see a stunned expression filter over his handsome face.

"You are the reason I chose this dress," I continue, drawing him closer to me. "It represents the gardens you long to be in. It was a nod to you, Roman, for helping me see I was hiding behind a colour. I don't want to hide. I'm going to reflect who I am and take chances. Monday was my first one, but today is the permanent leap to patterns and colour, and to expressing who I am. I can do my duties and let people see my work speak for itself, without trying to build that trust and confidence in white."

His lips part as if I've rendered him speechless. He takes a breath of air, almost as if for courage, before speaking. "You're wrong about one thing," Roman says, placing my hand over his heart. Goosebumps prickle my skin when I feel how fast it's beating underneath the starched fabric of his light blue dress shirt.

"What?" I whisper.

"My heart isn't only happy in the garden."

Now my heart beats as wildly as his. Roman drops his head and presses a slow, sweet, lingering kiss on my lips, and then breaks it.

"My heart is happy," he whispers, his lips barely inches from mine, "when I'm with you, Lizzie." Then he kisses me again, a hand wrapping around my back as his tongue tangles with mine.

I have never known such happiness as this. Knowing

he's being brave enough to explore a relationship with me despite how his heart was broken in the past makes me vow to protect him even more than I have already promised.

He breaks the kiss, and I smile up at him. "It's cold. Come on inside," I say, tugging playfully at his suit. "I have been remiss in not telling you that you are dead sexy gorgeous in this."

I watch as an embarrassed flush creeps up his neck. Roman follows me inside and shuts the door behind him.

"Well, if you had to stay in an evening gown, it was only fair that I show up in a suit," he explains.

Elation washes over me as Roman wraps his arms around me to hold me close. He's so kind, so thoughtful, and so aware, unlike anything I ever expected to find in a man.

"Well, you might regret that decision when you hear what I'd like to do tonight," I say, putting my hands on his suit lapels. Damn, he's beautiful, in both his work clothes and a suit.

"Hmm, why would I regret a suit?" Roman asks.

"I was wondering," I say slowly, curious as to how his reaction will be to my suggestion, "if you would be game to having some late-night pizza over at Christian and Clementine's. My sister Victoria will pop in as well."

Roman doesn't smile, and I wonder if meeting my family is too soon. Although, the squad are more like my best friends than family, but to an outsider, maybe it's weird.

Or too much.

"Princess Victoria?" he asks, a crease appearing on the bridge of his nose.

I know he's feeling the weight of my family now.

"Victoria," I say, dropping the princess title, "studies

fashion at the University of the Arts in London. She's always up for a good pizza and conversation."

The crease deepens. "What will your sister think of a gardener?" he asks, showing me his vulnerability.

"What will you think of a fashion student? It goes both ways, Roman," I say, raising my hand to his face to stroke it reassuringly. "You know how I am, and Christian. Victoria is like us, except she dresses like she should be in *Vogue*. That's the only difference. I promise you can trust me on this."

Roman takes my hand and draws it to his lips, kissing it. "Then that's all I need to know."

"To keep things fair, I'll wear my dress," I say.

His mouth begins to curve up in that teasing way I've come to adore. "You don't have to."

"I want to," I tell him.

Because it makes me think of you, I add to myself.

Before long, I'm wrapped up in my coat, and we make the short stroll through the Kensington Palace grounds to the cottage where Christian and Clementine live. As we walk, I feel Roman's palm go sweaty as we hold hands. I realise he's worried about what my family will think of him.

"I'm glad I wore a suit," he says, his deep voice fracturing my thoughts. "With Victoria studying fashion, my usual jeans and boots won't cut it with her."

"While Victoria loves fashion, she would never judge you for your clothing. Unless you wore a suit to work, because that would be ridiculous," I say. "She would be the first to tell you that."

"She sounds outspoken, like someone else I know."

I see the corners of his mouth turn up, and relief washes over me.

"She is," I say as I lead him up the path to Christian and

Clementine's cottage. "Victoria is a sharp judge of character. Which means she will adore you, Roman."

We stop at the doorstep. "Don't be nervous." I place my hands on his chest. Once again, I feel his heart, which is pounding at a rapid rate due to nerves. "You're friends with Clem. You're dating me. Christian and Victoria are no different. We're normal people born into an extraordinary position due to history. Victoria pushes a trolley, too," I say, smiling at him.

Now I get more of a turn-up on his sexy mouth.

"Right."

"It's true," I say, pressing the doorbell. I hear barking and know that Clem's Airedale, Bear, and Christian's spaniel, Lucy, are bounding towards the door.

"Bear and Lucy will be the first to greet you," I tell Roman. "I love them both. Lucy is sweet, and Bear is like a big snuggly teddy bear."

"I can think of something else you might consider snuggly," he says, his lips twitching mischievously now.

Heat flickers through me. Why, yes. Yes, I can consider Roman's hard, taut, athletic body quite snuggly indeed.

Clementine pulls open the door, and I can hear nineties pop music blaring in the background. I know without a doubt Victoria is here and has her playlist going.

"Um, you understood we are getting pizza and beer and staying here, right?" she asks as Bear and Lucy wag their tails excitedly upon seeing us.

"Yes," I say, grinning as she lets us inside. I begin stroking Bear's head while Roman bends down to pet Lucy. "I finished the reception, and Roman was already dressed, so here we are."

"Well, you look gorgeous," Clementine declares. "And look at you, snazzy man."

I grin as Roman's neck goes a deep shade of red.

"Terribly out of character, I know," he says, rising back up.

"It's fantastic," Clementine says. "Here, let me take your coat. Everyone is hanging out in the kitchen. Charlie is here, too. He's in London for the weekend."

"Charlie is one of Christian's dearest friends," I explain to Roman, "and has been since their days at Eton before going to Cambridge. He's like us, part of the squad."

Roman helps me take my coat off, and I turn around and see the trust in his eyes. I'm touched at how much faith he puts in me, considering he's still getting to know me. Then I realise he feels the same way I do, like he knows me even though his head is probably telling him he truly can't after only a few dates.

His heart, like mine, knows better.

Clementine takes my coat from Roman. "Go on back. You can give your pizza orders to Christian."

"Thank you," I say to her.

I lead Roman through the cottage, and he takes in his environment. I see him studying the sofas, the art, and the lamps before we move to the kitchen, where "Wannabe" by the Spice Girls is blaring from Victoria's phone. Christian is on his laptop, and Charlie is standing behind him, staring at the screen.

"Hello," I say cheerfully, bringing Roman into the kitchen.

And into the squad.

I squeeze his hand in mine to reassure him as I make introductions. "Everyone, this is Roman," I say easily, as if I pop in with a man at any given time.

Victoria, never one to be subtle, steps forward. "Hello, I'm Victoria," she says, giving Roman a welcoming smile.

She's dressed in tall black boots, a black corduroy mini skirt, and a cream wool jumper, with a black tweed newsboy style cap over her glossy, sleek, blonde locks.

"Your Royal Highness," he says, deferring to old tradition.

"Nope, Roman. I'm just Victoria, and it's a pleasure to meet you," she says, smiling and extending her hand.

He shakes it. "All right, *Just Victoria*, I've got it."

She laughs. Roman smiles.

And my heart is full.

"This is Charlie, a friend of Christian's," I say.

I watch Charlie, with his ginger curls and green eyes, as he shakes hands with Roman. His title is actually Charles Altham, Viscount Hallcourt, and he will become an earl someday and inherit the Hallcourt Estate in Northumberland, which has been in his family since 1506.

"Pleasure to meet you," Charlie says.

"Likewise," Roman replies.

"Good to see you again, Roman," Christian says, rising and shaking his hand as well.

Roman grips it back. "Thank you for having us over tonight."

"You're a welcome addition. You level the playing field for us gents here."

"Gents," I say, snickering.

Christian shifts his gaze to me; then a slow smile filters across his face as his eyes move from me to Roman and back to me again.

"Nice of both of you to dress up for us," he quips.

"It's a lovely dress. I couldn't bear to take it off," I say.

"Liz. This dress, it's *everything*," Victoria declares. "Sheer on the top? What are you thinking, you devilish woman?"

"I can tell you what she was thinking," Christian says,

and I see his blue eyes are dancing with mischief. "Liz was thinking, 'This dress will infuriate Her Majesty. Sold!'"

"Christian," I say, with a warning tone, "I do not live to make your mum furious at me."

"Please, go ahead. You realise you've moved ahead of Clementine now on the list of things that annoy her."

Inwardly, I wince. There is that wee problem about embracing my true self in the public light.

My dramatic change in fashion is gathering tonnes of attention.

Antonia perceives that attention would be hers, if only I would stay in my white dress and in my own lane. I'm sure I will be told to get back in that lane tomorrow when she serves me a watercress sandwich and cup of tea or suffer the consequences. I add it to the list of things to deal with later and come back to the moment.

"Roman, Liz, would you like to come here and study your pizza options? And would either of you like a beer?" Christian asks.

"A beer would be lovely, thank you," I say. "Roman?"

"Any pizza you order is good by me, and I'll have a beer, too, thank you."

"Any pizza? Oh, no, no, no, I need to see your pizza personality," Victoria declares.

I move around the table and sink down into Christian's spot. Roman moves behind me so he can study the menu, too. I feel the warmth radiating from him as he bends down low next to me, and I breathe in the sandalwood soap lingering on his skin. I shiver happily as I anticipate snuggling against his chest and drinking in his sexy scent when we're alone together later.

"What is your pizza personality?" Charlie asks Victoria.

"Precise and full of surprises. Layers of unexpected discoveries."

"How can something be precise and unexpected?" he wonders.

"I like things in a certain order, but they are things nobody else would expect," Victoria says, taking a sip of her wine. "My pizza has a tomato sauce, but not to the edge of the crust. The outer rim of the pizza has to have a lovely basil pesto. I get a combination of mozzarella ovalini, goat's cheese, and parmesan. Then I top it with torn basil, pepperoni, and pineapple. A light sprinkle of sea salt over the top, then it's finished with a drizzle of balsamic and more pesto. I'm *addicted* to pesto."

I glance up from the images of pizza on Christian's laptop and see Charlie staring at Victoria with a bemused expression on his face.

"That's gross," Christian says, plunking two beers down on the table for me and Roman. "Give me a pepperoni pizza."

"With a side of ranch," Clementine adds as she joins us.

Roman smiles at her. "The weirdest thing I have ever seen is Clem taking the pepperoni off the pizza and dipping it into ranch sauce. Isn't the point of having the pepperoni for it to be a topping on the pizza?"

"I give Clem points for not being predictable. That is so boring," Victoria says. "I like things that are unexpected. In food. In places. In people." She looks directly at Roman as a wicked smile passes over her beautiful face.

I blush. I know Victoria loves the fact that Roman is a gardener. She has mentioned over and over how Clementine was a fun, fresh breath of air in our world, and I know she'll think Roman is the same. We have both shied away from men in our usual social circles, but for different reasons. I had never felt the draw to any of them like I did to Roman, and I didn't want to be disappointed like I knew I inevitably would be.

Victoria, however, dismisses all of them up front as "posh polo boys" and has kept her eyes open for something different. So far, her choices have made my parents' hair stand on end, ranging from a poet who wanted her to pay for everything because he couldn't let a job interfere with his "creative process" to an up-and-coming social media developer who liked to use the beautiful princess to gain attention for his new messaging system. Once he sold the company to William Cumberland, who owns a massive media group, he dumped Victoria. Thankfully, she's decided to take a dating sabbatical and focus on her studies instead.

"You never did try the dipping method, Roman," Clementine chides. "I promise, it's a game changer."

He chuckles, and that familiar, low, reverberating sound sends goosebumps sweeping over my skin. "It would be, in the worst way," he teases. "What do you like on your pizza, Lizzie?"

My cheeks erupt with heat. Everyone in this kitchen knows I rejected that nickname as soon as the press adopted it. From "Luscious Lizzie" to "Lucky Lizzie," I hated every version.

But now it's my most cherished name when it comes from Roman's lips.

I decide to ignore the looks and speak directly to him. "Parma ham and rocket," I say.

"That works for me," he replies, rubbing his hand on my back.

The second he touches me, my heart flutters. I love the fact that he's not hesitant to show affection in front of others.

"Christian, I'll go ahead and add it," I say, as I see he already has multiple pizzas in the order.

Roman stays with me while I submit it, but after the order is placed, the guys gravitate towards the living room, to watch some football recap programme. I remain in the kitchen with Clementine and Victoria, where I know I'm about to get the inquisition from my sister.

"Lizzie? He calls you Lizzie?" she asks, her voice low.

"Trust me, they aren't listening now that soccer is on," Clementine says.

"Football," Victoria and I correct at the same time.

"Whatever you want to call it, we don't want to talk about it," Clementine says. "We want to talk about Roman."

Thanks to the renovations Christian did to the cottage over the summer, the floorplan is entirely open, and I can watch Roman from across the room now. "He's brilliant," I say, glancing at him as he takes off his suit jacket and makes himself comfortable with Christian and Charlie.

"He's dead sexy, I'll give you that," Victoria says. "He's a gardener?"

I turn back to my sister. "Yes. A master. He's incredibly gifted and has a passion for the earth. Roman treats me like I'm Liz, like you all do. He tells me what he thinks. He's gentle and passionate, and I knew he'd be special from the first words he ever uttered to me." The sentences tumble out of me, in sync with everything I'm feeling in my heart.

"Is he the reason you are pulling colours out of the wardrobe this week?" Victoria asks, pausing to take a sip of her red wine.

"Yes," I confess.

"Did you see all your press from tonight?" Clementine asks.

I shake my head. "No. Is it good?"

"It's fantastic, absolutely fantastic," Victoria declares, her eyes lighting up. "My favourite headline was 'SEXY LIZ WOWS IN DARING DRESS!'"

"I'm sure some people hated it," I say.

"It doesn't matter. You were sexy, elegant, and every bit the princess people want to see when they scroll through their royal feeds. Those are the people you are dressing for, don't forget that. You also can't discount how much attention you brought to the entrepreneur organisation," Victoria says.

"Yes, I had the same thought. Any publicity about the dress will mention the reception and the cause," I reply, taking a sip of my beer and shifting my attention back to Roman, who seems at ease with Charlie and Christian.

"I can't wait to get to know him," Victoria says.

"I worked with him all the way up until my engagement in November," Clementine tells her. "Roman is a good guy. He knows who he is, and he's comfortable in his skin."

"Well, I think it's time to get to know him now. Let's see if he gets the Victoria seal of approval," my sister says, moving into the living room.

Clementine leans in towards me. "Roman is so getting her stamp of approval."

I laugh softly. "I think so, too."

"Did Arthur congratulate you on your successful walkabout?"

"Arthur *and* Antonia did," Clementine says, arching an eyebrow at me.

"Oh? Do tell."

"She called me and said it was an acceptable appearance, and she thanked me for having the social sense to wear tights."

I snort. Clementine laughs.

"It's a breakthrough for us," she says. "I think she sees now that her only path forward is to embrace me and get attention for being the doting, loving, future mother-in-law to the American finding her way."

I roll my eyes. "Vomit."

Clementine snickers. "I know, but compared to the tea from hell I had last summer? We've come a long way."

"Speaking of tea, I have been summoned tomorrow, for wearing pink. Oh, and I was advised to wear white tonight."

Clementine flinches. "Oh, Liz, you threw gas on a fire."

"I know, but I want to be me. It's time to trust that I am enough with my work and what I do. I don't want to use white to play it safe anymore. If colours threaten Antonia, that's too bad."

Clementine is quiet for a moment, and my stomach tightens, as I know what she's thinking.

"Are you ready for what is to come from this?" she asks.

I glance back at Roman, who is smiling and talking to Victoria. "Yes," I say, knowing he will stand behind me and be there with me no matter what Antonia decides to do to me because of my revolt.

"It makes all the difference, you know, having someone who believes in you and is on your team."

"I want what you and Christian have."

"I think you're looking in the right place for it."

As I stare at Roman, I know she's right.

More to the point, my heart does, too.

"I love your family," Roman says as we walk back towards my cottage.

I smile happily, my arm tucked around his. It's late, after one o'clock in the morning, and the evening was beyond anything I could have asked for.

Roman fell into place quickly and talked easily with Charlie and Christian. I know Christian put on football as an ice breaker, and it worked. Nothing like a good, hearty debate about favourite football teams to pull men together.

Victoria monopolised him and, once she was finished, came over to me and said he was dead sexy and wonderfully down-to-earth and she was madly jealous I found all of that in one package.

The rest of the evening consisted of consuming way too much pizza and talking and sharing funny stories about our lives. In short, it was perfect, and I can't wait for us to have everyone over to my cottage for dinner soon.

"I'm so glad. They loved you, too," I say.

"I'm so grateful. I was worried. I'm not from this world, so I wasn't sure."

"You're a good person. They don't need for you to play polo or have an earldom in your future," I say, thinking of Charlie. "All you needed was to be you."

"This is still surreal, Lizzie."

"I know it is, but in time, it will be normal."

Roman chuckles. "It will never be normal, but I will get used to it."

I laugh, and he does, too.

"Have you noticed anything about Charlie?" he asks.

I glance up at him, for a moment taken by how beautiful he looks, and then refocus.

"What about Charlie?" I ask, curious.

"You actually haven't noticed?" Roman asks, his deep voice steeped in surprise.

"What are you talking about?"

"He's half in love with Victoria."

I stop walking. "What?" I say, stunned. "Charlie?"

Roman grins. "Yes, Charlie. It's so obvious."

"How? How is it obvious? I think I would have noticed."

Roman lifts his hand to my face and gently caresses it. "He watches her whenever she moves. He's attentive to her when she speaks."

I furrow my brow. "That's good manners."

"No, no, it's more than that," he insists. "Charlie gets her refills for her drinks and asks her questions about herself. I saw the way he stared at her when he thought nobody was looking. It's how I looked at you when you appeared in the newsfeed on my phone last summer. Something I wanted but was completely unobtainable."

My heart surges from his confession.

"I wasn't unobtainable," I say, sliding my hands up his suit jacket.

"I know, but I believed you were. All I could do was study your pictures and think about how you would never even remember me. Charlie looks at Victoria like that."

Charlie has known Victoria for a few years, and we have always hung out when Christian was home from university, but I never noticed this. Yet here is Roman, in his first meeting with my family and friends, and he sensed it.

"You're such a sensitive, observant soul," I say, rubbing my fingertips across his full lower lip. He captures my hand and presses a kiss against it.

"I know the look. Worse, I know the feeling," he says softly.

I frown. "Charlie is a great guy, but Victoria will never

see him as anything other than a future earl, and she wants nothing to do with that scene."

Roman's eyes widen. "He's going to be an earl?"

"His current title is Viscount Hallcourt."

Roman sighs, and I laugh.

"I'm dating a princess. And I spent the past few hours talking to a prince and a viscount. No, Lizzie, this world will always be surreal to me."

We resume our walk, my mind fascinated by the idea of Charlie having feelings for Victoria. I never noticed it. Never.

Yet my wonderfully sensitive man did.

As we reach the door, Roman draws me to him. "It's late."

I slide my arms around his waist. "I know."

"I have to be at work in a few hours. I don't want to go, but I should."

His mouth meets mine, opening it slowly. Roman's tongue slides inside, seeking mine, causing heat to coil inside of me from his slow, deliberate kiss. My hands find his face, feeling the stubble underneath my palms, scratching it lightly as I caress him. I kiss him back, his strong body pressing against mine. I feel his body heat and drink in his scent. I want more than time can give us.

I tear my mouth from his and find his neck, trailing my tongue along it, feeling his hot skin and tasting him. Roman's whole body grows more rigid as a result.

"Lizzie," he manages to gasp as I kiss him. "You're making me not want to go."

I lift my head. I see his lips are parted and swollen with desire. The gold flecks in his eyes are dominant.

"Then don't," I say, my heart racing. "Stay. Stay the night with me."

CHAPTER 16
DON'T DRINK THE TEA

R oman's eyes widen in shock at my invitation.
I asked him to spend the night.

My heart pounds with fury. I didn't think about the invitation. I didn't plan to offer it, but seeing him standing before me, feeling the passion that I do, my desire to have him took over.

He doesn't speak. Neither do I. All I can hear is my heart in my ears as I wait for his answer.

"Lizzie," he murmurs, framing my face in his massive hands and stroking me all over, "I've dreamt of this invitation since the first time I kissed your hand."

His lips find mine, and I melt into him, my body craving this intimacy with a fury I have never known before.

"I've thought about it," he murmurs, moving his lips to the side of my neck, "when I've kissed your lips. Touched your skin. Inhaled your floral perfume."

I shiver violently as his lips move torturously down my neck. I close my eyes and wrap my arms around his neck, savouring the sensation of his warm breath against my skin.

"I want you," I whisper. "I need to be with you, Roman."

"Unlock the door," he murmurs against my skin.

His mouth finds mine as my hand fumbles in my bag for my keys. I find them and slide my fingers to his lips to separate us. He laughs against my fingertips, and I force myself to turn around and slide the key into the lock. While I do, Roman slips his arms around my waist and begins kissing the nape of my neck. The second I feel his tongue flicker against my skin, I press my back into him, feeling his strong chest as his arms encircle me tighter.

It takes all my focus to get the door open, and when I do, we quickly step inside, shutting it behind us. As soon as it's closed, our mouths meet. Roman controls the tempo with demanding kisses that make me breathless. Dizzy. I feel wanted by him in a way no man has ever wanted me before.

His hands are in my hair, fumbling with the hairpins and dropping them on the floor as he undoes my messy bun. I relish the feeling of his fingers combing through my hair as his tongue continues to command mine to match his.

My body responds to his touch with a burning urgency. If he wanted to take me on the staircase, he could. On this hallway floor. I jerk his shirt out of his suit trousers, freeing it, and slide my hand up underneath it.

Roman shudders when my hand makes contact with his waist. I gasp. The muscles are hard. I can feel each ridge, every single sculpted cut in his skin. He's hot to the touch, and as my fingertips explore him, I feel his body go more rigid.

I draw his lower lip between my teeth and take a slight bite. Roman responds by returning the favour, causing me to whimper in ecstasy. My hand grabs his belt buckle, and I pull him forward. He chuckles against my lips, and I smile at the sensation. I walk backwards, guiding him towards the stairs. As soon as I hit the first step, and I become closer to his height, Roman abruptly stops kissing me.

"Lizzie, wait," he gasps, his face one of alarm.

"What's wrong?" I reply, trying to catch my breath. "Don't you want this?"

He appears anguished.

"Roman, please. Have you changed your mind?" I ask, confusion filling me.

He frames my face with his huge hands, his gaze making me feel like he's penetrating my soul.

"I've wanted this since the night you were at my flat," Roman whispers, his eyes searching mine. "You are the woman I never thought I'd find. I never thought I'd feel this way again. The way I want you, it's something I've never felt. I want to see the way you look at me. I want to hear your laugh. I want to hear your thoughts. I want your body to be mine when I make love to you. But are you sure you want *me*? I don't want you to do this and think it's a mistake. I haven't been with a woman in years. I... I don't want to be a regret."

Tears fill my eyes. Roman is laying out his heart before me, his deepest fear, his confession about not having been with a woman since his ex. His raw vulnerability, his ability to say these words to me, tells me he's putting his heart in my hands.

As I have put my heart in his.

I peer into his hazel eyes, the ones shimmering with concern, and I know my answer. "I want," I say, pressing my palm against his cheek, "to hear your chuckle in my ear. I want your hands in mine. I want to see the world through your eyes and share experiences with you."

Roman's eyes grow watery from my confession.

"I want you in my bed," I say, my heart doing all the talking. "I have no doubts, and I know I won't have any regrets. Not about you. Not about tonight. And not about us."

Not ever, I think.

I lock my hands around his neck and kiss him. Roman kisses me back slowly this time, gently. There's a sweetness now to his kiss. His hands cradle my face, making me feel protected. Cherished.

With a jolt, I realise what I feel.

Loved.

Before I can process it, Roman scoops me up into his strong arms.

"Tell me where to go," he whispers.

My head is spinning as I direct him up the stairs, to my room.

I can't tear my eyes away from his face. The face of a man I feel like I've known forever instead of days. The one who makes me feel alive and sexy and confident enough to be my true self. I should question my feelings. I should lay them out and examine them. Be logical and think about how there's no way I can be falling so hard and so fast in such a short period of time.

It's a recipe for disaster.

Isn't it?

Or is the old saying true, that the heart does indeed know what it wants?

Roman brings me into my bedroom and shifts his gaze to meet mine.

"You're so beautiful," he whispers, gently placing me down in front of him. He kisses me again, stroking my hair, his fingers combing through the waves that have fallen down the back of my gown.

He gives me a sizzling kiss before turning me around, so my back is facing him. Roman's mouth finds the back of my neck, and the second his tongue dances across my nape, I gasp in delight. His tongue flickers over my skin for a second before I feel his fingertips at the top of my dress, tugging on the zip.

His moves are deliberate. Slow. My heart pounds with each slow tug of the zip, easing it down until the dress falls open.

"My God," he whispers, his rough hands skimming over my back and sending ripples of desire through me. "You're perfection, Lizzie."

Roman draws me to his chest, and I feel the fabric of his shirt against my skin. His hands reach around to my stomach, stroking it, then moving up towards my breasts, which are covered with a black strapless bra.

"Roman," I murmur, arching my back against him.

Now his hands are caressing me everywhere, reverent touches that make me feel worshipped by this man. I record every gasp that escapes his lips, the hardness of his body, the warmth of his mouth now moving across my back and shoulders. His hands and lips are exploring, but I want to turn the tables.

I want to touch him. Taste him.

Make love to him.

I turn around and use his tie to pull him back towards my bed. Roman's mouth recaptures mine, and we tumble backwards, with his body pinning me to the mattress.

"You," I say, kissing him hard on the mouth, "are wearing way too many pieces of clothing."

Roman laughs. "Is that so?"

I unknot his tie and throw it aside. He pushes himself up and rips off his suit jacket. He unbuttons his shirt, and my pulse quickens as he reveals the sculpted abs I felt moments ago.

I gasp. My God, he's glorious. Bronzed and cut abdominals, massive pecs, with a light matting of hair starting from his chest and tailing down to a V-shape waist and the buckle on his suit trousers.

Roman is about to lower himself down on top of me, but I put a hand on his chest and playfully hold him in place.

"I believe your trousers are still on, sir," I say, cocking an eyebrow at him. "This won't do."

His mouth curves up. "No?"

He slowly undoes his buckle, driving me mad in the process.

"Faster," I blurt out.

Roman roars with laughter. "Oh, is that a command, Your Royal Highness?"

"Indeed."

He gets up and strips before me, dropping his trousers to the floor.

Oh. Dear. God.

He's cut like a sculpture. His legs are huge and muscular, no doubt from all the physical labour he does. He's muscled and taut and mine tonight.

"You're glorious," I whisper, taking him in.

Roman retrieves his wallet from his trousers and throws it on the bed. "I have a condom in there."

"Good," I say.

He finishes stripping and moves back over me, his skin against mine. Everything comes alive in me as our bodies entwine together. I stare up at him to find his eyes are locked on mine. God, the way he looks at me! I see desire.

Tenderness. I know this man wants not only the physical me but all of me, down to my soul.

"I adore you, Lizzie," Roman whispers to me. "I *adore* you."

As his mouth claims mine, tears of joy swim in my eyes.

"I adore you, too," I murmur against his lips, my voice thick. "More than you know."

And as I kiss him, I know Roman will possess more than my body tonight.

Roman Lawler now has my heart.

Most ardently.

⚜

I stare at Roman, breathless. His eyes are searching mine with the same expression of wonder. I stroke his face, memorising every feature about him while reliving the intense way we made love. I've never felt more cherished and powerful, all in one fell swoop. Cherished by the deliberate way he touched me, brought me to orgasm, getting as much pleasure out of it as I did. I did the same for him, driving him over the edge when I took the lead, making me feel sexy and strong.

Yet the whole time, I felt this emotional connection to Roman that I've never had with another man. The way he looked at me, touched me, kissed me, called out my name — it wasn't merely sex.

It was love.

My brain doesn't even try to fight it. I don't need to count a certain number of dates or conversations for "love" to be legitimate.

I love him.

And I'm sure this feeling in my heart will only grow

deeper with time, but I know him already. I do. As crazy as this is, I know this man. I know how he looks at me, touches me, and admires me.

And that is all my heart needs to know.

Roman reaches for my hand and presses it against his lips. Butterflies dance in my stomach when I see the adoration in his eyes. He lowers my hand and places it over his heart.

"It's still beating like mad," he says, a beautiful smile lighting up his face.

I lean over and kiss the bridge of his nose. "And you thought you were out of practice," I tease him.

The flush appears on his neck. "Lizzie?"

"Yes?"

"I've never made love like this before."

Elation bubbles up within me, pure joy that I made Roman feel this way.

"Me neither."

"Good."

I laugh. "So selfish, that you wanted me to have had terrible sex before you."

"Of course. It makes me seem like a fantastic lover by default."

"No, no more self-deprecating comments Roman," I warn. "You are an incredibly gifted lover, if you count the number of orgasms I had."

He blushes. I ruffle his hair affectionately.

"Come here," he says, drawing me into his arms and rolling over onto his back so I'm snuggled up against his warm chest. He drops a kiss onto the top of my head. "How am I supposed to go to work in a few hours when all I want to do is lie in bed with you?"

"I know, I would love to spend all day here with you," I

say, running my fingertips along his strong pectoral muscle. I replace my fingertips with my lips and press a kiss onto his hot skin. "But you have… gardening things to do?"

Roman laughs loudly. My stomach tingles as a result. "Yes. Gardening things. Like you have princess things."

"Oh, yes, I have big princess things today," I say, rolling over so I'm on top of him. Roman slides his hand up underneath my hair and begins playing with it. "I have tea with Antonia this afternoon. I will be reminded of my place in the family. Which is in white. And in the background."

Roman frowns. "I don't like the sound of that."

"I can handle her," I say, with confidence I'm not quite certain of.

"You're being braver than you feel."

I flinch. "How did you know?"

"Your eyes tell me everything. You want to be confident when you face her, but you don't want to jeopardise what you've been given."

"This is kind of scary, you reading my innermost thoughts."

Roman continues to stroke my hair in a comforting manner. "Don't let her bully you, Lizzie. You be who you are. Who you want to be. She can't change your role; you're protected by Arthur. And the public adores you. Good lord, ask my mum. She's always raving about how kind and well-spoken you are."

I feel my face grow warm from the compliment. "It's nice that your mum thinks that."

"Wait until I tell her I can vouch for that," Roman says, grinning at me.

Swoon. I love that he is already thinking of telling his mum about me.

"But back to your aunt. Lizzie, don't bow down to her,"

he says firmly. "You are doing a brilliant job for the monarchy. The only thing driving her is jealousy. You can handle that."

I think of the horrible things she did to Clementine when she first started dating Christian. She will do the same things to me, I'm sure of it. I simply have to be strong enough to weather the storm until it passes.

And the storm must pass before I even think about going public with Roman. Antonia would use him in her war against me. I know she would.

Fire fills me. I won't let her hurt him. I won't.

"You can do this. Don't doubt yourself," Roman says, interrupting my thoughts.

"You're right," I say, determined to keep him protected while she goes after me with the press. Once she realises I'm not changing for her, and eventually gets the adoration she needs with the upcoming royal wedding, she'll let it go. She'll have to, because I'm not backing down. Not now, not ever.

"One more bit of advice," Roman says.

"Yes?"

"Don't drink the tea. I'm picturing it poisoned, like Snow White's apple," he says wickedly.

I burst out laughing. "That's good advice."

"I charge for that, you know," he tells me suggestively, his hand sliding up underneath the back of my head.

Ooh, I like where this is headed.

"What form of payment do you accept?" I ask.

"A kiss," Roman says, drawing my mouth towards his.

As we kiss, all of my concerns fall away.

I love this man, and I trust him with my heart.

And that is all that matters.

CHAPTER 17
HER MAJESTY DOESN'T LIKE IT

I study my appearance in the mirror before I head over to Buckingham Palace.

The glow of the previous evening is gone, not that I have forgotten anything about making love with Roman.

Now I see a determined woman who will stand up to the person who will make my life hell for daring to draw my own lines instead of colouring in hers.

Ha-ha, colouring. I wish I could do that right now to centre myself before tea time. I wonder what Antonia would think if I brought her a gift of pencils and a colouring book and told her it was to help her unwind, as her rigid posture tells me she's stressed.

I get an image of every pin shooting out of her crafted chignon as her head explodes with anger.

As amusing as that thought is, I will not be bringing her a present. Sadly, I don't have time to colour, either. There's only time to make sure I'm immaculate in my appearance. Once again, I'm using clothing to send a message.

I run my hands over the fitted silhouette of the orange dress, one that Victoria got me for my birthday in an effort to shove me out of my white comfort zone. It has a beautiful cape overlay on the top, flowing to the body-conscious dress, and I feel vibrant in it.

Seriously, Liz, I think. *You can be such a twit. You live for pens and pencils and to colour, and you shoved this gorgeous dress in the back of the wardrobe, preferring your blank canvas instead?*

I can't even rationalise that.

Well, except for the fact that I can be a twit when I'm afraid of disappointing people.

I reach into the wardrobe, retrieve a camel-coloured trench coat I bought on sale last year, and slip into it, tying the belt around my waist. The camel is the coordinating colour to the orange, and I carry that through from my stilettos to my LK Bennett clutch.

I study my reflection. I see the fire in my aquamarine eyes. Oh, I know I'm going to pay for what I'm about to do. The next few months will be hell. I will pay for getting more attention than she does. Antonia doesn't like anyone upstaging her, and while she's had to settle for Clementine taking that light from her, she will not tolerate her niece — whom she never wanted to be a working royal — taking it, too.

Yet here I am, knowing the wrath I'm going to bring down on myself and doing it anyway.

I slip out of the front door and walk to my Range Rover, the sky dreary and grey above me. Despite the gloomy weather, and the task ahead of me, I'm happy.

A week ago, I wouldn't have even entertained this idea. I was convinced I had to prove my worth by keeping my head down and projecting I was good and trustworthy with my image. As if my speeches and work didn't matter — I thought I needed more to become the working royal I had always dreamt of being. But by being one-note, I lost myself. I was subconsciously making myself pleasing to Antonia, when I didn't have to.

I get inside my car, and as I drive to BP, I marvel at the change in my way of thinking. I can pinpoint it to one moment in time.

Everything changed the second I reconnected with Roman.

I'm amazed at how someone can come into your life and change it within days. It took his perspective — and him fearlessly sharing the truth with me — to make me see I was hiding.

A radiating warmth sweeps through me as I think of him. We've spent hours together — whether in person or on the phone — talking, sharing our lives, and growing what was a spark of interest into an all-encompassing desire for each other. Not merely physical, but this desire to share our interests, our fears, our dreams and vulnerabilities — I've never given so freely of my mind or my heart to any man in my life. I knew the moment I sat with him in the greenhouse, there was a good chance I'd fall in love with him.

And now I have.

I wrap myself up in thoughts of loving this man, this incredible man who is now mine.

One I suspect is falling in love with me.

My stomach flips upside down at the thought. Roman might not have said the words last night, but I felt his love. I know I did.

And the day he tells me he loves me?

I'll be the happiest woman in all of England.

I think of Roman during my short drive. We FaceTimed at lunch, and he told me how proud he was of me for standing up for what I wanted. He said he wanted me to text him when it was over and know he was there with me in spirit, holding my hand the entire time. I'm not alone in this.

Nobody has ever said that to me before.

As I'm let through the gates, with the press snapping pictures as I drive in, I visualise his hand on mine, knowing, without a doubt, I'm doing the right thing.

I park my car and glance up at BP, thinking of how it was built in 1705 by the Duke of Buckingham. It was made into a palace in 1820.

I wonder how many dramas have been played out behind its 1,150 doors. *Too many to count,* I muse as I head towards the entrance.

And today will add one more.

I enter, greeting palace staff as I do, and step into the lift to go up to the private apartments. The doors close, and I draw a breath in and exhale. I have no idea what she will say, but I'm prepared. I'll be calm and controlled—this is not the time for Angry Liz.

This is time for Toe-to-Toe Liz.

The doors open, and I move along the corridor to the queen's sitting room. I glance down at my watch. It's five minutes to five o'clock. Antonia will walk in on the dot, not a second earlier or later.

Talk about not colouring outside the lines.

I step inside the room, all done in cream with little pops of grey and navy. It's reflective of Antonia—colourless and rigid with no room for experimentation or something new. I slip out of my trench, and one of her maids appears out of nowhere and approaches me.

Good lord, this I cannot get used to. It was weird growing up, and it's weird now. People popping out of nowhere to assist with anything I need. I wonder where this maid was. Hiding behind the curtains?

Hmm. I wouldn't put it past Antonia to have someone hiding in there to record me if I were to be dumb enough to use my phone in here.

That sounds paranoid.

Or does it?

"Your Royal Highness, may I take your coat?" the woman asks.

"Yes, thank you," I say, handing it to her.

"You're welcome," she replies, whisking away as quickly as she appeared.

I sink down onto a sofa and peer out at the gardens through the window, which are now prepared for the cold weather. The flower beds are blown by the wind, moving back and forth against the gloomy backdrop of the day. I wonder what Roman would think of them. He would love being able to inspect them up close. I'll have to br—

With a pang, I realise I can't bring him here. Not yet. It would get back to Antonia, and she would use him against me. I refuse to let the man I love be a pawn in her game.

As soon as the clock on her mantle strikes five, the doors open, and she sweeps in. I rise so I can curtsy to her.

"Your Majesty," I say, lowering into a perfect curtsy.

"It's a pleasure to see you, Elizabeth," she says crisply, taking her seat on the sofa across from me. "Aren't you wearing an alarming choice of colour today?"

I sink down into the princess pose, i.e. sitting with my legs pressed together at the perfect slant, and find my position is mirroring hers to a T.

"Indeed," I say, smiling brightly at her.

Antonia is dressed in her standard sheath, today a navy tweed one, with a matching jacket. Her raven-black hair is pulled tightly back into her signature chignon, and her statement red lipstick is applied with precision. Strands of pearls from the royal jewellery vault adorn her neck.

A tea trolley is brought in, and we remain silent as the household staff begins placing everything on the table in between us. The standard afternoon tea menu is different today, featuring Christmas-inspired items. I see fruitcake — which makes me think of Roman — cranberry-studded scones, finger sandwiches, squash tartlets, mini panettone, and a glorious arrangement of macaroons, ones I bet are all Christmas-inspired flavours.

Antonia thanks the servers when they are finished, and she begins to prepare the tea. She remains silent as she goes about this task, and I watch her, thinking of Roman's advice to not drink the tea and nearly laughing out loud.

Perhaps I should watch her drink it first, I think wickedly.

"The chef did a Christmas assortment for us today," Antonia says, putting the silver pot down. "Sandwiches with ham and orange chutney, roast turkey with chestnut stuffing, mincemeat jam, cranberry and orange scones, butternut and sage tartlets, miniature panettones, and gingerbread and spiced orange macaroons. They're so *appropriate*, aren't they?"

And as Benedict Cumberbatch in *Sherlock* would say, the game is on.

"They are," I reply, selecting a turkey finger sandwich and placing it on my plate. "Of course, if you would have put something *fresh* and *unexpected* on the menu, oh, I don't know, like a candy floss macaroon, guests might find that *intriguing* and *exciting*."

I see her lips twitch ever so slightly. I take a bite of my sandwich.

"I do believe," she says with deliberation, "that the

hostess sets the tone. The tone is always set from the top, Elizabeth."

I pretend to mull this over. "Well, yes. When the hostess is hosting her own event. Otherwise, no. The tone is set by the individual. As long as that person is appropriate and doing his or her job to the benefit of the event, then the hostess shouldn't be threatened by that."

Zing! Her eyes slightly widen. If she didn't have so much Botox, I think I'd see a crease in her forehead.

"I see you want to be ugly about this," she says, "so I shall get to the point. You are not Clementine. If she insists on wearing patterns and going barelegged and being ridiculous and uncouth, she gets a pass—*for now*—because she's an American marrying a prince. She is living the movie, and for some reason I cannot fathom, both sides of the pond are eating it up. I will play the part of the adoring future mother-in-law because I have to. I have no such loyalty to you, however. If my husband had listened to me, you would be working in the public sector, my dear niece."

I reach for a miniature panettone like I'm picking up a chess piece and considering my next move on the board. I set it on my plate and pick up my knife, carefully slicing it in half.

"I have the support of Arthur," I say, "and the public. I'm here to stay, no matter how much you wish for me to be banished to a normal job."

I study her. She's contemplating her next move as she picks up the silver tea strainer and pours the tea.

"Clementine, the unfortunate disaster that she is, is here to stay. A broken engagement isn't an option now. But the public will turn on her when her golden period is over, and you know that."

She has no idea that comment has made a direct hit. My

stomach clenches, as this will not only apply to Clementine, but also to me, and down the line, to the man I love.

It's one thing for an American art curator to enter the House of Chadwick.

But a gardener from Shepherd's Bush is another.

I place a spoonful of mincemeat jam on the side of my plate as if I don't have a worry in the world, when the truth is, her words are chilling me. "We all go through those periods with the press," I say with a confidence I don't feel. "What would be lovely is if the women of this family could come together and support each other. Not only when there are downs, but in our successes and missions, too."

Antonia's face remains expressionless.

"Antonia, why can't you see me and Clementine as part of your team? Why do you have to see us as threats to your position in the public? You are the *queen*. We'll never surpass you in rank."

She laughs. "You are so naïve, it's comical."

"I'm speaking the truth."

Antonia puts the teapot down. She lifts her cup to her lips, taking a sip, and then focuses her dark brown eyes on me. "I have worked for years to uphold the mystique and standards the public have come to expect from royalty. I will not see it upended by a princess deciding to thumb her nose at tradition and seek all the press she can by wearing ridiculous clothing because she's young and beautiful."

"The media adores you," I say, confused. "How is my press coverage a threat to that?"

"Oh, yes, that article comparing our two appearances on Monday was oh-so-flattering to me," she says dryly.

Inside, I wince. She gets the chess piece on that one.

"Your grandmother," Antonia continues, "believes in the tradition of the monarchy. So do I. I refuse to see you, with no possible chance of ever sitting on the throne, *thank God*, ruin what I have worked so hard to maintain."

"How am I ruining the monarchy by serving the people? I'm not. This is all about you seeing anything or anyone different from you as a threat. Ones you believe will diminish your popularity with the public."

The lip twitches again. She's agitated that I landed a blow with that comment.

"You think you know everything because you are young, but you know nothing. I have lived my life to uphold these standards. Your side of the family, if the truth were to come out about your cheating father and pathetic, clinging, crying, hysterical mother, would be a bombshell to the monarchy. Who's to say you aren't going to dirty things up like they have? Why do you think I wanted you to take a nice job in an art gallery and merely be seen going to clubs in Mayfair? You *are* a threat, my darling niece. One I will not take lightly."

My face is burning in white-hot anger at her for dragging my parents into this, and for being right about the public's reaction to their marital drama, which is nobody's business but theirs.

"This is about me," I say, using every power I have to control my voice. "Not them."

"But does the apple fall far from the tree?" she says, taking another sip of tea.

"In the case of your sons, thank God it landed at the feet of Arthur and not you."

BAM! Her face cracks. I've infuriated her by giving her husband all the credit for how my amazing cousins turned out, and Her Majesty doesn't like it.

She sets down her cup with a clack—an unrefined, un-Antonia show of emotion.

"If you think you can bully me, you've underestimated me," I continue, blotting my lips with a linen napkin and placing it on my plate. I pick up my clutch, rise from my seat, and give her one last look. "I'm proud of who I am and what I do. I have chosen to wear colour, I have chosen to be me after months of being afraid to, and it's up to you to embrace who I am or not."

"I see," she says slowly. "Then you have chosen to embrace all the things that are going to come out in the press this month?"

My heart pounds in my ears. "You will leave my parents out of this," I warn.

"Oh, lord no. That would pull down the monarchy. Their stupidity is to be concealed. Yet you," she says, her eyes narrowing, "are ripe to be kicked off your golden girl pedestal, aren't you?"

I know what this means. She will start leaking rubbish to the press about me. My God, if she knew about Roman, she would destroy him.

"Hmm, I believe this troubles you," she continues, perfectly reading my expression.

The maid who took my coat earlier reappears with it.

"Yes, I'm troubled. By how pathetic it is that other women are seen as threats and rivals when we could be your biggest assets to ensuring the monarchy is standing long after we're gone. You're the one losing here, not me."

I turn and begin to walk out.

"What I'm most curious about," she says, causing me to turn and face her as she rises slowly from her seat, "is what has brought about this sudden, abrupt change in your wardrobe. Could it be a man?"

I go cold.

She smiles. "Oh, the fear in your eyes tells me this might

be true. If that is the case, I will find out. Something tells me he's not as lovely as India, the appropriate woman Xander has chosen, or we'd know about him."

"Like most *modern* women, I am independent. I make these decisions on my own. However, I understand you making that leap, as a woman who is stuck in time and refusing to modernise with the times."

Her nostrils flare. We are indeed going toe-to-toe.

"Good afternoon, my dearest Elizabeth. Do enjoy the positive press coverage today, while it lasts."

I stride out of her apartment, forcing myself to walk confidently despite how my legs are shaking. I reach the lift and press the down button. As I step inside, I know she will be leaking horrible stories to the press that are designed to hurt me or force Arthur to remove me from my position. I also know my cousins and Arthur will not allow that to happen. I will survive.

Until she finds out about Roman.

She will humiliate him and make his life hell. Tears prick my eyes as I visualise the headlines that will reveal him to the world in the tabloids. He has no idea what will come his way now. It would have been hard enough before, but with her leakers at work against him, I can't even imagine what they will say.

The lift reaches the ground floor, and I step out, wrapping my arms around me as I walk, my brain whirling with how to prepare him for what is to come. I know he'll say he can handle it, but can he? I merely thought my life would be a challenge before, but in the fight to be true to myself, I made his transition that much harder.

I blink back tears as I exit the palace. I reach my car, and as I put my hand on the door handle, I remember what Roman told me.

I'm right there with you, holding your hand.

I close my eyes and feel his fingers entwining with mine. I visualise the way he gazed into my eyes, the way he made love to me.

No. This love can withstand anything, I know it can.

Including a war launched by Antonia.

CHAPTER 18
CANVAS AND PAINT

A s I walk through Belgravia, the cold rain pelting down on my umbrella as it falls from the gloomy sky, I can't get Antonia's threats out of my head. I shiver inside my coat, not from the chilly air but from the fear that has been wedged in my heart since I left BP. This tea has made it clear I've started a war, and my brain is laying out how I will survive the incoming rain of bombs.

The most logical thing to do is to go to Xander and Christian. If they knew what she said, they would put a stop to it. Xander has the most power over her. He is not afraid to go to the media with counter stories about his mum. When Clementine was first attacked by her, he even threatened to step aside from the throne to protect her and Christian if that's what it took. Antonia backed down. Xander is a man of his word, and she wouldn't dare have that turmoil brought to the monarchy she has worked so hard to maintain.

While I might be his cousin by blood, we are siblings of the heart. I know he would protect me, as would Christian, but I refuse to put them in that position. I exhale, realising I was holding my breath anxiously. I don't want to be the woman running to her cousins for protection. I am strong. I am capable. I can find a way to solve this without their help.

More importantly, Antonia is their *mother.* I know from the past that she wasn't always this way. When Arthur met her, she was a young aristocrat from a wealthy English family. It was a love match, and when they were first married, she and Arthur were happy. She was not the controlling, insecure woman she is now but a duchess content to learn to uphold the monarchy the best way she knew.

Power and fame, however, can change people. While Arthur was off in the army for long periods of time, she carried out her work flawlessly. Nobody has ever said this, but looking at it objectively, I think this was when the dynamic changed. She received more attention. She realised her own power, and when she ascended to the role of queen, the monarchy mattered more than her family. My guess is, during Arthur's time away, the love faded, and she received everything she needed from the public and the press. While James hasn't accepted the reality of the family, I know Christian and Xander have. They know the truth.

And I won't rip open that painful wound.

I will handle this myself, I think, determination replacing the fear.

I round the corner, and for a moment, the sights ahead of me interrupt my thoughts. The beauty of Belgravia makes me pause. This posh neighbourhood has always been one of my favourite places in London. I love the stucco buildings, cobbled mews, elegant townhouses, immaculate streets, and beautiful window displays of the chic shops and boutiques.

I eye Elizabeth Street, all decorated for Christmas.

Lights twinkle above the shop fronts. Chandeliers strung up by wire hang over the streets. The shops have gone all out with elaborate displays in the windows, welcoming the festive season and inviting customers to come inside and partake of it.

I remember my focus on self-care and realise I have been giving Antonia power over me by worrying. I can't control what she does. By obsessing over it, I would let her rob me of moments like this, taking in this beautiful sight and living the magic of the Christmas season.

No more, I vow as I resume my stroll. *I'm going to think about how lucky I am to be able to head down this path to The Biscuit Cutter to get my surprise for Roman tonight.*

My thoughts shift to him, the man I love, and our date this evening. I block out the people taking my picture in front of me and smile, wrapped up in how magical it is to be in love. Roman makes me braver. I feel like I can take on anything, knowing he cares about me.

My heart feels lighter as I think of him. What we have is different. For him to open up to me like he has, when he's been so guarded for so long, tells me he cares about me in a deep way. I can't say if it's love for him, but I don't need that affirmation from him now. I know I fell ridiculously fast, and not everyone does so, but even though my heart has never had these emotions before, I know my feelings are real.

While the next few months will be hard, I also know we can survive it. My faith in his feelings is that strong. When he gazed into my eyes while we made love, I knew.

This is a man who cares about me more than anyone ever has.

And that is more than enough.

I continue on, heading towards The Biscuit Cutter. I'm

going to pick up something special for this evening, and I can't wait to surprise Roman with it. It's one way I can show him how I feel without saying the words he's not ready to hear.

Finally, the bakery comes into my view. It's a small shop, charmingly decorated for Christmas with fresh greenery and decorations around the doorway and Christmas trees in the windows. The café tables and chairs are vacant outside due to the weather, but inside, the shop is full of people.

I close my umbrella as I reach the entrance and shake it out. I pop open the door, with bells jingling against it as I do, and if I had any worries left, they are washed away by the scene in front of me.

The shop is magical. I move across the hardwood floor, the scent of cinnamon and sugar wafting through the air. I see rows and rows of exquisite iced biscuits, offering more selections than I had online when I ordered the basket for Clementine. Display tables are stacked with treats ready to take away, including thick, fudgy brownies and huge chocolate chip cookies. Another round table has gingerbread houses and iced biscuits in the shapes of Christmas trees, stars, and angels. Decorations hang down from the ceiling, and shoppers happily study the rows of cakes and cupcakes available under the glass while waiting in the queue to place their order.

Along another wall of the café, cosy booths and tables are full of people sipping hot chocolates and tucking into thick slices of Christmas cake. As I detect the sound of *The Nutcracker* playing, pure happiness takes over. I'm back in the now.

And not even Antonia can take me out of it.

As I study the shop, I think of what an Instagramable

place this is. I could totally envisage taking a quick video tour of the shop for an Insta story or Connectivity Story Share. I remember my earlier vow to approach Arthur about being the first royal to have a public Instagram or Connectivity Story Share account.

I take a video of the shop, zooming in on the lemon bars and Christmas cakes and every delicious seasonal goodie I love. I think of how it could connect people to me on a more personal level, even if it's something as small as sharing my love of lemon bars. My passion to make this happen takes over. I will show Arthur that this is a way of showcasing a personal side to the monarchy and connecting us with people globally, too.

I finish my video and take my place in the queue, hoping I can get what I want. I inhale the delectable scent of baked goods, wondering if I can restrict myself to getting the one thing I came for. I glance back at the lemon bars; I decide no, that is a feat for a person much stronger than me.

As I wait, my thoughts go back to Roman. I called him from the car park at BP and got his voicemail, as I knew I would. When he's working, his hands are full, and he's often dirty and not accessible for calls. I told him tea with Antonia was what I thought it would be, but I was okay. I ended the call by saying I was looking forward to dinner with him at my place this evening.

And surprising him with something special for dessert.

Finally, it's my turn. I step up to the till, and the young woman standing behind it recognises me. I can tell because when people do, their faces reflect surprise over seeing me in public. I'm sure they're used to famous clients in Belgravia, and she doesn't act any different. "Hello, how may I help you?" she says cheerfully.

"I have a special request," I tell her. "I'd like to buy a

Christmas cake, but I'd like to be able to ice it and decorate it myself. So I want a cake and the icing separate; is that possible?"

"Hmm," the woman says, wrinkling her nose in thought. "You want the fondant and marzipan on the side?"

"Yes. And I'd love to buy some icing that you could, you know, write with?"

"All right, I'll have to ask," she says.

Another woman approaches, and the girl at the till speaks to her. "Charlotte, Princes—I mean, this lady would like to buy a Christmas cake to decorate herself. With extra icings. Can she do that?"

The woman nods at me. "I think we can make that happen. I'm Charlotte, the manager. If you can move to the side, over here," she says, briskly walking towards a spot where there is a sign for special orders, "I'll have Poppy come up and talk to you. She's a biscuit artist here, and our master decorator, and I'm sure we can get this sorted for you."

"Thank you so much," I say, nodding at her.

I take off my gloves and stuff them into the pockets of my trench coat as I wait. Before long, a beautiful woman around my age walks towards me. Her hair is thick and dark brown, with caramel highlights. It's glossy and gorgeous. I can't help but stare at it.

She smiles as she greets me. "Hello, I'm Poppy," she says brightly. "I understand you want to decorate your own Christmas cake?"

My ears immediately detect a Welsh accent.

"Hello, I'm Liz," I say, smiling warmly at her. "And I do. Is it possible to get one that you haven't decorated so beautifully? Which seems wrong, by the way, as mine will look nothing like yours once it is complete."

Her dark brown eyes shine back at me. "Thank you. I consider cakes and biscuits my canvas, and my paint is icing. And I'm confident you will make your own beautiful creation, too. Which means you will need a naked cake."

"Yes."

She takes out a pad from her lilac apron, one that is covered in flour, and retrieves a pen from the cup on the counter. "Do you need everything, such as marzipan, marmalade, fondant?"

"I have marmalade," I say. "I do need marzipan and fondant. I also need the icing bags and decorations. And I saw some tiny gingerbread biscuits on display, so perhaps some of those."

"We don't sell piping bags and tips, but I think I can gift you some," Poppy says.

"Oh, no, I don't want to take yours. Perhaps I could return them?"

She smiles. "I assure you, I have plenty."

"Like a painter with paintbrushes?" I ask.

"Yes, exactly," she says. "If you'll excuse me, I'll get all your things boxed up."

"You have no idea how much I appreciate this," I say.

"It's not a problem. I like seeing people enjoy the art of baking."

I cock an eyebrow. "Even if they don't bake the cake?"

"Even if they don't bake the cake. It's about the joy," she says as she goes to the back.

Hmm. I wonder if she has watched *Tidying Up* with Marie Kondo. She's all about finding joy. Except Marie's idea of joy would have me throw out ten pairs of yoga pants and reduce my collection of fountain pens. I choose to ignore her on that point, as I can firmly attest that each fountain pen brings me a specific joy. And the joy of not having to wash yoga pants all the time? That's not only joyful but efficient.

I turn around and study the beautiful Christmas cakes in the case to my left, perfectly decorated from the icing to the "Happy Christmas" script and the snowflakes adorning the top. I smile as I peer down at them.

This was Roman's joy. Having his grandmother lovingly decorate a cake for them to all share. I know I can't replace those memories for him, but I don't want to. I want to give him this joy back, in a new tradition.

Decorating one with me.

And I can't wait to give him this gift tonight.

CHAPTER 19

PORT FOR THREE

"You promise me you will dress down this evening?" Roman asks. "I'm about to leave, and I'm in a checked shirt and jeans."

I smile as I finish tying the ribbon on the box with the cake and decorating supplies tucked inside. "I could wear nothing," I tease. "Would that be casual enough for you?"

There's silence for a moment. I know without a doubt there's a deep red flush climbing up that delicious neck of his.

"No," he says, his voice deep, "although I plan to see you in nothing later. For *hours*."

Now I'm the one who is flushed.

"Get over here," I say. "It's been too long since I've felt your lips on mine."

"I'll be there as soon as I can," Roman says before hanging up.

I place my phone next to the box. I straighten the ribbon, happy that I will be in his arms soon. I need those strong arms today. The ones that make me feel as if I'm the only woman he's ever held so lovingly or protectively.

I know Roman was in love before me. These feelings that I'm having, so bright and beautiful and new, are not foreign to him. But I know our time last night opened his heart to love again. There was no mistaking what was in his eyes. His touch. His kiss. Warmth fills me. I know he will fall in love with me, too.

My ringtone interrupts my thoughts. I glance down and see it's Mum. I sigh as the mobile continues to ring. For a split-second, I consider letting it go to voicemail. Then guilt for being a horrible daughter takes over, and I answer.

"Hello, Mum," I say cheerfully, hoping today will be a good conversation day.

"Liz, I don't know how much longer I can put up with seeing Sydney every day," she wails.

I mentally draw a line through the words *good conversation* in my head.

"Mum, I know it must be awful," I say, walking across the kitchen and leaning against the worktop.

"You have no idea. The torture of seeing her and knowing your father is sleeping with the staff, and that everyone at the palace knows? How can someone who loved me so much have these feelings after all these years? I look at Arthur and Antonia, and they fell out of love, too. Perhaps, it's simply what happens, Liz. Love fades and dies. It always *dies*."

Her words jar me. That's what happened with Roman, too. Could there be truth to her words? If he fell in love with me, I know there's no guarantee it would be forever. My chest grows tight. I can't imagine feeling the way I do now, and months later, years later, Roman telling me he doesn't feel the same way.

"I'm going to demand again that she resign. I'll go to the press with this; that's what I'll do. I waited all summer for your father to come to his senses and come back to me. I waited this autumn. I'm not waiting anymore. I will scream and yell and then scream some more until he realises what he's doing to this family he loves so much. I will tell him how cruel he is, how his daughters would be devastated if they all knew, and what it's doing to you."

Her threat brings my immediate attention back to her. "Mum. No. You can't make this about me because that's not true." My stomach has now contorted into a tangled mess, much like the earbuds in the bottom of my bag.

"It is true! I know you aren't on his side!" she says, the anguish going up a notch. "You would never approve of your father falling out of love with me!"

Oh, God, now I'm on the tightrope again, trying to somehow console my mother without attacking my father. Part of me is furious with him. For cheating. For falling out of love with Mum. But the rational part of me knows the truth. There hasn't been a divorce in the monarchy in hundreds of years. There's no way he could bring this on the family. Yet should he have to be miserable for the rest of his life because of the archaic rules of being born into this family?

I decide to focus on my mother. She needs help that I, as her daughter, am ill-equipped to give. "Mum, you can't go on like this. I hate that you feel this way. I think a good step would be seeing a therapist. You can't bear all this alone."

A sharp burst of hysterical laughter greets my suggestion.

"A therapist? I don't need a therapist. I need your father to keep his trousers zipped and that homewrecker kicked out of the palace!"

I swallow hard. Mum is starting to crack, and I don't know what else I can do.

"Besides, you are the only one I trust with this, Elizabeth. The *only* one."

More weight has been thrown on top of my shoulders. The kitchen worktop swims in my eyes as I try to fight back tears. "I know," I whisper. My phone beeps, letting me know I have a call. "Mum, I have another call coming through, but why don't we have lunch tomorrow? I can come over."

"Yes, of course. It will give me something to look forward to."

"I love you," I say. "See you tomorrow."

Then I accept the other call without checking who it is. "Hello?"

"Liz. It's India Rothschild."

My mouth drops. Is there a full moon out? Tea with Antonia, Mum going off the rails, now India is calling me?

"Uh, hello, India," I say, stunned. She has always been cordial with me at events and parties, but we are far from being anything resembling friends. I have nothing in common with a stuck-up party girl who merely wants to blow through her inheritance.

And become the queen consort someday.

"I know this phone call is a bit of a surprise, but I hope it's a lovely one," she says brightly.

I glance at the bottle of wine I have out on the worktop. Roman would understand if I started drinking now, right?

"It is a surprise," I say. "What can I do for you?"

"Well, you know I'm seeing Alexander," she says.

Alexander? Nobody calls him that. Not even the press.

"Yes," I say.

Maybe I should get another bottle out, I think.

Or a lemon tart.

Does red wine go with lemon?

Ha, no more than I go with this conversation.

"You're important to him," India says. "Alexander says you are like a sister to him. He told me what an important part of his life you are and how he loves you."

More tears prick my eyes, but this time, from learning that Xander said this to India.

Good lord. Roman is going to get here and find me drinking and crying and shovelling lemon tart into my mouth.

I've got to pull myself together.

And resist the urge to open that bottle or dive face first into a lemon tart.

"We're extremely close," I say. "That's sweet of him to say. I feel the same way about him."

"I know. Which is why I asked Alexander if I could ring you."

"What?"

"Liz. I feel we need to develop a relationship. Alexander is dear to both of us, so we should get to know each other, right?"

How do I answer this? How?

"Liz, are you there?"

I blink. "Um, yes, I'm so sorry. I got a bit distracted for a moment."

"I know it's a lot to take in. Alexander finally noticed me after all these years of me being right in front of him," she says, laughing happily. "My patience has paid off. He finally realised I was The One."

"He said that?" I gasp, alarmed.

"Well, no, but there are some things a girl knows without them being said," she says confidently. "Because of that, I'd like for us to get together. Maybe you could come over for dinner at my flat in Chelsea. As two of the most important women in his life, we should become better acquainted."

I can see I'm part of her plan to solidify her position with Xander.

Who might even marry her someday.

Antonia already loves her. She runs in our circles, she knows all the ins and outs, and unlike Clementine, Antonia will roll out the red carpet and give her all the support she needs to be a success.

Xander's choice, if this comes to be, will please everyone, but hurt himself. Because he will never know the feelings that Christian and Clementine share.

Or the feelings I have for Roman.

Oh, having dinner with India is going to be painful.

On a multitude of levels.

"Um, yes, of course," I say, vowing to have a long heart-to-heart with Xander as soon as I can get him face-to-face. "I have an appearance at the ballet one night next week, and another reception, but I should be able to make something work."

India says she will text me and hangs up. I stare at my phone in shock. I'm more convinced than ever about there being a full moon. Is there any other reason for all of this craziness to be unleashed on me in a matter of a few hours?

I exhale. I've got to be there for both my mum and Xander. I somehow have to convince Mum to see a therapist. I've got to make sure Xander is aware of the mess he's creating, not only for himself but for India, too, if he doesn't think he can fall in love with her someday. Because she is seeing the royal jewellery vault in her sights if she thinks Xander has decided she's The One.

Carrying all these worries, along with the impending storm that is brewing over in BP and about to head in the direction of my cottage, has made my shoulders ache. I run my hand up to my neck and rub it. I need another yoga session. I was going to ask the instructor to pass a message along to Jess, too. I pick up my phone and put in a reminder to do that tomorrow, and I also create an appointment to have lunch with Mum.

As I finish my entry, the doorbell rings. The second I hear the chime, my worries vaporise. The tension is replaced by pure electricity as I know Roman is here. I quickly hide his present in a cupboard so he won't see it.

As soon as it's tucked away, I hurry towards the door, goosebumps of anticipation sweeping over my skin. *I'll have to tamp down the urge to leap into his arms and kiss his sexy face the second I see him,* I think as I reach the door and open it.

My hand flies to my mouth. I gasp in surprise. Roman is standing before me, holding a huge Christmas tree beside him.

"I remember how you said you've never decorated a tree," he says softly. "I think you're overdue for the experience. We can save the poinsettia lesson for another time."

Fresh tears fill my eyes, but this time, ones of gratitude for the man who has brought me my first Christmas tree. I take him by surprise and give in to my urge by leaping up into his arms, causing him to drop the tree so he can catch me instead. Roman roars with laughter as I wrap my legs around him and lock my hands around the back of his neck.

"I take it you're pleased?" he asks.

"I am," I say, but I'm not even referring to the Christmas tree. "I'm so happy."

Roman smiles broadly at me. "That was the whole idea."

I kiss him sweetly on the lips, tasting mint as I do.

"You're making me dinner, and you brought me a tree. How perfect are you, Roman?"

He kisses me back. Mmm. I think I could happily stand in my doorway, wrapped up like this, and kiss him 'til the sun comes up.

"I'm not perfect," he says, chuckling as he puts me down. "Wait until you see the decorations I picked up. Terribly tacky. I chucked a whole bunch of things into the trolley."

"Terribly tacky makes it even better," I say, sliding my hands up to his face and feeling his five o'clock shadow graze my skin. "I can't wait to decorate our tree. It is ours, Roman."

He lowers his lips to mine again, and I melt into his kiss.

"Ours," he whispers against my lips.

"Ours," I whisper back, kissing him again.

He breaks the kiss. "I guess I should bring the tree in then."

I smile as he picks the tree up from the path, and I step aside as he brings it into the cottage. The scent of fresh pine fills the air, and I feel happy and content in this moment. I will tackle my list of problems tomorrow, but for my own health and happiness, I'm basking in this evening with Roman.

"Let me retrieve the tree stand and decorations," he says.

"I'll help you," I say. "Did you get fairy lights?"

Roman's mouth curves up, and I want to kiss the smile out of him.

"Yes."

"But did you get multi-coloured ones or white ones?" I ask as we reach the back of his car.

Roman opens the boot to reveal loads of shopping bags.

He pauses and peers down at me. "Do you have an opinion on this matter?" he asks, the curve still there on his luscious mouth.

"I do. Multi-coloured. We always have white fairy lights at St. James's Palace and at Sandringham, so as a little girl, I loved seeing the ones with all the colours."

Roman rummages through a few bags and pulls out a box of multi-coloured fairy lights.

"Colours," I cry in delight.

"You deserve all the colours," he says, gazing tenderly at me.

I don't say anything. I soak in his words, knowing he's referring to me coming out of my shell with my wardrobe, too.

He clears his throat. "All right. I've got decorations, lights, a tree stand, and everything to make dinner."

"Seafood?" I ask, arching an eyebrow.

"No, I don't want to get on the wrong side of royal protocol. I'm making curry. You said you had the best one of your life on a trip to India."

"I did," I say. "I love a good curry."

But the one I had won't compare at all to one made by the man who is standing next to me.

"I know it won't rival that," Roman says, unaware of the loving thought rolling around in my mind. "But I can make a red pepper and chicken curry."

"Sounds delicious," I tell him, reaching into the boot and picking up some of the shopping.

We make two trips to the car, and I take the groceries to the kitchen and lay out everything he needs to cook while Roman sets the tree up in my living room, right in front of the window and the sofas.

I can't wait to see it twinkling with fairy lights, I think. *It will be so cosy at night in my cottage. A tree. A fire.*

And Roman to share it all with.

He comes into the kitchen, heading straight to the sink to wash his hands.

"I can't wait to decorate the tree and see what you picked out for it," I say excitedly.

"You can replace the decorations I got when you go out exploring for things that make your cottage a home.'

I shake my head as he turns off the tap. "No. This is our tree, and I will treasure every decoration you bought for it."

He shifts his gaze to meet mine. I see the gold flecks grow brighter, and I know my words have touched him. I hand Roman a tea towel, and he dries his hands. "If I didn't know you as I do, I wouldn't believe that I could bring you a tree with awful decorations and you'd swear it was the best Christmas tree ever. But you see things through the lens of your heart."

I stare at him, my gaze unwavering, as his beautiful words resonate in my soul. "I do," I say, falling more in love with him in this quiet moment in my kitchen.

Roman lifts his hand and strokes my hair. "I feel like I've known you for years rather than days," he says, his voice low. "Is that crazy?"

"No, it's not."

He drops a sweet, gentle kiss on my mouth. "I like you more than I should, Lizzie," he whispers against my lips.

I kiss him back, easing his mouth open, my tongue sweetly caressing his, trying to convey with my kiss that his heart is safe with me.

I break the kiss and slide my hands up his chest. "As much as I'd like to keep kissing you, I'm famished."

Roman sweeps a lock of my hair behind one ear. "I'm going to fix that right now."

I help him make dinner by serving as his sous chef, chopping things up while he cooks. I give him all the details about tea with Antonia, and boy, Roman also gets a flush up his neck when he's pissed off.

"So she's going to throw her own niece to the wolves?" he snaps, angrily stirring the curry in the pan.

"Yes. It's going to get ugly."

"What about Arthur?" Roman asks, trying to work out a solution for me. "From what you say, I don't think he'd approve of his wife bullying you like she is."

I sigh. "Roman, he has enough to deal with right now. I want to prove to everyone that I'm an adult who can handle these situations."

"You are, but that doesn't mean your family can't help you. They would want to protect you. In fact, I remember a certain beautiful woman who came to Clementine's defence last summer when she was attacked in the press."

"But Clementine hadn't been prepared for what was to come. I've grown up in front of the media."

"So what? Your aunt is stacking the deck against you. You certainly didn't grow up prepared for that."

Gratitude for his honesty fills my heart. "You always tell me what you think. So many people throughout my whole life have told me what I want to hear, not what I need to hear."

"I'll always tell you the truth, I promise. And you need to go to your cousins if you don't go to your uncle himself. Christian will be furious."

"No," I say stubbornly. "I can do this, Roman. I can withstand anything she throws at me."

As long as I can protect you, I vow. *That's what matters above everything else.*

"I can see you're going to be stubborn about this," Roman says, dishing up two bowls of curry.

"Mmm hmm," I say, picking up a bowl as we head towards the dining room.

Roman sighs. "You can be exasperating,"

I grin. "I know. Which is part of the reason you like me."

"You're right."

We both laugh. We sit down to dinner—which is delicious—and I go on to tell Roman about Xander. He agrees there's no way Xander should settle for anything less than love.

"I don't know what I'm going to say at this dinner with India," I tell him, pausing to take a sip of wine. "I know Xander sees her as a solution to a problem. She sees Xander as her path to being royalty."

"Like I did with you," Roman teases, tearing off a piece of naan bread and popping it into his mouth.

"Right. Your master plan all along was to get a princess," I say dryly.

"If her name is Princess Elizabeth of York, then yes."

My heart flutters from his words, and he flashes me that full, brilliant smile.

He has no idea how much he does indeed have me.

"From what you are telling me, it would be an arrangement to get what they both want," Roman says.

I wrinkle my nose. "I can't imagine that. And of all people, Xander."

Roman is silent for a moment. "You can't take on this problem for him, Lizzie. Xander will have to sort this out for himself.'"

"I haven't even gotten to Mum's conversation," I say. "But tonight isn't about all of my problems, Roman."

"My time is yours," he replies, reaching for my hand on the table and squeezing it. "I will listen as long as you want to talk."

I shake my head. "We'll talk about Mum another time. Right now, I want to focus on us. And decorating the tree."

Roman puts down his fork and rises, grabbing my bowl and his. "Well, come on, let's clear this and get to it then."

Roman puts the last decoration on the tree and steps back from it, taking in the view next to me. He bursts out laughing, his deep voice filling the space and making me laugh, too.

"This is the worst tree I've ever seen in my life," he declares.

"No, no, it's beautiful," I challenge.

Roman's decorations from the shop are wonderfully awful. Our tree is covered in silver tinsel, multi-coloured lights, and a red garland. The show stopper, of course, is the collection of red and white striped baubles, which are everywhere, in all shapes and sizes.

"It's hideous," he says.

"I love it."

"Ah, wait, I have a tree topper in that last bag," Roman remembers, interrupting my thoughts. He moves over and pulls it out. "A fairy." Then he shoots me a sheepish grin. "They were out of angels."

"She's lovely," I say, giggling.

"You shall do the honours," he says, handing her to me.

"I can't reach that high," I say, gazing to the top of the tall tree.

"Then it's a good thing you have me around," Roman says, picking me up.

I laugh, and he does too, as he easily holds me up in his arms so I can put the fairy on the tree.

I place the fairy on top, and she immediately flops to the side.

"She's drunk," I say, laughing.

"Our tree is absolutely the most hideous one in England."

"I'd say the Commonwealth," I tease.

I turn back to him, and Roman doesn't put me down. I move my hands to his face and kiss him. I kiss him for this tree. For listening to me. For showing me what love can be.

His tongue moves against mine in increasing tempo. Heat begins to build in me, and within seconds, he's lowering me to the sofa. I moan softly against his mouth as his hand slides over my breast, caressing it as he deepens the kiss.

"Wait," I say, putting my hand on his chest and causing him to stop. "I have a present for you."

"Oh, I think I'm about to open a great present right here," he says sexily, his fingertips dancing around the waistband of my jeans.

"Roman, I'm serious. I have a special present for you. Please open it now."

A smile passes over his handsome face. He lowers his mouth to mine and presses a sweet kiss against my lips. "As you wish. As long as you don't forget where we left off."

"Believe me, I won't," I promise. "I'll get it ready, and then you can come in when I call for you."

Roman gives me a quizzical look but gets up so I can

slip into the kitchen. I take out the gift box, and then a bottle of port, and put three glasses next to it.

"All right," I call out. "Please come into the kitchen."

I hear Roman move across the hardwood floor and enter the kitchen, where I'm standing next to the box.

"Open this," I say excitedly.

A curious expression filters across his handsome face. "From The Biscuit Cutter, I see."

"What can I say? You have excellent taste in bakeries."

Roman slides off the ribbon, and I hold my breath as he lifts the lid and the layer of tissue on top. I watch him, waiting for realisation to kick in.

He peers down at the cake, his hands slowly moving over the items: the marzipan, the decorations and the ready to roll fondant.

"I think it's time to bring your Christmas cake tradition back," I say softly. "To celebrate your grandmother."

Roman keeps his eyes cast down. He swallows hard, and I panic. Did I make a mistake with this gift? Is it too much?

Slowly, he lifts his eyes to meet mine. I'm shocked to see that they are teary.

"This," he says, his voice thick, "is the best present I've ever received. Thank you. Thank you for bringing her back to me tonight with this gesture."

I fight back my own tears.

"I'm glad you like it," I say. "But there's one thing we have to do first."

I turn around to reveal the port and three glasses.

"We'll all have one. Even your grandmother, in spirit."

"You remembered," Roman says, his eyes searching mine.

"Of course I did. It was important to you."

He draws me into his chest, holding me tightly. I snuggle against his checked shirt, inhaling the sandalwood soap on his skin and listening to his heartbeat.

In this moment, I know I'm in the place where I'm meant to be. With this man. Celebrating his beloved grandmother and a tradition Roman thought he lost forever when she died.

This is what love is.

And this is what I will give Roman for the rest of his life if he falls in love with me, too.

CHAPTER 20

SPILLING THE TEA

The temperature has taken a strong dip as I make the walk from my cottage to Helene's apartment at Kensington Palace on Friday.

I shiver inside my coat. I'm cold and I'm tired. Yesterday was exhausting. I was up late with Roman on Wednesday night and then woke up early with him to have breakfast before he went to work. Then I had a meeting with Cecelia, followed by a draining lunch with Mum, who went on about how Father is destroying our family and the possibility of my sisters finding out.

I wince as they come to mind. They would be upset that I knew and didn't say a word, but it's not my story to tell. Victoria would explode. She would hate Father for what he did and hold on to that anger. Bella would be upended in a different way. She is incredibly close to Father. They are so similar in interests—both avid consumers of history—and how they see the world, it would destroy the perfect picture she has of him—and a huge part of her heart, too.

My hair blows straight back as the biting air cuts across me. I managed to put my worries aside to attend my board meeting this afternoon, for a culinary arts organisation for teens in trouble. It was a great meeting, and I loved working with the board to come up with ideas for fundraisers. One is going to be a dinner created by the students this spring, which I will host at St. James's Palace. It will be a black-tie affair, with the price of the tickets going towards the expansion of the programme. The students will get to man the palace kitchen for the night, and I can't wait to see what they will do.

After this busy day, I should collapse on my bed and settle for a bowl of Frosted Shreddies and my joggers, but I always rally when it's time for tea at Helene's. I smile as I gaze at the Clock Tower wing, which is where apartment 1A is. It's actually is a four-storey house with 30 rooms. I'll have to remember to tell Roman this; he'll find it amusing.

I tuck my chin down as the wind whips up again, trying to stay warm. Tea sounds so good right now, and nothing warms my heart like spending a Friday evening with Clementine, Helene, and Jillian. Since Clementine introduced Jillian to Helene, they have become thick as thieves, and she has become part of the weekly afternoon tea.

I walk up to the door and ring the doorbell. I'm ushered in by her butler, Thomas.

"Good afternoon, Your Royal Highness," he says.

I smile at him. This is our routine whenever my schedule permits me to come to Friday tea.

"You know to call me Liz," I say, as I always do.

The older man with salt and pepper hair smiles sagely at me. "Yes, ma'am."

I slip out of my coat, and he takes it, carefully draping it over his arm. "Thank you," I say, "and the day you call me Liz will make me incredibly happy."

He chuckles. "That, my lady, won't happen."

"Well, it should," I say. "But I know you will not let down that royal guard of yours, will you?"

"No, ma'am."

I shake my head and cross the expansive foyer, with a black-and-white marbled checked floor and equine-inspired art on the walls. I hear my aunt's laughter coming from the living room, and my heart is happy as I approach the doorway.

As I stand in the entrance, I find myself still amazed at the renovation that has taken place in this room. Helene let Jillian, a retired interior designer, go to town on her living room, and now it's refreshed and chic. There's a large tartan Chesterfield sofa with zebra and silver pillows and a round, rosewood coffee table with a lush arrangement of white flowers and greenery in a crystal vase. Two houndstooth armchairs are across from the sofa, on the other side of the table. A plush silver chair is next to the roaring fire, and the same deep shade of silver is used for the long, floor-to-ceiling curtains. On the other side of the room is a gorgeous, sophisticated Christmas tree, the opposite of mine, with white, twinkling fairy lights and modern decorations in silver, tartan and zebra patterns. It's a complete departure from the stuffy chintz and gold that was here before.

I'm the last to arrive, and as I walk into the room, Helene rises to greet me. "Oh, my darling Liz, you're finally here," she says, pressing a kiss on my cheek.

"You know this is the best part of Friday," I say, returning her kiss with a warm hug.

I take my seat next to Clementine on the sofa. "Hello," I greet her, smiling.

"Hello," she says, smiling brightly back at me.

I turn to Jillian. "How are you, Jillian?"

"I'm wonderful. Dragging this apartment out of the thirteenth century has been my biggest design challenge ever."

"She lies," Helene says. "Eighteenth century is more like it."

"This room is more you," I say, thinking of my fun-loving aunt, who has a wicked sense of humour and modern tendencies.

"Who knew I liked zebra?" Helene asks. "Well, I like it on almost everything except boxers. If I saw a zebra print on a seventy-year-old man, I'd scream in horror."

"I'd pass out if I had the pleasure of seeing boxers, zebra pattern or not," Jillian declares. She shifts her attention to Clementine. "Live the dream, darling."

Clementine laughs. "Oh, I am."

I smile. I love how easy it is to discuss anything with Jillian and Helene.

"So I've done a thing," Jillian says, leaning forward in her chair.

"What?" Clementine asks.

"I've joined a dating website," Jillian announces.

"Get out!" Clementine cries in joy.

"She needs to," Helene says. "You should see these men. Older than dust. Too horrid for our vibrant Jillian."

"I thought I would have to do some swipe thing," Jillian says. "But no. They send you a list of matches."

"They're all dreadful," Helene complains as the tea trolley is brought in.

"Are you both looking at the profiles together?" I ask.

"No, Jillian sends me the candidates on WhatsApp."

"You have a WhatsApp account?" I ask.

"Of course I do," Helene says as Kim, one of her household servers, begins setting up the coffee table for tea.

I smile as I see a carafe for hot water and an assortment of tea bags. Helene hates dealing with tea leaves, so she doesn't. Antonia would not approve of using tea bags for an afternoon tea. I glance around the revamped living room. She'd hate this design, too. And she would be aghast at the idea of Helene using WhatsApp and checking out men with her friend.

In fact, Antonia might form two wrinkles in her forehead with that thought.

"Why are we not all on a chat then?" Clementine asks, picking up her phone. "We need to have a chat."

"I need to see these men this site is suggesting for Jillian," I say, opening my bag and retrieving my own phone.

"No, you don't," Jillian groans. "It figures. I'm finally brave enough to put myself back out there, and all my matches are rubbish."

"Surely not all of them?"

"Yes," she and Helene say at the same time. Then they collapse into a fit of laughter.

They truly are the best of friends, two brilliant women in the next act of their lives, and I'm blessed to be a part of this scene.

I see I have a new message from Jess, the girl I met last Saturday at greenhouse yoga. The instructor passed her a message from me, and now I have received one directly from her, as I decided I trusted her enough to give her my contact information. I read her message:

What a great surprise to hear from you... I feel like I should say Your Royal Highness. Is that

right? I've seen that there is going to be a pop-up yoga class at the greenhouse again tomorrow. You game? Then maybe lunch at the estate café afterwards?

Ooh! I don't have anything scheduled for tomorrow, so I can do this. I can also see Roman, as he likes to work Saturday mornings.

"There's another greenhouse yoga class tomorrow at Cheltham House," I tell the group as I begin to message Jess back. "I'm going to meet a friend I made there last week if anyone wants to come."

"I'd say you met a *friend*," Clementine says knowingly as Christmas cupcakes are placed on the table.

Helene and Jillian's heads swivel in unison to look directly at me.

"Friend?" Helene asks, arching her eyebrow up.

I can't help it. I beam.

"Yes. His name is Roman, and he's a gardener on the estate. I met him briefly during the time Clementine worked there, and I reconnected with him last week."

"I think it's time you spilled the tea," Helene says.

"If you had added me to your secret WhatsApp, you'd know," I tease.

"Valid point," Helene says, her blue eyes twinkling. But you have been added. Now tell me about Roman," Helene says.

"I will, but first I need to reply to Jess. Does anyone else want to go tomorrow? Eight o'clock in the morning?"

"I'd like to go," Jillian says as Kim takes the tea trolley out of the room.

"Christian and I are meeting with our wedding planner at nine," Clementine says, reaching for a tub of hot chocolate, which Helene provides because Clem hates tea.

"I'm giddy imagining the response Her Majesty had to the fact that you and Christian hired an outsider to take the reins," Helene says. "Did she get a crease in her forehead?"

I burst out laughing. "I'm sure she wanted to. How dare you not use her people?" I tease.

Clementine sighs. "She wasn't happy, but Christian said she didn't have a choice."

"Wedding planning is hard enough when it's a normal wedding," Jillian says. "I can't imagine planning one for the world to see."

Clementine's face freezes. I see panic over what her new reality truly is—a rare occurrence. My stomach flips. If I married Roman, it would be a royal wedding, like this one, with crowds and global television coverage. He would have to say his vows to the world and ride in an open carriage afterwards to a cheering public.

He would hate that, I think in a panic. *It's not him. At all.*

"My dear Clementine, all will be well," Helene assures her. "All that matters is that you are marrying Christian. You've handled all your appearances beautifully. You are going to be fine. Even better when you imagine Christian waiting for you inside the church."

I see Clem's shoulders lower. She exhales. "Yes."

"And we'll be right there with you," Jillian promises.

I reach for her hand and squeeze it. "You are going to be a gorgeous bride, with a beautiful wedding and a dream life, not because my cousin is a prince but because you are marrying the man you love."

"Thank you. Most days I'm fine—better than fine—as I do realise I'm living a dream. But a royal wedding is insane. I have sketches coming from the top five designers of my choosing for my gown and a choice of historic chapels. The world is interested in my vows, and I am both humbled and happy."

"I was in your shoes once," Helene says. "When I married Paul. I grew up along with the royal family, ran in the same social circles, had been to Buckingham Palace many, many times, and I was still petrified on my wedding day."

"Hell, I was, and I didn't have a royal wedding," Jillian says.

I can see Clementine putting all this into perspective, and at least for now, she doesn't seem so overwhelmed.

"Are you all right now, sweetheart?" Jillian asks with grandmotherly concern for her.

"Yes, thanks to all of you," she says.

"So I can send this text," I say, coming back around to the topic at hand. "Clementine is a 'no' for yoga. Jillian is a 'yes.' What about you, Helene?"

"No. I'm going to the Welsh National Opera in Cardiff tomorrow night, so I'll be getting my hair done and then travelling. I'm leaving out the fact that my body is so stiff, it would fold like a bad hand of cards."

"Pfft, that is why you need yoga," Jillian says.

"That is why I *don't* need yoga," Helene retorts. "Now, tea time. Pour."

"I hope you have more than one cup, because I can pour the tea endlessly about Roman," I say, sighing happily. "He is smart. Confident. Quirky. Protective. Gentle. He loves the earth and finds his happiness in the garden, nurturing plants to grow and thrive. That comes across in how he treats me, too. I feel like he wants me to be myself and thrive in my role, but on my terms. I've only known him a week, but we've spent so much time together, Helene. I know this man, and I know he's for me."

"I think I need another cup, because the tea is spilling over about him," Helene says, smiling. "You're like Christian, you know that?"

"How so?"

"You both walled yourselves off from romance for so long. Then all of a sudden, you meet that right person, and I see the light come on in both of you. You have never spoken so animatedly about anything other than your work, Liz. But now I hear the excitement in your voice. Your eyes are shining, and you are glowing with joy. Which makes me so happy, because you deserve all the happiness in the world."

"Don't make me cry," I say, blinking.

"I could cry for you, because Roman is wonderful," Clementine says, grasping my hand and squeezing it affectionately. "I always hoped you two would find your way together."

"I do worry about how he'll handle the media attention," I confide. "He loves working in quiet. How will he handle the press waiting for him when he leaves work? Or when they are waiting for him outside his flat?" The joy is sucked right out of my heart as reality hits. "Or when the press mocks him for not being who a princess should be with."

"Liz. Don't underestimate him," Helene warns. "You talk to him about your fears. You prepare him. It's dangerous to start writing reactions for him."

I nod, although I don't want to spook Roman with all this talk after a week.

"I'm always here to talk to him, as I know his experience from the commoner side," Clementine adds. "The squad, once they all know, will help him adjust."

I exhale. "What about Antonia? You don't think she'll make his life hell?"

I keep my tea with Antonia a secret. Otherwise, Helene would be dialing up Arthur, and Clementine would be telling Christian, and that's not what I want. This is my adult problem to handle.

Somehow.

"Oh, she can bloody well piss off," Helene says.

I can't help but giggle, as does Clementine.

"Helene!" I cry.

"She's a miserable woman who is desperately wanting her family to remain as elitist as possible," Helene continues. "She and the old dowager queen can get their knickers in a twist about a gardener ruining the bloodlines, which is ridiculous. Who cares? The world is changing, and they are utterly tone deaf to it. Do you see how people love Clementine? The modern love story? You would be the same. The gardener and the princess. I think it sounds lovely."

"Love will always have challenges," Jillian says. "However, your position is a bit different to Christian's, as you are more removed from the throne. There will be an interest in you, but Roman will never gather the attention that Clementine, as an American becoming a duchess, will."

I absorb the advice of these wise women and decide they are right. If Roman falls in love with me, he'll go through these challenges. It won't be easy, but I know if his heart is involved, he can do it.

"Enough talk of what can go wrong," Helene advises. "Let's talk about what can go right."

"Talk? I think we need to *celebrate*," Jillian declares. "Liz has found a good man, who I doubt would wear zebra boxers."

"Oh, no, he doesn't," I say without thinking.

All eyes shift to me.

Now my face is on fire.

"You've slept with him!" Helene says gleefully.

I know my raging red face has provided the answer.

"How come you didn't tell me?" Clementine squeals, although I can tell she is delighted.

"I take it it was good?" Jillian asks, leaning forward in her chair.

"Isn't the old saying 'a lady never tells?'" I ask.

"Nobody here is a lady," Helene teases. "I think there's more tea to be spilled."

"Oh, forget tea. It's time for champagne," Jillian says.

"Splendid idea," Helene says, picking up her phone. "Kim? Please bring in some champagne… Yes, that is all, thank you."

"We're having champagne because I had great sex?" I ask, laughing.

"Oh, so it was great?" Jillian asks. "We must have a drink to that!"

"I'll celebrate anyone who is having sex," Helene declares.

"You could be having sex," Jillian points out. "You are a vivacious, witty, spectacularly attractive, mature woman."

Helene shoots her a pointed look. "Yes, but I'm aiming for a man who has teeth. The last man who hit on me was Lord Hampshire, and I'm sorry, when his dentures slipped during dinner, I could imagine that happening during sex."

"He could have taken them out for you," Jillian says, her eyes sparkling.

"Oh, yes, I'd love nothing more than to look over at the bedside table and see his dentures in a cup."

"Wouldn't he put them at the sink, by the toothbrushes?"

"He can put his teeth anywhere he likes. I'm not sleeping with him. Besides, I think he has a saggy butt. Oh, I miss a nice, tight bum. You should put that on your dating profile, Jillian. Seeking to date a nice, lovely man with a glorious bum."

Now Clementine and I are dying with laughter, and Helene and Jillian join in. I feel as though my life is so much richer with these incredible women, who have faced all kinds of challenges in their lifetime and have come out the other side as strong, funny, witty, engaging people. Friendship truly knows no age boundary.

As they continue to laugh and joke, I know I'd be a wise woman to take their advice to heart. Clementine has been in Roman's shoes. Helene and Jillian have decades of life experience for me to take in when it comes to romance and relationships.

If I take their word, and Roman falls in love with me, we'll be okay.

And that thought is worth a glass of champagne indeed.

CHAPTER 21

READY FOR HEADSTANDS

I head across the grounds of Cheltham House, ready for my yoga class this morning. I'm truly impressed at the grasses and flowers still in bloom in December. I know from Roman that it takes a lot of planning to keep the grounds beautiful all year round, and he does a lot of research to ensure they are colourful and enticing no matter what time of year it is.

Thinking of Roman and meeting my friends for this class are what is keeping me going despite the headlines that have hit this morning. They painted me in a negative light and are complete rubbish and untrue, which normally would make me laugh. But not this time, because I know where this leak came from.

Antonia has launched the first attack in her war against me.

In her lies, spun by her allies to more than willing tabloid ears, she has pitted me against Clementine. My stomach churns as I remember seeing the articles that appeared in the squad chat this morning. The headlines are imprinted in my brain:

COLOUR OF JEALOUSY?

GREEN WITH ENVY LIZZIE LEAVES WHITE BEHIND AS CLEMMIE'S POPULARITY SOARS.

ROYAL FEUD: THREATENED BY CLEMMIE, LIZ VOWS WAR

TROUBLE AT KENSINGTON PALACE?

TRUE COLOURS—LIZZIE IN A TIZZY OVER CLEMMIE

I get furious as they flash through my head. Amelia called me, pissed at how ridiculous the press was being, dreaming this up within a week of Clementine's first public appearance. Roman, who likes to arrive early on the estate, hasn't seen them yet and won't until he's done with work. He'll be as furious as Amelia when the alerts come up on his phone.

The squad, on the other hand, thought it was hysterical, as they don't know it was Antonia who planted the stories and thought the press had been eager for a good duchess versus princess cage match.

But I do.

I also know this is a warm-up for her real attacks.

I pop open the door to the greenhouse. I've arrived early to make sure Jillian and Jess will be able to put their mats by mine. I find a spot in the back and unroll my mat. I think about all the articles and comments and tweets and posts that are going to happen while I'm in here this morning, with no way to stop it. I must shrug it off and stay the course.

And keep Roman under wraps until I'm sure he can handle the press and public scrutiny that is going to come his way.

A few more students arrive, and I know I'm recognised. I smile and say "hello," they do the same, and I wonder if they've seen the headlines. Do they think I'm evil? That I honestly hate Clementine? That I am nothing more than a spoilt, jealous cow?

I haven't even looked to see what Twitter is saying.

Ugh, I don't want to know.

Well, I kind of want to know.

No, I do not!

The door opens again, and in walks Jillian, so I leave the stupid idea of retrieving my mobile and scanning Twitter aside.

For now.

I watch as she approaches. Jillian has mastered chic on a whole new level. Her silver hair is swept back into a chignon. Her warm-up jacket is a fitted pale grey, with zips on the sides and thumb holes on the sleeves, and her yoga leggings are amazing. They are shimmery and slick and seem like a wet second skin.

Endlessly cool.

Jillian smiles as she sees me. "Good morning," she says, taking the space to my right. She eases off her black yoga rucksack and sets it next to her feet, which are adorned with grey New Balance trainers. She unzips her jacket to reveal a black and grey camo vest, and when she takes it off, I see her arms are perfectly toned.

"What is your secret?" I ask. "Your body is incredible."

Jillian ties her jacket around her lithe frame. "This body is built by yoga, lots of laughs, a balanced diet, and by finding ample joy in simple things. And gin and tonics," she adds with a wink.

I love the truthfulness in her answer, and I know she has provided me with a wonderful roadmap to keep in mind for the rest of my life.

As we chat, out of the corner of my eye, I see a woman holding up her phone. She is acting like she's reading it, but I know she's taking a picture of me. I know I can't control this, but with the media in the mood to kick me around, will the fact that I'm revealing my stomach in a cropped yoga top in public be considered un-princess like? Too showy? Even though half the class is full of them, will I be held to a different standard?

I already know the answer to that.

Part of me is angry. Angry because I can't be a modern woman working out in clothes that make me feel happy and comfortable in my own skin. Angry that I will be judged on something so stupid. And angry that I'm the one who provided the trolls with this ammunition instead of wearing a more modest top.

Wait a minute.

I stand up a bit straighter. I am a role model for younger women. Modern women. I'm wearing nothing that no other woman would wear to a yoga class. It's no different than wearing a bikini at the beach.

So screw it.

The door is continually opening now with students streaming in, and I spot Jess. I smile, nodding to my left, where I parked my yoga bag to save her a spot.

"Good morning," she says cheerfully.

I wonder if she has seen the articles yet.

Liz, shut up, I will myself. *You can't spend the whole morning wondering if people have seen that you are an evil, jealous cow on their Facebook feed this morning.*

"Good morning," I say, smiling at her. "Jess, I'd like to introduce you to my friend, Jillian Park. Jillian, this is Jess Lui."

Jillian smiles at her. "Hello, Jess. It's a pleasure to meet you."

"Likewise," Jess says, her face lighting up in a warm smile.

"I'm so glad you wanted to meet up," I say to Jess. "I'm excited about eating afterwards."

"Me, too. Have you ever been to the café here? All the produce and herbs are grown right here on the estate."

Pride for Roman takes over. I know he's laid out the culinary garden, and the project has been his baby. His kitchen garden was designed with thoughts on what the chef here could use season by season for sustainability. Every seed, every plant, was put into the earth by his own hands, with each one having a purpose.

"I haven't, but I'm looking forward to it," I say.

I shift my attention out the windows of the greenhouse. Not for paparazzi like last time, but for Roman. He did say he was working this morning, and when I told him I'd be here for yoga, he said he wouldn't be able to resist stealing a look at me, which made me happy.

A tall, elegant woman steps to the front of the room. "Hello, my name is Grace, and I'll be leading our practice today," she says. "Please put all your belongings at the back of the room, and make sure your phones are put on silent as I want you all to be in the moment."

People begin moving around, and I wonder how much I can stay in the moment when I know Roman might be watching me. A triumphant feeling takes over. Now I'm pleased I wore my black, strappy crop top and long black yoga pants. If Roman is going to sneak a peek, I want it to be a good one.

Class begins, and I do all I can to focus on my practice. How is it I can walk down endless stairs at BP in high heels, but when I'm in yoga poses, I get wobbly?

As soon as we start, I know my mind isn't in the right place. I'm thinking about those stupid articles. Trolls. Antonia. Roman. I go through the motions, but I'm not into it. We work through sequences, and finally, we are at the point where we are going to do a headstand. I had mastered this previously in my private yoga sessions a few weeks ago, and I'm eager to see if I can do it as well as last time.

I move my hands into position and lower my head to the floor. I lift my hips, straighten my legs, and then walk them towards my head. I've done this twice before, so I'm feeling confident about my ability to do it in this class.

I lift one leg towards the ceiling, moving it into proper alignment. Then I lift my other leg. I don't get it up right. I try again. No. Now I'm frustrated because I know I can do this. I hate nothing more than knowing I can do something and having problems doing it. I lift my leg again, and as soon as I get it up to the top, I lose my balance and BAM! I flop over on to my back, landing on my mat with a huge thud that echoes through the greenhouse. I accidentally kick my water bottle into the woman in front of me, sending it rolling into her bum as she's completed her stand and is in child's pose.

I gasp, as the pain shooting through my bum and my back is excruciating. But that is nothing compared to the mortification I feel. I had the most ungraceful fall ever. Yet despite my whopping fall, everyone else in the class is going about their practice as if nothing has happened.

How are they not laughing?

I glance over at Jess, who has gracefully lowered herself out of her headstand, and her dark-brown eyes dart over to me for a second. "Are you okay?" she whispers.

I force myself up to a sitting position and nod. She tries to stifle a laugh, and it comes out in a snorting sound, and then she begins to have a coughing fit.

Now Jillian starts laughing, and I do, too.

We can't stop.

"I need to leave; this is rude," I whisper to Jess.

"I think it's time for a coffee," Jillian says.

Jess nods.

I feel as if I'm being watched again. I turn and glance out the window. There, I find Roman, watching me with a huge smile. My embarrassment increases tenfold. I know from the amusement on his face, he saw my epic headstand fail.

The three of us roll up our yoga mats, and since we are at the back of the room, we're able to slip into our shoes and jackets without distracting the class. I'm the first one out the door of the greenhouse so I can say hello to Roman.

He has a shovel in his hands, which he is casually leaning forward on, and a slightly curved smile on his face. His boots are covered in mud, and I see his red and black checked shirt is stained with it, too. There's a swipe of dirt across his cheek, and I long to brush it away with my fingertips but resist the urge.

Oh, Roman is gloriously sexy when he's working in the garden.

I lead Jess and Jillian over to him. "Before we get our

drinks, I want to introduce you both to a friend of mine who works here."

"Hi," I say, smiling at Roman but not touching him because we are in public. "Roman, I'd like you to meet Jess Lui."

"I'd shake your hand, but for obvious reasons, I won't," he says, smiling at her.

"Thank you," Jess says, smiling back. "It's nice to meet you."

Then I present Jillian. "And this is Jillian Park, a dear friend of Clementine's."

"Pleasure," Roman says, nodding.

"Likewise," she says. "Both Clementine and Liz speak highly of you."

I watch as that cute flush climbs up his neck from the compliment.

"Thank you," he says softly.

"So you might have seen my, uh, ungraceful fall out of my headstand," I say.

Now a huge smile lights up his face. "Hmm. Ungraceful is one way to put it."

"Stop," I warn him, laughing.

Roman gives me a deep, sexy chuckle, and goosebumps sweep over my skin.

I see another member of the gardening staff come down the path towards us. This man is older, with thick, silvery hair and a tall frame, and he's carrying a pair of huge clippers in one hand. As he nears us, I can clearly see his full lips and strong jaw. There's no doubt in my mind who I'm seeing.

This man is Roman's grandfather.

I hold my breath. I wonder if Roman will introduce us, and if so, will his grandfather know who I am? Maybe not, since we've only just started dating. He stops next to Roman, and now the resemblance is even stronger. Same height.

And the same hazel eyes.

"Grandfather, I'd like you to meet Liz," Roman says.

"A true pleasure, Your Royal Highness," he says.

"Oh no, call me Liz, please," I implore.

"Roman told me you'd say that," he replies, smiling broadly at me. "He's told me a lot about you."

Happiness radiates through me from this confession. "He knows me well," I say, glancing at Roman. I turn my attention back to his grandfather. "But please, I beg you, call me Liz, Mr. Lawler."

"I shall call you Liz as long as you call me Clive," he says warmly.

"Grandfather, these are Liz's friends, Jess and Jillian," Roman says, introducing them.

Clive says hello to Jess, but when his gaze shifts to Jillian, his eyes linger for a moment.

"Jillian," he says slowly. "Lovely to meet you."

"Clementine used to rent a room in Jillian's flat," Roman explains. "Until recently."

"It's so dreadfully empty without her," Jillian says. "It's me prattling around with the telly turned up for sound."

"I do the same thing," Clive says, nodding. Then he smiles, and my heart melts when I see that it's the same smile that Roman bestows on me. "If you rented a room to Clementine, you must have seen Cheltham House before."

"I was here at the house for a tea last month celebrating caregivers," Jillian explains. "My husband passed away from Alzheimer's years ago."

Clive's eyes widen. "My wife did as well."

I watch this exchange with interest. I steal a glance at

Roman, who seems to be studying the interaction between Jillian and his grandfather as much as I am.

"So you understand," Jillian says, her eyes bright in acknowledgement.

"I do," Clive replies, nodding.

There's a brief pause as they stare at each other, and I know we have all faded away in their awareness.

Clive clears his throat. "Have you seen the gardens here, Jillian? I'm slowly shifting into retirement, and Roman has done an amazing job taking over much of the planning and design. His culinary garden is a masterpiece."

I don't even need to look at Roman to know he's flushed from the compliment.

"No, I haven't, but I'd love to see that," Jillian says. "Whenever you have time. I don't want to impose if you are working."

"No, I'm nearly done. Easing into retirement means I can have Roman pick up the slack."

Roman grins and shakes his head, and Jillian turns to me. Before she can say anything, I beat her to the punch. "Enjoy the tour," I encourage. "Jess and I will be in the café."

Jillian gives me a warm smile, and I think she's eager to get to know Clive better.

"Let me take you to a place where you can put your bag," Clive says. "Then, after I wash my hands, I'll show you the winter garden."

As they head off down the path, I turn to Roman. "Your grandfather is smooth," I tease. "Tour of the garden?"

"Says the woman who took a yoga class with a mission to find me," Roman counters.

Jess is watching with a furrowed brow. I didn't intend

to discuss Roman in public, but now I must. I decide I will take my chances and confide in her.

"I'm seeing Roman," I say quietly.

"Oh," she says.

"We're keeping it under the radar for now," I continue, keeping my voice down. "I ask that this stays between us, and we not talk about it further until we are alone."

"I completely understand," Jess says. "I will keep this a secret."

I feel Roman's gaze on me, and I glance at him. He's studying me with a furrowed brow, and I don't understand what the look is for. He has to know why I want to keep us under wraps.

He clears his throat, and the dynamic between us has shifted. He stands straight up, almost rigid now, in opposition to the easy way he normally carries himself, and there's no smile on his face. I don't like the unsettled feeling coming over me, and I want to pull him aside and reassure him as to why I want to be secretive about us.

"I should get back to work," Roman says abruptly.

My chest draws tight. He's obviously hurt by how I explained us to Jess. But if I pull him aside to talk to him now, the longer I'm seen in public with him, the more opportunity there is for pictures of us to show up on social media.

"Okay," I say softly. "I'll see you tonight." Roman is going to spend the night over at my place.

"Yeah," he says simply. "I'll see you."

I shoot him a pleading expression with my eyes.

Roman, you know me. You have to know I'm not hiding you for any other reason than to protect what we have.

"Jess, it was a pleasure meeting you," he says.

"Likewise, Roman," she replies, nodding.

"Enjoy the café. I recommend the pumpkin pasta with fresh sage oil."

Then Roman turns and walks away.

If I were a normal woman, I would stop him. I'd tell him to hold up because we're talking this out, right here, right now. I wouldn't care who saw or snapped a pic or gossiped about it. I'd tell him why I did what I did and that he might not like it, but it was done for him. For us.

But I'm not a normal woman.

I'm Princess Elizabeth of York, who can't be seen talking to a man alone for even a minute without it showing up somewhere. There will already be pictures of me from the yoga class as soon as it's over. I can't even imagine the glee of the tabloids if they found out I not only have a man, but one who is a gardener. While, to a lot of the public, this is nothing, to those in the inner circles of the monarchy, it is unheard of. There'd be whispers about how Roman would fit and how I should have dated up. All crap, all rubbish, all ancient in thinking.

I will be the one to break this ceiling, I vow.

But this will take time. Roman will need to adjust to this world. I want our love to grow and deepen first. He must be ready for how his life will change. His feelings for me have to be strong and secure before we go public, because if they aren't as strong as mine, he could decide I'm not worth it.

With a gut punch, I realise it could be like Dad with Mum.

His feelings could change.

It's getting harder to breathe as I watch Roman fade from view and come face to face with my deepest fear: that he could grow disappointed with me, the constraints of my life, and his feelings could change.

With Antonia lurking about, being exposed right now

will be a thousand times worse. Roman's the perfect tool for her to use to destroy me. If I'm to protect him, to protect what I love, I can't be normal.

I have to be a princess.

And for the first time in my life, I hate who I am.

By the time I get back home, an edginess takes over that won't resolve itself until I can explain my actions to Roman. I sigh heavily as I slip out of my jacket, hanging it up in the cupboard. Tea followed by lunch with Jess was fine, despite my worry over what Roman was thinking. If one thing being a royal has taught me, it's that I can compartmentalise my feelings and expressions so nobody knows if I'm bored. Irritated. Anxious.

Or upset.

Putting my emotions aside, I did enjoy Jess's company today. She's an interesting person, who has the same passion for working with children as I do. She told me about her days teaching at a nursery school, and I loved hearing her inside stories and struggles, mentally taking notes to see if there was anything I could help with on a larger scale. She's single, twenty-three, fluent in Cantonese, and emigrated with her family from Hong Kong to London when she was four. As an only child, she is bombarded with weekly checks to see who she is dating and if she will ever get married, and Jess was so funny and dry about it, I couldn't help but laugh. My instincts were right. She is someone I'd like to become better friends with.

I didn't see Jillian for the rest of the day, but I did get a text during lunch that made me smile. I retrieve my phone and read it again:

Isn't Clive GORGEOUS? We're going to lunch.
I'll see if there's depth to this silver fox like I hope
there is.

I already know the answer to that.

If Clive is anything like Roman, the next text will be to tell me she's smitten with him.

I tap my phone to my chin and sink down onto the sofa, gazing at my wonderfully beautiful Christmas tree, given to me by the man who has my heart in his hands. The heaviness I had shoved away returns as I think of Roman. If it were anyone else, I'd text him a message about what happened, but he has always made it clear he would rather FaceTime or hear my voice. I'm sure this sentiment is stronger when he's hurt.

I glance down at the time. Roman won't be finished for hours yet, but I can't imagine him working that whole time and thinking I was keeping him a secret for any reason other than to shield him. I decide to leave him a voicemail. I sort out the thoughts in my head first; then I call his number, waiting for his greeting to come on.

"Hello?" Roman says suddenly.

I gasp in shock. "You… you aren't working?"

"Were you hoping to get my voicemail, Liz? Would that make things easier for you?"

Liz.

If I didn't know he was angry by the edge in his voice, I

surely know it now by him choosing to call me Liz. It makes *me* angry.

"Roman, I know you're cross with me, but you are leaping to all kinds of conclusions that you shouldn't. I was calling because I know you prefer to hear my voice rather than receive a text. I also know you're working, and I didn't want to wait until tonight to explain things to you."

"Explain things," Roman repeats. "Why? Because I'm stupid? I'm not from a posh circle so I can't possibly understand that you're embarrassed of me? Was being in public with me the reality check? You made that abundantly clear by not standing within five feet of me on the path, Liz, and by telling Jess to keep me a secret, like I was something dirty you didn't want people to know your gloved princess hands have touched. After all I've said and shared with you, you treat me like that? That was humiliating, Liz. And yes, I'm angry. I'm not something for you to dabble in while you figure out how to date. I won't be your walk on the normal side. I won't be embarrassed like this."

Ooh! I'm furious now.

And I let him have it.

"You are an idiot," I say through gritted teeth. "I *adore* you. I've never cared about anyone in the way I do you, which is insane after a week and should utterly terrify me, but it doesn't.

"What does terrify me," I continue, my voice shaking, "is that you think I could ever be embarrassed of you. You know me. At least I thought you did. You know me better than anyone, and if you think that I was doing anything other than protecting you, then I question what we're doing."

"Protecting me? What are you talking about? This is about you."

"No. I *was* protecting you. The press came out with a bunch of horrible headlines about me today. Antonia has launched her attack, and she's made it out that I am a wretched cow who is jealous of Clementine. I'm the monster on social media, and if she knew anything about you, saw one picture, got one tidbit off social media that her minions could find, she would make your life hell, Roman. She'd take away your privacy. You'd be stalked, and slapped on headlines making fun of you like they do me. You've only been with me for a week; do you know how utterly scared I am that this would drive you away, and you'd find someone normal? *Do you?*" I shout at him.

I hear Roman suck in his breath on the other end of the line.

"You don't," I say, my voice shaking. "So, yes, I kept my distance, and I didn't make a big deal out of us while people and their phones were around. And as much as I wanted to stop you from walking away and explain everything, I couldn't do any of that without the fear of being recognised and bringing you into this world without any preparation. My actions had nothing to do with me. It was about you. You don't know this world. You don't know how hellish it can be. I was hoping you'd be committed to me and in love with me before I dragged you into it."

All I can hear is silence.

"Lizzie," he finally says, his voice thick. "I —"

"No, you said what you thought in that outburst," I say. "I don't need to hear any more about how I'm ashamed of you, or toying with you. Nothing could be further from the truth. The fact that you thought, even for a second, that I was playing with you, after everything I've said to you, makes you someone I don't wish to speak to."

Then I hang up.

My phone immediately rings back, and I throw it down on the sofa in anger. I'm bubbling up inside, and I need to walk, to clear my head, to hear something other than Roman hurtling out those accusations at me.

I don't even grab my coat before I fling open the door. Then, I stop, stunned at who is coming up the path.

It's Xander.

I haven't seen him for weeks, and now here he is, bundled up in a cashmere jumper, scarf, and jeans, with his dark hair blowing in the breeze. He's giving me the brilliant, perfect smile that has charmed women around the world, but it fades the second his deep blue eyes lock on my face.

"Liz, are you all right?" Xander asks quickly, moving up the path to me. "No, you're not. What's wrong?"

The anger that was overflowing abruptly stops with his concern. His observation and attention remind me of how Roman acted towards me.

When he thought I was real.

Before he thought I was a princess merely taking a spin with a man outside my gilded walls.

Hurt fills my heart. My eyes swim with tears, and before I know it, Xander has his hands on my arms, holding me tight.

"Liz, what is it? Talk to me," he pleads.

I stare at the older brother of my heart, the one who chose India because she understands his life. I never thought he could be right about that, but now I'm not sure.

But the second I think it, I know I'm wrong to doubt myself. Roman is the man for me. Hard-working, sensitive, strong Roman. Like Christian, I don't want easy. I want true love. But what I thought I found with Roman isn't what Christian has with Clementine. She never doubted his sincerity.

With my anger stripped away, the harsh reality of this fight slams into me. For Roman to doubt my heart, when he's the only man who has ever held it, tells me all I need to know.

He is the man I love, yes, but he doesn't even *know* me, let alone love me.

And as I understand this, there's only one thing to do.

I collapse against Xander and burst into tears.

Xander doesn't say anything. I cry into his jumper, the soft fabric caressing my cheek, which reminds me again of Roman, and I wish it were him I was clinging to instead of Xander. A sob escapes my throat. He remains still for a few moments before speaking.

"Let's go into the cottage," he says firmly. Like the military man he is, Xander doesn't wait for my response but takes action, guiding me into the house. He leads me to the sofa and instructs me to sit. "I'll bring you some tea."

I'm too upset to protest that I don't want tea, so I let him do it. I hear him rattling around in the kitchen, opening various cupboards, retrieving items, and running water. Within minutes, he has returned with a mug, which he places in my hands.

"Drink," he commands, sinking down onto the sofa next to me.

I do as I'm told, letting the hot liquid slide down my throat, but it gives no comfort.

"Liz, what's happened? Did you and Roman have a row?" he asks, his blue eyes searching my face for clues.

With a shaking hand, I put the mug on the coffee table. "He thinks I'm ashamed of him," I whisper, reliving the words he flung at me over the phone, "because I wouldn't acknowledge him in public."

"Why didn't you?"

My attention snaps back to Xander. "What?"

"Tell me why you didn't acknowledge him."

I feel my chest grow tight. "Xander, we've only been seeing each other for a week. I want to protect him as long as I can from this world. You see what the press is doing to me right now. What do you think they would do if they found out I was seeing a gardener? They would have a field day with stupid headlines and stories all designed to humiliate him."

"But this *is* your world, Liz," he says simply. "Roman knew that from the day he asked you to come to dinner."

"Roman doesn't understand what that truly means," I say. "We do, because our first moment in the public spotlight was when we were on the steps of the hospital ward as infants. It's all we've known. Roman understands there will be attention and things written about him, but he doesn't know how that will actually feel. His life will change because of who I am."

"Liz, this isn't your choice to make," Xander says gently. "It's Roman's. You can't keep him hidden forever, because that's not your life. All the publicity and social media write-ups *are* your life."

A solitary tear escapes my eye. "What if he changes his mind about me?" I ask, reaching up to wipe it away. "This institution is hard to live in. You know that."

"Which is why I'm seeing India. She knows this life. Mum adores her. She's well-versed in society and knows the work she would undertake in this world. India," he says with resolution, "can handle this."

"You realise what's missing from that comment, don't you, Xander?"

He blinks. "What?"

"Love," I say. "Do you love her?"

"We've just started seeing each other," Xander says. "It takes time for that."

"Sometimes," I say. "But when you talk about her, there's no spark. You don't light up, not like a man who is happy or who is falling in love."

Xander rakes a hand through his hair. "We both know that's not an option for me."

"Why do you say that?" I cry, terrified that he is thinking this way. I'd rather have Xander the Philander back than this man, who is convinced he has to live his life without love.

"You're worried about Roman, but Liz, your path is different to mine. Yes, you will have attention, but the light on Roman will fade, and it will never be as bright as one put on the future queen."

"You are telling me about love and saying Roman should have the right to make that choice, yet you won't allow your heart the same option?"

Xander turns back towards me. "No."

"Xander, don't do this," I say, shaking my head. "You cannot. You deserve to be in love with someone who loves you."

He gives me a sad smile "That's the problem. Everyone wants the Prince of Wales. Women think they know me. They love me before they even see me in person."

"And India's different?"

"No. I can see it in her eyes. She thinks she loves me,

but she loves the monarchy. And that's going to have to be enough."

"Do you hear yourself?" I say, leaping off the sofa in anger. "Do you? Because you are being a *fool.*"

Xander's eyes widen in surprise.

"You are going to be the king someday. You can change the future. Don't you see that?" I cry, exasperated. "You could be the first king to find love outside the circle. Christian has kicked the door down, and you choose to ignore that? He has changed *everything.* Whoever you give your heart to, you will help her adjust. If she loves you, like Clementine loves Christian, she won't care. And what would the world say? That you married for love?

"The people you want to represent are diverse and modern," I continue. "Don't sacrifice your heart when you don't have to. You deserve the world, Xander. And that includes a woman who loves you. For you. Don't you dare believe she doesn't exist, because I know she does. You will regret it for the rest of your life if you don't find her."

Xander stares back at me in shock. He's silent as he takes in my words.

I sit back down next to him. "Please don't give up on love. I never knew what that meant until now. I know I love Roman, and I never thought it was possible, the happiness I have now. He makes me feel alive, Xander. You deserve this same happiness. I can't imagine you spending your life without it. I wouldn't wish that fate on anyone, let alone my brother."

I know I've verbally slapped him. He sits still, unmoving, my words hanging in the air between us.

"I don't want to talk about India," he finally says.

My heart breaks. Xander is determined not to hear me.

"But what you said," he continues, "can apply to Roman, can't it?"

Now it's my turn to be silent.

"You're right," he says. "Christian has changed everything. Not only for me, but for you. There will always be critics. Trolls. My mum. It takes a special person to overcome all of that, but you will never control it. I know you're terrified Roman will get into this and then leave you."

I blink back tears. "He could leave before he ever falls in love with me," I say, forcing the words out.

Or he could fall out of love with me if he does already love me, I think with anguish.

"If what you say about love is true," Xander says slowly, "Roman will find a way to handle this. It won't be easy, but as Clementine told me, she never wanted easy. She wanted Christian. According to you, this is what we should want. Roman could be that man, Liz, but you have to let him decide what he wants. If he doesn't want the protection of secrecy, you'll have to respect that and trust that if he loves you, he will get through it."

I know Xander is right. I should have talked all this through with Roman, even though it's early on in our relationship, because of my situation. He always should have been a part of the conversation. I confused him and kept him in the dark, and that was wrong.

And now it's time to make it right.

Xander rises from the sofa. "Are you okay?"

I stand. "Where are you going?"

"That wasn't the question," he says.

I smile. "Thanks to you, I will be. I'm going to go visit a certain gardener now."

Xander gives me a hug. "Tell Roman I want to meet him."

I step back from him, and he goes towards the door.

"And where are you going?" I inquire.

Xander gives me the most serious look I've ever seen on his face.

"I need to talk to India," he says slowly. "It's time to end this charade."

My heart is filled with relief. He did listen.

"If you have no chance of loving her, it's the right thing to do," I reassure him.

"I only hope you're right, Liz."

"About breaking up with India?"

"No. About someone out there being able to love me for me."

Then he opens the door and leaves, shutting it behind him.

I walk with purpose towards Cheltham House. I'm throwing all caution aside in what I'm about to do, but Xander made me understand I have to let Roman have a say in how we move forward. As much as I want to protect him, to shield him from the humiliation Antonia and the press will no doubt throw upon him, I can't hide him forever. He needs to see the ugliness of my life.

And make his own choice if he can love me enough to live with it.

I stand in the queue to buy an admission ticket. I'm still in my yoga clothing, my hair in a ponytail at the nape of my neck, my face blotchy from crying, but I don't care. This is what a modern princess who had a fight with her boyfriend looks like, and the world can put it all over social media for all I care.

I pay for my admission, and the woman puts a wristband on me. I bypass the entrance to the house and head straight for the gardens, my heart hammering inside my chest. Roman didn't leave a message on my phone, so I have no idea if he called me back to apologise or argue some more or break up with me.

The last option brings new tears to my eyes. Because where I'm about to go with Roman is faster than I wanted. He could hate what is about to happen to him. He could decide I'm not worth it.

But that is a risk my heart is more than willing to take now.

I stroll down the path, desperate to find the one person I'm searching for. I'm oblivious to the people around me, not caring if they recognise me. I head towards the walled garden, past the shrubs and topiaries, hoping I'll find him. Maybe I should go to the greenhouses first, or find a staff member to ask where he is. I'm about to turn around and head back towards the house when I see him.

I stop on the path. Roman is working on branches against the brick wall, ones with no blooms and bare for winter. I can see he's cutting them back, no doubt preparing for a beautiful bloom this spring.

My throat goes dry. My chest aches. I will myself to move forward.

He hears my footsteps and lifts his head in the direction of the sound. When he sees me, he drops his pruners in shock. I cut across the grass, as it's the shortest path to him. I can't hear anything but the pounding of my heart.

Roman's eyes stay locked on mine as I get closer. But

this time, I don't stop five feet from him. I close the gap so we're only inches apart.

"Lizzie," he says, his voice thick, "I'm — "

"If you want me to touch you right now," I say, interrupting him, "I will."

His hazel eyes widen with my words. "What?"

"I promise you, Roman, I only wanted to protect you, and us, by delaying the intrusion that is about to come into your life. You say you know what is about to happen, but you don't. My deepest fear," I tell him, my voice wobbling as I force the words out, "is that it will be too much. That you will leave. Which I understand you might do, and you have every right to. But that is why I wanted to keep us quiet. Half the reason was for you, but in truth, half the reason was selfish. I was afraid I would lose you. I still might."

"No," Roman whispers. "You won't."

The tears I vowed not to shed rush back, and I blink. "You say that, but if we go forward, in public, Antonia will humiliate you. You might hate what your life becomes. I thought, with time, I could ease this transition for you and prepare you the best that I can. I'd do everything in my power so you wouldn't resent me, or become disappointed in me," I say, my voice breaking, "and decide being with me isn't worth it."

The second I finish speaking, Roman's hands frame my face, and his mouth captures mine in a desperate kiss. I feel the tears fall from my eyes as his tongue tangles with mine, making a statement with a bold, passionate kiss for anyone to see.

I'm his.

I kiss him back, liberated by his declaration. His kiss tells me he's not afraid of the storm that is to come. He's willing to take this on, all of it—the press, the monarchy, the queen.

Because I'm worth it.

I savour every moment, imprinting this kiss on my brain. I smell sandalwood and the fresh dirt that is on his skin. He tastes of mint, and I feel the wetness of tears on my cheeks and the soft fabric of his checked shirt sleeves, which I am gripping onto as I kiss him back with the same passion and intensity.

Making him mine.

Roman breaks the kiss, and I see desperation in his eyes, the golden flecks now coming alive in them. "I am so sorry I was such an arse to you," he says, his deep voice tinged with regret. "I'm so sorry. I know you, Lizzie. I do. I know your heart, and it was my own past coming up and warning me that you would leave me, too."

The penny drops for me. This was about his own broken heart.

I move my hands to his face. He lowers his forehead to mine.

"I thought it was the beginning of you seeing I didn't fit in your world and being disappointed in the man I am," he whispers as I caress his face, stroking the stubble that has shaded his skin. "While I survived that happening once, this time I couldn't. I couldn't because *you* would be the one to break my heart."

Roman stands up straight so he can gaze into my eyes. "You could break my heart because I'm falling in love with you, Lizzie. I'm falling in love with you."

CHAPTER 24
GRAPE VINES

He's falling in love with me.

Never have any words given me such elation as those beautiful words he said out loud.

Twice.

My feelings, the ones I hoped he would reciprocate in the future, are closer at hand than I ever dared to dream.

I'm about to erupt in giddiness when Roman speaks first. "I know it's only been a week," he says, continuing in absence of me saying anything. "I know you might think this is mad or careless, and I don't expect you to feel the same way. I never thought I'd say this so soon, but after what an idiot I was, I wanted you to know my feelings are real, Lizzie. That's why I reacted so badly earlier when I thought you were embarrassed of me. But I know you would never, ever feel that way."

"Roman," I say softly, gazing up into his hazel eyes, "I'm falling in love with you, too." I decide not to tell him I'm already there, as that might put pressure on him to feel something he's not quite ready for yet.

Surprise lights up his handsome face. "You are?"

I laugh. "Well, you are falling in love with me; isn't it natural that I'm falling in love with you, too?"

I'm rewarded with a brilliant smile. "I can't stop what I'm feeling," he admits. "Every time I talk to you, every time I'm with you, I find myself handing over pieces of my heart to you. More to the point, I want to give them to you. Only you."

I think my heart is about to burst right open with love for this man.

"You have made me so happy," I whisper so only he can hear me, even though it's just us and the barren branches in this part of the garden.

"I want you to know something," Roman says, cradling the back of my head with his large hand. "I'm not scared of social media or the press. They can say what they want. I don't care."

I wince from his words. "Roman, you say that, but you don't know the world that I live in."

"I think I do. I was there when the press descended on Clementine. There will be an interest in me. People will make fun of the dynamic of a gardener and a princess. They will say I'm not good enough, and that you are digging through the rubbish bin for a man. So what, Lizzie? The only thing that matters to me is what *you* think."

Tears fill my eyes. "I'm afraid you won't feel that way once your life is out there for everyone to read. I don't ever want you to be hurt because you are with me."

"No, no, don't say that," Roman says, shaking his head. "You don't understand. They can mock me, attack me, I don't *care*."

Now the tears fall.

"Roman, it's going to be rough right now because Antonia will come after you. She will purposely have stories leaked to humiliate you. She will dig into your past. I thought it would be easier to insulate you during this time, so maybe she can get over herself. While it will never be easy to be in the spotlight, I thought if she wasn't so fixated on me, it wouldn't be as horrible for you."

Roman is quiet for a moment. "What if we beat her to the punch?"

"What do you mean?"

"We go out in public. If someone happens to post a pic of it, we've taken the wind out of her attacks on you with something else for the public to talk about. That Her Royal Highness," he says, stroking my face, "has a love interest. That's more interesting than any rubbish she can say about you. I saw the headlines about you today after you hung up. It is bullshit that they came after you like that, when you've done nothing but work so hard on behalf of your organisations. And you jealous of Clementine? It's absurd. But our story? It's *real.*"

I take in his words. I never thought about taking the discovery of Roman away from Antonia.

Then I realise what he is offering to me.

He's willing to put himself through the hell of the tabloid press, of social media comments and attacks, to make my situation easier.

"Do you understand what you are offering to do?" I ask, searching his eyes. "The sword you are going to fall on for me?"

"You're wrong," Roman says, his eyes growing dark. "It's not a sword. Showing the world what we have is not a sacrifice. It's an honour to be able to say you're my girl. Not Your Royal Highness. But my girl. Because you have been since that day we sat on the floor of the greenhouse."

He kisses me, lightly brushing his lips against mine.

Tears stain my cheeks, and I can't believe what Roman is willing to do for me.

He steps back and brushes away my tears with his calloused fingertips, ones that feel rough against my skin. "Whatever you want to do," he says softly. "This choice is yours."

I think on this briefly, but as I stare up into the face of the man I love, I know what I need to do. "You always said the world needed to see more of Angry Liz."

Roman's mouth begins to curve up in that teasing smile. "I did."

"Then I think it's time for me to leak some things to people who are favourable to me in the press. Not a tabloid, but a respectable royal reporter. Perhaps in time for the Sunday edition tomorrow."

He rewards me with a beaming smile that takes my breath away.

"I like your style, Your Royal Highness," he teases.

I continue to think. "Can you get off in a couple of hours? For a strategic photo op?"

"Yes, I can leave soon. I'll get cleaned up and meet you at your place."

I slide my hands up to his face. "Thank you."

"Do you have a headline in mind for this photo?" Roman teases.

"The gardener and the princess. I love the sound of that."

"Me, too," he says, dropping another kiss on my lips.

"I should let you get back to work," I say, staring at the branches.

"Yeah, I've got to pick up the slack for Grandfather, who ran off with Jillian and texted me to say he's taking the rest of the afternoon off."

"Really?" I ask, loving this bit of information.

"Apparently us Lawlers have a thing for elegant ladies," Roman says, bending over to pick up his tool.

"Yes. I'm the image of elegance flopping out of a headstand," I say dryly.

He chuckles. "I was thinking of you in that evening gown, but you did manage that flop with spectacular style."

"I did, didn't I?" I tease.

"The kicking of the water bottle into the woman's bum in front of you was a spectacular finish."

Now I blush, and Roman winks at me.

I seriously love this man.

I clear my throat. "What are you pruning back here?" I ask.

"Grape vines," he says. "This is the only thing I prune in December. But there's something kind of beautiful about the bare vines, the simplicity of them, knowing they will bear fruit in the season."

I gently place my hand against one. "I love seeing the earth through your eyes. You see possibility and growth in the land."

Roman wraps his hand over mine. "I see possibilities everywhere right now," he says.

I see the adoration in his eyes, and I'm absolutely breathless.

This man, this incredible man, is falling in love with me.

And I can't wait to share our love story with the world.

"Are you ready for this?" I ask.

Roman watches me from my bed as I pull my hair up into a topknot. "To take a walk around Kensington Palace

Gardens with you? I've been looking forward to it, despite the fact that it's gloomy this afternoon."

I bite on my lip as I tuck my locks into place. Doubt about our plan to beat Antonia to the punch has come back to the surface.

Because after our conversation next to the grape vines, fear began to creep into my heart. I know Roman says he doesn't care, but how can he not? Not when the nasty, rude, insulting things about him are put online and in print for anyone in the world to read. I know he says his feelings for me are greater than that, but I also know feelings can change. Especially when they are tried by public opinion and the restrictive rules that govern the world I live in.

Roman glances up at me and meets my gaze in the mirror. "Lizzie, don't worry about me. I don't care."

I sink down next to him on the bed, my stomach twisted into an anxious knot. "I know you don't," I say, placing my hand on his thigh, feeling his muscular leg against my palm through the fabric of his jeans. "But even putting the press aside, you're entering my world, with family rows and screaming matches. There are rules for everything when you are inside the palace. I... I don't want to lose you because of what comes along with being with me."

Roman places his hand over mine and lifts it to his lips, brushing them sweetly across my knuckles. "I'll tell you a million times over. I'm not worried about any of this. The media attention I can handle. Now, will I be nervous the first time I attend any kind of dinner with you? Of course. But I would be nervous meeting your parents if your name was Liz Smith, because you matter, and what they think matters. That's what will make me nervous."

I love this man so much.

"I had Amelia tip off the reporter I trust so she has the

exclusive. I told her to say that we walk in the park late in the afternoon. Vivian said she would send a photographer out and have the story ready to hit Sunday's paper."

"Lizzie, with this move, you're doing two things. You're taking the weapon away from your aunt, and you're showing that you don't take any crap from her, no matter what crown she wears on her head."

"I've always been so good at staying out of her lane," I say softly. "The second I got more attention than her, she turned on me."

"It was a matter of time. First it was Clementine, but now that she can't take her anger out on her, it's going to be you, until the next woman who comes along and threatens her."

I stand up. "Well, at least that won't be India. Antonia liked her because all India wanted to do was be Antonia two point oh. India would have stayed in her lane, following all directions Her Majesty barked at her."

Roman rises. He towers over me, and I have to say, I find his massive frame wonderfully sexy. "But if India was going to become the future Princess of Wales, Antonia would have turned on her as well. Can you imagine the attention that will come to the girl Xander does fall for? It will be *massive*. And because Antonia is threatened by the younger women around her, that girl will be the biggest threat of all."

"Well, whoever she is, Xander will protect her. He's the one who has the biggest sway over the queen."

Roman furrows his brow at this comment. "Have you told Xander what his mum has said to you?"

Crap.

I shake my head. "No, Roman, I want to prove to her

that I don't need to go running off to the men to fight my battles for me."

He exhales loudly. "Lizzie. Xander and Christian would want to know this. They would have your back. From the way you talk about Arthur, he would, too."

"I have no doubt of that, but I'm not going to be weak," I say defiantly.

"Why is that weak?" Roman persists.

I move away from him and begin to pace. "I want to prove to everyone that when I took on this role, which she said I was not needed for, I took on everything that came with it. Including her."

"I disagree with you. I think you could nip all this right now with one phone call."

"No."

Roman sighs heavily. "Is it weird that we've been together a week, and I already know by that tone that I won't be able to sway you?"

I stop walking and smile. "I love that you do know that."

And I love you, I add to myself.

"Come on, let's go act like we don't know people will be watching us," Roman says dryly.

I swipe a pair of sunglasses that are on my dresser and put them on. "I'm hoping the updo and sunglasses will help hide my identity so social media pics don't leak out tonight, but they might."

"I'll need to call my parents when we get back," Roman says. "They won't believe it, but Darcy can confirm I'm dating you. The pictures will come in handy, because my mum will have to believe I'm not making it up. That or we could FaceTime them, but Mum might pass out."

I giggle as I pull gloves out of my pockets and slip them on my hands while we head downstairs. "I think my parents are still in recovery over the fact that I have a boyfriend," I say.

I told my parents earlier, swinging by St. James's Palace after I left Roman at Cheltham House. To say they were shocked would be an understatement. Not so much by him being a gardener, as they knew I didn't like the guys I knew from my social circles, but by the fact that I had a man at all, since I never showed interest in one. I also gave a heads up to Cecelia, who was giddy over the fact that I had met someone.

I think about the next steps, which would be to meet each other's families. Christmas is coming soon, and if this were any other man, I'd be stressed about how to bring up Christmas, wondering if we should spend time together with them so soon, blah blah. But I'm not worried with Roman.

While I know it's not protocol for "boyfriends" to be invited to Arthur's Christmas celebration at Sandringham, I have a feeling if I asked him whether I could bring Roman —at least for Boxing Day—he would allow it.

Which is exactly what I intend to do.

And if Roman asks me to meet his family around Christmas, I would happily agree. His family sounds amazing. Normal. Happy. I can only imagine how much I'd enjoy spending time with them, as opposed to the drama show that I get on a regular basis from my parents or when the whole family gets together at Buckingham Palace or Sandringham.

Honestly, it's more dramatic than a final episode of *Is it Love?* on the telly.

We leave the cottage and stroll towards the park. I'm

nervous. But part of me is excited to be sharing Roman with the world.

"May I hold your hand?" he asks.

I respond by linking my gloved hand with his. I watch his profile, and his mouth curves up in happiness. My heart zips with joy. It feels good to be like this in public, for all the world to see.

We enter the park, and despite the gloomy day, people are milling about with pushchairs and dogs and taking walks.

"I told my official leaker," I say, smiling as I think of Amelia, "that we love to hang out at a specific place in the gardens."

"For our strategic photo op," Roman says.

I notice some people staring as we walk by. I glance at Roman, who seems completely unfazed by the attention. I lead him to the spot I had picked, where I know Vivian will have her photographer situated.

As we approach the Italian Gardens, I stop. I take off my glasses and drop them inside the pocket of my coat. "This is where I told them we'd be, at the ornamental water gardens."

"Why did you pick this spot?" Roman asks, his voice laced with curiosity.

I shift my gaze out to the pools of water and fountains that lay before us. "Legend has it," I say slowly, "that this was created by Prince Albert for Queen Victoria. He was quite into gardening, like someone else I know."

I feel Roman's eyes on my face. I turn to face him, and his expression is one of tenderness. "You picked this spot for me," he says quietly.

"I did," I tell him, reaching for both his hands and squeezing them in mine. "It seemed perfect for you."

"Perfect for *us*," Roman corrects, staring deeply into my eyes. "For the start of a love story. Not for a king and queen, but for a gardener and his princess."

I feel lightheaded from his words, absolutely dizzy with happiness. "Yes," I whisper.

Roman is silent for a moment, then lets go of my hands so he can frame my face with his. "May I kiss you? Or is that too much for a princess to do in public?" he whispers as he holds my face.

Happy tears prick my eyes. "I'm a modern princess. You may kiss me."

Roman lowers his head and brushes his lips against mine in a gentle kiss.

When he raises his head, still holding me, gazing at me with adoration, my heart swells with joy. I know pictures were taken from a distance. The world is about to know that I have given my heart to Roman.

But in this moment, it's not a staged kiss. The emotions here are real. I picked this spot for him, and it is significant.

As he draws me into his chest, hugging me, I can't think of a better place in the world than to be here, with this man, in this spot, letting the world know how we feel.

Right now, it doesn't feel like a preemptive strike.

No. It's not.

It's the beginning of a love story, I think happily. *One that I know will end with my happily ever after.*

And with that thought in my head, I decide to live in this moment.

With the man I love.

CHAPTER 25

PRINCESS IN LOVE

I listen to the rhythmic beating of Roman's heart, his chest rising and falling as I lie cuddled against him. One hand is wrapped around me, holding me to him. His body radiates heat, keeping me warm early this morning.

Normally on a Sunday, I'd be content to sleep against him, staying in his arms as long as I could, but I'm dying to grab my phone and bring up the online Sunday edition of *The London News* and see what Vivian wrote about me and Roman. Amelia provided all the facts, which, in this case, means the truth—and I desperately want to read it.

The room is still dark, so if I do get my phone, the light will wake Roman up. I've discovered he's a light sleeper, and he loves the fact that I have blackout curtains in my room. However, I do have a nightlight that I keep on in case I have to get up. That doesn't seem to bother him, though.

Hmm. If I move, I'll have to do so gently, because that wakes him up, too.

Don't wake him up, I tell myself. *He works so hard, and he deserves to sleep.*

I lie still and listen to his heart, grateful that I am in his arms and intimate enough to have my ear pressed against it. How is it, with Roman, everything has meaning? How is my view of life so different? I lightly trace a heart over his chest with my index finger, thinking of the love I feel for him. I value his steadiness, and his unflinching desire to stand by my side, where other men in his position would have walked away. He's brave and fearless, and while I've always thought of myself that way, he makes me feel even more so.

I love you so much, I think, as I absently trace heart patterns on his chest. *I can never love you enough for what you are willing to do for me and for what you are giving up to be with me.*

"Going to go for four hearts?" Roman asks, scaring me to death.

I gasp and pop right up, my own heart racing inside my chest. He laughs, that deep sound reverberating against me, and I tingle with happiness.

"Did I wake you?" I ask, guilt for doing so making me feel awful.

Roman grins and slides his hand up and down my bare arm, sending goosebumps sweeping over my skin. "No. I've been waiting for you to get up so we can check the newspaper. But if you fancy drawing more hearts on my chest, I can wait."

Embarrassment takes over. "No, but are you ready for this? To see your name in print and things written about you?"

A thoughtful expression passes over his face, barely illuminated from the nightlight. "I admit it's weird. From nobody knowing who I am to everyone knowing I exist because of one article."

"I know," I say, biting my lower lip. "And this article will be favourable. A lot will be hateful. And even on the positive ones, there will be horrible comments from people."

"Hey." Roman sits up. He slides his hand underneath my hair and cradles the back of my head in his hand. "I don't care. I'm not going to read those. What do I care what some troll behind a keyboard says? I care about what our friends and families think. But even more than that," he says, his voice growing more impassioned, "I care most of all about what you think, Lizzie. You are the most important person in my life."

My heart stops. I realise how much he loves me with that confession.

I'm his person.

"I feel the same way about you," I say, caressing his face with my palm.

"So are we ready to read it?"

"We are."

Roman reaches over and gets his phone off the bedside table. My heart goes from still to racing as he begins swiping things on his screen. I watch his face as he stops. He begins to read, and now my heart is thundering as I try to see what his reaction is.

The brow furrows. Eyes widen.

"Is it good?" I ask, impatient to know how this is impacting him.

Then I see the sight that makes me ridiculously happy.

Roman's mouth curves up.

"Tell me!" I shout.

He laughs. "Apparently, you love me."

He hands me his phone. I can't breathe. I gather my courage and glance down at the screen:

LOVE BLOOMS FOR PRINCESS ELIZABETH

The working royal finds love in a familiar place — the same estate where Clementine Jones worked!

Then there's a picture of Roman kissing me in the Italian Gardens.

My heart is giddy with joy upon seeing that picture. It captured a moment that is readable even to anyone who doesn't know us.

We love each other.

"Go on. Read about how impossibly good in bed I am," Roman teases. "And fit."

I giggle. "That will be in *Dishing Weekly* in a few hours, along with hideous gardening references."

He chuckles and begins stroking my hair as I read:

Princess Elizabeth has found the man of her dreams — at the same place where Clementine Jones, the fiancée of Prince Christian — used to work!

A close friend of Princess Elizabeth revealed details of the romance after Princess Elizabeth strolled in public with Roman Lawler, a gardener at Cheltham House in London, on Saturday afternoon in the Italian Gardens at Kensington Palace.

"They met through Clementine and Prince Christian last summer," the source told The London News exclusively. "But the romance didn't take off until they re-connected this month."

This is the first time any man has been seen in public with the princess, which, according to her confidant, shows how real this romance is to the princess.

Lawler, 25, attended The University of Glasgow in Scotland, where he earned his degree in horticulture. The friend of the princess says while the match doesn't seem likely on paper, it makes sense to everyone who knows the couple.

"He's a grounded, even-keeled soul," the friend tells The

London News. "*Roman makes Liz incredibly happy. I always knew she'd fall for someone who spoke to her heart, and Roman does.*"

I stop reading and hand Roman back his phone. "It's all true," I say, adoration swelling within me. "I told Amelia you were the man I never thought I'd find."

He is quiet. "There's one thing missing from this article."

"What's that?"

"How I feel about you."

My heart does a flip-flop inside my chest.

"Tell me what the article would have said if your source had spoken to Vivian."

"Well, that would have been Darcy, and he would have cocked it all up."

We both laugh at that.

"But," Roman says, his fingertips gliding across my cheekbone, "I would have said you were a woman with a quick mind and a passionate heart. And that I adore you."

His mouth finds mine, parting my lips and slipping his tongue inside in a deep, slow, sensual kiss. He draws me closer to him, so my bare breasts are pressing against his chest. Roman's arm wraps around my back, holding me close as his tongue continues to tangle with mine.

I move my hand over his back, feeling all the powerful muscles, gloriously created from the physical labour he does. He eases me back on the bed, his body covering mine, and I shiver in anticipation as the weight of him falls on top of me.

Roman slides a hand down to my breast, and his lips find my neck, his tongue now sweeping over my skin and sending my pulse skyrocketing. He reclaims my mouth, kissing me, tasting me, teasing me. I respond in kind, yearning for more of him. His skin is hot to the touch. He moans against my mouth.

"I lied to you yesterday," he whispers against my lips as he kisses me again. "I already love you, Lizzie. I love you."

I gasp against his mouth from his confession. Roman pushes himself up so he can gaze down at me, trying to gauge my reaction in the darkness.

"Lizzie, please don't feel like you have to say anything. You don't have to say it back," he pleads with urgency. "I was about to make love to you, and as I'm kissing you and touching you, I *had* to say it. I had to be honest. I won't say it again until you say the words back. No matter how long it takes for you to get there."

I look up at the man I love, my heart never so full as it is in this intimate moment between us.

"I love you, too," I whisper. "I love you with all my heart, Roman. I have from our first date. You are mine. You have my heart."

"And you have mine."

He claims my mouth again with his. As we kiss, tenderly and sweetly, I know, without a doubt, this love is strong.

It can withstand anything.

Including the monarchy.

With my heart the fullest it's ever been, I make love to the man who is my everything.

My person.

And he always will be.

I nervously walk down the corridor towards Arthur's office on Monday morning. After the article hit, I was called by his private secretary to a meeting as soon as possible. Which turned out to be breakfast at eight o'clock sharp, before I have my own meetings with Cecelia to review my diary and plan outfits for my functions this week.

I got ready as soon as Roman left for work this morning. He texted me when he arrived at Cheltham House, gleefully saying the paparazzi were mounted at the car park and the entrance, and he zipped right past them all on his motorcycle — completely unnoticed.

Of course, more articles have come out this morning with some outrageous headlines. Like **LIZZIE GETS HER HANDS DIRTY WITH GARDENER ROMANCE** and **GARDENER PLUCKS THE ULTIMATE ENGLISH ROSE.** Cringeworthy ones. Articles that I thought would make Roman doubt this romance but, instead, made him laugh deeply.

I smile. He has continued to surprise me with his response. When I first met him, I thought he would hate this. But he's taken it well so far.

So far.

As soon as the doubt creeps in, I make a furious effort to bat it away. Roman loves me. He will find a way to deal with this life long after the articles aren't humorous anymore.

Antonia has remained silent. Probably furious that I'm flying in the face of her rules of finding an appropriate man to date, lowering the monarchy by dating a mere gardener, and getting heaps of publicity, which she is horrified by. But is she horrified about what is being said? Or by the fact that people are more interested in my love life than her being queen? I have no clue which answer might be right.

I continue down the familiar hall towards Arthur's private suite, my stomach twisting with anxiety. I'm nervous. Is he upset with me for being so open with my affection for Roman? He is supportive of Christian being openly affectionate with Clementine in public. Of course, Christian hasn't been spotted kissing her in public, either. Did I cross a line? Was that too much for a royal to do?

I think about this as I walk through the palace. But I wasn't working when I kissed Roman. A sense of righteousness surges through me. I won't back down from this. If I'm going to help keep this monarchy relevant, that means being true to myself when I'm not working.

Including sharing sweet kisses with the man I love and showing the world I have a man who respects and values me. I think that's an important lesson in itself, too.

I reach his doors and find them open, with Arthur sitting at a table, reading his mobile. I smile. Talk about a modern king. He reads the news on his phone, preferring it to a stack of newspapers.

He glances up and rises. "Good morning, Elizabeth."

I dip into a curtsy. "Arthur."

He moves around the table and pulls out my chair for me. I sink into it, and he resumes his place at the table. "Thank you for agreeing to this meeting today," he says.

"Of course," I reply.

I study my uncle, with his vivid blue eyes and thick blonde hair, thinking of how strikingly handsome he is.

"Poached eggs on avocado toast with a cup of Earl Grey?" Arthur asks.

"How do you remember these details?" I ask, laughing.

"Makes my job easier, having an excellent memory. You know how it is. The more you can remember, the easier every function is."

He picks up his phone and sends a text. I know it's to the kitchen, as Arthur prefers texting his food requests, much to Antonia and my grandmother's horror. I fold my hands in my lap, but instead of staying still, I twist the rings on my fingers in anxiousness.

"I'm sure you know why I called you here today," he says, pausing to take a sip of his coffee.

I gulp. "Because of the papers."

"Yes."

Arthur traces his finger absently around the rim of his china cup. "Tell me about him. He must be incredible if you've decided to go public with him."

I furrow my brow. He doesn't sound angry.

"I don't know how you feel about showing affection in public, Arthur, but I love this man. I've never been in love before, but when I'm with Roman, he makes me feel like I can take on the world. I want people to know I love him. I want to be like any other young woman in love, and to me, if that means giving and receiving affection in public, I will do so." I exhale after my rambling speech.

"You have always been headstrong when it comes to doing the right thing," he says with a grin.

"Excuse me?"

"You are willful, but it suits you well. When you feel passionately about something, it leads you to make the best choice."

I exhale with relief. "Thank you."

"Now your cousin, on the other hand, is determined in the wrong ways. I'm worried about Xander now that he's leaving the army. The army kept him structured and gave him purpose. Now he's got to figure out how to be a king in waiting, and that is a tough hand of cards to be dealt. He can't do what he wants, and in his role as the Prince of Wales, he will be, god willing, waiting a long time to ascend to the throne."

I wonder where Arthur is going with this.

"His first stumble was this thing with India," he continues.

"You saw it, too?" I ask, shocked.

Arthur gives me a sad smile. "I know my son. He doesn't need a 'yes' woman. He needs a partner who will challenge him and who will be strong in her sense of self. India isn't that woman. He was doing the easy thing by selecting her. The last thing I want is to see history repeat itself, so you can imagine my relief when he told me he broke up with her yesterday."

My mouth drops.

"I feel I can tell you these truths in confidence," Arthur says slowly. "You are ready to help us be the monarchy of the future, and that means not selecting the partner right for this antiquated world, but the partner right for you. Which is why I want you to know that I fully support this romance of yours."

My heart leaps. Arthur understands.

He's going to support me and Roman.

But his statement about history repeating itself is one I need to know the answer to.

"What do you mean by history repeating itself?" I ask quietly. "Are you talking about my parents?"

Arthur's eyes widen. "No, no, I was talking about me."

Now I'm shocked. This is an extremely personal conversation we're entering into.

"I did love Antonia once," he admits quietly. "But we were introduced for our suitability, not because people thought we'd be good together romantically. We were encouraged to be together because our families wanted it. The public wanted it.

"Over time, I convinced myself I was in love with her

because she was driven and smart and she ticked the boxes. Now I can see they weren't the right boxes. While I did love her, it wasn't the right love. I can see that so clearly now. I think it was the same for her. We fell out of that love with each other only a few years after we married."

My heart slams into reverse. "You fell out of love with her so soon?" I ask, the cold fear creeping through every inch of me as my own fear is brought out as a truth.

"It was both our faults," Arthur explains. "I was away in the navy, and she was abandoned here, at this palace, with my mother and father, who were very much in the old way of thinking. Nobody helped her adjust. I'll give her credit; she found her own path. But when I came home, we were different people. We grew apart. While I was ready to come home and pick up where I left things, she had already found her role. The attention she craved was no longer from me, but from the public. Which is why she is so fiercely protective of her position.

"If this man suits you, if you think you could love him, you are going to have huge challenges ahead of you," Arthur continues. He pauses to take another sip of his coffee. "It won't be easy. He will be frustrated, but remember, it's not at you, but the attention. Unlike Clementine and the woman who will marry Xander, Roman won't have to give up his career. I don't think the attention will be on him for long, not like the way it will be on Clementine and whoever Xander chooses for a wife."

I nod, grateful Roman won't have to give up his job.

"I worry about the fame side of being with me. About the rules. Roman is used to being his own man. I hate knowing what will be said about him, and how his life will be examined because he chose to be with me."

"You will help him through that, Elizabeth," Arthur says.

The door opens, and staff enter with cloche plates. Arthur is served porridge and fruit, while I'm presented with avocado toast.

"What if I can't?" I admit as soon as he dismisses the staff.

"If he loves you, he will find a way. I know your cousins will help him, and Clementine is the best of all as far as understanding how he feels."

"Clementine has been such a gift to all of us," I say.

Now Arthur beams. "She is. I adore her."

We chat a bit longer about Christian and Clementine before he clears his throat. "You do know there will be people in this palace who think you are lowering the mystique of the monarchy by dating a gardener," he says.

My body goes cold again. "Yes," I say, understanding that he is speaking of Antonia's camp.

"If anyone gives you problems, I want you to tell me. That includes your grandmother as well as your aunt. I know your grandmother loves you, but she believes in a traditional relationship, meaning Roman needs a title in front of his name or he's nothing."

"I know," I say, my heart hurting at the thought of her discrediting Roman before she's even met him.

"Don't worry about that. She'll get over it. Now, in regards to your aunt, if she does anything to make you uncomfortable, or to embarrass you, I want you to come to me immediately."

My face burns. I would sooner die than run to Arthur with a report of how Antonia is trying to force me back to being a dutiful princess who will do what she asks.

"I mean it. I'm not speaking to you as your uncle, but as your boss."

I manage a small smile. "You are a good man, Arthur."

"So I've been told," he says, his blue eyes twinkling at me.

We continue to talk about the week ahead and my visit to Leeds, where I'll be opening a library and attending a conference on children's nutrition. I'll also be hosting a tea at St. James's Palace for early childhood educators. I ask him about his schedule, and as we talk, I see his genuine excitement over the events where he is hands-on with the public. I can't help but wish he would divorce Antonia, so they could each live a life true to themselves. Most of all, so Arthur could find the happiness he deserves.

But someone else will have to kick down that door before he'd do that. Arthur is moving the monarchy forward, but I don't see him filing for divorce and causing that kind of scandal. My head and my heart know the monarchy would overcome that. I believe, with all my heart, that it would show him as a mortal man. But he's worked so hard to be the loving father, the king of the people; he would never want to disappoint the public with a divorce.

It's the same reason my parents are staying together.

Out of duty.

I feel the heaviness come crashing over me, of four people who chose each other and chose wrongly. Or were in love and fell out of it. It happens all the time.

I simply can't imagine it happening with me and Roman.

I push the thought away. I can't let that dominate my mind, or I'll go mad.

Then something else comes to mind.

"Arthur, I do have one thing I'd like to ask of you," I say.

"Fire away," he replies.

"I'd like to have an Instagram account or Connectivity Story Share. It's silly to think I can't have one. It's a growing platform that can keep me connected with not only younger people but with people of the world. I could share my events, little inside pics of my life with my friends, and I'd like to show Roman, as the kind of partner people should believe they are worthy enough to have."

Arthur takes in my words and is silent for a few moments. "I think it's a good idea. You are a wonderful role model, Elizabeth. You understand how to make personal connections in a way that will make you not only relatable but shows your true self. I approve on one condition."

I nod.

"I think you need to get that picture from *The London News* and make it your first post. Let true love reign," he says, winking at me.

I laugh, and he does, too.

There is no doubt what my first picture will be on Connectivity Story Share.

Let true love reign indeed, I think happily.

CHAPTER 26

My mind is racing as I walk with Roman in Shepherd's Bush. Another week and a half has flown by, and now Christmas is coming quickly.

I've survived days of ridiculousness in the press, with such lovely headlines as:

SACKED! KING ARTHUR VOWS TO TERMINATE JEALOUS LIZ TO PROTECT CLEMMIE

IN LOVE WITH THE HELP

SEXY GARDENER ON CALL FOR PRINCESS LIZ!

WHO IS ROMAN LAWLER? Meet Princess Elizabeth's new love!

A COMMONER TREE TRIMMER FOR HER ROYAL HIGHNESS

ROYAL WAR: JEALOUS LIZZIE TORMENTS POOR CLEMMIE

ROYAL SPENDER? Princess Elizabeth racks up massive expenses on new clothing that the public is footing the bill for.

NOT IN LOVE Sources close to the Princess claim Liz is dating a London gardener to get attention.

DO WE NEED MORE WORKING ROYALS? If buying new clothing and running around with her boyfriend is all she does, let Princess Elizabeth get a REAL JOB.

I glance at Roman as we walk. He's oblivious to my thoughts, content to be wrapped up in his own as we head down the path. I only hope he's not thinking of all the things said about him last week.

He assured me he didn't care. He went about his life, even while photographers surrounded Cheltham House and waited outside his flat to get a picture of him. Not once has he complained. In the pictures snapped of him, he's shielding his eyes from the glare of flashbulbs and is expressionless as he walks, even as the paparazzi screamed insults at him to get a reaction. In fact, he's only voiced concern about me, as sources from Antonia's camp have leaked all kinds of hideous things, resulting in those awful headlines and even worse stories.

I study his profile, remembering when I caught him going through his phone while he was waiting for me to come to bed. He stopped scrolling, began to read, and then his expression completely changed. His face paled. I know his expressions like I know my own. Roman read something that upset him. I asked him about it, but he said it was "rubbish" and put his phone aside.

I know it was something bad, but he refused to tell me. He remained quiet and within his head the rest of the night. It killed me knowing I was doing this to him. If he were with anyone else, there would be no embarrassing stories about him in the press. He wouldn't have photographers stalking him. He wouldn't have trolls on social media mocking him.

Whenever I relive this moment, I wonder how many more he's had in private. Roman says he doesn't care, and most of the time, I believe him. But I know from experience, some articles do hurt. They do get under your skin, even if it's incredibly thick.

My chest aches as I stare at him. How many moments will it take before he decides I'm not worth living the rest of his life this way? When will he begin to resent the goldfish bowl I've put him into?

"What are you thinking?"

I blink. Roman must have felt my gaze on his profile.

"I'm nervous," I say.

"You have nothing to be nervous about. My family are going to love you," he reassures me.

I shift my attention to the present. Because I'm going to be at Sandringham with the whole family for Christmas Eve and Christmas Day, we've decided to split our family time. I'm having dinner tonight with Roman's entire family, and Friday night, he is invited to Arthur's friends and family pre-Christmas dinner at Buckingham Palace. We'll spend Christmas apart, but Roman is going to come up to Sandringham for Boxing Day on the 26th.

"I'm actually more nervous than you about this," he continues.

I blink. "Why?"

Roman sighs. "To me, you're Liz. You've become that to Darcy, too. But to them — especially my mum and my aunt — you're royalty. My mum has changed the menu three times already, worried about what to serve a princess. I'm worried they'll make you uncomfortable by being star-struck. In my head, all I see is my mum and my aunt staring at you like you are an apparition, my uncle saying he doesn't understand the fascination with the monarchy, my father saying everything has gone to pot with society, and Darcy trying to wind me up about you by quoting Jane Austen love lines."

I feel a lightness return to my soul. Roman has no idea I find all these things endearing rather than something that can make me run away.

"They sound lovely," I say. "I'm excited to meet them."

"I've already warned them that the palace prohibits you from taking selfies."

Now I can't help but laugh. "I would have done it."

"I don't trust my mum and my aunt to not post it on Connectivity or Facebook. You're too good not to share. Which I understand."

I reach over and put my hand on his arm. "It's going to be wonderful."

I only wish I could say the same kind of thing about my family dinner that Roman will be joining on Friday. He comes from such a normal, grounded world. The idea of bringing him into mine is terrifying. That will be the first time he will meet my parents, and it will be in a palace, with cocktails, formal attire, and menu cards in French. With the exception of himself and Clementine, everyone is a family member or insider to the royal circle and all of its tightly held secrets and illusions.

The light in me is extinguished as I picture Roman being in BP, not only grabbling with all of that, which is imposing enough, but with the vipers on Antonia's side judging him, being rude and cold, and doing everything in their power to make him feel awkward.

I think of all the things that can go wrong, and a wave of sickness washes over me. What will Roman think of all that? Will he wonder if I'm worth putting up with the rules of being a York and the people that come with it?

He slows in front of a house where the door is wrapped like a present, with a huge red bow and ribbon on it. "This is where Mum and Dad live," he says. "Easy to find because of the tacky door."

"I see," I say, smiling.

"I think pilots on approach to Heathrow can see it," Roman quips.

I laugh. "It's cute."

"It's awful."

He leads me down the path to the decorated door, and nerves kick in. I'm carrying the box of mince pies I picked up from The Biscuit Cutter earlier today as my gift for his parents, and I grip it a little tighter as we get closer.

As we reach the doorstep, Roman turns towards me. "I hope they don't freak you out," he says, his eyes imploring me to understand. "My parents are good people, but my mum and my aunt are so excited to meet you that they might be... overwhelming."

"I promise, I can handle it," I reassure him.

Roman rakes a hand through his hair. "Right."

"Right!" I cry with enthusiasm.

His mouth curves up a bit, and he presses the doorbell.

The door swings open, and I'm greeted by a woman in her early fifties, with blonde hair and blue eyes, wearing the biggest smile on her face and a Christmas jumper with a blinking light-up fireplace on it.

"MUM!" Roman gasps. "What are you wearing? It's not Christmas Eve!"

It's all I can do not to laugh. The jumper is so bad, it's brilliant.

His mother immediately dips into a deep curtsy, ignoring Roman's horror, and then rises to greet me. "I can't believe you're here, Your Royal Highness. In my home! It's truly an honour, and while I know it's humble, I hope you will be happy to celebrate with us!" she says in a rush.

She steps aside to let us in. "Please, please, I insist you call me Liz. No curtsy needed. It is my pleasure to be here."

"Christmas Eve is not for a few days. What are you talking about, 'celebrate with us?'" Roman says, fixated on what is happening here.

He has told me that, like with my family, Christmas Eve is the night everyone gathers and opens presents.

"Roman, this is the first time you've brought a woman home in ages. Shouldn't we celebrate together?" she says.

I peek into the living room, where everyone is staring at me. Well, except for Darcy, who is grinning as if he's enjoying watching Roman squirm.

"I'm Eden, by the way," his mum says. "Oh, goodness, I can't believe you are dating Roman! I could squeal with joy. You are the princess I've always loved best!"

"I think you *are* squealing," a man says, rising to greet me. He is wearing the exact same fireplace jumper as Roman's mum, the LED lights on the fire blinking away. He's tall, with thick, dark hair that is beginning to grey, and as he comes nearer, the same hazel eyes I saw in Clive shine back at me. "Hello, Liz, I'm Thomas, Roman's father."

"It's an honour to meet both of you," I say.

"It's good to have you celebrate with us," he says warmly.

"Did anyone think to tell me we were doing our Christmas Eve celebrations tonight?" Roman asks.

"Well, I didn't know you would be seeing Liz," Eden says, "so I didn't have the chance to order her a matching jumper, and I didn't want her to feel weird being the only one without one. Not that a princess would wear a Christmas jumper, you know."

"Need a drink yet, Roman?" Darcy calls out from his seat in the living room.

"Maybe five," he replies.

Darcy snickers. Roman looks like he wants the floorboards to swallow him up.

"Oh, Roman, you know your mum loves Christmas more than anything," another woman says, coming up to me. "Hello, Princess Elizabeth, I'm Lisa, Roman's aunt." Then she squeals, her hands flying to her mouth. "I swear I'm dreaming this. Roman and a princess, whoever could have foreseen this? I waited for your mum and dad to come out of the Lindo Wing with you. This is so exciting! Our Roman! You picked our Roman!"

I glance at Roman, who has a deep flush climbing up his neck. "I am the lucky one," I say, smiling. "Roman is an incredible man, who was obviously raised well by amazing parents."

"I'm Clark," Roman's uncle says. I notice he and Lisa are in different Christmas jumpers. Lisa's has a pug in a Santa outfit on it, and Clark's has a Nordic pattern with trees and reindeer.

"Pleasure to meet you," I say.

"Here, here, I've forgotten to take your coat, oh my goodness," Roman's mother says, flustered. "I'm in a kerfuffle right now!"

"I've got it, Mum," Roman says.

"Oh, first, these are for you," I say, extending the box to Eden. "Mince pies from my favourite bakery."

His mother's eyes light up. "Mince pies are my favourite. Did Roman tell you?"

I smile. "He might have."

"Oh, this is wonderful, wonderful," she says. "Let me put these straight in the kitchen, and I'll check on the turkey."

Roman helps me out of my coat and then removes his. His father takes them, along with my bag, and whisks them away to another room. I feel Roman's hand find the small of my back, guiding me into the living room. It's small but cosy. There's a Christmas tree in front of the window, filled with multi-coloured fairy lights and all kinds of decorations. There is a fire in the fireplace, and Christmas bunting strung across the mantle. I see the table is set in the adjacent dining room, with Christmas crackers on every place setting. He leads me to the sofa, so I take a seat next to Darcy, and Roman sits on the other side of me.

"Hello, Liz," Darcy says, smiling at me. "Lovely to see you."

"Hi, Darcy, how are you?" I ask. "Glad your exams are over?"

I've rarely seen Darcy, as he's been studying the past couple of weeks.

"I'm excited to not be in a book or in a library," he says, shoving back a lock of wavy hair that has fallen over his brow.

"Where's Grandfather?" Roman asks, glancing around.

"He'll be here for Christmas pudding," Darcy says. "He said he had something to do when I called him, though I don't know what he could be doing on a Wednesday night, but said he would make it for pudding."

I don't look at Roman. I know for a fact Clive and Jillian had a date set up long before this dinner was on the calendar. Those two have taken to each other as fast as Roman and I have, and I've never seen Jillian glow like she has since she started dating Clive.

"What would you two like to drink?" Clark asks, smiling at us. "Wine?"

"Ask Liz if she would like wassail!" Roman's mum calls out from the kitchen.

Wassail? What is wassail? I rack my brain for an answer, but I honestly have no idea.

"What is *that?*" Roman asks, a crease forming in his brow.

Roman's mum pops her head in the doorway. "Liz, I have a cookbook based on royal family Christmas traditions, and the royals drank wassail at Christmas during the Tudor period."

Oh. Good to know.

"Are we having a beheading after pudding, too?" Darcy quips. "If we are adding Tudor traditions and all?"

"Darcy! You are speaking about her history!" Lisa chides. She turns and gives me an apologetic look.

Ah, yes, dear old Henry VIII. While we do share the "belonging to the royal family" bit, luckily, I do not share the urge to behead people.

"I would love to try the wassail," I say, wanting to please Eden.

"Splendid," she says, clasping her hands together. She

stares at me from the doorway, as if I'm a mirage, before she blinks and scurries back into the kitchen. "Thomas! Please come here and bring Liz a wassail!"

"A what?" he yells from the other side of the house.

"Wassail! Don't you remember the song?"

"No," he shouts back.

Roman groans. Darcy laughs. Lisa and Clark are staring at me.

"Why don't you bring us a bottle?" Darcy says. "Roman here looks like he might need it."

"A bottle it is!" his uncle cries cheerfully.

"I'll help," Lisa says, and they both scurry from the room.

"I'm so sorry," Roman whispers.

I put my hand on his knee. "It's okay. Thankfully, the Tudor period is way back in the history of the monarchy," I tease.

"Roman, if she's going through that cookbook, you don't think she'll throw down a boar's head on the table, do you?" Darcy asks.

"I hope not," he groans.

"Well, that would top dinner at home," I tease. "We have turkey."

My eyes wander around the room, and they settle on the bookshelves, which contain rows upon rows of books about my family. Picture books of Arthur and Antonia's wedding. Of my parents' wedding. A book of Arthur's coronation. Biographies, including one about Xander that is so full of mistruths, we quote it all the time in our group chat to crack ourselves up.

It's surreal.

Then my eyes land on a spine that says: *Princess Elizabeth: Growing up Royal.*

Roman grew up in a home with this book about me on the family bookshelf.

Whoa.

"Roman? Can you come here for a moment?" his mum calls out, interrupting my thoughts.

"I'll be right back," he says, leaning over and brushing his lips against my cheek.

As soon as he's gone, Darcy shifts his attention to me. "Is our family freaking you out?" he asks, concern in his voice.

I turn to him. "No. I understand their reaction. I only hope they grow to like me for me. Because I love Roman, and because they think we are good together. I hope they will like me for those reasons above all else."

A confused expression passes over Darcy's face. "Why wouldn't they love you for being Liz? You are incredible, and you don't need the title for them to see that. Right now, they are awestruck. That will pass soon enough. But what you've done to change Roman? They already see that."

"What do you mean?" I ask.

"We all thought a part of Roman died when Felicity broke his heart," Darcy says quietly, referring to Roman's first love. "It went on for years. I've never seen anyone shut down the way he did. It was like one woman broke him, and he put himself in a self-imposed exile. Nobody was worth taking that risk for. Until he met you."

My heart quickens.

"Liz, we've all talked about the change in him. Roman loves you. For him to even date you was a huge deal. For him to bring you here, to meet his mum and dad, means he loves you."

I blink back tears.

"I know Roman as much as I know myself," Darcy

continues. "I've seen him with Felicity, and I've seen him with you. He loved Felicity, don't get me wrong, but his feelings for you are more intense. When he talks about you, it's with a deep respect for the things you do to help people. How you are passionate and assertive in pursuing issues you believe in. How you face all these challenges that have been put upon you since birth, and you are okay with that because you know the good you can do. He not only loves you, he *admires* you."

I clear my throat, hoping I'll be able to speak.

"I love him," I confide to Darcy. "I know Felicity let him go, but I never intend to."

"So you know after only a few weeks?" he challenges.

"I do."

Now Darcy flashes me a huge smile, and I once again see the resemblance to Roman when he does.

"Brilliant. Will you introduce me to some available women at your wedding?"

I flick him on the arm. "I doubt you will need my help."

"Roman has that fit gardener thing going on. All I have is architecture. Girls don't find that as exciting."

"Darcy. This conversation tells me you love your cousin. You have depth, like he does. There's a romantic soul in you. Plus, you know Jane Austen. You should have women banging down the door to your flat."

"As you have seen, you are sadly mistaken about that," he says. "The only woman banging down the door for me is the one who is delivering my pizza."

I burst out laughing, and Darcy does, too.

Roman reenters the room with a mug in his hand that has a picture of Antonia plastered on it. "What's so funny?" he asks. He hands me the mug. "Wassail. Drink at your own risk, because Mum went extra heavy on the spices. I picked this mug for you because it would be awkward for me to see you drinking out of a mug with your own face on it."

I look at the mug. Antonia smiles creepily back.

I add this to the list of surreal moments of the night.

"Did you find an animal head in the kitchen?" Darcy jokes.

Roman sits down next to me, draping his arm around my shoulders. "No. Just one dry turkey, per Christmas tradition."

"Are there stuffing balls?" Darcy asks.

"Indeed."

"Excellent."

I take a sip of wassail and give thanks that that tradition has died, as the clove is about to choke me. Soon, wine is brought in, and we're all drinking and laughing. Lisa asks me a million questions about my family, gushing about how much she loves my mum and dad and wanting to know if the papers were right about Xander and India breaking up. I answer her questions carefully, not tipping my hand at all to any behind-the-scenes drama or indicating that I'm glad Xander has finished with India. I've found that most of the time, when people say they will keep a secret, they can't. It never hurts to be safe.

"Time to eat," Thomas says, carrying in a carved-up turkey on a platter.

"Mum, we can't all sit around this table," Roman says as we enter the dining area. "It seats four, not seven."

"I'll eat in the living room," Darcy says.

"Nonsense, we'll all gather round, nice and cosy!" Eden declares.

"Cosy? We'll be in each other's laps," Thomas says.

I bite my tongue to keep from laughing.

"Roman, Darcy, come on, grab more chairs," Eden says, ignoring the fact that we'll be more crowded at this table than walking on Oxford Street on Christmas Eve for last-minute shopping.

Nevertheless, we all squeeze in, shoulder to shoulder, to eat.

"Crackers first," Eden says excitedly.

I pick up the shiny, wrapped cracker on my plate, one imprinted with Father Christmas, and turn to Roman, who takes the other end. We both tug and it snaps, followed by a pop. Others around the table do the same, and after I help Roman open his, I sift through the contents of mine. I have my joke, of course, my paper crown, and a bright pink plastic ring, which I immediately slip on.

I extend my hand to Roman. "It's gorgeous," I say, laughing.

"I got a paperclip," he says, showing me his.

"Now, everyone, paper hats on," Eden says excitedly.

"Mum, really?" Roman groans.

"Why not? We do it every year," Lisa chimes in.

I pick mine up, open it, and place it on my head, and I watch as Roman struggles to get the hat to fit his head.

"They never fit," he declares as it sits lopsided atop his dark brown locks.

"It's your massive head," Darcy chimes in.

I giggle. "I'll add this to my vault of tiaras," I tease Roman.

"I thought you wouldn't wear a tiara until you got married," Eden says.

"That is true," I say, nodding. "The first tiara I'll wear is on my wedding day."

"Oh, and you get to pick out of the king's collection!" Lisa says excitedly.

"Yes," I say. "But Roman thinks I have a vault of jewellery at home, which I don't, so I like to tease him about it."

"Now everyone, read your joke!" Eden commands.

I get to go first, and we all read our incredibly bad jokes, groaning often in response. Then the conversation carries on as food is passed around the table. There's turkey, of course, and roast potatoes and veg, and the stuffing balls Darcy asked about earlier.

Darcy takes a stuffing ball for himself, then passes the platter to Roman. "Make sure you give Liz one of these. Liz, these are the best part of the meal."

Roman takes two for himself and turns to me. "Would you like one ball or two?"

Darcy roars with laughter. Roman realises how that sounded, and within a second, his neck is turning red.

I burst out laughing, and Roman curses under his breath.

"What will it be, Liz? Roman is offering you one ball or two," Darcy says to wind him up further.

"Shut up, Darcy," he snaps, his neck now the colour of a double-decker bus.

"Darcy Lawler! Stop talking about Roman's balls at the table!" Lisa snaps.

"He's not talking about my balls!" Roman insists.

"I can't believe you. We have royalty here. Can we not have a normal conversation that doesn't revolve around testicles?" Eden cries, her own face now turning pink in mortification.

"This is a normal conversation for us," Thomas says, winking at me.

"Talking about testicles?" Darcy says, grinning. "You're

right, usually we slide that in right after the weather and before the latest episode of *Strictly Come Dancing.*"

"We do not talk about balls!" Lisa insists.

"Stuffing balls. We're talking about stuffing, not *testicles,*" Eden declares.

Roman pulls his lopsided crown down over his eyes. "I can't even look at you, Liz," he mumbles.

I reach over and push his crown back up on his head. "No, no changes for me, I love this. I'll take two of your balls," I say, playing along.

Now the whole table erupts into laughter, and in that moment, I know I've kicked down a huge chunk of the wall in them seeing me as Liz.

Dinner progresses, and I was right. The questions shift to getting to know more about me, and not me as a royal. They share stories about themselves and Roman, and the evening is fun and full of laughs.

As promised, Clive shows up in time for dessert, cheerful and excited to see everyone. As soon as he spots me, his face lights up, and he extends his hand to me. "From everything Roman has said about you, I feel like I know you," he says, his hazel eyes shining at me. "I feel like I should hug you instead of shake your hand."

"I accept hugs," I say warmly.

Clive laughs and gives me a bear hug. As he does, he whispers in my ear, "Thank you for giving me the gift of Jillian."

I'm touched by his words. I move back and smile at him. "Nothing makes me happier than knowing that," I whisper back, as obviously Clive hasn't told the family yet.

"This was a night for you and Roman," he says quietly. "After Christmas, we'll have another dinner I'm sure." And from the twinkle in his eye, I know Jillian will be the guest of honour at that one.

"Shall we have dessert now that Dad is here?" Clark asks. "You know I have to have my sweets."

"And port!" Thomas adds.

"Liz brought mince pies," Lisa chimes in with eagerness. "Oh, those are my favourite."

"Liz? Want to help me in the kitchen?'" Roman asks.

I wait for half a second to see if Eden bolts up and yells "no" and instructs me to sit and be waited on, but she's giggly from wine and smiles at both of us.

I've become one of them.

I watch Roman's family, all laughing and joking and warm with each other, and my heart sees how I fit in. I am happy here, not only with Roman but with these people, too.

But as soon as I think it, the reality of Friday night weighs heavy on my heart. Roman won't be embraced by a portion of my family. Worse, while my parents will accept him, we'll never have this type of family experience with them. How can Roman go from this to that without wondering why he's putting up with everything?

"Liz?"

I blink. Roman is waiting for me in the doorway, his face studying me now with concern. "Yes, coming," I say, moving over to him.

As soon as we're in the kitchen, he entwines his fingers through mine. "You're worried about something."

I don't even try to deny it, as Roman would know the truth in a second. "I look at your family and compare them to mine. That table, that living room, is filled with people who genuinely enjoy and love each other. My immediate family doesn't act like this. Throw in my extended family, and I'm mortified at what you will think, Roman. The lies. The secrets. The judgement. Why would you want to take that on for the rest of your life?"

I gasp after the words are out. "Um, I'm not saying you will marry me, or that you have to think about that right this second. Sorry, I didn't think before I spoke."

"Exactly," Roman says simply.

"What?"

"You spoke from your heart," he explains, drawing my hand up to his lips and pressing them against my knuckles. "You aren't asking if we've known each other long enough, or making sure to tick off all of Princess Elizabeth's boxes first. You spoke as Lizzie, the woman who has my heart."

He takes one hand and slides it around my waist, drawing me closer. "I do think of that future. It doesn't scare me. Your family doesn't scare me, and Her Majesty doesn't scare me. I promise you, there is nothing they can do on Friday night to change that."

Roman kisses me as if to punctuate the point, but worry still consumes me.

My heart believes him.

My head tells me he has no idea what he's getting into.

I tuck my head against his chest, listening once again to his heart.

And praying it will remain true to me after Friday night at Buckingham Palace.

CHAPTER 27
BAUBLES AND GARLAND

R oman slows as we make the last turn towards Buckingham Palace. He's behind the wheel of my Range Rover, and we are headed to the point of no return. Crowds are lining the streets. Paparazzi have their cameras out, filming each car slowly heading into the open gates of BP.

And into my landmine-filled world behind palace doors.

My stomach tightens as we move closer and closer to the palace. I glance at Roman, whose brow is furrowed as he drives.

"Look at all these people," he says quietly.

Flashbulbs start going off as we are recognised in the car. It seems like hundreds of them, and the light blinds us as we head towards the gates. Roman puts his hand over his eyes, trying to shield them from the continuous flashes of brightness.

People are cheering for us, but Roman keeps his eyes straight ahead. I do, too. We follow slowly behind another car, and the flashes of light don't stop until we have passed behind the gate and through the secure walls of the palace.

Once we are in the car park, Roman remains frozen at the steering wheel. People in cocktail gowns and tuxedoes are entering the palace, ready to celebrate Christmas with Arthur and Antonia with a five-course dinner in the State Dining Room.

"Do I look ridiculous?" he blurts out.

My heart crashes into my stomach. I see the expression on his face. In his eyes. It's written all over him.

I know, in this moment, Roman understands I'm not just Liz.

I'm Princess Elizabeth of York.

"You," I say, putting my hand on his freshly-shaven face, "are insanely hot in this tuxedo."

"One I had to rent."

I furrow my brow. "So?"

"I'm sure Antonia will love this; the gardener who had to *rent* a tuxedo."

I see the man I love slipping away from me in this car park. My confident man, the one who hasn't cared what the press have said since we went public, is realising the full impact of my world now that he is behind the gates of BP. Kensington Palace is my world. Where Liz, the woman he loves, lives by her rules.

But now he's seeing the other side of my life, and it has a whole new meaning to him now that he's here. This is a part of me. Rules and hierarchy and a whole new world beyond the one he's experienced with me so far.

It's new to him and scary, but he must accept it if he is going to be with me.

"Roman," I say turning his face towards mine, desperate to reassure him. "I love you. You are dashing in your tuxedo, and I'm proud to be with you. I'll happily shout from the top of the Grand Staircase so everyone can hear it."

He exhales. "Right."

"I know this is weird," I continue, hoping I can ease his nerves somehow. "This is your first time meeting my family."

Roman shoots me a wry look. "Yeah, your parents, who happen to be a prince and a duchess. And oh, the king and queen."

"*Aunt* Antonia and *Uncle* Arthur," I say defiantly.

"Who happen to be the king and queen."

"You know what I mean."

He exhales.

"Roman. Please don't worry. The people who love me don't expect you to be anything other than who you are. An incredible, insightful, grounded man."

"I know you're right, but sitting here, seeing these people, being on the other side of the fence of Buckingham Palace... I know there will be people tonight who hate me for being here. I... I don't want to embarrass you, Lizzie."

My heart further wrenches in my chest. "Roman, take that thought out of your head. That's not even possible. You be the man I love, and I will proudly be by your side."

He gazes into my eyes but doesn't say anything.

"I will," I reiterate. "And, yes, tonight will be surreal and weird, but then it will be done. Like Cinderella, we'll go down those red-carpeted steps and back to the coach, and I'll turn right into Liz again."

This gets the corners of his mouth to turn up, which gives me such relief that I almost audibly exhale.

Roman nods. "Okay."

We get out of the car and follow the other guests to the entrance. As we walk across the courtyard, I take his hand in mine, finding it clammy. My relief is short-lived. I know what this world is and how brutal it can be. Roman is getting stressed just being on the edge of it.

How can I expect him to live it?

Guilt burns within me the second I think it. How can I expect him to be anything but nervous? He's meeting my entire family tonight, while having to wear a tuxedo and make small talk with people he's never met, who happen to have intimidating titles like Your Royal Highness.

We reach the entrance and step inside. Roman helps me with my coat, which is whisked away by household staff. Guests are strolling through the Grand Hall, with its deep red carpeted floor, marble fixtures, and guild on the walls and ceiling.

But Roman isn't looking at any of that.

His eyes are fixated on me.

"You did it when you opened the door, but you're doing it again. You take my breath away in that dress," he says, his voice low.

His compliment makes me feel radiant. I'm wearing a floor-length, platinum-coloured sequined gown with cap sleeves and a cowl back that drapes down, exposing just enough skin to be alluring.

"Thank you."

Roman leans over and whispers in my ear. "Seeing your back is sexy. It's taking all my willpower not to touch it."

Heat swells within me as I inhale the sandalwood on his skin. "Later, it's all yours."

"Promise?"

"Oh, I do."

Now I get a smile.

"So, welcome to the Grand Hall," I say as we walk. "I

hope you like red and gold, because you will see a lot of that tonight."

"I think I prefer silver," he says, arching an eyebrow. I smile, and he shifts his gaze straight ahead. As he does, I see his expression change from teasing to awe.

"Those stairs," he whispers. "The staircase is even more impressive than on TV. And more *golden.*"

I nod as we walk towards the sweeping Grand Staircase. "It's quite dramatic, isn't it?"

"Slightly," he teases.

We reach the landing and step onto the Grand Staircase itself. The golden scrolled banisters are wrapped in greenery and baubles for Christmas.

"Look at that," Roman whispers, gazing up at the domed glass ceiling.

"You should see it in the daytime. The light comes through, and it's so beautiful."

He nods, his attention shifting to the walls as we continue our climb upwards. "And the paintings?"

"Queen Victoria's family."

His eyes are wide as he shifts his attention back to me. "Your family."

"Yes," I nod. Then I lower my voice. "Xander likes to get under Antonia's skin by telling her he'll replace all of them with modern art when he's king."

That gets a slight smile out of Roman. "Can you imagine?"

"No, she would *die,*" I whisper.

Once we reach the top, we step through the Guard Chamber and then enter the Green Drawing Room, which is filled with family and close friends of my aunt and uncle. A string quartet plays Christmas music in one part of the magnificent room as people laugh and drink cocktails and champagne underneath a brilliant chandelier suspended from the modelled ceiling. It's a sea of tuxedos and gowns, with servers wandering through the crowd, offering guests canapés off silver platters.

I know the first thing I need to do. I need to get Roman with the squad to relax him and make him feel welcome. I scan past the vipers that are in Her Majesty's inner circle, past Arthur's friends, and then I see Helene. Perfect! She's the perfect person to —

"Liz, I'm so glad you're here," I hear a voice from behind me say.

I freeze. I know that voice.

I slowly turn around to find myself face-to-face with India. I use every princess trick I have in the book to keep my face neutral instead of showing surprise. "India, hello. It's a pleasure to see you. This," I say, turning towards Roman, "is Roman Lawler. Roman, this is India Rothschild."

She gives him a tight-lipped smile. "Pleasure."

I know Roman knows who she is from my stories, but his face doesn't show it.

"Likewise," he says, nodding at her.

"Liz. I need to speak to you," India says urgently. "Privately. It's of the upmost importance."

No. No. I don't want to talk to India.

"We've only just arrived," I say. "I need to introduce Roman to my family."

"It will only be a moment," she presses. "Please, Liz. I'm sure Roman will understand."

Dammit. Now she's put Roman in an impossible position to say no. I look at him.

"Go ahead," he says, with a flick of his head. "I'll get a drink."

"I will be *right back*," I assure him.

"I'll be fine," he says.

I glance around the room. I see some of Antonia's allies eyeing us up, their heads bent in not-so-discreet whispers. "I won't be long," I tell him firmly.

"Thank you," India says. Then she escorts me through the crowd and into the Picture Gallery. As soon as we're there, she blurts out what is on her mind. "You have to help me get Xander back, Liz. You hold sway with him. Xander listens to you. You can help me."

"No. I can't do that, India. I'm sorry that you're hurting, but this is Xander's decision to make, not mine. Now I need to get back to the party."

I make a move to go, but India calls out after me. "What if you were in my shoes?" she asks.

I turn around. "What?"

"What if your *handyman* suddenly dropped you, and you knew I'd have sway with him? Wouldn't you want me to help you?" Her green eyes flicker at me. The cling film holding her perfect image has been peeled off, and now I'm about to see a whole new side to India Rothschild.

"Roman is a gardener, not a handyman, and I wouldn't want him to be swayed. I'd want him to choose me."

Her mouth draws into an angry line, and she practically spits out her words at me. "Well, you probably don't have to worry about him. He moved up from the potting shed to the palace—quite an accomplishment. But for you? To go dig in the dirt? You are embarrassing your family. In front of the world."

"You," I say calmly, "are the embarrassment. You're shallow and vapid, and you wouldn't know love if it showed up and slapped that tight smile off your face. Xander dodged a bullet with you. My cousin, my family, and potentially the entire Commonwealth dodged a bullet. All of us deserve better than you."

"The queen was right about you," India says coolly. "You are a self-destructive twit with a taste for rubbish. You'll drag everyone down with you so you can have the gardener plough your field."

Rage consumes me. "I won't engage you. Say what you want about me, I don't care." I turn around and angrily stride towards the doorway, shaking as I do.

India hurtles one last insult at me as I leave her behind. "Even though you repulse me," she says, "I hope you never feel as heartbroken as I do right now. Because I wouldn't wish this feeling on anyone. Even you."

Her words send a sharp chill through me, but I keep walking, determined to find Roman in the Green Drawing Room. I quickly re-enter, searching for him. Within minutes I spot him, and I breathe a sigh of relief as I see him next to the marble fireplace talking to Christian, Clementine, and Bella, who is back from Scotland for Christmas.

Thank God, I think. *He's protected with my family.*

I'm stopped a few times before I can reach them, by friends of my parents and relatives, painfully making small talk before I can be by Roman's side. As I approach, he spots me, and his eyes light up. "Hello, everyone," I say. I move in and give Bella a hug, breathing in her familiar perfume as I do.

"It's been too long!" I cry into her neck as I hug her. "I'm so glad you're home."

"Me, too," Bella says, stepping back from me.

I study her. She has her golden locks piled up on her head, and she's dressed in a crimson red dress with a V-neck and ruffles falling down the front of the gown. It's a soft look that accents the curvy body she was blessed with.

"You've met Roman?" I say, smiling at her.

"Yes," she says, smiling at him.

"And you've met James?" I ask him.

"Not yet," he says.

I glance around the room. I see James and Victoria, who are engaged with Helene, but no Xander. "Where's Xander?" I say.

"Hiding from the country you paid a visit to," Christian says dryly before taking a sip of his gin and tonic. "Mum apparently forgot to mention she was on the guest list."

"Lovely," I say.

"What happened?" Clementine asks, her eyes wide.

I exhale. "I will never talk to her again, I'll tell you that much."

I feel Roman's gaze on me. If he knew what she said... no, he can't ever know that. What India said will never be spoken of to Roman.

"I could do with a drink," I say.

"I'll get you one," Roman says. "Wine?"

I nod. He walks towards the bar, and when he's out of earshot, I speak. "India went after Roman. He can't ever know what she said; it would upset him."

"For what? Not having a title?" Clementine says. "For being a commoner, like me?"

I glance at Christian, whose piercing blue eyes flicker angrily in response to the idea of India attacking someone for not being an aristocrat.

"Roman is nervous enough. He doesn't need the rubbish opinion of people who don't matter," I tell them quickly. "Please don't say anything."

I'm met with quick nods all around.

"I need to introduce him to Mum and Dad," I say, searching the crowd for them.

"It's the weirdest thing. Dad was running late and sent me and Mum on ahead," Bella says, wrinkling her delicate nose. "But he hasn't arrived yet. Mum is angry and has been on her phone the whole time she's been here. I asked her if something was wrong, but she said it was a little spat, nothing to worry about."

My chest hurts. A "little spat" in Mum's words means they had an argument that could be heard in an entire wing of St. James's Palace.

And Bella has no idea.

I'm so disappointed in them. They knew tonight was a big deal for me, to introduce Roman to them, and they can't even manage to pull it together for one night?

No, I think painfully, *they can't.*

Mum isn't even in this room. I have no idea if she left or if she'll come back.

"Liz."

Roman's voice interrupts my thoughts as he hands me a glass of wine. I gratefully take it and have a deep sip. I glance up at him. "Mum is here—I mean, not in this room but somewhere here. Dad is late. I… I don't know when he'll make it."

Roman's eyes study mine. "It's all right." Then his hand lightly presses against my bare back in a measure of comfort.

He knows.

Tears of gratitude prick my eyes for this man, who knows what is in my heart without me having to say a word.

I love you, I think.

A buzz goes about the room, and I see my grandmother has entered, dressed in a long cream gown embroidered with crystals. Arthur is dapper in his tuxedo. By his side, of course, is Antonia. She holds her head regally. Not a hair is out of place in her chignon, and her long, navy column dress fits her like an elegant glove.

Antonia smiles that magical smile she bestows on her beloved fans and scans the room. I hold my breath and wait for her to see me. As her head slowly turns in my direction, her eyes lock in on mine.

The smile doesn't waver.

But the eyes tell me everything.

I've seen that look before, when we were at Windsor last year for Ascot. It was Clementine's first outing with the family.

My heart accelerates. My stomach turns into a knot.

That was the start of her war on Clementine.

But Antonia's battle with her future daughter-in-law is over now.

The new one is against me.

And the cold expression in her eyes tells me she is going to do everything possible to ruin what I have with Roman tonight.

CHAPTER 28

BATTLE LINES

M y breathing grows rapid. My mind is racing. The anxiety grows within me as I watch Antonia talk to guests, her head tilted at the right angle to indicate interest, her facial expression on point with the conversation at hand. As I watch her, I remember the glance we exchanged a few moments ago.

She has put a target on my back.

And the weapon she will use to destroy me is Roman.

I feel sick. I've made a massive mistake bringing him here. I should have waited. Now I understand I've walked into a minefield, and I don't know where she's hidden the bombs.

"Liz? Are you all right?"

I blink. Roman is watching me, concern flickering in his hazel eyes.

"Yes," I lie.

He can see through my answer, and a crease forms in his brow.

Before he can say anything else, Victoria and James approach us.

"What is wrong with Mum?" Victoria asks.

"What do you mean?" I say, my panic now rising on a different front.

"I ran into her in the loo," she says. "She said she didn't feel well and was going home."

I feel the colour drain from my face. "She *left?*" I cry, aghast that she would do this when she knew I wanted her to meet Roman. "She was supposed to meet Roman!" I take a quick glance at him. He appears shocked that my mum abruptly left.

"Is Henry here?" James asks, glancing around.

"No," Bella says, frowning. "But he assured me he would be."

An awkward silence falls over the squad.

"You must be Roman," James says quickly, switching gears. "I'm James, Liz's youngest cousin."

Roman extends his hand and shakes it. "A pleasure, Your Royal Highness."

"You can quit that bit," a baritone voice from behind me says. I instantly know it's Xander.

Roman and I both turn around, and he is grinning mischievously at us.

"Xander," he says, extending his hand to Roman. "No bow, no titles. Just call me Xander."

"Roman," he says, shaking Xander's hand. "Pleasure to meet you."

"Likewise. I've heard a lot about you from Liz," Xander says.

"So you've come out of hiding, brother?" Christian asks.

Xander rolls his eyes. "Dinner will start soon. Thank God we don't have assigned seats at this one."

I couldn't agree more. Because this is an intimate friends and family event, Arthur—I'm sure to the dismay of

Antonia—doesn't do a receiving line or have assigned seats at the table. It's not like parties at Windsor for Ascot Week, or charity dinners or receptions, where that is a normal part of the proceedings.

I shift my attention back to Antonia, who is now talking to India. I clench my jaw. India is no doubt making me out to be a complete cow, and I'm sure Antonia is agreeing with utter empathy that she had to even speak to someone as wretched as me.

Well, they can say what they want. I'm more upset with my parents right now. They knew I planned to introduce them to Roman tonight, and they couldn't even put aside their own drama to do something important for me.

To meet the man I love.

I glance at Roman, who has a worried expression on his face. I need to pull him aside. I need to reassure him that their disappearance is all them and has nothing to do with meeting him.

As I'm about to lead him away, Arthur taps on his champagne glass to get everyone's attention. The quartet stops playing, and the conversation in the room comes to a standstill.

"Good evening," he says, smiling warmly at everyone gathered in the Green Drawing Room. "Happy Christmas to all of you."

Everyone says "Happy Christmas" in return.

"On behalf of Queen Antonia and myself, thank you for joining us tonight for dinner. As you know, this is a special night for only our closest family and friends, and we are so blessed to have all of you here. With that said, let's adjourn to the State Room and have a great evening."

Everyone applauds Arthur's speech, and he and Antonia wait at the edge of the doorway to greet guests as they enter. So while there is not an official receiving line, there kind of is an unofficial one.

And this is when I will introduce Roman to them.

"Come on, let me introduce you to my aunt and uncle," I say, leading him away from the squad. I walk by his side as we head to the doorway. His whole body is rigid with tension. My anxiety goes up another notch as a result.

We fall behind other guests, my heart in my ears with each step we take. I know Antonia won't be outwardly rude in front of her husband, but she will send her message. Finally, I am standing in front of Arthur, whose blue eyes regard Roman with both an understanding of who he is and genuine warmth in meeting him.

"Arthur," I say, dipping into a curtsy. "I'm so happy to be here this evening." It's a lie, of course.

"It's good to see you, Elizabeth," he says, smiling brightly at me.

"Arthur, allow me to present Roman Lawler," I say.

He bows to Arthur. "Your Majesty, it's an honour to meet you."

"Roman, Liz has told me so much about you," Arthur says, extending his hand to shake Roman's. "I'm glad to meet you at last."

"Thank you, Sir," Roman replies. "I know Liz thinks highly of you."

I clear my throat to do the dirty work my parents have left for me. "Arthur, I'm sorry, but my mother has left for the evening. She is feeling unwell."

As soon as I mention my mother, Antonia shifts her complete attention to me.

"Oh, I'm sorry to hear that. And Henry?" Arthur asks.

"He has been delayed, unfortunately," I lie.

And I feel like crap for having to lie to a man I deeply

respect. Crap for how my parents have put themselves first tonight and put me in this position to cover to Arthur. And crap for having to explain their ungracious behaviour to Roman later.

One of Arthur's aides approaches him. "Sir, His Royal Highness Prince Henry has requested to speak with you."

I perk up. "Is he here?"

"No, Your Royal Highness. He's on the phone."

My heart breaks again.

He's not coming.

"I'll take it," Arthur says. "Please excuse me."

He leaves, and as the squad are still gathered in conversation by the fireplace, I am left to face Antonia alone. I dip into a curtsy. "Antonia, thank you for having us this evening."

Her tight-lipped smile is nothing more than a polished smirk, and anxiety begins to shift towards anger inside of me.

"Yes, so wonderful to see you Liz. And this dress," she says, carefully eyeing me up and down, "is so... *different*. It reminds me of tinsel. How *quaint*."

Oh! That was a direct slam, because I know she thinks tinsel is hideous and terribly tacky. She continues before I can respond to her barb. "It's a pity to hear about your mother this evening, I sincerely hope nothing has made her ill. For both your parents to be so noticeably absent at a family event makes me think she must be seriously under the weather."

Her eyes lock on mine. It's her way of saying she knows it's a row that is causing their disappearance.

"Of course, I know they'd love nothing more than to be here," I lie again.

"It is the season for sickness," Antonia says with false understanding.

"Unless," she continues, shifting her attention to Roman and staring directly at him, "there are people here they'd rather not interface with."

I nearly gasp out loud from her obvious insult. A flush begins to climb up Roman's neck, and I'm so angry that I can't find the right words to level back at her.

Roman bows to her. "A pleasure to meet you, Your Majesty."

Antonia's smirk widens. "Thank you. Do you know what I love about these parties that Arthur has? That we get to interact with such a wide variety of people. Clementine is our first American to attend one. And now we have you, a *gardener*. It's so... charming, our new *cross-section* of attendees."

Rage is about to swallow me whole. Roman's neck is so red that it looks like it would feel hot to the touch.

"I think we're the lucky ones," a voice from behind us says.

I turn, and from the expression on Xander's face, it's obvious he's heard what Antonia has said.

"Xander, darling, how lovely to see you," she says.

"Mum," he says, moving around me to greet his mother. He leans in to kiss her cheek, then steps back and gives her a stern look. "I sincerely hope you were welcoming the new cross-section of invitees as a much-needed breath of fresh air, which they *both* are."

Her eyes laser in on Xander, showing disapproval. "Of course I was."

"Good. I'd hate to get drunk at dinner and embarrass you in front of our old pollination of friends," he warns.

I suck in my breath. He is daring her. If she missteps with Roman, Xander will embarrass her on purpose.

Antonia's nostrils flare ever so slightly, her small slip showing that her eldest son has the upper hand now. Xander is the only one with some power over her. She views anything that the heir to the throne does as a reflection upon her. If he misbehaves in front of her closest friends, she'd be mortified.

"Don't be silly, Alexander," she says, using his full name as her own warning back. "Now go on, dinner is about to start."

We move out of the doorway, and I turn to Roman. "I'm so sorry," I murmur.

"Maybe I'm the one who is sorry," he says, his eyes locking with mine.

I can't breathe as we walk through the Picture Gallery, en route to the dining room. What does that comment mean? Is he sorry to be here? To be in this situation?

Is he realising he's sorry to be with me?

"She should back off now," Xander says to us quietly, interrupting my panicked thoughts. "Nothing gets Mum to behave more than the idea that I won't."

We enter the Blue Drawing Room, which we must pass through to enter the State Dining Room, and under a normal situation, I'd love to stop and show Roman the Table of the Great Commanders, but my mind is a racing mess of fear. I need to have a private conversation with him, to talk about that comment and reassure him that all of this will pass with time.

Roman is silent as we walk with Xander, and soon we are entering through the doorway of the State Dining Room. It is fully lit for a Christmas celebration. The chandeliers are aglow, bathing the red room in light. The long table is set with elaborate candelabras, bowls of sugared fruits, and greenery. Each place setting is set with precision, each piece of cutlery spaced to an exact measurement. Menu cards adorn each place setting, an —

Wait. Why are people walking around studying the table instead of sitting down?

I gasp. Those are place cards.

My face grows hot. We've never, ever had place cards at this party in all the years I've come to it. It's supposed to be sit where you want, as we're all here to enjoy the night.

I glance towards the doorway, where Antonia is entering the room with Lady Violet Clark-Hampton, one of her closest friends. As they are talking, her eyes meet mine from across the room. A triumphant smile passes over her face.

She's done this to torture Roman.

With panic rising, I now fear who she has seated him with.

"What is this?" Christian asks, glancing down at the table and picking up a name card.

"Oh, well played, Mother," Xander says under his breath.

I see the understanding in Christian's eyes. "She's separating Liz and Roman. Sounds familiar, doesn't it, Clementine?"

I flash back to the party at Windsor during Ascot, where Antonia seated Clementine as far away from Christian as she could. She made the fatal mistake of putting Clementine with Victoria instead of someone who would make her uncomfortable. Antonia won't make that mistake twice. She'll put Roman with someone who will make him miserable.

"Roman," Clementine says, dropping her voice, "this

isn't about you. Anyone who is outside of this world is treated like this. I was, too."

Roman peers down the length of the table. "Right."

I hatch a plan to switch places with someone seated next to Roman, but before I can speak, Antonia approaches us.

"Please, take your seats," she says smoothly. "Unless there is a problem with your seat."

"Yes," I say, "Th—"

"Liz, let's find our seats," Roman says, cutting me off.

I stare at him. His eyes are dark. He's upset. But right now, I don't know if it's with me or the seating arrangement.

"Excuse me," Lord Gordon Oliver says. "I believe this is my seat."

Roman walks around the table, searching for his name. I follow behind him, wishing I could speak, but with so many ears now around us, I don't dare say a word.

I spot mine, and I'm wedged in a seat between India's mother and Lady Violet. While normally I would say this was the worst seat at the table, I know it's not. Antonia will have saved that for Roman.

He continues to search for his name. At the opposite end of the table, we find his place. On one side of him is my grandmother, the dowager queen, who will hate him. And on the other side is India.

Oh, no. No, no, no. Grandmother will be rude enough, but after what happened in the Picture Gallery between me and India? She will do everything she can to make him feel like he's not worthy of being here.

"No," I say out loud.

"I'm fine," he says firmly.

"No, I'm not allowing this," I continue, not caring who hears me.

Roman puts his hand on my arm and lowers his head towards my ear. "Stop treating me like I need protection. Just stop it."

I freeze from his words. Roman is angry. Irritated. Or both.

I'm rooted to my spot, as people find their places and take a seat. I stare down at the menu card, all in French, and I know Roman doesn't know French. I think of how awful this would be, stuck on the other end of the table, with no one who wants to talk to you.

Grandmother approaches, and as she sees me standing with Roman, her face draws into a scowl. I've seen that scowl before. She used to use it on Clementine, until Arthur told everyone to get on board or risk losing Christian.

But my father isn't here to support me, I think with anguish. *On a night when he knew I would need him, his irritation with my mother superseded me.*

The frown remains intact as Grandmother reaches us.

"Grandmother," I say, dipping into a curtsy.

"Darling Elizabeth," she says, leaning forward and kissing my cheek. "What's this I hear about your father being indisposed?"

I shake my head. "I heard he was delayed. Mum went home ill."

She arches an eyebrow but says nothing.

"Grandmother, I'd like you to meet my boyfriend, Roman Lawler," I say proudly. "You will get to know him during dinner tonight, as he is seated next to you."

Roman quickly bows. "Your Royal Highness, it's a pleasure to meet you," he says.

She locks her eyes on him. "You're quite away from the potting shed tonight, aren't you?"

"Grandmother!" I hiss.

"No, she's right," Roman says evenly. "It's a long way from Shepherd's Bush to Buckingham Palace."

"A gardener. From Shepherd's Bush. Dating *my* granddaughter? Dear God, I need a drink," she says at that news.

My face flushes red with anger. I love my grandmother, but her superiority complex is an ugly side of her that I hate.

She's my grandmother. And the dowager queen. This is a dinner thrown by the king. We're in Buckingham Palace.

But I don't care. I'm not allowing her to treat Roman like this.

"To be honest, you're lucky to be sitting next to a man like Roman," I snap. "And he's the one who will need a drink before you do if that is your attitude towards getting to know him."

"Liz!" Roman gasps.

My grandmother's face reddens. "I can see he's already changed you. And not for the better."

Roman's face darkens as he watches the exchange. He politely pulls out the chair for my grandmother, who accepts it with a huff, and then he turns to me. "I think it's best," he says, his voice low, "that you go and sit down now."

I feel tears prick my eyes. Now it's wrong to defend him? Am I supposed to stand by meekly and let my grandmother humiliate him? Apparently I'm only allowed to be fiery, passionate Liz when he wants me to be?

Anger takes over. "Perhaps it is."

I turn around, and nearly bump into India as I do.

"Oh, Liz, you seem upset," she says, drawing her lower lip into a glossy pout. "Sad that you won't get to sit with your day labourer?"

This time, I don't defend Roman. I brush past her, angry at this whole situation. I'm angry at my parents. At Antonia. India.

Worst of all, now I'm angry at Roman.

I go and take my seat, not even daring to glance down towards the end of the table where he is with India and Grandmother.

As soon as everyone is seated, the courses begin. I put on my Princess Elizabeth best, forcing myself to be engaged in conversation with people I do not like, all for the sake of what people expect from me. I might be pissed off and upset, but this is Arthur's night. I won't ruin this dinner for him.

By the time the second course has come out, my anger has subsided. All I want is to talk to Roman. This evening has been stressful and exhausting, but I want him to understand that I had his best interests at heart. By pushing back, I showed how much I loved him. Grandmother did not have permission to be rude to anyone, let alone to my boyfriend, and I want to apologise for all of the awful treatment he has received this evening.

The dinner lasts for an hour-and-a-half, the time crawling by, and with each course, my anxiety increases over what Roman is thinking. I wonder how he is handling the rude and degrading comments that my grandmother and India are no doubt saying to him.

Finally, Arthur finishes his dessert, and the staff immediately begin sweeping plates away. While we've been dining, more desserts and tea have been set up in the Picture Gallery, and guests begin making their way out. I leap up, wanting to get to Roman as soon as I can, but once I'm out of my chair, I'm stunned at the sight before me.

It's my father.

I watch Arthur greet him. They talk, with their blond heads bent together in a sibling confidence. I turn around in time to see Roman walking quickly past me, straight out of the State Dining Room.

Wait, what is he doing? Is he going to leave me here?

"Roman," I call out.

He stops, and the expression on his face sends me into a fully-fledged panic. The face I know every trace of, the face that is so expressive when he tells me he loves me, is one of agony. My throat swells. My heart begins hammering.

He's already had enough of this.

He comes over to me. "I need to get some air. I… I'll be back, all right?"

"I'll go with you," I say.

"No, give me a few minutes alone. Please."

Roman quickly moves out of the room before I can argue with him.

I begin to shake. I'm not worth this. No man should suffer the abuse he has simply by choosing to love me. He's dealt with the press and social media, and that was bad enough, but now this? My own family treating him like rubbish?

I glance at my father, who is now talking to Bella, Christian, and Clementine, but my brain is too worried about Roman to wonder what they are discussing. Does he want to be alone so he can figure out how to break up with me? Is that why he tried to slip past me unnoticed?

No. I need to follow him. I need to talk to him.

"Liz!" I hear my father call out.

No, no, not now! But there's no escape.

I make my way over to my father, who gives me a hug. "I'm sorry I'm late," he whispers in my ear. "But you know I wouldn't miss meeting Roman for anything."

I quickly blink the tears away before I step back from him. "I'll have to introduce you in a bit. I honestly didn't think you were coming."

My father exhales and pulls me aside from the group. He lowers his voice so only I can hear him. "I had to calm down. I didn't want to meet Roman when I wasn't myself. I had a bourbon. Sat in solitude for a bit. Let go of the feelings I had so I could come here tonight and give him the reception he deserves. Knowing he is important enough to come to Buckingham Palace for us to meet him tells me how much he matters. It tells me Roman," he continues, with a twinkle in his eyes, "is different."

It takes everything I have not to burst into tears.

"Yes," I manage to get out.

"So, where is he?" my father asks.

"He went to get some air," Helene says from behind.

I quickly turn around to find my aunt with a knowing expression on her face.

"W-where did he go?" I ask, my voice coming out in a strangled sound.

Helene focuses all her attention on me. "I followed him. He was in a hurry. Heading down the Grand Staircase."

I can't breathe. The room begins to sway around me, my heart and mind making the connection I don't want to make.

He didn't simply step out into the hallway or the Picture Gallery for air.

Roman is leaving me.

"I didn't like his expression after dinner. Lord knows there wasn't enough wine served to get me through sitting between those two. I followed him and introduced myself. My darling, the boy is visibly upset. He said he needed to clear his head and begged my forgiveness."

No. No. I shake my head. This isn't happening. Fear renders me unable to move.

"Go," Helene commands. "Liz, go now. You need to catch him. Go!"

I bolt from the room, hitching my dress up to make running in heels easier. My worst nightmare is coming true. One night with my family was enough to break him. I know he loves me, but that isn't enough.

I was delusional to think it was.

I hurry through the rooms, cursing the design of the palace that forces me to go in the most indirect route possible, and finally reach the massive staircase. I run down the flights of red carpeting, finding myself alone as everyone continues to celebrate upstairs.

As I reach the last little flight of stairs, pausing on the landing to catch my breath, I find Roman seated on a mahogany bench, his head in his hands. I gasp. My strong, silent man, who told me he didn't care what anyone said about him, has never appeared more vulnerable than he does to me right now.

I can't move. I can't.

Because I know what he's going to tell me as soon as he lifts his head.

That no love is worth living in this prison.

Even mine.

I stare at him, rooted to the spot, tears swimming in my eyes. Roman must feel someone watching him, because he lifts his head. A shocked expression passes over his face as he sees me. He slowly rises.

I take the stairs with wobbly legs and force myself to meet him, but as soon as I see the hurt look in his hazel eyes, I know what is about to happen.

I'm about to say goodbye to him.

Roman turns away from me, and I fight to breathe as he does. My heart is throbbing in anguish. My throat is full of tears. I'm trembling and cold, and I fear what is about to happen next.

Because I know my heart won't survive it.

"I'm sorry. I... I had to get out of there. I was suffocating," he spits out, the words tumbling out in an uncharacteristic fashion for him. "The things that were said to me, no man should ever have to hear. *Ever.*"

The anger he was repressing when I first approached is rising back up within him.

"Your grandmother loathes me. She flat-out refused to speak to me after telling me she thinks I'm going to drag you down. I'm rubbish in her eyes."

"Then why wouldn't you let me defend you?" I cry, finding my voice. "You were furious at me, don't deny that!"

Roman stares at me. "Because she is your *grandmother.* You have to respect her, Liz. I would have handled it. You needed to let me do that!"

"I respect no one, family included, who acts like an aristocratic snob," I say, my voice rising. "What happened to you liking fiery Liz? Does that disappear when I stick up for you? Does that threaten your manhood?"

Roman's brows shoot straight up. "What? Is that what you think? Don't you know me? No, Liz. I didn't want you making it worse."

"How much worse could it have been? Do I even want to know what India said to you?"

Roman clenches his jaw.

"You're not even going to tell me, are you?"

"No."

"You didn't mind protecting my honour to the paparazzi, so why can't I defend you?" I point out.

"This is different," Roman insists. "This is your *family.*"

"I don't care who it is," I say, my anger returning. "But none of this matters. Your face tells me everything I need to know."

"What?" he asks, his brows knitting together. "What do you mean?"

"You don't want this life," I cry, my throat thickening again.

"*What?*"

"You don't," I say, the tears overflowing in my eyes. Now the words are coming out in spurts, as it's hard for me to say them. "Roman, you were miserable up there. You deserve better than this. Y-you thought you knew what you were getting into with me b-b-but you didn't! You were so upset you didn't even want me to go with you. You were heading out of here, I know it."

Roman's expression changes in an instant as my words tumble out. "Liz, no, no, you're taking this the wrong way," he pleads. He grabs my arms and clutches on to me. "Don't mistake my frustration for something it's not. I honestly was trying to clear my head. I wasn't leaving. I love you."

I shake my head violently. "You won't continue to do so!"

My voice is sounding hysterical to my own ears.

"Lizzie, stop. I *love* you, do you hear me?"

"You deserve better," I sob, ignoring his plea. "It's only a matter of time before you fall out of love with me because of this." I gesture around at the columns and guild that have become my prison. "You will leave me. You will stop loving me. I can't expect you to pay this price to be with me, Roman."

"No. You are overreacting," he insists, his voice as firm as his grip on me.

I shake free of him. "I'm not. You will miss your old life. Before you get sick of being snapped by photographers. I saw your face the other day, Roman, when you were reading an article. You were so hurt."

"You don't understand," he says, shaking his head. "Liz, th—"

"You will eventually stop loving me, Roman. You will. You will resent the world I've trapped you in. Most of all, you will resent me, and this will end, don't you see that?"

His neck colours, and to my shock, he seems furious.

"So you get to decide what I want? What I will or will not put up with? Because my first night was rough, you assume I want to end things?"

I don't know how to answer that accusation.

Because his words are true.

"You need to look in the mirror," Roman says, his voice shaking with anger. "I'm not looking into the heart of the woman I love. I see a scared woman who is watching her father fall out of love with her mother. One who can't see the man who loves her but the man she fears will leave her. Don't blame this royal world for that. That's the easy way out. You are afraid I will be disappointed or fall out of love with you. You're afraid I will leave, like your father wants to do. Instead of trusting me, you are banishing me. How utterly royal of you."

I reel backwards from his words. My heart shatters inside my chest, and my body is crushed under the weight of my actions.

"You should *know* what is in my heart," Roman says, his voice shaking with raw emotion. "The fact that you don't is more cutting than any insult I've heard this whole evening."

"You're right," I whisper. "I'm so sorry."

I see the despair in his hazel eyes, and I know I have destroyed the love of the only man I will ever give my heart to. Roman will never trust me after this, not after I decided his future and pushed him away.

With no trust, there can never be love.

I'm about to be sick. I need to throw up. I need to bawl. I need to get out of here.

I turn and pick up my dress, running back up the stairs.

"Liz!" he yells after me, his voice echoing down the hall. "Liz, no!"

I reach the first landing and turn around. "Words can never say how sorry I am," I say, sobbing.

"No," Roman says, taking a few steps towards me.

"Goodbye, Roman," I tell him.

Then I run as fast as I can, ignoring his anguished pleas to stop, and knowing my own self-imposed prison, not this royal one, has cost me the love of my life.

And my heart, the one I smashed into a million fragmented pieces with my own actions, will never love again.

CHAPTER 29
THE 1844 ROOM

I seek solace in the 1844 Room. I hurry inside the famous room, resplendent in blue and gold silk-covered furniture. This room often shows up in the media, as it is where Arthur receives his most important guests. And now it will forever be the room where I went after shoving Roman out of my life.

The torrent of tears I had somehow held from breaking now burst free, racking my body with heavy, crushing sobs. I drop to my knees on the carpet, pushing my hands out to hold myself up, and cry for everything I have lost — and lost because of one simple reason.

I decided everything for Roman, instead of listening to him. To what he wanted. To his feelings, his concerns.

Why did I do this?

Because I didn't think I was worth him going through all this hell for. I thought there was no way he wouldn't hate this life, and eventually hate me for it. I was certain he would fall out of love with me.

In an instant, I see the look in his eyes when he said I had banished him. Those eyes were a mixture of fury and hurt as I decided not to trust his heart, not to even let him speak, and, instead, decided our future out of fear.

Fear.

A word that has never been associated with me. I've been known as strong. Brave. Confident. Fiery.

But nobody knew of the inner turmoil that ran under the surface. I was so afraid of Roman being disappointed in this life, of being harassed by the media, of stupid rules and constraints and archaic policies, that when I saw glimpses of his frustration, it brought this buried fear right to the surface. Because of this, I was sure his frustrations were the beginning of the end.

The beginning of Roman falling out of love with me.

The tears subside, as I don't have any left, and I drop my head on to my knees and draw a shaky breath. I kneel on the floor for a long time, with only the light from the garden terrace illuminating the room, wondering where Roman is. I remember how he begged me to stay, but how could I? I didn't trust him. I didn't believe in his love. I didn't give him a chance to vent his frustrations as I should have. He said that cut him more than any of the atrocious behaviour he was on the receiving end of tonight.

I squeeze my eyes shut. How do I live now, without Roman? Without his smile, his passion, his gentleness? My stomach wretches at the idea of never seeing him again. Of never hearing his voice, his laugh. Never again hearing him tell me how much he loves me…

Oh, I've made the biggest mistake! I was so afraid of losing him that I didn't see that he was here, willing to live this life because he wanted to be with me.

I was so afraid of the future, I lost sight of the present.

And lost Roman because of it.

Fresh tears swell in my throat, and another sob escapes

me. Then another. The pain I feel in my heart is unlike anything I have ever known.

Suddenly, a light comes on, startling me. I whip my head around and find Christian standing in the doorway.

"Christian," I gasp, rubbing my hand across my face.

"I knew I'd find you here," he says, shutting the door behind him and walking across the room. He sinks down onto the floor next to me, as if it's totally normal to find me a hysterical mess.

"How?" I ask, sniffling.

Christian arches an eyebrow. "I remember you telling me when we were kids that someday you were going to have meetings with important people in this room like Grandfather used to do."

I manage a small laugh. "I was bold."

"Well, I might not be an important person, but I'd like to have a meeting with you here," he says gently.

Christian blurs in front of my eyes. "You know."

"Roman came looking for you," he explains, his blue eyes holding steady on mine.

"He did?" I ask, swallowing hard.

"He was desperate to find you. He said you two had a row, and he didn't know where you were. Roman was worried, Liz. Really worried."

"Roman's kindness after I broke his heart is more than I deserve," I say, my voice shaking.

"Liz, I don't know about the row you had, but he didn't act like a man who was only worried about your welfare. Roman was *stricken*. Helene ordered her driver to take him home, and that took a lot of convincing. If we would have let him, I think he would have searched every single one of these seven hundred and seventy-five rooms until he found you."

I feel my breathing pick up with Christian's words. My heart begins to beat with a tiny, fragile stirring of hope.

"Roman loves you," he says. "For him to come back upstairs, to tell us you had a fight and he absolutely had to find you, when he knew all of Mum's spies and palace allies were watching him, is proof in my eyes."

"Christian," I say, my voice thick, "I shoved him away tonight. I saw what this life, this gilded prison, was doing to him. He was anxious about being here. Then the insults he suffered from—"

I stop short, not wanting to put Christian in the position of hearing things about his own mother.

Understanding flickers across his face. "Mum. I know. She did it to Clementine, remember?"

I nod. "Grandmother was rude to his face. He wouldn't even tell me what India said."

"Cow," Christian snaps.

"All I could think," I say painfully, "was that I was doing this to him. Roman loves me now, but how could he not grow to hate me because of the circus that has now entered his world? I've never seen him so unsure, so shaken, and I brought him into this. All I could see was that this," I wave my hand around the room, "would make him resent me. His love would die. And he would leave me."

Christian contemplates my words for a few moments and then speaks. "I understand this more than anyone. I was terrified to bring Clementine into this world. I tried to protect her, and that led to some rows between us. I hated myself for what my position did to her."

"You're the only one who understands this," I say, blinking back tears.

"I do. So I want you to listen to me when I tell you this. Roman loves you. Living in this life is hard. People never understand what these walls are like until they are on the other side. They can't comprehend what it's like to have the media love you and praise you and then take square aim at the pedestal you are on and find happiness in kicking you down to the ground. Yet, Clementine's love for me is greater than all of that. She will wear the uniform and play the part, suffer through attacks in the press, deal with social media trolls, and give up a job she loves and find new passions through our foundation. She would do this a million times over because, at the end of the day, when it's us and the dogs and we're watching a quiz show on TV, we are together. Her love for me is greater than the monarchy. And from what I saw of Roman tonight, I'd say his love is the same for you."

Tears run down my cheeks. "I broke his heart tonight. I didn't trust his feelings. How do you have love when there is no trust?"

Christian stares at me. "Because he loves you. It's that simple. But you have to allow yourself to believe that he is making the choices that he wants. Roman is with you because of you. You are what he wants, Liz. Not Her Royal Highness. Not this palace. Not the monarchy. You have to believe you are worth the sacrifices he is willing to make to be with you, or this won't work."

His words hit me in the heart. I know he's right. Christian is absolutely right. I need to be confident in myself as the woman Roman loves, and will love, if I let him. Roman chose me. He fell in love with me. And he's strong enough to survive everything that comes along with falling in love with a princess.

Roman loves me for being fearless. Fierce. Passionate.

And this woman is one who will own her mistake and fight to make it right.

"I need to go to him," I say, adrenaline pumping through my veins.

Christian rolls his eyes. "Finally. That's the Liz I've been waiting for."

I punch him lightly on the arm. He laughs in response.

"I love you," I say to him. "I'm so grateful you're my cousin."

Christian smiles warmly at me. "I love you, too."

He rises to his feet and gives me a hand to help me up. I take it, and he pulls me to a standing position. I throw my arms around him and give him a hug, which he warmly returns. He takes a step back from me, putting his hands on my shoulders. His face grows serious, and I bite my lip as I look at him.

"Go to him, Liz. Tell him everything. Own up to your fears. I would say fight for him, but I don't think you have to do that. Just love him."

I nod. "I do, Christian. I love him with all my heart. And I will never, ever doubt his love for me again."

"That's the Liz I know."

"That's the Liz I *am*," I say determinedly.

And not wasting a minute, I hurry out of the room, with one mission only in my mind and my heart.

I'm going to get Roman back — and I'll never let him go.

I run up the path to Roman's flat in Shepherd's Bush. I have mascara down my face, my lipstick is worn off, and my coat isn't buttoned, but I don't care. I have to see him now. I have to make this right. I have to tell him I'm a fool for shoving him away when that is the last thing on earth that I want.

I locate the doorbell for his flat and ring it. I pace on the doorstep, my stomach knotted in anxiety, my heart pounding inside my chest. Impatiently, I ring it again.

"Hello?" Darcy's voice comes on the intercom.

"Darcy, it's Liz. I have to see Roman. It's urgent. Will you please let me in?"

There's a pause from him.

"Darcy!" I shout back at the intercom.

"Yes, come in."

The main door unlocks, and I jerk it open. I head straight towards their flat and rap on the door. Darcy opens it, and his eyes widen at the sight of me, all disheveled and blotchy from crying.

"Liz," he says, stepping aside.

I enter the flat, and as soon as he shuts the door, I approach him. "Is Roman in his room? Did you tell him I'm here?"

Darcy seems uncomfortable. He rakes a hand through his unruly locks, making them more of a mess on his head.

Panic begins to build inside of me. "Darcy?"

"Liz, Roman has left."

My heart freezes. "What do you mean?"

"He came back here a short while ago, extremely upset. I've never seen him so upset, and I was here for the Felicity years."

I'm going to be sick. I reach out and put my hand on the back of a chair to keep from falling.

"He packed some bags and left," Darcy continues. "Said he was going away for a few days, to tell his mum to ignore what was in the press, and he'd be back after Christmas."

"What?" I cry, aghast. "Where was he going? Darcy, if you know, I beg for you to tell me. Please. Please, Darcy."

Sadness fills his eyes. "I asked him that same thing.

Roman wouldn't tell me. He said he needed to be alone. Then he took off on his motorcycle and promised to return on Boxing Day."

A knife is run through my heart. Boxing Day was the day Roman was going to spend with me up in Sandringham. Now he's making plans to come home that day instead of spending it with me.

My breathing grows rapid. I feel dizzy. I clutch harder onto the chair, my knuckles going white. "Will you... call me when he contacts you? So I know he's all right?" I manage to ask.

"I can't," Darcy says, inclining his head towards the coffee table. "Roman chucked his phone to me on the way out. Said he didn't need it or the rubbish that would come across it regarding you."

I stare at his phone in shock. It's blinking with messages.

He didn't want to hear from me, I think with anguish. *Whatever Christian thought, he was wrong. Roman might have looked for me, but it was out of his protective nature. It wasn't,* my heart now understands, *because he wanted to make up with me.*

It's over between us. The damage I did, my lack of trust in what we had, is irreparable.

As is my heart.

CHAPTER 30
SANDRINGHAM

I glance out of the window from my room at Sandringham on this Christmas morning. Tiny snowflakes swirl in the wind. The sky is grey. Soon, I will walk with the entire family to St. Mary's Magdalene for Christmas Day church services.

I turn away from the window, my eyes brimming with tears, as they have been practically non-stop.

Roman hasn't called me. Not that I expected him to after what Darcy told me, but every time my phone rang, there was hope. Maybe Roman had changed his mind. Maybe he was calling from wherever he was. Maybe he had gone home.

But those were merely desperate wishes.

I catch a glimpse of myself in the mirror. I have done nothing but blink back tears and force down the nausea that has risen within me this whole time at Sandringham, missing Roman with every inch of my heart and soul. Watching Christian and Clementine, who is spending her first Christmas at Sandringham despite not being married to Christian, has been painful to my broken heart. They kicked another door down for us young royals, as the normal rule calls for only spouses to come to Sandringham for Christmas Eve and Christmas. Thanks to Arthur declaring that rule stupid and vetoing Grandmother and Antonia on it, they are here and blissfully happy.

As Roman and I should be.

But never will.

I think of how I had to tell Father that night, after I returned from Roman's flat, that Roman and I had an awful row, and he had left London because of it. He was reassuring, telling me that all couples fought, and that if we were meant to be, we'd work it out. Mum, in a phone call the next day, apologised for her disappearance and told me if Roman couldn't handle this, I was better off without him.

They were both wrong.

We weren't meant to be.

And I'm not better off without him.

My heart only knows anguish now. The smiles I had at the elaborate Christmas Eve dinner were fake, much like Mum and Dad's show of affection and happiness this weekend.

This is what my life will be now: holding the smile, the princess pose, and acting happy because that is what everyone wants to see, while inside I'm dying and desperately wishing for the man I love.

Jillian did tell me Clive had heard from Roman, and that he's fine but needed to think about things and wanted to do it alone.

The press, however, thanks to palace insiders on Antonia's side, have had a field day, declaring Roman was out of place at the party, we had a row, and I fled in tears. Now they will be looking for those tears as we make the traditional walk to church.

I close my eyes. The cameras won't lie on this one. I'm pale. I have dark circles under my eyes. It's obvious I'm devastated.

How do I learn to move past this? How do I get over a man like Roman?

But I already know the answer.

I won't.

There's a rap on my door.

"Liz? We're leaving," Xander announces.

I grab my coat off the end of the bed. "Coming."

I slip into a rich aubergine coat that matches the wool dress I have on and take one last glimpse in the mirror. My matching fascinator is perfectly in place. Oh, I see a bonus. The deep purple brings out my undereye shadows. The TV people will love it.

I open the door to find Xander waiting for me, dapper as always in a black suit and sharp cashmere overcoat.

"I thought we'd walk together," he says.

"Thank you," I say, stepping out into the hall.

Xander truly is the best person for me to walk with today. He's witty and will keep me distracted as people take our pictures.

The whole family is gathered downstairs, ready to make the short walk to church. Everyone is dressed in their finest for the hundreds of well-wishers who will line the walk to greet us, along with the heavy media coverage.

I glance across the room to see Clementine speaking to Christian. She is gorgeous in a tartan coat and black beret. I smile. Antonia is furious she is attending without a wedding ring on her finger but will put on her best smile and act as if she's overjoyed her future daughter-in-law is sharing Christmas with the family.

"Liz, you look awful," Victoria says, coming up to me, concern flashing in her eyes.

"I feel awful, so it works."

We begin filing out the door into the cold. I tug on my gloves as we fall into step, with Bella, Victoria, and James walking together, followed by Clementine and Christian, then me and Xander. Leading the procession, of course, are Arthur and Antonia, my grandmother next to her. My parents are walking arm in arm, their charade as grand as mine, with Helene next to my father.

If people only knew the truth, I think, forcing a smile on my face as I walk with Xander. All the senior members, with the exception of Helene, are miserable. I count Grandmother with them because of her miserable attitude.

Now I will join them with my own heartbreak.

I push that feeling down, knowing that while this is Christmas Day, we are technically working, giving the public a parade of us in our finery as we smile and stroll joyfully to church.

University-aged girls who have lined the path scream when they see Xander come into view, calling out "Your Royal Hotness!" as he strolls past.

"You're such a rock star," I tease as we walk.

Xander grins. "There are perks to the job."

"I'm glad you woke up about India. Don't worry, I wasn't going to let you marry her."

Xander keeps the smile on his face. "Momentary life crisis. It's passed."

The snowflakes grow puffier and swirl around us as we have our pictures taken by the crowd and media that have assembled for us.

"Well, I'm glad. You deserve love."

"Like what you have?"

I strain to keep the smile plastered on my face. "I don't have that anymore."

"I think you do."

Xander flashes another adoring grin to the crowd, and more hysterical screams follow.

"I don't want to talk about it," I say through my faux smile. "My heart is shattered."

"I don't think it will be for long."

"Xander, please drop it."

We draw closer to the church.

"You don't have to talk to me, but I think you'll want to talk to Roman. It's kind of rude not to since he's been waiting here."

"Wh-what?" I gasp, stunned by this news.

"He's at the top of the line near the church on the left," Xander says.

I frantically search the crowd for him as we move closer.

And then I see him.

Roman is standing behind a barricade, dressed in a suit, staring straight at me.

Holding a bouquet of red poinsettias in his hand.

My heart slams to life against my ribs. Roman is here. At Sandringham. Waiting behind a barrier to see me. And holding the flower that was in the greenhouse the day we met again.

I fight every urge I have not to run to him. I'm shaking as I continue my walk with Xander, and as the others head towards the church, I break away, heading towards Roman.

The crowd begins murmuring around us.

"It's him! The gardener!"

"Didn't they have a falling out?"

"He loves her!"

"Princess Elizabeth, we love you!"

"Don't believe everything you read; it's all rubbish!"

"It's a love story, a real-life love story!"

I lock eyes with him from across the rope. He is on one side, and I am on the other, the rope representing the royal rules that I was so certain would somehow divide him from me.

"Officer, please let this man through. I know him," I say.

The officer nods, and Roman moves to my side of the rope.

And the royal rules no longer separate us.

We take a few steps away from the rope, and he hands me the flowers. I accept them with a trembling hand.

"I love you," he blurts out. "And I have no problem knowing my place in your life. I accept the rules. If that's behind a rope on Christmas Day, so be it."

I gasp as I take in his words. I understand now why he's here, in this spot, at Sandringham.

To prove to me that he can handle my life.

His hazel eyes search mine. There is so much that needs to be said, but I don't want to say it here.

"You are coming to church," I say, taking his hand in mine.

"What? I can't. We aren't even engaged!" he protests.

"I don't care. It's church, you're the man I love, and you are coming with me."

I defiantly walk with him to the church, which sends the crowd cheering and going into a picture-taking frenzy. I lead him towards the steps, where the rest of the royal family has gathered outside the doors of the medieval church to go inside.

All eyes are on us as we approach. I glance over my shoulder. We are still in the straight view of those telegraphic lenses, so I lead Roman down the path, to the back of the church, where those prying eyes can't reach us.

As soon as we round the bend and stop, Roman's hands frame my face. I drop the flowers. He gazes down at me with such a need, I cannot breathe.

"I love you," he repeats. "I have been in misery since our row. I waited until today so I could be here and show you I can deal with rules I don't agree with but are a part of loving you. I know what I'm getting into here. I not only accept it, I want it. Because this means I'm a part of your life."

The tears fall again. Roman's calloused thumbs sweep them away.

"I love you, too," I say, "You were right. My fear of the future, of you feeling the way my father does now, terrified me. I thought for sure that night was the beginning of the end. I didn't see how you'd want to live under those rules, that scrutiny, or with my family, who do not respect you. I didn't see why you would, when you could have so many other women who would love you the same way without all the rubbish that comes with loving me."

My cheeks burn in shame. Roman continues to hold my face, his hazel eyes bright with intensity.

"The party was hard, harder than I ever thought it could be," he admits. "I've never had people hate me upon sight, or degrade who I am in public."

I wince, and he strokes my face to comfort me.

"But Lizzie, I never, for one second, thought about leaving you," he says, his voice firm. "There isn't, and there will never be, anyone else but you for me. Ever. Did I worry about not being enough for *you?* Yes."

I stare up at him, some of his remarks from that night

now making sense. "Is that why you were angry when I tried to defend you?"

His neck begins to flush. "Yes," he admits, his voice low. "I'm sorry. I was an arse about that."

"I will always defend the things I'm passionate about," I say, "and the people I love."

"Which is one of the things I admire in you," Roman says. "I never want you to change that. That was about me more than you. I hated that you had to defend me in the first place."

"That," I say, my voice flickering with anger, "is on them. Grandmother is my grandmother, but that doesn't excuse her snobbish behaviour."

"I know," Roman says.

"And you are the man I love. The only man I've ever loved," I say.

"I have never loved anyone the way I love you," he declares.

He pauses for a moment and places a gentle kiss upon my brow. I close my eyes, relishing the feel of his lips on my skin, and vow to treasure every single kiss he bestows on me for the rest of my life.

Roman stands back up. "While I had those doubts, when you started to push me away, they vanished. I realised I could lose you, and when that started happening, I knew I couldn't let you go. I can't be without your heart."

I collapse against his overcoat, the wool scratching my cheek as I cry into his chest. He cradles me, and I cling to him, thinking of how much I love and need this man in my life.

I eventually stop crying and step back from him. His eyes are rimmed with red.

"I was wrong not to trust your feelings," I admit painfully. "I will never do that again."

"I will have bumps getting used to all of this," Roman admits. "I will struggle and get frustrated, or even angry, but don't ever doubt that I am where I want to be."

"Roman, when you were upset reading something on your phone and I asked you about it—did the press finally get to you? The media trolls?"

A flash of recognition dawns in his eyes. "No, that's what I was trying to tell you. It was an article about you, and it pissed me right off. I promise you, I can deal with people on social media or in the press thinking poorly of me. I know who I am. Will I be upset or angry like I was at the palace? Sometimes. I'm human. I can't help but want the people closest to you to want me to be a part of your life. But I will always take it as long as I know you love me."

"I do love you. I'm impossibly mad about you, Roman. You rode into my heart at Kensington Palace last July, and you have been there ever since."

"I will always want to be with you, Lizzie. I love you. What we have, I want forever."

"I love you, Roman," I say, my heart pounding, "and I want forever with you, too."

"You know what this means. You'll be wearing that tiara at last while I wait for you at the end of the aisle in the future," he whispers.

Zing! My heart is giddy at the thought of Roman proposing to me, marrying me.

"That idea," I say, "makes me the happiest woman in the world."

A smile lights up his face. "Is it improper to kiss you at church?"

I answer by drawing his mouth towards mine, stealing the best kiss I've ever known from the man I'm going to marry someday.

The kiss is gentle and sweet and most of all, full of love.

I end the kiss. "Come on, let's go break some more rules by going to church."

Roman throws his head back and laughs. "Yes, going to church. Only in your family can that be considered scandalous."

"Oh, I'll hear about it later, but the public that backs the younger generation will love it."

Suddenly, Xander flashes in my head.

"Wait. How did Xander know you would be here?"

Roman's mouth begins to curve up in that smile, and my heart is truly at home again.

"Wouldn't you like to know?"

"Roman! Hurry, church starts in a few minutes, and I need to know."

"I called Grandfather from my hotel room. I asked him to have Jillian get Xander's number from Helene. I knew I could trust him to keep a secret. I love Clementine, but she would have told you. I had to keep it a secret because if I had gone to you straight away, you never would have allowed me to stand behind that rope. And that was important for me to do, so I could show you I understand the rules and will live by them if that means I get to love you."

My heart swells with love and admiration for Roman's conviction in what he needed to do. It was symbolic and right, even if it took longer to do so.

"I love you," I say again.

Roman lifts my hand in his. Much like that first date, he

brings my gloved hand to his lips and presses a kiss across my knuckles.

"And I love you. Most ardently."

He bends down and hands me my bouquet of poinsettias. I make a note that while most royal brides carry forget-me-nots, I will break another rule and carry poinsettias.

Roman offers me his arm. "Ready to go cause some trouble in the name of modern love?"

I grin as happiness soars in my heart. "Most ardently."

And with those words, I walk with the man I love, ready to celebrate the first of all future Christmases as we should.

Together.

For the rest of our lives.

Balmoral Castle, Scotland

"This was the most perfect day," I say, cuddling up against Roman in front of a roaring fire.

Nightfall has come in the Scottish Highlands, on the first full day of our weekend getaway. On Friday night, we caught a flight from London to Aberdeen, drove the fifty-three miles to Balmoral, to spend the weekend at one of the cottages on the majestic property. The castle, set against the backdrop of some of the most gorgeous views of nature I have seen anywhere in the world, was purchased by Prince Albert for Queen Victoria in 1852.

And it seemed like the most natural choice for my first weekend away with Roman.

We spent all day in the gardens, which we loved despite the cold weather. The grounds don't open to the public until April, so it was like having a spectacular private castle all to ourselves.

We took our time, hand in hand, exploring, with me telling Roman the history of the castle and the gardens. The grounds also include greenhouses and a beautiful conservatory filled with potted flowers, which he especially loved.

Now, we've settled into the cottage for the night. Roman made a rustic beef stew for dinner, and we are cuddled up under a blanket in front of the fire, sipping wine.

"Do you realise," he says slowly, brushing his lips against my temple, "that we have been together two months now?"

"I do," I say with a smile, turning my face towards his. "And I've never been so happy as I have been with you."

Roman drops a sweet kiss on my lips, and then we're both quiet as we watch the flames dance in the fireplace.

The past two months have done nothing but solidify our relationship. After Roman attended church with me on Christmas Day, Antonia went ballistic at Sandringham. But this time, I was not the only one to stand up for myself, Christian and Xander were right by my side, too. Xander said we were a team, and in that moment, I realised it was no sign of weakness to have the support of my cousins. It was a sign of strength to accept their support. Antonia continued her leaks to the press for the entire month of January, but I held my head high and did my work. And proudly held the hand of the man I love whenever we were out and about. This trial strengthened us. It made both of us realise how we could have lost our relationship out of fear and leaping to conclusions instead of talking things through.

To be honest, it was probably the best thing to happen to us. We know how to face adversity together while understanding how we tackle things as individuals.

Roman did tell me what India said to him when I asked a second time; he confessed that she referred to him as rubbish that would tarnish the reputation of my family. Did he want to be in history books as the first gardener to marry up into the monarchy? Did he even have any idea of what to talk about to the other people at the table besides dirt? She told him he stood out in the worst way and would do nothing but derail the work I was doing on behalf of the crown. Then she refused to speak to him for the rest of the dinner.

When I found out about this, I was livid. I was ready to confront India that very moment, but Roman said she wasn't worth it. We were together, that was never going to change, and her thoughts were irrelevant. I did tell Roman I would confront her after Christmas, and I did. The first day I was back in London, I paid her a visit. And told her that if she ever spoke a negative word about Roman again, I would make my thoughts known to all members of my family about her petty, vindictive, elitist ways, which might be becoming to Antonia but not to Arthur, who happens to like Roman.

The fury which laced my voice scared her, and when I got to the part about Arthur, her eyes nearly popped out of her head. India was just what I thought she was: Someone who spread gossip and hate, but as soon as someone stood up to her, she freaked out and backed off.

I think of what else has happened since Christmas Day. Mum and Dad are still living separate lives under the roof of St. James's Palace, and my pleas for therapy have fallen on deaf ears. I don't see how they can go on indefinitely like this, but as Roman said, that will be their problem to sort out.

Clementine and Christian have completed another engagement, this time in Northern Ireland. Another smashing success for the family business, and the change in

Christian is remarkable. He's actively engaged in the walkabouts, shaking hands and dropping down to eye level to greet children. Clementine has brought out the best in him, and that makes me happy.

Xander left the army and has begun to undertake more royal duties. He is now living full-time in Nottingham Cottage at Kensington Palace, and it's a welcome sight to have him pop over to hang out with me and Roman.

Luckily, he hasn't been out clubbing or hitting on girls, but I detect there's something missing in his life now that the army is gone. However, I have full faith Xander will figure it out and eventually blossom in his role as the Prince of Wales. In fact, I have a meeting with him, Christian, and Clementine to determine the group goals for our foundation next week, and I can't wait for him to take a more hands-on role in it.

"Lizzie?" Roman asks.

I turn and gaze up at him, watching the flames from the fireplace illuminate his gorgeous face. "Yes?"

"Do you think we could go back to the conservatory tomorrow? I'd love to take another look at it. I don't think I studied it properly the first time."

I smile and slide my hand up his face, loving how his gardener's heart needs more time there. "I think that can be arranged. For a fee."

His mouth curves up. I swear I'm going to kiss the smile out of him.

"I think I have the currency for that," he says, dropping his mouth on mine.

And as we melt into each other, I have no doubt the admission will be paid in full right here in front of this fireplace.

❦

I hold Roman's hand as we walk through the morning mist. The conservatory is ahead of us, the beautiful white and glass building filled with all kinds of flowers. As we step inside, vibrant geraniums in all shades of colour surround us.

Roman takes a few steps ahead, his hands shoved inside the pockets of his coat, then he stops and gazes out of the glass windows onto the grounds.

"I'm embarrassed to admit, I'd never been inside this building despite all of the summers I spent here," I say, taking in all of the blooms around me. "It took you to show me how special this place is."

Roman turns around. "Do you remember when I told you I loved you for the first time?"

I smile at him. "Of course I do."

"I remember that I had to tell you how I felt. And I didn't care that to most people, it wouldn't seem long enough to know if it was love or infatuation. But I knew. Now there is something else I know."

Roman steps towards me, taking one of my hands in his. "I told you on Christmas Day that I'd be waiting for you at the end of an aisle one day."

My heart begins thundering in my ears.

"I'm not one to wait on my emotions. If I feel it, I feel it. More than that, with you, I know it. I love you, Lizzie. I only thought I knew what love was before, but I was wrong. The love I have for you is the greatest thing I have ever known. I've opened my heart to you, and I have been rewarded for it every minute I've spent with you. I want those minutes to be infinite. I want to marry you and call you my wife. I want to be with you on this journey, and I don't care if that means attending a fancy event or watching you colour with your pencils at night when you think I'm reading. I want us, forever."

Now I'm shaking as Roman retrieves a velvet box from his pocket and drops down on one knee in front of me, surrounded by all these beautiful flowers in bloom on this misty February morning.

"I spoke to your father last week. I told him I intended to marry you, but if he wanted me to wait, I would do so before I asked. Your father said the look in your eyes and the way you are with me was all he needed to know about how you felt."

I swallow past the lump that has swelled in my throat. He went to my father. I can't even imagine how intimidating that was, yet he did it because he loved me.

"This ring," Roman says, his voice thick, "belonged to my Grandmother."

He reveals a ruby and diamond ring to me, and I'm shaking all over.

It's his grandmother's ring.

"Grandfather picked a ruby because it matched her fiery spirit," Roman says softly. "And he said you have that same fire that she did. That you should have this ring now. I can think of no greater honour than for you to wear it. I began to fall in love with you in a greenhouse, Lizzie. Now I am here in front of you in a conservatory because it reminds me of the day that changed everything in my life. For the better."

Tears fill my eyes as I stare at the ring. Never have I seen anything more beautiful than Roman kneeling before me, offering me a forever I never knew I wanted until I fell in love with him. With a ring that was chosen because of the woman who used to wear it, and the woman he wants to wear it now.

"Roman," I gasp, my voice shaking. "Oh, my God."

"Elizabeth Alexandra Grace, will you marry me?"

I nod frantically, as I don't trust my voice at first. Then the words come pouring out of me. "I love you so much. And I want nothing more than to marry you, Roman Joseph Lawler."

Roman slips the ring on my shaking hand, and I stare at the red ruby in awe. He rises and frames my face in his hands, kissing me with all the love he has in his heart.

I kiss him back, grateful for the moment he rode into my life on a motorcycle and changed everything. This man has given me the courage to be myself.

And to love.

He breaks the kiss and drops his forehead to mine. "I know we can't announce this just yet; I don't want to take anything away from Christian and Clementine's wedding."

I take a step back from him and link his hands with mine. "Normal protocol is that you announce an engagement about six months before you have a royal wedding. But I'm not one for convention, are you?"

Roman's mouth curves up in that teasing way that I love so much. "What are you thinking?"

"We'll announce the engagement in a few weeks, and then we can have the wedding in the autumn. It won't take anything away from Clementine and Christian's wedding build up, trust me. And they will be thrilled for us. Everyone will be. And I'm the luckiest woman in the world because I'm living a fairy tale."

Roman's eyes shine brightly at me. "The one about the princess and the gardener?"

"The best one ever written," I declare happily.

As his mouth captures mine, my happiness knows no bounds. I love Roman, he loves me, and we are going to get married and share our lives together.

A happy ending indeed, I think.

THE END

The next book in the series will be Xander's story, called *Royal Icing*. To receive updates on this release, follow me on BookBub, Goodreads or sign up for my newsletter.

CONNECT WITH AVEN

Amazon Author Page
Website
Facebook Page
Twitter
Facebook Reader Group
Newsletter
GoodReads
BookBub
Instagram